PUNCHBAG

PUNCHBAG

Robert Llewellyn

Hodder & Stoughton

First published in Great Britain in 1999
by Hodder and Stoughton
A division of Hodder Headline PLC

10 9 8 7 6 5 4 3 2 1

British Library Cataloguing in Publication Data
A CIP catalogue record for this title
is available from the British Library

ISBN 0 340 70791 7

Typeset by Hewer Text Ltd, Edinburgh
Printed and bound in Great Britain by Mackays of Chatham, plc, Chatham, Kent

Hodder and Stoughton
A division of Hodder Headline PLC
338 Euston Road
London NW1 3BH

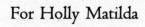

For Holly Matilda

PREFACE

There is an unusual male odour I have experienced in two very specific locations and nowhere else. One is in my dressing room at the side of B stage, Shepperton Studios in Middlesex after a long day on a *Red Dwarf* set wearing the plastic and rubber Kryten suit.

The other was in the changing rooms of the Bay Area Model Mugging group in Redmond, California as three men stripped off their padded impact suits after a multiple assailant self-defence class.

I have discovered that if you clad a man in non-porous nylon and foam and make him exert himself for long enough, you can achieve this peculiar brand of odour. That is the only connection between my work and the work of these very remarkable, dedicated men.

I believe working as a padded assailant has to be one of the hardest jobs in one of the most contentious areas a man can do. It is also one of the most important. So I would like to thank in particular Eliot Nemzer, Stu Sofield, Rick Gibbins and all the other men I met and talked to who spend so much of their time attacking women for the very best reasons.

I am also deeply indebted to Cori Couture and the teachers who allowed me to watch their classes, and to the many women who allowed me to witness at first hand the phenomenal transformation this training engendered. I was humbled to a point of complete inactivity by what these women had been through and survived, only to be further impressed by their ability to overcome and defeat their demons.

I would finally like to dedicate this work to all the women I have known who have suffered from the violence of men, and hope against reality that this book will promote in whatever tiny way, a more peaceful and non-violent future for all our children.

Knees and elbows! as they say in model mugging circles.

Robert Llewellyn
December 1998

Chapter One

'What I need you to do,' said Tara Kennedy, 'is stand in a room with fourteen women and have them take turns at beating the hell out of you for five hours a day.'

'Come again,' said Nick, his mind failing to conjure up an image of what this beautiful woman was talking about.

'You'd be well paid. I'm not saying you'd make a fortune, but a good living.'

'Sorry,' said Nick. Nothing she was saying was registering.

'Let me try and explain,' said Tara. 'Come into the café and have a cup of tea.'

That was really how it started for Nick Gardener, although, if he ever thought about it, he considered that it truly started a little earlier. The night before their first meeting, Frankie Jessop, his boss at All Areas Security, called him. As usual the call came just as he'd really got relaxed in the bath. Frankie's dulcet tones crackled through the knackered old answering machine in the kitchen.

'Oi, Nicky, you 'ome or what?'

Nick hopped down the stairs, one wet leg in his black, fighting-weight jeans, picked up the phone just in time.

'Yo, Frankie, what's up?'

'Ah, you're there, then. Thought I'd missed you, son. Got a bit of a job on, last-minute gig, mate. You're not a family man, are ya?'

'No way, mate,' lied Nick.

'Good. This is a last-minute door security job, all day tomorrow, in Brighton.'

'All day!' said Nick, disappointed. 'That sounds like a get-up-in-the-morning job to me, Frankie.'

'It is. Got to be there for eight thirty, mate.'

'Frankie, I don't come off Trash till gone three.'

'It's all sorted, mate. I got Mickey to cover for you tonight.'

This was coming as a horrible surprise. Nick wasn't happy. He was in the process of getting himself ready for his nightly stint outside Trash on Charing Cross Road. Head of security – responsible position with a bunch of right nutters to keep in order.

'Mickey's a psychopath, Frank, you know that. He's gonna kill some little raver soon.'

'Let me worry about that. You just worry about getting your hairy arse down to Brighton tonight. I've booked you a hotel on the seafront, you lucky bastard. The Clarion. 'S not actually in Brighton, it's in 'ove. Bit of a fleapit, but it's only one night. Pack your bags and get going.'

'Well, where's the job on?' asked Nick.

'Conference centre. Didn't I tell you?'

'No, you didn't.'

'Okay, well, I have now,' said Frankie, between puffs on his Camel untipped. 'It's a oner for the day, can't be bad. Bunch of lezzos having a conflab or some such. Bunch of poofs want to get in. Can't make head or tail of it myself. You're there like shit in the old sandwich as usual, my son.'

'Thanks,' said Nick.

'I'll 'ave a word with management there so as they expect ya, alright? Gotta go, got a rush on.'

He heard Frankie start to talk to someone else before he put the phone down and the line went dead. One hundred pounds for one day's work. For a security guard that was manna from heaven. Even compared with office cleaners the job was scraping along at the bottom of the heap, Nick knew that. He'd had plenty of other jobs in his time, he'd raked it in on occasions, but standing outside Trash was a regular gig, four nights a week, free food and booze and the life of the street to keep you amused all night.

He did as he was told, packed a bag and caught the Tube to Victoria, got on a train to Brighton. It was just getting dark as he hit the streets. He'd been there before, as security at gigs – he'd hung out with his mates in a pub. He followed his nose through the maze of small lanes, trying to remember where it was. Eventually he found it – large windows, bright lights and loud music.

'Nicky, mate, what you doin' 'ere?'

It was Billy Turrel, a huge barrel of a bloke Nick had done a door with at a Drum and Bass concert.

'Yo, Billy,' said Nick. They shook hands – two big hands, two big arms, two very big geezers. 'Doing a door tomorrow, conference centre.'

' 'Ow come I didn't know about that?' asked Billy.

'Search me, mate. Frankie Jessop sent me. Just doin' my job, mate,' said Nick.

'I never get gigs like that, you lucky fucker,' said Billy with just a hint of malice. Nick shrugged, patted Billy on the back and entered the noisy bar.

An hour later Nick Gardener was walking along the lanes with a girl who worked at the NatWest bank around the corner from the pub. He went back to her place, a small flat on a steep hill she shared with a fat girl. Within an hour Nick was sleeping heavily by her side, his hugely built arm resting over her frail body. They'd had sex, with a condom, very quickly. She told him he was the best lover she'd ever known, she wanted to see him again. They swapped addresses and phone numbers. He worried about her ringing him – he didn't need the hassle.

He woke up early in the morning and looked at her, sleeping quietly, the pretty girl from the bank. She was cute but he felt like shit, and for the life of him he couldn't remember her name. He sighed – he'd done it again. He'd promised himself he wouldn't, but he had.

He crept out of the flat, didn't even take a piss in case he woke her. Checked his diver's watch as he walked down the steep street – 6.35 in the morning. Bright sunlight dazzling him, his bladder bursting. He got to the corner of the street before he found a tree and relieved himself, only a passing milkman giving him a dirty look.

As he walked along the seafront he got a lump in his throat. He was still alone. His life was shit really, nothing going on except he was getting more porky than built, more wrinkly than rippled. True, he could still go into a pub and pull, but so what? It made no difference, he still felt like a waste of space. He found himself wishing he hadn't shagged some unknown bank clerk the night before.

By the time he got to the conference centre it was already busy. Hundreds of women standing outside the door talking excitedly. A woman inside opened the doors and the crowd swilled in. Nick followed them, feeling awkward and noticing some of the women giving him the evil eye. He shrugged it off, he wasn't doing any harm, but he felt exposed, standing a good foot taller than most of the women.

'Nick Gardener?' asked a face in the crowd, a battered face that for a moment Nick couldn't put a gender to.

'That's me,' he said with a smile.

'Nice one, Nick,' said the woman. 'Want a smoke?' She offered him an open packet of Marlboro Lite.

'No, ta.'

'Fair enough,' said the woman, lighting up. 'Wendy, by the way. We're running security here but we needed a big geezer as a bit of a deterrent. Got a bunch of blokes threatening a bit of a disruption. My money's on fuck-all happening, to be honest with you. Anyway, if you just do the door for the time being, I'll have a word later. All right?'

'Fine by me,' said Nick. It was the normal thing – someone in some insurance company had said they needed a bloke on the door. There was nothing to do except be bored shitless all day, standing up and looking ready.

That day Nick Gardener held the door open for four and a half thousand women and not one of them managed to say thank you. He didn't want them to grovel or think of him as some sort of worshipful entity, but in his experience a little politeness in life went a long way. Standing there, holding open the double glass doors of the convention centre, being taken for granted; who needed it? Keep the money – he could have stayed at home. He felt like he needed a bath, he hadn't washed since he'd worked up a sweat the night before. He loved having baths, steam baths even better. He liked being clean and he could tell his pits were heading towards wiffy. He hoped none of the thousands of women who were ignoring him could smell anything.

Chapter Two

Occasionally the mixing of distinct gene pools throws up
anomalies in the human form. Some are interesting but not
immediately attractive to either racial group, some very rare.

In mixing Celtic Irish fishing folk from the bleak Atlantic
coast and Native American Arapaho from the Pacific North-
west, not forgetting a fair-sized trace of Spanish blood for good
measure, it is just possible to make someone who, when walking
through the average shopping mall, will make most people miss a
breath.

Tara Kennedy: thirty years old, five foot ten inches tall, bone
structure a model would suffer surgery for, teeth from a dental
floss advert, a build that would not disgrace an Olympic
swimmer, and thick, really thick and very dark red hair. She
was astonishing-looking, to say the least. The Arapaho/Spanish
blood-line, from her mother, gave her the fine-boned face and
the wonderfully smooth, tanned skin. A casual observer might
find that the pronounced Native American cheekbones appeared
to push her eyes closer together than normal, it was a facial
characteristic she was acutely aware of, but she worked hard at
ignoring it and had been reassured so many times she was
beautiful that she suffered no lost sleep. Her height, the light
grace and strength of her limbs and her thick dark red hair came
from her father, third-generation Irish American.

'Thank you very much, Germaine,' said the woman who appeared to be running things on the large podium. Tara was standing by the side of the stage behind some blue drapes. A smiling Germaine Greer walked past her as she left the stage. Tara was nervous now. She had been woken a little closer to the time of her appearance than she would have liked. Landing at Heathrow airport that morning and being rushed to a train to Brighton, maybe she had cut it a little fine. She just had time to give her slide carousel to the technical crew backstage, put on her lecture clothes, wash her face, clean her teeth and gulp some water before she was called to the stage.

Her travel companion and assailant, Tim Renaldo, was already in his suit, standing next to her. He was beaming away as usual.

'How you feeling?' he asked.

'Jet-lagged out of my brains,' she replied.

'Me also. Man, it's like being on PCP. This is gonna be great.'

She smiled at him and raised her eyebrows naughtily. 'Let's knock 'em dead, Tim.'

'Way to go.'

'Before we break up the show,' said the stage presenter, 'I'd like to welcome our final speaker, all the way from the United States of America, the facilitator of Winning Strategy, a women's self-defence organisation from San Francisco, please welcome Ms Tara Kennedy.'

There was a fierce round of applause as Tara bounced up on to the stage. Tall and lean, wearing black training pants and a plain shirt, she took the podium with casual grace. She looked around the hall. Over four and a half thousand women were clapping and looking up at her.

'Thank you, Jenny.' She had checked the woman's name with one of the assistants. 'It's great to be here and to see so many women from all over the world. They say this is the post-feminist era, to which I can only respond with a very British term. Bollocks.'

The crowd erupted with laughs and cheers, hoots of mirth and fanatical applause.

'I'm not sure what it means but it sounds kind of appropriate. It's great to be here and all the women and men at Winning Strategy send their warmest greetings. The reason I am here is not so good. Last year, in the United States, every three minutes a woman was raped or sexually assaulted. Of those women, over five thousand were murdered after the event. To say that sexual crimes against women are at epidemic levels would be an understatement. For every woman who gets a better job, better housing, better childcare, there are ten women whose lives have been destroyed, their dignity removed, their confidence shattered, their sexuality permanently damaged. In the US there have been many responses to this never-ending crisis – capital punishment, chemical castration, group therapy. It may help stop the individual male rapist, but it does nothing to alter the rapist mentality of men and the rapist structures in our society.'

A loud cheer ripped through the now totally attentive crowd.

'I know that the self-defence movement does not have the total answer to these problems, not on a national or international level, but on an individual level it is, I believe, the very best thing women can do for themselves and each other. The reasons men use their anger and frustration in such an appalling way are complex and, as we all know here, deeply rooted in our societies. The extraordinary thing about what we do is that we confront those issues head-on in our work with men. To give you a brief background on where we're coming from, I'd like the first slide, please.'

A picture appeared of a woman in a black-belt karate outfit, holding a stance on a training mat. The only unusual thing about the picture was that her face was blacked out. Tara turned to look at the picture then back to face her audience.

'Okay. The system of self-defence we teach, known as full-impact defence training, started out way back in 1972 after the brutal rape of this woman, an award-winning black-belt karate student. In a real-life attack situation she had what we call a freeze response – she was simply unable to overcome the learned use of self-control which is of course essential when practising with friendly partners. On the mat she could really kick ass, but when her attacker used foul language and sudden unprovoked aggression, she did nothing to defend herself or to dissuade him. She was more than capable of rendering her assailant uncon-scious and yet she did nothing. Slide, please.'

Tara turned to see a picture of a man in full kit on the thirty-foot screen behind her.

'This is a highly trained, extremely dangerous attacker. I have been working with him for seven years and in that time he has sexually assaulted eleven thousand women.' An audible gasp went through the auditorium. Tara waited and then continued. 'He has screamed a torrent of sexually explicit abuse in women's faces, pulled knives on them, tried to put his hand in their panties, tried to rip off their clothes. He has pinned them down on the floor and tried to force them to perform oral sex.'

Another pause. Tara turned to look at the picture to let what she had said sink in. She turned back to the now silent audience.

'In response to this Tim has had the hell kicked out of him more times than he would care to remember. Please welcome on stage Tim Renaldo.'

As Tim stepped into the limelight, Tara experienced the familiar sound of an audience in crisis. The women didn't know how to respond. They had just heard a litany of offences committed by this man and he suddenly appeared before them – big, huge in fact, monstrous in proportion, and carrying a huge helmet almost the size of a dustbin. Tim waved as one or two women clapped. Tara smiled and turned to look at her audience again.

'Tim Renaldo is one of the most courageous, dedicated and honourable men I have ever met. He is a padded assailant, one of a small band of men who have helped train over seven hundred thousand women in the United States in the past thirty years.'

She turned and looked at Tim, who was standing calmly in front of the huge crowd. She raised her hands and clapped, instantly joined by the other four and a half thousand women in the room. Tim nodded slightly and moved to the back of the stage, where he knelt down.

'Can we have the mats on, please,' said Tara, and two women dressed in black rolled two huge crash mats on to the stage.

'The best way to describe what we do is to show you. Tim and I are going to go through some very basic routines for you, to kind of give you some idea of what you'd learn were you to take the course.'

Tara took the microphone off the stand and walked to the mat. 'Now I'm not going to be able to hold this as I fight Tim, but I think you'll get the general idea.'

She placed the microphone on the floor and walked on to the mat. Tim put in a gumshield and pulled on his helmet. He walked up to Tara and shouted. 'You been teasing me too long, bitch, you gonna get what's coming to you!'

He grabbed her by the hair, but with two swift blows, the sound of which bounced off the rear wall of the auditorium, Tim was on the floor.

Tara picked up the microphone again. 'If Tim had not been wearing the suit, he would have been taken to hospital at this point. Those blows were delivered at full force. How hard did I hit you, Tim?'

Tim back-flipped over into a standing position, pulled off his helmet and spat out his gumshield. 'You hit real hard, Tara,' he said, leaning towards her to make use of the microphone.

'Thank you, Tim,' she said, then nodded curtly. Tim replaced his helmet and walked to the other side of the mat.

'Now, as you will all know, I'm sure, the vast majority of assaults against women are carried out by men known to the woman. We deal with this too, by role-playing.'

Again Tara put down the microphone and stood on the mat. Tim walked up to her and stroked her hair softly. Although most of the audience couldn't hear what he was saying, they knew the scene. Tara stepped back with both her hands raised in front of her, palms flat.

'Step back, you're too close!' she said clearly. The auditorium was silent. Tim shrugged and moved towards her a little, this time stroking her shoulder.

'I said step back. You are too close.'

Again Tim shrugged, still cajoling her, assuring her he meant no harm. A small whimper could be heard as a woman in the audience started to cry. Tim put his arm around Tara's shoulders and then grabbed her hair. His movements suddenly become more energetic and angry. Tara's response was sudden and terrible. Five or six blows rained down on Tim's collapsing form, followed by a knee into his padded face. He rolled motionless on to the floor. Tara stood by his head and looked around.

'Look, assess, no!' she shouted. This was the three word mantra she taught her pupils, to encourage them to remain aware after an attack. Then she ran to the side of the mat and said, 'Dial nine nine nine!'

There was a moment of silence followed by an instantaneous explosion of applause. When the roaring had subsided enough, Tara picked up the microphone and said, 'It may be cool to watch, but believe me, it's fantastic to do. All the women who do our course have been transformed by the experience. Women who walk tall in the streets, not scared, not cowering, not looking for trouble but knowing they are allowed to be there, that they belong to the streets and the streets belong to them.'

Another round of applause and cheering, some impressive whistling mixed in. Indeed, it had barely stopped as she spoke. Tara was enjoying herself immensely. Finally it started to die down. She held the stage.

'Of all the women who have completed our course we know

of one hundred and sixty-six graduates who then faced physical assaults from men. Over one hundred and thirty were able to make graceful exits from the assault, i.e. they used psychological tactics we teach to diffuse the situation and leave the danger area. Around twenty managed to show that they were not going to be overpowered, and their assailant either fled or backed down, and the rest were forced to use a physical response. Every single one of those women knocked their assailants unconscious within five seconds of the initial assault taking place.'

Another huge round of applause.

'Thank you. The trainees are taught exclusively by women – the men only offer advice when called upon by the teacher. The woman trainer is with the student all the way through the assaults. This is not just a toughen-you-up self-defence class. We also offer a great deal of emotional support through group and one-to-one therapy. What we create in class is, in fact, a safe place to fail. It's only through admitting we're scared, using our fear as a strength, as something that helps us survive, that we can find a way through a situation. Notice I did not say out of a situation. The way out is through. This is a term we use a great deal in our classes. The way out is through. That means leaving your assailant in a position where he can no longer cause you harm.

'There are forty full-force self-defence groups in the US – in total we have trained nearly a million women. There are groups in Canada, Australia, New Zealand, Japan, France, Germany and Italy. There isn't one in England and that's why I'm here. Winning Strategy self-defence is about to kick butt in Britain. Thank you.'

The auditorium erupted. Women were on their feet, cheering, shouting and clapping. For a moment Tara wasn't sure what to do. She took a small bow and beckoned Tim to join her. They both stood centre stage in the glare of a brilliant spotlight. She held Tim's hand, they lifted their hands together – what a team. She had done the demonstration and made her speech a hundred times before at countless college campuses and women's events around the US, Australia and New Zealand, but this was her first time in England. She hadn't expected this response at all, had expected just the opposite, that the women would say it was so American and crazy. Only wealthy Americans could afford the time to indulge themselves so. What she could sense in the crowd was huge enthusiasm – and adoration, there was no point denying it. Creating that kind of response was a buzz.

Chapter Three

'Tell them they've just got to have some muscle on the door,' said Alice Moreton. She had a report in her hand and another up on the screen in front of her. It was Friday afternoon and suddenly everything had to be done at once. She had seen a faxed leaflet from an organisation called DAD-E, Dads Actively Demand Equality. It looked tragic but they had threatened to disrupt some feminist shindig in Brighton. Her police contacts had told her there could be anything up to five hundred men turning up. There was a women's security firm guarding the place but it wasn't enough, anyone would know that.

'Look what happens at football matches. You need a presence. The ladies' security company are just going to raise the stakes – these blokes are going to see that as a direct challenge. Get some heavies in for the day at least. I can't suggest cover without it, the risk is off the scale. Okay?'

'Okay,' said the tired voice of an insurance broker on the other end of the line.

Alice Moreton hung up and glanced back at her screen. What was up there, recently decrypted from a US government CD, was the latest findings from the wreckage of Flight 455 from New Orleans, the 636 that blew up off the coast of Miami, with total loss of crew and passengers. A wiring fault above the central fuel tank had finally been blamed. An insurance nightmare, a risk assessor's dream come true. She had raised the issue of this particular wiring loom with the Civil Aviation Authority in the UK and the US Senate Subcommittee on Aviation Safety two years previously. She intended to remind them of it, but the immediate problem was how should she assess the present risk. Over three thousand 636s in the air, all with a similar problem. No airline was going to ground its entire fleet. The manufacturers had found a way to solve the wiring problem but it was going to take years to fix every aircraft. Lloyd's and the other major world insurance houses were very tense. What if another one went down? 636s were the cheapest aircraft to insure in the air, owing to their immaculate safety record. What was more, everyone liked them – they'd been around for years and carried millions of people every day. This was a very serious matter.

Alice was just glad she wasn't flying anywhere that weekend. She was very aware of the mass of dangers all around her but managed to keep it in perspective. She had to, she knew too much about how dangerous everything was. She had lived for twenty-eight years without breaking a bone, having a stitch, an operation or anything more serious than a bit of cream and a bandage for a scratched knee. As a fourteen-year-old she tripped during a gym class at school and knocked a front tooth loose. A lot of dental intervention at the time saved her from having a false tooth, but she did have a wonky one. She was embarrassed about it and had learned to smile without showing her teeth.

Alice was a small-built, fit woman, her hair neat, something about her whole being tight and tidy. She had, during her student days, finished a marathon, and as an adult in the working world still managed to swim regularly using the YMCA pool on Tottenham Court Road in central London. She wore a lot of black and it suited her, made her look taller.

Everything about Alice Moreton was self-contained. She was well designed and left no mess – her desk in the Central Risk Assessment Office on Chancery Lane was the neatest in the room. Her computer, were its contents not classified, could have been used as an example to all who used them of best practice. Maximising hard disk storage and ease of file acquisition, she used her machine as a pianist used their instrument. Alice Moreton was very good at her job and she knew it. She had risen through the ranks of the insurance industry very fast. Risk assessment was her favoured field and she was one of the top ten assessors in the country.

She arrived home that evening at about the same time she always did, in her VW Golf – twin air bags and top of its class for safety. Home was an apartment block off the North Circular Road in Finchley, very neat and comfortable, fashionably decorated with not a great deal of blatant individuality.

The phone was ringing as she walked in. She didn't panic; she put the car and apartment keys in the large Ikea glass bowl by the TV set and picked up the cordless receiver.

'I knew I'd catch you now. They could set atomic clocks by your movements.'

'Hello, May,' said Alice happily, pleased to hear the reassuring squawk of her oldest friend. 'How's the baby?'

'If I want to talk about the baby I'll ring my mum,' came the curt reply. 'I ring you because you're the one person I know who doesn't give a stuff about bloody babies. He's asleep.'

'I do care about babies.'

'Yeah, yeah. But I want to hear about Peter.'

'Peter? What about him?' asked Alice.

'What's he like?'

'Oh, he's all right. He's nice.'

'He looked gorgeous.'

'Oh, of course, I keep forgetting you've seen him.' Alice remembered that she had last parted company with May outside Covent Garden Tube station where she had also arranged to meet Peter Welbeck. 'No, he's very nice. A real boy.'

'Oh God. I just thought about the two of you all the way to bloody Luton. Why did I have to end up with a bloke from Luton? Why couldn't I meet someone like Peter?'

'He lives in High Wycombe. Is that any better?'

'Oh well, you go out with him in London. God, I miss my life.'

'You've got Oscar.'

'I know, and he's gorgeous. It's just seeing you being so, well, alive. God, it's boring being a bloody mother.'

'You've only been doing it three months.'

'Five. Oscar is five months old. Seems like a lifetime, and look what you've done in that time. Dumped that dreamboat you met in Greece and found some even more dishy hunk. God, you're lucky.'

'I'm not lucky. I've got a really dull life. I spent the whole of last weekend doing nothing.'

'That's what I mean, lucky. I didn't even notice a weekend except that David was here being grumpy. Why did I marry him, Alice? Eh? Why?'

'And why did I listen to you and wear that revolting bridesmaid's outfit. God, that was embarrassing.'

'You did look bloody awful. I'm very sorry.'

Alice was cheered by the pointless conversations she had with May. She missed her friend. May had left her dumpy old flat in Kensal Green and moved to Luton with David. Her weekends had taken a marked downward shift since Oscar's arrival, and Alice had no one to go out with after work. She generally rented a video she didn't really want to see, went home and heated some soup. Nothing unusual. She spent many evenings like that.

The previous weekend she had spent hours swimming in the YMCA pool. As she felt the water rush past her ears she slowly became aware that she had a life and wasn't sure what she was doing with it. She came from a strictly Christian background. However, her beliefs, once heartfelt, had been challenged by her knowledge of the mechanical and structural design failures that beset the human race. How could a God allow such disasters to be created, how could so many innocent people suffer so much, and how could He allow insurance companies to make so much money?

Alice's father, although he worked for Smiths Industries in Cheltenham designing fighter aircraft undercarriages, was choirmaster at Tewkesbury Abbey. Alice had grown up in the shadow of the beautiful old church, living in one of the ancient monk's houses tucked behind a stable yard. One of the buildings that Henry VIII didn't knock down when he trashed the place.

As a child she went to church every Sunday and listened to her father's powerful voice lead the choir. She went to Sunday school and read the Bible and she didn't mind it at all. She never really thought about it. The world around her wasn't like the Bible – very few people she knew went to church, no one seemed to believe anything, and there was no pressure on her either way. She still loved going to Christmas services at the abbey – the smell of the place brought her childhood close, and she'd had a happy one.

Having no siblings, she spent hours playing alone, making secret dens in the tangle of outbuildings, watching the town boys ride their noisy motorbikes in the field that bordered the ancient house.

Why she had been put on the earth had never been an issue for Alice Moreton. Being part of God's wonderful creation was enough, and part of that creation, as she had learned from her quietly spoken mother, was to have children. The realisation that she didn't want children made her feel as if the whole edifice of her life had come slowly apart.

By the time she had got out of the pool the previous weekend she felt terrible, almost physically ill. She sat in the changing rooms, naked, damp towel at her feet, looking at the tiling on the floor. What was the point? She had a job, good money, a flat she called her own, she was healthy. She even had sex when she wanted, courtesy of Peter. None of this added up to anything. She felt cold and hollow, and yet the prospect of going to talk to a priest or a man of the cloth filled her with further despair.

Their response would be so easy to predict she didn't even bother. She had no faith in anything man made – cars, planes, computer systems, trains, boats. They all crashed, burned, sank, broke and failed at some point, and if God made man then God made everything man made, and everything man made failed. It was just too daft.

'Is this sad?' asked Alice. 'You know what? On Monday morning, when I sat down at my desk again, typed in my password and started work, I realised I was happy again. People are supposed to hate work and only live at the weekends, aren't they, but for me it's the other way around. I hate weekends.'

'Oh, Alice. You're so complicated.'

'Am I?' said Alice, who always thought of herself as being supremely straightforward.

'Yes. You don't really know how to enjoy yourself, do you? You never have.'

'Haven't I?'

'No, you never let go. But then look at me. I let go with a boring old fart who lives in Luton, and look what happened to me.'

Chapter Four

'Brought you a cup of tea,' said a gruff voice from behind him. Nick turned around and looked down. A short but very sturdy woman in her mid-forties was holding out a polystyrene cup to him. It took him a moment to recognise her. It was Wendy, the bruiser who'd welcomed him when he arrived.

'Oh, cheers, ta very much,' said Nick.

'Thought you might be a bit parched.'

'You're not kidding. Everything all right, then, is it?' he asked, nodding towards the door of the auditorium.

'Sweet as a nut, chief,' said the woman. 'Not really expecting any trouble, but you never know. A lot of weirdos around.'

'Tell me about it,' said Nick. He sipped his tea. It was sweet and hot, just as he liked it. 'Fuck me, this is a good cuppa.'

'Nice one,' said the woman. Wendy was not the name Nick would have chosen for her. 'Killer' or 'Kosher' maybe. With a bashed-in face, short-cropped, bleached blond hair and shoulders like a Sumo wrestler, she did not strike him as a Wendy.

'I'm Nick, by the way,' he said with a big grin.

'I know, mate. Checked you out.'

'Did you!' Nick was slightly alarmed and wondered exactly who she could have checked him out with.

'Had to. Nothing personal, couldn't have some perv in a place like this.'

'Fair enough.'

'I've known your boss for years. I run VWW.'

'What's that, Beetle enthusiasts?'

'No, mate, stands for Very Wide Women. Security firm.'

'Blimey,' said Nick.

'Yup. Been going nigh on fourteen years now.'

'Bloody hell. I've never heard of you. Is it all, well, ladies?'

'Women, Nick, women. Catch up, mate.'

'Sorry.'

'Yeah, all women. We do gigs, events like this, parties, anything and everything really. Bit of bodyguard work.'

'Really?' said Nick.

'Yeah, but that's the discreet end of the business,' said Wendy, tapping the side of her nose. 'Yeah, I've known old Frankie Jessop for years. He's a decent bloke.'

'Yeah, he's a good bloke. Drives me mad sometimes. I didn't hear about this job till last night.'

'Yeah, well, that's my fault, not Frankie's. We got a warning very late in the day that there might be trouble from some group of sad nutters. Insurance people thought a bit of serious muscle might put them off before they started anything.'

'Do the law know about it?'

'Oh yeah, it's no big issue. Insurance company insists and all that stuff. There's only about ten of them, the group's called DAD-E, Dads Actively Demand Equality. Heard of them?' asked Wendy, staring at him carefully.

'Only from Frankie. What do they do?'

'Moan a lot mostly, if you want my opinion,' said Wendy, taking a Marlboro Lite packet from her sleeve pocket. She offered one to Nick. He shook his head. Wendy lit up and inhaled like an old lag from Parkhurst.

'Sensible man,' she said, then blew a fine blue cloud to one side, avoiding Nick's face. 'Nah, they've probably got a point, you know. Kiddies need a dad around, I suppose, but they're full of shit really. They've linked up with the anti-abortion mob.'

'Oh, right,' said Nick, not sure what he felt about the whole abortion issue. He didn't need to worry about proffering an opinion. Wendy filled the available airspace.

'Anyway, if there's any trouble, don't worry about it. My "ladies" will back you up.'

Nick glanced up the stairs at the assortment of hard-looking women standing smoking and drinking tea.

'I'm sure they will.'

'See you later. We'll have a bite of scran in the staff canteen later if you're interested.'

'Might take you up on that, Wendy,' said Nick, holding his tea up. He watched her almost waddle to the stairs and then spring up them with her short but very powerful legs. He tried not to shake his head in disbelief because he could see the other security women looking at him. He smiled and waved and scratched his head. She must have been a lezzo, but she was really friendly, so who gave a stuff? She looked like a woman who enjoyed a good time, her face as lived-in as a face can be without being dead. What she did in her private life was no business of his.

He turned and looked out of the large glass doors. A few tourists were passing, an old man with a dog. Although the sun was shining there was a strong wind blowing. A young woman walked past wearing lightweight black trousers. The wind blew at her from behind, and the cloth pulled tautly on her buttocks. He looked at the line, the gentle curve. Beautiful. He remembered Wendy and the Very Wide Women, looking at him from thirty metres away. They'd notice – he'd better watch himself. He glanced at the woman as she moved down the pavement. Why should he watch himself? He wasn't doing anything wrong. What could be more natural than a man looking at a woman? On the other hand that was probably what they spent their whole time doing. Lezzo security guards – whatever next?

He leant against the glass, Tiffany suddenly coming to mind. He found she did if he got bored. If he got bored he got horny and if he got horny he thought of Tiffany. He'd had such a good time with her. Not always — they had a bad time too. Once.

Tiffany Smooth must have seen Nick serving behind the bar at the Circus, a singles joint he worked in for a while a year and a half previously. On one of his many breaks from security work, Nick had landed a job mixing drinks in Joe Allen's restaurant in Covent Garden. There he'd met a blond hippie barman from San Francisco who told him about the Circus, what a great place it was, and how there was more pussy there than between the covers of *Playboy* magazine. Nick made contact, got a job there illegally, and flew to San Francisco.

As a committed Ameriphile he'd been to the country on many occasions, but never to San Francisco. The Circus bar, situated on the corner of Front and Market, was wild, energetic and (the hippie barman was right) crawling with totty. It was like *Loaded* magazine come to life. He couldn't believe that virtually every drink he served went to a woman he would pay good money to for a zipless fuck.

And then within two weeks of getting off the Virgin flight, one of them asked him on a date. Nick's entire fleet had come in. Tiffany Smooth was a babe, if a bit young for him really — he was pushing thirty-three and she looked as if she should have been at school. When she said she was at school he blanched until she told him she was twenty and he realised she meant college.

'I want to study law, so I'm doing a degree in politics,' she said. Nick flashed back to the students he had known at Oxford, who always had their future planned out, as if they always knew what they wanted to do. He'd never had a clue.

'I never went to college. Too busy working,' he said, hoping she wouldn't be put off by his uneducated status.

'I'm working,' she said sharply. 'No one is putting me through college, 'cept yours truly.'

'What d'you do, then?'

'I'm a dancer, at the Crazy Horse.'

Tiffany was sharing an apartment with a grungy girl whose

name he could never remember. The place was cramped and dirty; he felt at home. It was three days after they had spent their first night together that he walked past the Crazy Horse and realised what kind of dancer Tiffany was. He felt so thick that he hadn't picked up on it sooner. There was something about her that was almost professionally horny. He had never met such an extreme lover.

Nick was shocked at first. He had always considered establishments like the Crazy Horse to be full of ugly women and unpleasant desperate men. Tiffany seemed so streetwise and sassy, such a hip millennium babe, the last place he expected her to work was a tacky old topless joint

'D'you wanna come watch me work?' she asked as he was cleaning up the bar in the early hours.

'I don't know. Don't know if I could handle it. Never been in a place like that.'

'Oh, come on. Guys always go to places like that at some time.'

'Well, I haven't.'

Nick finally visited the Crazy Horse on his night off. The idea did make him horny and he decided to go for it.

It was a dive, just as he had expected, but the atmosphere was very unlike that of a seedy topless pub in England. It was boisterous, energetic, loud. The men shouted out encouragement to the girls on the huge catwalk that half filled the crowded room. There was a stainless-steel pole at the centre of the stage, and the women seemed to try to outdo one another with the naked, spread-legged gymnastics they were prepared to undertake using this device. The lighting was brighter than he had expected, the drinks cheaper, the whole place cleaner. He decided it wasn't too bad. He checked the girls cavorting naked on the stage and couldn't believe he was having a scene with one of them. He realised he quite looked forward to seeing her there. He was beginning to get a thrill out of it, then decided this was too sad.

He had started to have strong feelings for Tiffany, and he

knew that one sure-fire way to stop having a good time was to start having strong feelings about anyone. Especially if the woman you had the feelings about worked somewhere like the Crazy Horse.

The music changed. Alanis Morissette came on and he felt his stomach churn as Tiffany Smooth walked on to the stage wearing combat trousers, a tight T-shirt and no shoes. Within the first couple of lines of the song, the trousers were ripped off in one Velcro-ed reveal. The crowd went wild. Nick felt sick. There was something wrong with the whole thing. She was smiling but it was fake, she wasn't enjoying it. She was working, but what shit work.

'D'you want a beer, honey?' asked a woman in a swimsuit carrying a tray. Nick didn't speak. He didn't want a beer, he didn't want anything. He wanted to get the fuck out. He felt humiliated; he wanted to tell the woman he wasn't like all the other tragic individuals in the place, he was actually having sex with the woman on the stage, who by now had pulled up the T-shirt and was wriggling out of it in an inconceivably sexy way. He wanted the woman in the swimsuit to know he was way too cool to come into some shithole like this for a surreptitious wank.

Tiffany's thick mop of hair flipped back. There was an expression on her face he'd seen before. When she was with him, when she was coming. At least when he thought she was coming. His stomach turned over. For one of the first times in his life Nick Gardener had a really bad time. Tiffany clung to the pole and swung around, bending over, showing herself to everyone. Everyone.

'Oh God, yeah, baby. Do it to me,' screamed a scrawny man with a protruding Adam's apple who was standing next to Nick. The man was holding out a carefully folded ten-dollar bill. He looked as if he was about to lose it. Nick wanted to punch him in the face, smash his stupid American teeth down his perverted throat. Then he got angry with Tiffany. He watched her gyrations as she bent down and allowed the men in the front row to delicately tuck folded bills into the stupidly skimpy panties she was wearing.

Nick felt sad, lonely, a long way from home, from anyone who understood him. He turned and left. He had no idea Tiffany did that. He imagined she did a bit of go-go dancing or something, in a cage up in the sky, while cool people smoked and talked and pretended not to look. He had even imagined it was sexy, Tiffany in a miniskirt maybe, her pants showing occasionally. She had never told him she more or less fucked the punters. He shook his head and hit the street.

Nick took a taxi — not a normal occurrence, but he needed to get home. Two hours later Tiffany turned up at the house he was staying in in Beulah Street.

They stood in the kitchen together. He chain-smoked and felt terrible.

'I never want to have sex again after that. Put me right off,' he told her.

'It's just a job,' she said. 'I'm independent, I do it 'cos I want to. I get paid ten times more than if I waited table. Give me a break, Nick. I really like you. Don't screw up on me with some moral shit. You sound like my mom.'

'Maybe your mom's got a point. She ever seen you working?'

'Of course not, asshole.'

They didn't have sex. For the first time they spent a night together just holding each other until she slept. Nick looked at her beautiful face, so clear. No scars from what she'd been doing all night. How could this be the same woman?

He definitely did not have a good time that night.

It had been a year and a half since their bitter-sweet parting, Tiffany crying at the airport, Nick almost sobbing as he sat crushed in his economy seat to London. He'd spoken to her on the phone, even written her a letter once, and that took some doing. They had both promised to visit the other but neither of them had got it together.

Nick sighed as he looked out over the sea wall to the grey

waves dribbling against Brighton beach. The wind made a lonely howl through the cracks in the glass doors. It was still bloody freezing and yet it was supposed to be spring. Bollocks to global warming.

He scanned the promenade, tried to imagine what it would be like if ten thousand irate men with placards charged down the road towards the door, armed to the teeth, screaming like psyched-up rugby players. What was he going to do? For the money he was on he'd open the fucking door and leg it, that's what he'd do. Let the Very Wide ladies deal with it.

This had to be the weirdest job Nick Gardener had ever undertaken.

Chapter Five

'Hey, hon, how you doing?' asked Tara, sitting in the office at the back of the stage. The window looked out on a deserted street and the backs of a few old buildings. She had called Adrian in his hotel in Houston, knowing he'd be awake. Adrian didn't sleep much; he worked a lot.

'Not so good.'

'Oh, babes, have you had the results?'

There was a silence on the other end of the line. She could almost hear the room he was in, in the Houston Raddison, big and dark, cold from air-conditioning with a huge bed and ugly paintings on the wall.

'Babes. It's okay. I'm sure it's okay.'

'It's not okay, Tara,' he said without a hint of aggression. 'It's not impossible but it's not good. I have a very low count, very, very low, like one in three million. I asked if it was because of sitting in front of a screen for ten years. It's kind of as low as it gets. It's very common now and all that bullshit. It's nothing to do with VDUs. They reckon it might be Bakelite or some shit they used in electric motors when we were kids.'

'Oh, babes.'

'It's left me feeling kind of flat.'

'Hon, it doesn't matter. I mean, sure it matters, but it doesn't matter to me. Truly. I love you, d'you hear me?'

A short silence and then, 'I hear you. Likewise. Okay. It's like four in the morning here, I should try and sleep. Thanks for calling, Tara, you know it means everything.'

After she had hung up she stared out of the window a while, at an empty street, and then, as if on cue, a young woman walked up the street pushing a baby buggy. Tara snorted to herself.

'You were fantastic, man!' said Tim as he entered the room carrying the enormous holdall that contained his suit. He dumped it on the floor and flopped on a chair, rubbing his tired face with his hands for a few moments. 'They really loved you, the whole place is buzzing.' He stood in silence for a moment. 'You had news?'

'I had news.'

'Not good, huh?'

'Nope. Not good at all.'

'You called Adrian?'

Tara nodded. 'He's like really depressed. And he's not even at home, he's at some convention in Houston. Hotel blues.'

'Oh, man. Poor guy. What did they say?'

'He said it was like one in three million.'

'One in three million. Do they really count the suckers? Oh, man. This is really bad, Tara,' said Tim, looking her right in the eye, his face full of concern. 'Oh, man, that must be tough.'

'I guess so,' agreed Tara. Tim had no children and had always seemed happy about it. Maybe men didn't get the same kind of urge, but there was something happening inside her now, some urgency that filled her to which she could put no name.

'Oh, man,' said Tim. 'I'm real sorry to hear this. What are you going to do, man?'

'I don't know. Not have kids, I guess.'

'You could maybe consider adopting a kid if Adrian really can't, you know. I love the kids I'm stepdad to, even though they're kind of grown-up. But that's like me adopting them, and it's a really good way to relate to kids. You're not quite so fucked up as a parent. You know. It's worth thinking about.'

'Sure,' said Tara, smiling at Tim's kind face. 'We talked about that. But, well, I guess I kind of wanted to have a baby. That whole biological clock thing.'

'Sure. No, it's real hard. You and Adrian, I mean, it's like an institution, man. It's real hard on him, but, well, what about a donor?' said Tim.

'Oh, wow,' said Tara, her face creasing up. 'No, that's way too heavy, Tim.'

'Sorry, man. I was just suggesting, you know. That's what some people do.'

'No, we'll try something, something will work out. I'm sure.'

'Okay. You hungry?'

'Sure. Let's go eat.'

Chapter Six

About fifty men appeared around the corner of a side street and started walking towards the convention centre. They were, to put it kindly, a motley crew. Mostly over thirty-five, Nick guessed, but other than that, nothing seemed to tie them together. About six of them were holding handwritten placards which bent double in the fresh breeze blowing off the sea. After a while he could make out what they read. 'It's a man's right to help choose' and 'If men are so bad, and mothers have all the rights over children, who's fault is it?' and the most difficult to understand, 'Men demand the right to live longer'.

The group, who were escorted by two happy-looking police officers, walked up to the large glass doors. Some of them looked a little embarrassed and awkward, some had very red faces and appeared very angry.

'We demand the right to be heard!' shouted a thickset man in his forties. He was wearing a T-shirt boasting the logo 'I'm a normal dad. No rights, no home, no access to my children'.

The men stood staring furiously through the door. There was an awkward silence after the initial shout. Nick had no idea what to expect. Suddenly, and with no clear warning, the thickset man in the T-shirt shoulder-barged the door. It was locked but it was right next to one that was open. Nick couldn't help smiling at this. He started to move towards the open door to have a word, and noticed how some of the men stood back when they saw him coming. He raised his hands to show he meant no harm. The two police officers stood well back. They watched in a casual way, clearly not wishing to get involved.

The thickset man understood and kicked at the unlocked door. He marched through and started shouting immediately. 'Men have rights too. We demand the right to look after our children. Women like you are emasculating the population. The pendulum has swung far enough! Men exist, get used to it!'

Nick moved between the man and the now edgy security women at the top of the stairs. The man didn't seem to see Nick; his eyes were fixed on the women. He shoved Nick harder than Nick had expected. It threw him off balance a little and his adrenalin kicked in big-time.

'Sorry, mate, it's a private event. You can't come in here.'

'I demand the right to be heard!' screamed the man, still not really registering Nick's presence. Two other men started to push their way through the open door. Nick saw it for what it was, classic door-bursting tactics. Why hadn't he seen it coming? It was rhino time.

He forced the pushy man in the T-shirt back towards the door with a continuous double-handed shove. The man offered little resistance, clearly not expecting the move. In so doing, Nick trapped the three or so other men who were trying to slip in.

'Oi, oi, oi!' shouted the man in the T-shirt. 'Get your hands off me!'

Nick realised with some surprise that this bloke was actually quite posh, army officer type, which might mean he could rumble.

'I'm sorry, sir,' said Nick, holding the man back with one arm while holding the sleeve of another man who was slipping through to one side. 'This is a private, woman-only event. I have to ask you to wait outside.'

'Who the hell are you!' asked the T-shirted man, as if for the first time realising that the person who had stopped him was a man and was standing right in front of him.

'I'm head of security for this operation and I am under the strictest instructions not to allow you access, so I am asking you to wait outside.'

'Who gives you the authority to suppress our right to free speech?'

'You can say what you like out there,' said Nick, very used to all the arguments punters might throw at him in a situation.

'We demand to be heard,' said the man in the T-shirt, looking over his shoulder for support. He received it, and Nick felt the force from behind the man as the crowd started to push forward. He acted swiftly and fiercely, the only way when things reach an impasse. He used his right knee to dead-leg the man who was trying to slip in through the side. He went down hard, gripping his leg and moaning. The move freed Nick's left hand to grip the door frame while his right started to force the door shut. The glass was pushed into the face of the now near-hysterical man in the T-shirt. His nose was comically squashed to one side. Nick hyperventilated and then, with a jerking movement, managed to get the door shut. His right boot jammed against the bottom edge, he found the bolt and slid it home. Then he looked down to see the man he had dead-legged lying on the floor holding his thigh.

'What are you doing in here?' asked Nick.

'I think my leg's broken,' said the man.

'Blimey, mate, you all right?' asked Nick, and ignoring the hammering and screams from outside he bent down to tend to his victim. It didn't take long to ascertain that the man's leg was fine except for some painful bruising. Nick helped him to his feet and ushered him along the row of glass doors, constantly reassuring him and not letting him say anything. 'You'll be all right, mate. God knows what happened then. It was a total nightmare. Soon have you out of here. Don't you worry, mate, I'll look after you.' They came to a door that had no protesters outside. Nick opened it and, without obvious aggression, quickly ejected the man, then closed it again. The man stumbled outside, turned to see that he'd been ejected, and then charged the door. The other men all ran up to him and tried to help him push the door. It was too late – Nick had closed it firmly. The two police officers could now sense that things were getting a little heated and started to move in amongst the men. Nick was very glad to be on the quiet side of the doors.

A small round of applause came from the Very Wide Women at the top of the stairs. Nick glanced up. They were all looking at him, beaming.

'Nice one, Nick,' said Wendy. He smiled back, not sure how to feel. Then he noticed someone else standing next to the women – taller, slimmer, in fact bloody gorgeous. She had short-cropped dark red hair and eyebrows that were thicker and darker than he'd ever seen before. She was looking at him, just standing there looking at him.

Suddenly, behind this stunning woman, hundreds more delegates started to appear. It was clear that a lot of discussion was taking place between the women delegates and the security guards. Nick couldn't hear, but he guessed they were having a break and some wanted to go out the front for a cigarette. Some of them started to come down the stairs and move towards the door. Nick walked towards them.

'Can you open the door, please,' said one of the women.

'I don't know if it's a good idea to go out there right now. Those plonkers are a bit mad about something.'

'The demise of patriarchy,' said the woman flatly.

'If you say so,' said Nick happily.

'Open the door, please. This is not a prison.'

Nick shrugged. By the time he had reached for the fire escape bar on the stout door at least another fifty women were waiting, some of them rummaging through bags looking for lighters and cigarettes. The men outside were waiting too. Nick checked the women. They all still clearly wanted to go outside.

'It's amazing what nicotine can do to people,' he said as he pushed open the door. The end of his sentence was drowned out by the chants and screams of the men outside.

'Look who's sexist now!'

'It's a man's right to choose too.'

'Take your fucking rights off our children's bodies!'

In the main the women ignored them, just walking past them and talking to each other, but as Nick had almost expected, the man with the T-shirt proclaiming him to be a normal dad stepped forward and pushed one of the women.

'Take your fucking rights off my body, you fucking cow!' he screamed. Nick's arm automatically shot out to protect the woman, but too late; she fell into the crowd. Nick was brushed to one side by a solid force as two of the Very Wide Women barged past him. The man in the T-shirt was pushed with such force that he seemed to be lifted off the ground, his angry red face turning paler as he accelerated backwards.

A man in a duffel coat who was standing next to Nick shouted in his ear. 'How can you support these so-called women! Eh? They're a fucking disgrace.'

'Calm down,' said Nick. 'Someone's going to get hurt.'

'We're already hurt,' said the man. 'They've destroyed our lives, taken our jobs, taken our children. We have no say over anything any more. The future is female, mate. Get aware.'

The man was shoved to one side by a woman who had bared her teeth and exhibited such hatred that even Nick backed off for a minute.

'How dare you, you Neanderthal!' she bellowed.

'Calm down, lady,' he said, but he might as well have been trying to reason with an inanimate object. The man and woman were now engaged in a rapid exchange of insults and soundbite political slogans. Nick wanted to listen and see what the hell they were all so angry about. He felt as if he'd missed some cataclysmic event that had set all men and all women at each other's throats, and yet there had been nothing about it in the *Daily Mirror* that morning.

The scuffle rapidly turned into a rumble. All around Nick the women piled into the men with surprising ferocity. He saw at least three very nasty blows to the head delivered by women, one of whom was clearly holding her cigarette out of the way behind her in her left hand.

'Calm down,' he said, trying to hold the men back and receiving a glancing blow on the back of his head. It felt hard, like an elbow. He considered giving the perpetrator a discreet return elbow in the solar plexus, but decided against it as a policeman was suddenly standing right next to him.

'D'you mind going in and closing the doors, sir? We'll deal with this,' said the officer before shoving the men back away from the door.

'Fair enough, chief,' said Nick, and he turned and tried to get back into the building. By now so many women were leaving it was impossible to move.

'You're not from DAD-E, are you?' asked one of the women who was shoving against him.

'Stroll on,' said Nick.

'DAD-E. Very clever, isn't it? Not. They're like a radical activist offshoot of Families Need Fathers.'

'Fucking Ada,' said Nick under his breath.

He turned around and watched the men back away from the building, partly because the two police officers had now been joined by a dozen others, some with riot protection on, partly because of the sheer number of women who had appeared. They were so overwhelmed by noise and open displays of hostility that they had finally quietened down. The placards were still held high but the fight had gone out of them.

Nick eventually managed to get back into the building. He stood to one side of the door as the women continued to stream out. Wendy the bouncer joined him. She was puffing hard on a cigarette; he noticed that her hands were shaking slightly.

'You all right, Wendy?' he asked.

'Yeah. Got a bit shaken up by one of them, had to put the nut on him.'

'I saw,' lied Nick. 'Nice technique.'

'He had it coming, tosser,' spat Wendy.

'I don't get it. What are they on about?'

'Search me, mate. They all need a good kicking if you ask me,' said Wendy, pulling on her Marlboro like a tommy in the trenches.

Nick decided not to respond. What the man in the duffel coat had said had alarmed him slightly. He did feel as if he'd missed something. Clearly all these women at the conference were up to something. Much as he'd like to assume they were all white middle-class lezzos it was pretty clear that they came from all backgrounds and all races. He'd seen Indian women, black women, Far Eastern women, and bloody gorgeous women. What were they doing that got the sad little crowd of blokes so upset? Clearly something to do with the kids, but all that had ever happened to Nick was some woman desperately trying to dump his kid on him, not keep him away.

'Excuse me, may I talk to you for a moment?' asked an American voice from behind. Nick's heart skipped a beat. The voice sounded a little like Tiffany's, maybe a little deeper. He turned and his heart skipped another beat – it was the eyebrow woman who had looked at him from the top of the stairs.

She held out her hand. He shook it. She was fucking gorgeous.

'Hi. My name's Tara Kennedy. I'm one of the convention speakers,' she said, staring straight into his eyes.

'Oh, right,' said Nick. 'Nice to meet you, Tara. I'm Nick Gardener from All Areas. What can I do for you?'

'I'd like to talk to you for a while, away from all this,' she said, not a hint of flirtation in her voice, very matter-of-fact and businesslike. Nick had never been more confused. He couldn't even tell if he fancied her. She was gorgeous-looking, but there was something about her manner he couldn't make out. And she wanted to take him away from all the clamour.

'Oh, right. Well, I knock off at six,' said Nick.

'Right, okay. You can't leave right now?' she asked. Nick smiled at her and gestured outside to the continuing barracking and name-calling taking place only feet from where they stood.

'Don't think it would be entirely appropriate,' he said. 'It's my job to keep the building secure until everyone has left.'

Tara nodded. She then tapped Wendy the bouncer on the shoulder. Wendy turned and smiled a big yellow-toothed smile.

'How can I help you, darling?' she asked, a smile on her battered face.

'I need to talk to this gentleman for a moment. Would it be okay if we just found somewhere quiet?'

'You take him, darling. Everything's fine here.' She turned to Nick. 'You're all right, Nick, take five, mate, have a smoke. Oh, you don't, do you. Well, have a mug of tea.'

'Ta, thanks a lot,' said Nick. He turned back to Tara. 'Thanks,' he said. 'I was feeling a bit parched.'

Chapter Seven

When she had first met a padded assailant, Tara Kennedy had felt nothing but distrust. Why on earth would any man willingly allow himself to be beaten, kicked and punched by twenty women in a row? The only possibility she could imagine was that he managed to get off on it in some sexual way she couldn't, and had no desire to, understand. Men were weird like that, she had always known it.

Tim Renaldo looked harmless enough as he joined the circle of women at her first class, eight years before her appearance at the Brighton women's conference. Tim was about five ten, one hundred and eighty pounds, greying hair tied in a neat ponytail. He looked kind and soft, like a hippie potter or organic fruit farmer from Skagit Valley in Washington State. When it was his turn to speak Tim explained what he did and why he did it. He wanted to help women learn to defend themselves; it was all he felt he could do as a man to rectify the damage so many men had done so many women. Tara wasn't convinced. When he returned to the room after they had done their warm-up she was even less sure. Seemingly doubled in size and carrying a huge helmet under his arm, he looked very weird. Like a figure in a dream. Strangely threatening.

After her first class she experienced a complete turnaround in her feelings about Tim. In what was now a familiar phenomenon, she went from hatred to almost teeny-bopper adoration in the space of a five-hour class. Her confidence from that moment had hugely increased. She had done it, she had successfully fought off a large aggressive male using all his strength to overpower her.

During her preparation for the trip to Britain, Tara had been in touch with numerous schools of martial arts in and around London. She was looking for suitable male candidates to become padded assailants. She had singularly failed to find anyone, and she felt defeated by the stonewall lack of interest from all the people she contacted.

Although no one was actually rude to her during her numerous international phone calls, she could sense that behind the politeness the instructors she spoke to thought Winning Strategy represented a daft Californian fashion thing, a crazy cult, a trendy hiccough that would soon pass. What the people she spoke to practised was traditional, tried-and-tested martial arts. Karate, judo, kendo, tae kwon do – it didn't matter which, anything that challenged their orthodoxy was seen as faddish and of lesser quality. A little like devotees of religious faiths, martial arts people tended to be very evangelical about their own particular system of belief. Tara didn't really care what they thought, but she did need men to help her teach. She needed men like Tim Renaldo, and they were few and far between.

Tim had left the building through a rear exit and had promised to meet her on the seafront. However, events had overtaken her. She had watched the security guard during the whole of the incident at the entrance to the convention centre. Something about him had caught her eye, something familiar. She guessed it was the raw material she had seen so often sitting in the corner of the room during a class back home. Men who had been inveigled into coming along to watch the process of training, often moved to tears on their first encounter with the emotional turmoil that was stirred up by the experience. It was rare that she saw the necessary qualities in men needed for the job, but she thought she might have seen them in this guy. She guessed it must have been his quiet confidence – he didn't get mad when things got out of hand, he didn't take revenge when a woman punched him on the back of the head. He dealt with a very ugly situation surprisingly calmly. Plus he was fairly tall with a heavy build – not a prerequisite, but definitely an advantage.

She had asked the security women about him. They'd had him vetted – he was a single dad and had no convictions; he seemed 'above board and kosher', as the squat bouncer Wendy had put it.

As she walked up the stairs towards the restaurant Tara was aware that most of the women she was passing recognised her from her presentation. She was used to admiring stares from men and women, but this level of public adoration was harder to take.

Their passage was slowed by the constant stream of women who wanted to do the course, but eventually she and Nick made their way into the busy restaurant. She noticed many women turn and look. The conference was a women-only event but men were allowed in the café and crèche. She saw a man in the corner holding a baby, but it was still clear that Nick's presence wasn't altogether welcome. Tara turned around to see Nick holding the door open for a group of women who were leaving. He held it in such a way that they had to pass under his arm, and he arched his body to give them room. He was smiling at them, not lecherously, but flirting in some way she wasn't sure she understood. Could have been an English thing.

She bought two cups of tea and two doughnuts from a self-service counter and sat down at a table with Nick. He pulled off his padded black bouncer jacket revealing some disturbingly large, pumped-up arms. She pursed her lips and wondered if she were making a very big mistake.

'Nick . . . is that right?' she asked. He nodded silently. 'I liked what you did out there.'

'What?' asked Nick. He seemed genuinely not to know what she was referring to.

'You handled yourself very well. You didn't get mad, you didn't let them win, you kept neutral. I like that.'

'Oh, right, well, that's my job,' said Nick, taking a sip from his tea. The delicacy of the movement was peculiar; the size of his arms made the cup look pathetically small.

'Great. Well, let me tell you about my job,' said Tara, deciding to press on regardless. 'I help run a women's self-defence teaching system in San Francisco.'

'Oh, great,' said Nick. 'I've been there.'

'Where?' asked Tara, confused.

'San Francisco. Used to work behind the bar at the Circus on Market Street. D'you know it?'

'Can't say I do,' said Tara, knowing that Market Street was the area where in the past she had taught free self-defence classes for sex workers. She wondered exactly what the Circus bar was like. 'I don't go to bars that much, I guess. But let me ask you something. Have you ever heard of Winning Strategy?'

'What's that?'

'It's the women's self-defence organisation I help run.'

'Oh, I see. Can't say I have, but then I'm not a woman.'

A bit prickly, she thought. Leave it for now.

'Right,' she said. 'But d'you know any women who've taken our course?'

'Don't think so.'

'So you know nothing about it?'

'Sorry,' said Nick.

'Okay, that's fine, I'll explain,' said Tara. 'I help run a full-force, full-impact self-defence training system for women, although we do also teach children and some men. Our students don't practise in the air against an imaginary assailant as in all other forms of self-defence or martial art, they practise, with full-force blows, full-impact defence, against living men.'

'Bloody hell,' said Nick with an embarrassed laugh.

'The men are wearing a state-of-the-art body armour called

an impact suit. And they are carefully trained to take the blows. We call them padded assailants.'

'Padded assailants, bloody hell,' said Nick.

'It is only through using the techniques we teach that a woman really can experience what it's like to fight off an assailant. They can overcome their inhibitions and they can effectively fight back.'

'Right,' said Nick. She waited. He said nothing else, sipped his tea and looked at her.

'I just wondered how you felt about what we're trying to do.'

'Sorry?' asked Nick.

'I guess I'm trying to ascertain your attitude to the work we do.'

'Oh, right. Oh, well, sounds really good.'

'Fine. Okay.' Tara wasn't sure how to continue. She couldn't judge if Nick was just plain dumb or nervous and guarded. The arms were a big no-no. Most of the padded assailants she had worked with were martial arts experts, not body-builders.

'Have you had any martial arts experience?'

'Blimey, don't think so.'

'Oh. You looked like you knew what you were doing.'

'Oh, I see. You mean have I been to martial arts classes and stuff like that?'

'Yes,' she said. Maybe he really was something of a Homer Simpson, an embarrassing 'doh'-brain.

'Yeah, I've been to loads. Not for years, though. I did Shotokan karate when I was a youngster, got a brown belt. Bit of tae kwon do.'

'I thought so,' said Tara.

'When you said experience I thought you meant have I ever used martial arts techniques like in a rumble, a confrontation. Which I haven't. Well, not in an organised way. In my experience, you know, violence is a whole lot messier in reality than it ever is on a blue mat. Or in the movies, come to that.'

A ray of light shone. This was exactly what Tara wanted to hear.

'Right. That's great you think that.'

'Is it?' He smiled.

'Yes, because what we teach isn't smooth technique, it's about surviving a messy, ugly struggle, finding targets in the confusion and delivering knockout blows.'

'Wow.'

'Does that sound frightening?'

'Sort of a bit weird.'

'It is very disturbing,' agreed Tara. 'But not as disturbing as an actual assault.'

'Oh, right. Have you, like, been assaulted, then?' asked Nick quite gently.

'I don't want to discuss that right now. What I'm trying to work out is if you'd be interested in getting involved.'

'Who with?' he asked cheekily.

'With the programme. I wanted to find out if you'd be into joining a training course.'

'Me!'

'Yes. It would mean coming to San Francisco for about a month.'

'Would it?'

'Yes. The course is very intensive. You would be paid, of course, but we're not talking a fortune here. Our company is a non-profit 501 organisation, like a charitable foundation here in England.'

'I'd get paid!' said Nick.

'Yes. All your expenses, of course, and a small fee.'

'Fucking hell,' said Nick. He sat back in his chair with his hands on the table. 'I thought you wanted me to . . . well, I don't even know what I thought now. This is totally weird.'

'I'll give you a brochure and all my contact numbers. Give yourself a few days to decide. I'm not going back until the end of the month.'

'I see. Bloody hell. I mean, I have got a regular job, security at a club, nightclub. West End joint called Trash. I'm a bouncer. I mean, it's a shit job. I mean, I'm bored out of my tiny mind and I'd love to go back to San Francisco, believe me, but I don't know about all this getting punched in the head stuff.'

'Nobody is going to punch you in the head. They'll punch a specialised helmet you wear. We are very careful about protecting you. In the class you're our most valuable asset.'

'Bloody hell.'

'You'll think about it, then?'

'Yeah, sure,' said Nick.

Tara delved in her bag and pulled out a stack of leaflets. She handed one to Nick while she wrote the telephone number of where she was staying on the back of an envelope.

'Looks bloody lethal,' said Nick, studying the pictures of women fighting with padded assailants.

'It is very effective,' said Tara, passing him the envelope. 'This is where you can get hold of me.'

'Oh, right,' said Nick. 'I s'pose I should give you my number.'

'It's up to you. It would be very handy for me, but I respect the fact that you don't know me. If you want time to check out the whole thing, please do. You can ring the number on the leaflet to talk to our administrator. She'll confirm who I am. You can e-mail me.'

'Wouldn't know how to e-mail if my life depended on it,' said Nick happily.

The English were so retarded, thought Tara, but delightful.

'Okay, give me a couple of days to mull it all over.'

'I'll be waiting to hear from you,' said Tara. Nick stood up and pulled on his jacket.

'Better get back to the front line,' he said. 'Anything could be happening.' She smiled and held out her hand; he shook it. 'Nice to meet you, Tara. Thanks for the tea.'

'No trouble. Okay, speak to you soon.'

Nick walked back out of the cafeteria, swaying to miss the dozens of women standing around talking. One or two of them watched him go. Tara sat still and chewed her lip. Everything about his appearance said no, everything he said told her yes. She couldn't make him out at all. He seemed very open but then his answers made him seem very distant. She had never really known any English men, they seemed completely different to the wonderful men she worked with, but then Nick might not be typical. It was as if he'd learned the openness from spending time working in America, but he didn't really understand what it meant. He was terribly guarded – the arms were part of that, surely. To walk around with his arms and no doubt the rest of his body so heavily muscled was surely saying keep away, I'm frightened in here. She imagined him seeing a class. He was going to have a hard time, that was for sure.

Chapter Eight

Barney Mulberry was waiting in the kitchen when Nick got home from Brighton. He knew where the key was hidden, under the flowerpot with a dead flower in it by the twenty milk bottles that one day Nick would get round to taking back to the supermarket on Caledonian Road. Barney was just about to turn sixteen. He was nearly six foot tall, with great gangly legs that seemed to take up all the space in the kitchen.

'Yo, Barney, me old mate. What are you doing here?' said Nick, trying to hide his surprise at seeing his son.

'It's Friday night, Dad,' the boy said, sounding, as always, posher than Nick remembered. 'I'm staying with you this weekend.'

'Yeah, of course,' said Nick. He dropped his bag heavily and looked around. Everything seemed to be all right – didn't look like Barney had been taking drugs or turning the place over. 'Bloody hell, sorry I'm late, mate, it's been a mad rush to get back.'

'Don't worry, Dad, I know you'd forgotten,' said Barney.

'No, I hadn't forgotten,' Nick lied. 'I just got a bit delayed. Been on a job in Brighton.'

'Bodyguard?' asked Barney enthusiastically.

'Sort of, yeah. Big security operation.'

'Brilliant.'

'But not quite a bodyguard.'

'Dad, when are you going to get it together? It would be so cool if you were a bodyguard.'

'Yeah, yeah, all right, all in good time.'

'Dad!' said Barney, shaking his head in disbelief, the way his mother would have done. In fact looking more and more like his mother as he grew up and thinned down.

'Look, I've got to apply for the course, but I'm so busy at the moment. You know, I made bloody good dosh, mate. We can have a Thai takeaway if you want.'

'It'll be better than your cooking,' said Barney flatly. Nick smiled. He was always slightly scared of Barney's cruelty. The first thing he felt when he saw Barney was guilt. His son was completely right, he had forgotten about the weekend visit. The kid must have caught the train from Oxford and made his own way to the flat. So different from when he was a little lad in corduroy shorts, going to Oxford to get him on the train. Sitting beside him holding his little duffel bag full of clean pants and socks.

He had sometimes wondered what it would be like to have a kid if he lived in a family, with a wife. Like a mum and dad and kid. With a sort of grandma and granddad and pet dog. He'd seen it, watched other people go about their lives with prams and picnics, birthday parties you remembered, Christmas all together. His life was completely disjointed; nothing connected. He hadn't even told his mum and dad about Barney until the boy was nearly eight months old.

He'd been working behind the bar in Browns restaurant in Oxford when he'd met Sally. She was a student, studying English at one of the myriad of colleges he could never distinguish. She had been a face in the crowd, one of the many women flirted with as they waited for their tables in the frantically busy eatery. He hadn't paid her much attention because at the time his heart belonged to a blonde waitress who was still dithering about going to bed with him. The romance had blossomed between her serving table and him filling her drinks orders. But then Sally had asked him out and made it very clear that she fancied him.

'You are the most sexy man I've ever seen,' she said into his ear as he put a vodka and fresh lime in front of her.

She waited for him one evening, pointedly sitting at the window table where all the staff could see her.

'She's just a friend,' he had told Sarah, but within an hour of leaving the restaurant he was in bed with Sally, in her parents' house off the Banbury Road in north Oxford.

In his memory there was no other time he had slept with her; in fact they had coupled repeatedly for two months. However, it seemed very shortly after the first time when she had turned up at the bar as he was making lecherous noises to the waitress.

'I'm pregnant,' she said.

'Oh,' he replied. It was then that Nick first learned how quickly you could go off someone. Before his eyes Sally turned into a sharp-featured harpy, a difficult, annoying, tedious cow who was trying to destroy his life. He felt a little guilty about these feelings but they caused him to be very defensive.

'What d'you expect me to do about it?' he said as he tipped ice into a large bucket beneath the bar.

'Not be a bastard,' she said with a smile, and left.

He first saw the baby when Barney was just ten weeks. He walked into the big front room of her parents' house and saw a cot. Inside, a little pink head was wrapped in a blue blanket, eyes closed, one tiny hand protruding, sleeping and breathing with toy breaths. He remembered the incident with electric clarity, so it must have made an impact, but he didn't remember feeling anything at the time. It didn't look like him. In fact Nick thought the little thing was pretty ugly and smelled of that special sweet, slightly sickly smell of babies.

Sally, Barney's mother, made a vague attempt at reconciliation. She held out an arm languorously and he walked up to her. She looked fat, and she had an ugly spot on her forehead which looked sore. She pulled his head down and kissed him. He jerked back a little. It didn't seem right, to start shagging in front of a kid. She smiled at him, an expression that really didn't suit her. She looked better scowling. When she asked him to change Barney's nappy, he held the baby at arm's length for fear that it might shit all over him. She turned on him without warning and told him he'd better start giving her money or she'd go to the family solicitor and have him done, whatever that was supposed to mean.

He did give her money when he was able, or when he remembered, which wasn't often. Three hundred pounds here, fifty there, just enough to keep her away. Sally was always phoning and moaning – it was enough to put anyone off. Nick only saw Barney twice between the ages of one and five. Months would pass when the child's existence would never cloud his mind. He never felt sentimental about him, didn't have a picture of the young boy in his wallet, didn't tell the myriad women whose beds he passed through about his little Barney.

Sally went back to college when Barney was three years old and attending a nursery. She got her degree, and by the time Barney was attending the Dragon School, paid for by her father, she found a teaching post at Headington School for Girls. However, she was still living in her parents' large house and things were not happy at home. Although Nick felt completely uninvolved in her life, he heard all about it, at least three times a week.

When Barney was six years old, Sally had to go to a conference in Sheffield. Her parents were off somewhere posh-sounding. Venice probably. She asked Nick to look after Barney for the week. She had no choice, and it was about time he did something useful. He argued that he couldn't fit it in. It was too much hassle and he was very busy. The phone calls went on and on. The threats, the cajoling and the constant moaning slowly wore him down. He finally said he'd give it a go.

Nick was working in Bournemouth, a fitness trainer and tennis coach at the Woodman Hotel. He asked the hotel manageress if he could have some time off to look after his son. It was all arranged and it was all a big hassle. He was not having a good time and the kid hadn't even arrived.

During this period he lived in a caravan three miles outside Bournemouth with 'filtered' views of the sea. This meant the caravan was stuck in the corner of a field and he could just make out the sea through a hedge. He was too embarrassed to take anyone there – it made him seem too poor. However, the boy was so enchanted by the sea and the little den-like caravan that the two of them suddenly made friends.

It was a thankfully sunny week in late October, a half-term; Nick had forgotten they existed. They spent hours on the beach each day, playing strange games that the posh-accented Barney liked to play. They built things out of sand, not castles but boats, cars, mermaids. Nick bought a disposable camera and took some pictures. He actually started to have a good time. Barney looked after himself pretty well, reading books in the morning while Nick slept off the cans of lager he'd had alone the night before.

From this time on, once or twice a year, Barney would visit his dad, just for a couple of nights. They didn't seem to have anything in common and very often Nick found it extremely awkward. Somehow the timing of Barney's visit would always clash with the prospective arrival of a new lover. He did start carrying a picture of the boy with him, and when he mentioned Barney to a young woman in a pub the reaction was positive, so much so that he started lying about how much time he spent with the child.

Through all the years during which Nick was slowly getting to know his son, Sally remained a constant and painful thorn in his flesh. The understanding that he knew he would never be rid of her caused him the most hurt. She was as awful as only an Englishwoman can be. Frigid, cold-hearted, unwashed, annoy-ingly bad-tempered and fearsomely clever.

Barney wasn't like her, not really – there were enough of his genes swilling around to soften the boy. He was growing so fast, and as he did even Nick could see the resemblance. He was a Gardener as much as a Mulberry.

'How's school, then?' asked Nick when he had phoned his order for a Thai meal for two from the little restaurant around the corner.

'Shit,' said Barney sullenly.

'Why's that, then?' asked Nick. 'I thought you were getting on all right.'

'I'm just sick of all the work. I never get a break. You should see my homework. I've had to drag piles of it here. There's so much pressure, Dad, I really don't need it, d'you know what I'm saying?'

Barney could not utter the oft-used London phrase 'D'you know what I'm saying' without sounding slightly off-key. He wasn't exactly poshly spoken. As a little kid he had sounded like royalty to Nick, but as he grew and his voice broke he started to drop his aitches and slur his speech a little. Anyone could tell he had a bit of class in the background, though. He didn't sound very convincing, but Nick felt better about himself if he didn't put the boy down for trying to sound more street. He could clearly remember how life was hard enough for a teenage boy without having your dad do your head in.

'That's a bit worrying, though. You know how important education is, to your mum especially.'

'She goes on and on all the bloody time. Drives me crazy, Dad. It really does.'

'Well, she's got your best interests at heart.'

'Oh, please, Dad, that's so clichéd,' whined Barney, jumping back up the social ladder in one phrase. Nick hadn't realised what he had said was clichéd; he worried about how many clichés he used without knowing it.

'I mean . . .' he said slightly angrily. 'Look, I mean, look at me. No, look at your mum.' Barney really could run rings around him. He persevered. 'Look, your mum, right. She earns a good living, she's very bright, she worked hard at school. Look at me. Fucking dead loss, mate.' Got it out in the end.

'You're not,' said Barney angrily, his face flushed.

'I am, Barn. Face it. What am I, thirty-five, heading for thirty-six, getting bald and fat, and what have I got to show for it? I don't even have a motor.'

'You have, you've got the Triumph Stag.'

'Oh, the Stag, yeah, fat lot of good that is. A rusting heap in a garage in Pinner. I'll never fix it, I don't have the cash. The convertible roof's totally shot to ribbons. I've blown it, Barn, I'm too old to repaint and too young to sell.'

'It's old enough to repaint and young enough to sell if you're quoting the Neil Young song. Slightly different meaning.'

'Fuck. Listen to yourself. You're not like me. You're dead bright. You know stuff and you can't pretend you don't. Now your mum, let's face facts, Barn, if it wasn't for your mum you'd really be in the shit. When you leave home she'll be able to chuck you a bit of money so you can get your own place, you'll be able to get a job 'cos you'll have qualifications. Not like me. I've been a barman and a bouncer, a tennis coach and a swimming instructor. I've got no pension, no savings and a rented maisonette in a shit part of town.'

'This place is brilliant,' said Barney.

'Barn,' said Nick. He didn't want to go too far but he had done this before, reminded the boy that his life was not a bed of roses. 'I know Mum's difficult, but she really loves you, mate, and she knows what's best. Even I've realised that, and you know me, I'll always give her the runaround.'

'She deserves it.'

'Look, if you lived with me all the time, you'd soon realise what a good woman your mum is.'

'Well, I want to.'

'What?'

'Live with you.'

'Do you?' This news had come completely out of the blue.

Nick felt a shiver run through him as he realised Barney was now of an age where he would start to decide what he wanted to do rather than be told.

'Yeah, I'm sick of living at Grandma and Granddad's. They still think I'm a little boy. They just don't understand what I'm going through.'

'Yeah, well, they're fucking ancient, but your mum understands.'

'She doesn't!' shouted Barney. 'She really doesn't, Dad. She still thinks I'm a little boy. I'm taller than her now and she still talks down to me all the time. At least you treat me like a grown-up, you respect my opinions, don't always put me down with some clever history stuff. I can't begin to express myself back there. For a start everything's sexist in our house. Grandma and Granddad live in some weird time warp, they think it's still the seventies. It's ridiculous because actually they're all fascists!'

'All right, Barney,' said Nick. He realised his brow was furrowed, which in turn made him realise he was genuinely worried about the boy, which then made him realise he wasn't having a good time. The prospect of a trip to America had really raised his spirits, but Barney's arrival and anger had rapidly removed that good-time glow.

'I'm not joking, Dad,' said Barney, standing up. He was a big lad now, willowy but with a bigger frame than Nick's. He'd be taller in a few months.

'All right, mate. I hear you,' said Nick. Barney threw himself at Nick and embraced him.

Fucking hell, thought Nick. It was all so difficult. He didn't feel he could comfort him as he had done after a knee scrape at the adventure playground or a frightening experience at the cinema. He held him gently, patted his back.

'I'm serious, Dad,' said Barney. 'I hate Mum. I really fucking hate her.'

'Whoa, whoa.' Nick couldn't help feeling relief that he had

an excuse to break the tight embrace. 'You don't hate your mum. Come on. What's happened? Have you had a fight?'

'I told her I wanted to live with you and she just went ballistic, totally ballistic.'

'Oh. Right. I suppose she was bound to. Bloody hell, Barn. If you did move here it would mean a big change in her life, you know.' He glanced at his answering machine. Twenty-two messages – he was pretty sure they weren't from the girl from the NatWest in Brighton or the red-haired woman he'd met at the conference centre.

'You see, mate,' said Nick, holding the now tearful Barney at arm's length, 'she can't let go of you. It's going to be difficult for a bit, but she loves you.' Barney nodded as the tears flowed down his cheeks. 'It's all gone a bit pear-shaped, hasn't it, mate.'

'Tell me about it,' said Barney, wiping his eyes.

Nick smiled. Children were mirrors, showed you how naff you sounded. The thousands of times he'd said 'Tell me about it' to Barney in just the same way.

'Look,' he said, 'I'm about as reliable as, well . . .'

'Something that isn't very reliable,' said Barney. 'I know you're useless, Dad, but I don't need to rely on you. Listen, I can go to sixth-form college in September – there's a local one, Willesden. I've checked out their website.'

'Fucking hell,' said Nick, impressed that his son even knew what a website was. Nick certainly didn't.

'I could live here, keep studying for my A-levels after I've done my GCSEs. I'd go and see Mum at the weekends. I'd still see Hugo and Joey. They could come and stay, couldn't they? They think it'd be brilliant if I lived here. They could come up to London more often. Go to concerts and clubs and stuff.'

'Look . . .' said Nick. Then the doorbell rang. He struck a dumb pose that he and Barney had performed to each other after they had watched *Dumb and Dumber* on video. 'Duuuh, dinner,' he said, and went to the front door, took the food and paid the delivery boy from the thin wad of twenties he had just received for the Brighton job.

'Look,' he said when he entered the kitchen carrying the bag of steaming food, 'let's have a think. I mean, I'd be happy to have you live here for a bit, you know that. I mean, I'm hardly ever here anyway, but I'm worried about upsetting your mum. She makes my life hard enough as it is.'

'She'd come round to it if you talked to her, Dad. She listens to you,' said Barney, who had already put plates and forks out on the small round table.

'You'll have to stay with your mum for now though, Barn. I'm going to the states.'

'What! Are you going to train to be a bodyguard?' asked Barney.

'Sort of. Yeah.'

'Brilliant.'

They ate their meal and Nick heard about what Hugo and Joey, who he took to be Barney's best mates from school, got up to. Not really like he had been, these kids seemed to get their kicks from sending cryptic e-mails to TV stars in America, or shooting arrows at each other on Port Meadow, a huge stretch of open grassland on the outskirts of Oxford. No mention of girls, snogging, getting a bit. Still, he was only fifteen. Plenty of time for that.

Barney watched television in the bedroom while Nick cleared up the kitchen. His biggest fear was that the boy would find his magazines. They had just been lying in a pile next to his bed – he'd had to make an excuse earlier and dive upstairs to stash them under the bottom drawer of his old dresser. It wasn't so much that he was embarrassed about them; he just thought that they'd do the boy's head in. Nick hadn't set eyes on hard-core pornography until he was in his mid-twenties. He'd tried to imagine what he'd have thought if at fifteen he'd seen close-up penetration and ejaculation shots as opposed simply to semi-naked women in *Fiesta* and *Men Only*. Maybe it wouldn't have been such a bad thing. Sex was such a minefield, and nothing he'd seen or read by the time he got around to doing it had prepared him one tiny bit.

They watched an American sitcom together, lying on the bed, Nick with a beer, Barney with a Diet Coke as very beautiful young women were being sassy and quick on the screen, Barney laughing and yelling to his dad that he'd e-mailed this girl or that boy. Nick imagined being in New York with the dark one; he felt he half knew her already.

'Bedtime, mate,' said Nick when it was after eleven.

'All right, Dad,' said Barney. 'And before you say anything, I'm going to clean my teeth.'

'Nice one,' said Nick.

Barney climbed off the bed and sloped out of the room. Nick lay watching a chat show. A snippy English actress flicked her hair around as she spoke, reminding Nick of Barney's mother. He heard Barney climb into his bed in the next-door bedroom and waited a while. He eventually got up, took a leak and crept downstairs. He entered the kitchen and shut the door, plugging the phone back in – it was a habit to unplug it when he got home and couldn't face the earache. He switched the answering machine to Play, turning the volume down.

Message after irate message from Sally, asking him what he'd been saying to Barney and gasping in overdramatised disbelief that he'd suggest Barney should live with him. Did he know what he was saying? Nick ran his hands over his close-cropped head as he listened to the endless tirade. There was one message from his mum – it was his dad's birthday and his dad wasn't very well. His cough was back. Nick had forgotten that his dad was ill and forgotten his birthday. One message from a club-owner who'd got his number from Frankie Jessop, a door job in Notting Hill. Too late. Then another half-dozen short, bitter messages from Sally. Where was he? Where was Barney? What were they up to? How could he do this to her after all she'd done?

He clicked the Erase button and climbed back upstairs. He

checked on Barney as he passed his bedroom door; the boy was already deeply asleep, curled up in a foetal position with his left hand draped off the side of the bed. Not a trace of anxiety on his young face.

'Clever little fucker,' Nick whispered affectionately as he pulled the door to. Once back in his own room he turned the sound down on the clever chat show host and checked his watch.

It would be about mid-afternoon in San Francisco. If he rang Tiffany now, she just might be in. He dug the phone out from beneath a pile of clothes, held the receiver and hesitated. She was bound to be with someone else now. He was living in a fantasy land if he thought she was going to wait for him, but then she did write all those amazing letters.

He checked his battered address book and dialled the number. It rang clearly — three rings. She wasn't in. The answering machine clicked in, her voice.

'Hi, can't take your call right now, please leave a message after the tony-tone-tone. Bye!' So bright and young. The tone sounded.

'Hi, it's Nick, in England. Hi. Um, just thought I'd give you a bell. How you doing and all that . . . ?'

The sound changed, a click. 'Nick, you asshole!'

'Oh, wow, you're there!'

'Oh, baby, I can't believe it's you. You've actually rung me up!'

' 'Course I have.'

'I thought you'd forgotten all about me!'

'I can't forget about you. Even if I wanted to I couldn't. How are you?'

'I'm good. I'm good. I miss you, though, baby.'

'Oh yeah,' said Nick. Although he wanted to hear this, he didn't want to — it made the pangs he felt for her hurt so much more.

'It's true. When are you coming to see me?'

'Well . . . Oh shit, it's so complicated.'

'Oh, hon, it's always so complicated.' She imitated his voice as best she could.

'Well, I've just had the weirdest job offer today,' said Nick. 'Guess where I'd have to go for the job.'

'Baby?'

'A city called San Francisco. D'you know it?'

'You're kidding me!' she squealed.

'God's honest truth, Tiff. I just don't know about the actual job.'

'Oh God! I love hearing your voice so much. You make me wet, just hearing you.'

'Oh, please,' said Nick, his hand going to his crotch without hesitation.

'So, what's the job?' she asked.

'Well, it's this weird thing, I don't know how to explain it, like a women's self-defence thing where they get to beat up a bloke, and I'd be the bloke and they'd pay me for it.'

'Winning Strategy!' said Tiffany as though it were obvious. 'Shit.'

'You've heard of it,' said Nick, his spirits lifting.

'Sure. I didn't know it was still going.'

'It's been around, then?'

'Sure. They've got some place over in Berkeley, or is it here? Mom would know.'

'Your mum!'

'Sure. You know I hate all that pious shit my mom's into, but a job's a job, and if it means you get to live here, who gives a shit?'

Nick didn't want to tell her that the job was actually going to be in England. 'You think I should do it, then?'

'Oh, please, babe, I miss you so much.'

'Do you?'

'Of course I do, you asshole. What d'you think! Don't you miss me?'

'Terribly.'

'That's so sweet.'

Once Nick had finished cooing to Tiffany on the other side of the world, his little room seemed very small. Very lonely. He reached over and pulled out the bottom drawer of his dresser. Tiffany had bought the magazines for him in San Francisco. Not a moment he'd ever forget. He couldn't imagine an English-woman ever doing anything like it.

It was the sheer hard-core nature of the publications which was so shocking, but then Tiffany was a pretty hard-core sort of woman.

Jizz-Glazed Cheerleaders was on top – a blonde woman whose features were almost completely drenched in freshly spent sperm. She was holding an erect penis in each hand and smiling at the camera. He let each glossy copy slip through his fingers as he took in the lurid images on the covers – *Sperm-Soaked Babes, Girls Who Like It up the Ass* and *Trailer Trash on Heat*.

'I know what you boys like,' Tiffany had said happily, as she snatched the magazines off the shelf in an adult bookstore just off Market Street. Nick was partly appalled and partly fell freshly in love as he watched her hand over hard-earned dollars for the magazines, he guessed in the vain hope that with those pictures to occupy him, he wouldn't be off chasing tail.

The effect of the images on the glossy pages was predictable and fairly rapid. Moments later, with the lights out, his heavy arms resting above his head, Nick stared into the darkness. At the end of the day, sex and women, money and kids, age and youth, life and death, it was getting increasingly difficult to have a good time. All in all it was pretty fucking complicated.

Chapter Nine

Tara had slept for something approaching fourteen hours. She slipped out of the guest bedroom and ran herself a lovely, hot, English bath, overflowing with herby bath oils from the Body Shop. She couldn't really remember the last few hours of the previous day. She had stayed up as late as she could to try to combat the effects of jet-lag. The house she and Tim were staying in belonged to a scatty but charming Englishwoman called Yolanda Tintern. The small terraced house was full of heavily printed cloth, pictures, driftwood sculptures and cats. Too many cats for Tara and far too many for Tim. His eyes were swollen like cracked Jaffas as soon as some fluffy ginger moggy entered the room.

The previous evening had been noisy. Tara had spoken at length to an enthusiastic woman from London who'd achieved a black belt in tae kwon do but was frustrated with the system. She was an ideal candidate and a great find.

She had watched Tim gently flirting with a woman from the conference, and had smiled to herself. He just couldn't help it, he was wired that way. The conversation was hectic, fascinating and very well informed. She wasn't sure she could keep up with these brainy, fast-spoken people any more. Maybe she was a Californian girl after all. She just wanted to chill.

'Tara, phone for you, man,' said Tim's voice from outside the door.

'For me? Who is it?' Tara asked.

'I don't know. A guy,' Tim said between sneezes. The door opened a fraction and his arm appeared holding a cordless receiver. Tara pulled herself slowly out of the bath and wrapped a towel around her. She opened the door and took the phone. Tim was averting his gaze very dramatically.

'I am not naked, you dumb ass. Anyway, you've seen me naked before. What's the big deal?'

Tim pointed at the receiver and made faces.

'What?' said Tara. She looked at the receiver. It seemed pretty normal. 'How do I switch it on?'

'It's on, man,' said Tim, jumping up and down on the spot. 'It's on, it's on, he can hear you!' The jumping caused the floor to move slightly, which made Tara tense, coming as she did from an earthquake zone.

'Oh,' she said, and held the phone to her ear. 'Hello.'

'Oh, hi there, is that Tara?' said a deep male voice.

'Yes. Who's this?'

'Nick Gardener. I met you yesterday. At the . . .'

'Oh, right. Nick. Hello.'

'Sorry, is it a bad time?'

'No, it's fine,' said Tara. The towel started to slip off her. She tried to grab it with her free hand and keep the phone wedged to her ear. Tim kept staring at her with his big, inane grin.

'I've had a good think about this course you talked about,' said Nick. 'I'd like to say yes.'

'Oh, great. Okay, Nick, well, okay, let's meet up.'

'All right.'

They arranged to meet in a pub in London, Tim looking increasingly horrified as he heard Tara's side of the conversation. When she had hung up, she handed Tim the phone and discreetly adjusted the towel.

'Is that the dude you met yesterday?' asked Tim, now staring resolutely out of the window.

'Yeah. Good news, huh? He sounds real keen.'

'You want I should come with you?'

'Why, Tim, I thought you wanted to go see some castle thing.'

'Yeah, but you don't know who this guy is. You know, I mean . . .'

'I've checked him out,' said Tara proudly.

'Oh, Tara, man. You are too much. How d'you do that?'

'The security firm at the conference — what were they called?'

'The VWW women. Bunch of tough broads there, man.'

'I spoke to their co-ordinator. They found him through a reputable company, they know his record, he's clean.'

'Well, take care. You hear me? I have to look out for you. Adrian made me promise.'

'You guys,' said Tara with a smile as she walked to the bathroom door. She noticed Tim glance at her body, and caught his eye.

'Oh, man,' he said to himself.

'What?' asked Tara. She knew what, but it was fun all the same.

'I love Adrian, man, you know that, but he's the most morose guy I've ever met, and he's with you! It doesn't make sense.'

'He's not morose. He's wonderful,' said Tara. Tim laughed loudly and covered his face with his hands.

'What?' squealed Tara.

'You. You're so goddamn sexy. If I was Adrian I'd be walking around like I just finished a weekend course on finding inner happiness.'

Tara had known Tim long enough, had seen him go through enough in his own life, to trust him and for this outburst to be acceptable, but even taking this into consideration, it was on the edge of what she would tolerate.

'I am not going to fuck you, Tim. Okay?' she said flatly. It was a boundary she thought could do with a little reinforcement.

'Hey, I didn't say that. I know, man. I'm sorry.'

'It's okay.'

'You want a coffee?'

'I would kill for one.'

'But you wouldn't fuck me for one.' Tim stared at her with a kind smile. Such a creep, but such a wonderful guy at the same time. In another life, maybe she would.

'No.' She smiled back. They were, after all, very good friends.

'Cool. See you downstairs,' said Tim, now staring at her unashamedly, grinning from ear to ear.

'Now, please,' said Tara loudly. 'Let me do my toilet!'

'Okay,' said Tim as he slipped out of the door.

She sat motionless on the side of the bath for a while after Tim left, wrapped in the big green towel. She tried to absorb the moment — the softness of the towel, the way the light fell into the small, steamy room. The smell of soap. It didn't come naturally. Tara's life wasn't very sensual, had never been so in fact. Adrian was a complicated man, complicated but delightful, deep and clear in his thoughts, in his early forties, greying a little, naturally slim, tanned and very Californian.

He was so very cerebral, working on some indecipherable computer project at Palo Alto. Tara loved going out with him because he was so calm, so completely absorbed by the enormous thoughts taking form in his head. But there was little physical demonstration of affection between them. At first this had been exactly what Tara was looking for. She had told her friends and work colleagues that at last she was happy with someone. A man she really fitted with. It was accepted by all who knew them that she was a beauty and Adrian was devilishly handsome, but that neither of them was that impressed with the other's looks came as a blessed relief to both.

They went jogging together, they went to the movies together, and every now and then, quite rarely, they made love together. The stress of the struggle for a child hadn't killed the relationship as much as slowly diminish it in both their lives to a point where it was no longer tenable. Adrian had moved back to his own apartment in Palo Alto and slowly all his possessions followed him. It was only when he stopped in for coffee one day and walked out with a box of clothes, books and his laptop computer that it finally hit Tara. She sat down on her large red bed and wept for hours. She had never, in all her twenty-nine years, felt so utterly lonely.

She made an effort. She rang Adrian and they started talking – they hadn't talked for what seemed like years. He started e-mailing her regularly; she would log in and get forty messages from him, which he'd sent in one morning. In one or two succinct lines he would explain that he'd left her so she could find a breeding partner. He realised that his damaged gene pool was being removed from the continuance. As an individual he felt depressed about that but he knew it made sense for the continued development of the species. Each message made Tara sob. She fell freshly in love with a man so unselfish as to sacrifice himself for her. She had seen this in the faces of the padded assailants, men who understood what sacrifice really meant – she had utter respect for such behaviour. It had helped her understand how men fought wars. She had run to Adrian's house one evening. It was over five miles from her apartment, she could have driven, but it was important to run. Their reunion was passionate and prolonged. Adrian seemed charged by what she'd done. Waves of debauchery and pure lust swept over these two normally restrained people – they did things to each other they'd never done before. Afterwards they agreed there was no going back, they were together for life and needed to work on the problems facing them. Adrian agreed to have a sperm count, which he'd promptly organised.

Now she was in a bathroom in Brighton, England, with a view over a damp little garden and a row of brick houses going down the hill. It was a Sunday morning and she was tingling from her bath. She was in love and her love was reciprocated.

But Tara had a big, hollow sensation in her belly. It didn't seem to matter how many people she knew, how many people fell for her, told her they adored her – when given the time alone, only a few minutes, she felt incredibly lonely.

Chapter Ten

Alice knew that at any one moment in time, upwards of 2.3 per cent of the world's population was involved in sexual activity. Although this did include illegal public displays of masturbation by lone men in parks, rape and bestial acts, prostitutes with their clients and nocturnal emissions, it was still a sizeable amount of people. Even reducing the input exclusively to acts of standard sanctioned heterosexual copulation, you were looking at 2 per cent. That was about half a billion people. Half a billion people grinding and pushing and gripping and twisting around with each other. It didn't make her depressed that she was part of this statistic, in fact it gave her a warm feeling of involvement. She arched her back the way she knew Peter liked and felt his hands run over her buttocks, sliding up her thighs. It was a ritual, it was a ritual that worked.

'Oh Christ,' he said, as she felt him lose his balance and rest against her. As his hard body made contact along her back she could feel his erection pressing against her, feel his heat and his immense need. He moved her legs apart with his big, muscular thighs and slowly and smoothly entered her. She took a breath as she accommodated him and remembered that Pete was a master of hands-free entry, his erections so rigid he had no need to guide his penis manually.

She breathed deeply as his irresistible rhythm started. Within seconds she could feel her orgasm laying its foundations, and it seemed only moments later when she climaxed long, hard and loud. No one previously had done that for her. It seemed to be something almost magical, as if not Peter the individual but some peculiar physiognomy she wasn't aware of just made it happen. Alice had never believed in the vaginal orgasm, she had never even considered it a possibility, but no other man had ever made her come so fast merely by being inside and thrusting as Peter did so powerfully.

The explosion and sudden loss of tension made her lie spent and weak, flushed and tingling as Peter mounted her in every way he could, picking her up and bending her, always watching with totally absorbed fascination as his penis disappeared inside her, his face contorted slightly by the effort and concentration, his short fringe forming a sweaty zigzag of dark hair above his wonderful eyes.

He withdrew suddenly as he liked to do. There was no need, she was using her cap, but it was his favourite method. He did it annoyingly at the point when she could feel every contour of his astoundingly hard erection and the tingling tension of another orgasm. She watched, slightly removed from the whole thing as Peter's sperm flew out and landed in hot blobs on her stomach.

'Darling,' she said, making the word long and somehow devoid of emotion. He collapsed on her, turning the creamy gobbets of liquid into a sticky lubricant between them.

'Oh God,' he said. 'Oh God, Alice. I wish we could get on.'

He was right, of course. She and Peter didn't get on very well at all. She had never known a man she had less in common with but could have such nice sex with.

Peter Welbeck sold life insurance, investment and pensions products for Victoria Life Assurance. She didn't understand what made him want to do it, except that he earned a lot of money and was quite a good talker. He was thirty-three, very fit because he played rugby and golf at every available opportunity. He had a maths degree from Warwick University, a sixteen-valve

Ford Mondeo 1.8 GLi with alloy wheels, and a collection of ties that on first inspection made Alice pretend to gag with revulsion.

In terms of status within the industry she was leagues ahead of Peter. As a statistician, a number-cruncher, a data-provider to the government, to Lloyd's and to insurance companies the world over, she was highly regarded and highly paid. She knew how dangerous it was to send a diver down under a sea-based oil drilling rig; she knew how safe a Boeing 737 was during take-off with three hundred thousand gallons of fuel sloshing about in the wings. She could walk into the kitchen of a restaurant and see that it was a fire hazard waiting to happen. She spent her time looking at disasters, working hand in hand with crash inspection teams, fire inspection teams, sinkings and flood inspection teams. She had her own hard hat, life jacket and thermal clothing. She tended to flit around the world at a moment's notice, so maintaining things like relationships for long enough to settle down and have children was not something on her immediate to-do list.

That wasn't to say she never thought about it, but as soon as any picture of how life could be emerged, the phone would ring and she would fly to Malaya and walk through the steaming rainforest looking at pieces of aeroplane, people, children and babies strewn through the dense vegetation. An experience that intense tended to remove the everyday to a safe distance.

Of course, this was a well-known phenomenon. People who worked in the 'disaster trade' managed to keep real life at bay for years by travelling from one dreadful disaster to the next. Their home lives, if you could call them that, were always volatile or sterile — volatile as the marriage broke up, then sterile as they lived alone for longer and longer.

Alice had met Peter the previous year when she had appeared as a guest speaker at a Victoria Life Assurance sales convention which had taken place in Deauville, Normandy. She had been flown to Deauville in a twin-engined Piper Comanche, a sturdy American-built plane with a relatively good safety record for its class. The pilot was French and clearly very experienced, ex-military, which meant an increased safety factor.

Her talk had gone well. She had the capacity to make people laugh as she explained the processes involved in risk assessment. She used her laptop computer which contained her display material and some gory photographs which always captured people's attention and she knew made her seem just that bit more glamorous. Her favourite was a photo of her in the huge hangar where they had put together the fated Flight 800 from New York to Paris which had blown itself to bits twelve thousand feet above Long Island.

Peter Welbeck had spoken to her in the banqueting room after her talk. She didn't have any great desire to stay but there was no flight out of Deauville until the morning and the Hotel Normandy had a certain tacky charm with its huge casino and topless dance displays. He had enjoyed her talk and thought that what she did must be fascinating. He looked like all the other men in the room, freshly scrubbed in their executive bathrooms and uncomfortable in their evening dress. She noticed that he was quite trim and had nice eyes.

She asked him about his personal fitness and they discussed issues relating to male health, life expectancy and heart disease. She discovered that he loved rugby. She hated rugby. Statistically so dangerous, a virtual guarantee of multiple injury for anyone who played it, and so dull to watch. She was convinced that all men who played rugby had a missing gene. She told him this and he laughed, which was nice. He agreed with her, and then tried to assure her he wasn't a typical rugger bugger. He mentioned golf, and when she told him that all forms of competitive sport gave her a headache he laughed again. She liked him – he confounded her prejudices, sidestepped her criticisms skilfully and confounded her deadpan responses to his flirtations.

Somehow she gave him her number, not a thing she would normally do, but there was something about him which appealed.

A thing she couldn't assess owing to lack of data – just a small flutter of excitement registering in the lower abdomen.

A week later they met at Tuttons in Covent Garden, his choice. He lived in High Wycombe, so she assumed it was just through lack of knowledge of her native city. She forgave him his naffness and in fact they had a nice meal.

'There's a great deal of artistry in rugby,' he said matter-of-factly during this first date. 'There's even ballet involved, if you'll only give it a chance, Alice. God, I love that name. But listen, I just find rugby's a really powerful way for me to express myself, to use a mixture of raw power, body weight and speed, with agility and cunning to get a ball through a series of hazards. It's . . . look, honestly, it's an almost spiritual experience when I score a try.'

'Almost spiritual, that is so tragic,' she said, warming to him more every minute.

'I know,' he said. 'I know and I don't care.'

They did go back to her place and they did make love for hours and it was brilliant. They saw each other irregularly for three months. He put very little pressure on her, never mentioned anything about formalising the relationship, never hinted at jealousy or uncomfortable emotions, he just supplied her with very intense sex whenever she needed it, which wasn't often. To her never-ending amazement, Alice actually accompanied Peter to a rugby match after he had pleaded with her gently for weeks. It seemed to be his attempt to build a bridge between them based on something other than sex.

The experience of standing through the spectacle was as appalling as she had feared. She couldn't understand what was going on; found the attitudes it fostered in the men on the field as barbaric, dunderheaded and annoying as she had expected. She sat in the car listening to Radio 3 as he changed. She imagined him singing songs about jolly girls with big tits with the lads in the shower.

'I never want to see you doing that again. I cannot bear it. I literally cannot bear it. I have never been so bored and upset in my entire life,' she said as he sat down beside her in the car, smelling of soap and underarm deodorant of a slightly claggy nature.

'Right,' he said, holding the steering wheel with both hands and staring into the dusk. 'Okay, well, at least we know where we stand.'

'I'm sorry, Peter, but I am allergic to rugby.'

'Okay, you don't have to watch again. You do know we won, don't you?'

'Sorry,' said Alice, feeling genuinely so. 'It's such a shame. I mean, I really, really like you. But I just can't abide it. It makes me depressed to think you love it so much.'

'Oh,' said Peter. They drove back into London in silence.

Rugby was a wall between them. After one visit to his clean and strangely empty house in High Wycombe, Alice knew it was insurmountable. A very large photograph of a rugby ball sitting on greensward had been Blu-tacked above the fireplace. On a delicate and, she guessed, IKEA shelving unit were a cup and three photographs in frames of rugby teams, all presumably including Peter, although she couldn't actually bring herself to bend and look at them. There was an old teddy bear on the top shelf and a picture of a red sports car. That was all – no books, no pictures of his mother and father or brothers, or anything. Sport, cars and sport. Surely there had to be something else to this man.

'Drink?' he asked.

'Tea,' she said.

'Nothing stronger?'

'No, Peter, nothing stronger. You don't have to get me drunk in order to have sex.'

'I wasn't trying to get you drunk.'

'Yes you were.'

'I might not want to have sex.'

'Of course you do. You always do.'

74

'I might not now. Today, I might not be in the mood.'

It would go on and on. They enjoyed each other's company but there was nothing resembling affection in their encounters. Their bodies so mutually satisfied each other that it almost removed the need for affection. In fact, as time wore on Alice found it was better to nurture a healthy dislike for Peter and everything he stood for. It was almost as if she enjoyed having sex with him more if she held him in low regard.

Alice found that her day-to-day life had improved during the time she had been with him. The world seemed better, less dirty and problematic if she had been making love into the early hours the night before. She could cope with life, the bulk of her work being computer-based and fairly dull. She had a spring in her step, and when she made progress with a problem she really felt she was making a difference in the world, no matter how small.

Alice knew she hadn't found happiness, she hadn't found her mate, and she certainly hadn't stumbled across the perfect man. She fought down the desire to scream out at him, tell him she thought he was a low-brow, narrow-minded rugger-bugger moron whose very existence bored her to tears. It didn't matter, that was the conclusion she came to. He was very polite and respectful, he was brilliant in bed, clean, never late. In fact, in so many ways he was less annoying than all the men she had known before. Cruel really, and not explicable in any statistical sense.

Chapter Eleven

Nick stormed through the crowds at Heathrow carrying an enormous yellow nylon shoulder bag. He had got to the Tube station on Caledonian Road and gone through the classic panic pocket-pat. He frisked himself only to find he'd forgotten his passport. It was on the kitchen table, he could see it, burnt into his retina like a flashbulb going off in his face.

He'd had to leg it back down the Caledonian Road and up Offord Road, barge back into the flat, grab the passport and leg it back to the station.

The first ten minutes on the Tube were spent trying not to sweat too much in case the packed carriage occupants thought him some sort of nutter.

He knew he was going to be late so he decided that when he got to the airport he would do without baggage check-in at the gate and just go for it at full pelt.

'Would passenger Gardener due to board BA flight 371 for San Francisco please go immediately to Gate Fourteen where your flight is waiting to depart. Passenger Gardener to Gate Fourteen, please,' said the announcement as soon as he'd made it into the departure lounge.

'I'm passenger Gardener and I'm seriously late,' said Nick as he approached passport control. The woman was very friendly, let him through and pointed him in the right direction. The staff at the security check were equally helpful. Nick felt blessed – he had often been the recipient of grief at such places.

'Straight up there and to your left, sir,' said the man in the cap by the baggage X-ray machine.

'Ta, thanks a lot,' said Nick, shouldering his bag and sprinting. For a man of his size, Nick Gardener could put on an impressive turn of speed. He ran along the moving walkways feeling serious wind in his face. People heard him coming, shouting 'Thank you very much!' and 'Ta, sorry' as he barrelled past them.

Gate 14 – not far; he could see the worried officials waiting, walkie-talkies at their mouths. A British Airways woman held her hat as she ran with him down the passenger tunnel. He stepped through the door and into the wide-body 747 without any of the trepidation he normally felt as he entrusted his life to the giant machine and its crew.

'Really sorry,' he said as the door was immediately swung to behind him. A completely bald purser in a crisp white shirt smiled genuinely. He held up his smart gold watch.

'You made it, sir. We could have waited another three seconds and that was it.'

The plane started to move off as Nick apologised and slowly moved down the corridor between the rows of packed seats. When he was halfway down he realised he was sweating an enormous amount. He had a heavy American quilted denim jacket on, over a sweatshirt and a shirt. He was soaked through underneath – he could feel sweat pumping out of him as if he were a leaking plastic bag.

Suddenly Tara Kennedy's head appeared in a seat in the central section. She looked up at him and raised her eyebrows very slightly. All the anxiety Nick had been experiencing on the way to Heathrow airport suddenly evaporated. Tara Kennedy was a deeply attractive woman. He'd forgotten that bit.

'So, you didn't change your mind,' she said when he finally finished stripping off and stuffing his bag in the already cramped overhead locker.

'No. Thought I'd drop in at the last minute,' he said, wiping the seemingly endless torrent of sweat off his forehead.

'Looks like you may have run a little in order to get here,' said Tara.

'Tell me about it,' said Nick, then, remembering his son's use of the phrase, he added, 'Like a bat out of hell. Must have lost two stone. Frightened the living daylights out of some of the passengers. Bloody hell. They must have thought I was some sort of terrorist nutter.'

'Glad you made it anyway. I was real worried for a while back there.'

'Sorry,' said Nick.

'I was just trying to make up my mind how I was going to tell the guys back in the office. "I met this guy that I thought would make a great assailant, so I bought him a ticket and he never showed up. Sorry about that." It would have been kind of embarrassing.'

'Yeah, well, don't bear thinking about, does it,' said Nick, not really knowing what to say.

'Anyway,' Tara said as she delved into a leather bag at her feet, 'I've bought you something to read on the flight.'

'Oh, great,' said Nick flatly. Reading had always been a bit of a chore. Tara handed him a thick pile of paper bound together with a metal clip at the top left-hand corner. The cover said 'Outline History of Winning Strategy, the San Francisco Women's Self-Defence Organisation'. Nick's dread only increased when he saw what he was required to read. He turned the first page – no pictures, just great wads of writing. At least he might find out what he was getting himself into.

'You don't have to read it all,' said Tara, 'but it gives you a very good idea as to why we do what we do and how we know it works.'

'Great,' said Nick. 'Great.'

He had already started reading.

Hard Plastic and Feminism

Winning Strategy, although not then known by this name, was started, to all intents and purposes, in July 1975. In early 1975 a female black-belt karate student was violently attacked and raped in her home by an unarmed serial sexual assaulter. She had just been placed second in her style at a state championship, she had the ability to fight back, the technique to render her assailant incapable of harm, and yet, on her own interpretation of events, she did nothing. She experienced a freeze response to an assault. Her training had not prepared her for the emotional and physical realities of an actual situation.

This woman's karate teacher was Hugo Chang, a triple-dan karate, kendo and judo trainer from Los Angeles. The attack confirmed Chang's worst fears. The woman had closed in on herself, not using any of the techniques he had taught her over many years. It made no sense to many people, but Chang felt he knew what was wrong. The woman had never actually hit anyone. She had been brought up in an environment where this was not seen as appropriate behaviour for anyone, but most especially for a woman. Chang felt very strongly that this was what had to be changed.

Over the next few months, using football padding, helmets and crudely improvised groin protection, he started working on a self-defence system where a pupil could use full-force techniques to experience far more realistically the effects of unarmed combat. The technique, although crude by today's standards, had remarkable results.

Once women experienced a 'fight' as opposed to merely practising against air, once they experienced applying full-impact blows to a violent, abusive and physically larger opponent, their confidence and ability increased exponentially. New methods and techniques sprang up which suited the female body and convinced everyone who witnessed the classes that Chang was on to something.

Over the next fifteen years the Winning Strategy self-defence system was buried deep in the research and development process until it became established into the format and organisation we see flourishing today. Many more people have become involved, many have moved on and left, but the principle behind the training system has only ever strengthened. There are now over 600 police-verified examples of women who have been trained by the full-impact movement around the United States using the techniques to protect themselves successfully.

Winning Strategy self-defence has come about due to a combination of feminism and hard plastic. The feminism is the philosophy behind the class; the development of hard, high-density plastic padding making light, flexible body armour has been the catalyst for this type of self-defence teaching and made it possible for students to use full-impact techniques without causing injury to the assailant in the class.

This is the story of feminism and hard plastic.

Nick sat scrunched up in his seat, utterly absorbed in what he was reading. An hour later he looked up as a British Airways cabin crew member lowered his table and placed a meal tray before him.

'I chose the fish for you,' said Tara. Nick smiled. He glanced over at the window to see the familiar brilliance of the sunlight over white clouds. He had no awareness of the take-off, so completely absorbed had he been by the Byzantine history of the Winning Strategy self-defence movement in America. He'd never heard of it before, and yet it had clearly touched thousands of people's lives. As the system had grown and evolved, still based in the San Francisco Bay area, people moved out to other cities and started 'chapters' there, some successful, some less so, but always developing new techniques of teaching, new operating procedures, using therapeutic methods from the burgeoning self-awareness movements that swept the States during the eighties.

He could easily see, hidden between the lines of the glowing history, ugly disagreements that had caused rifts to develop between opposing groups. The movement, started in the seventies, had by the early nineties grown into a huge and unwieldy organisation. Each separate group, or 'chapter', a term Nick had only previously heard in relation to Hell's Angels motorbike gangs, was located in and served a specific area. There were stories of chapters in certain cities changing their name and thereby infringing on a neighbouring chapter's territory. It was all pretty strange; Nick couldn't get a handle on what these people were like. He couldn't understand why they had to have all this organisation. They didn't strike him as people who were having a good time.

Fearful hatreds and mistrusts seemed to develop between chapters of differing views. Scandalous gossip spoke of teachers taking advantage of students while giving them one-to-one training at home. In a bedroom, at night. Weird stuff. Then whole sections on transference, which seemed to mean that some of the students started to crack on to the padded assailants, which sounded well good to Nick. Then, as he read on, he started to get more depressed – they all sounded barking, like they were fighting over nothing and not having a good time. However, the paper ended on a high note. By the mid-nineties it seemed everyone had sorted out their differences and had agreed common goals. He noticed Tara's name occurring more and more during the latter half of the paper. She had obviously become a big noise with the chapters in recent years.

'Good afternoon, ladies and gentlemen, this is Captain Mark Allen speaking. Hope you're enjoying the flight. We are presently cruising at thirty-seven thousand feet and we have a bit of a tail wind so our arrival at San Francisco today should be slightly ahead of schedule. We are presently about thirty miles off the coast of Newfoundland and will be heading down past Calgary, on our way to San Francisco. I hope you are enjoying our in-flight service and I wish you a very pleasant journey.'

'This is bloody amazing,' said Nick when he'd finished reading the pile of paper. 'I had no idea.'

'Well, I thought it would give you a kind of background, just to show you this wasn't something we made up in the last couple of weeks.'

'But you all seem to have been fighting each other,' said Nick. 'I don't understand all the battles that have been going on. Why can't people just do whatever it is they do?'

'Okay, well, most of that is in the past,' said Tara. 'A lot of stuff happened before I even got involved, and it is a kind of primal experience, as you'll find out. I don't mean that in therapeutic terms – we're not an Arthur Janov encounter group.'

'Who's he?'

'Arthur Janov? You've never heard of him?'

'No. Is he a martial arts bloke or something?'

'No, he wrote a ground-breaking book called *The Primal Scream*.'

'Never heard of it.'

'Okay, forget it,' said Tara. 'What I mean is, the training tends to bring out some very deep-seated emotions, in both the teachers and the students. That's why when people got mad about technique or process in the classes, they got real mad.'

'Bloody hell.'

'Are you wondering what you've let yourself in for?' asked Tara with a smile.

'And some,' said Nick. 'I'm shitting myself. I don't understand the half of it. Reading this thing has just made me more confused than ever. I mean, I'm with you on the whole women shouldn't be raped thing. I'm with you on the whole teaching women to look after themselves. It's just all this other shit.'

'Well, the other shit is the detail,' said Tara. 'Like who teaches and how. When the first classes happened in the early seventies, it was still men teaching – women were just pupils or assistants to the male teacher. A lot of trouble started when the women said "We want to teach", and the trouble got worse when they said we want to teach and we want you to be merely an assistant, a padded assailant who makes what we've got to do possible. Without a fully grown male to fight, we're never really going to know what it's like. Just how strong you guys are and what it takes to put you on the ground.'

'Fucking hell.'

'So that's where the trouble started, and some guys who were involved, for all the best reasons, got real mad at what they saw as their marginalisation, and some were cool, and so you got splits and factions. Once that was settled, some of the women teachers were real good, and some were not so good, you know, and some of them maybe should have been administrators, but the charge you get from teaching is so intense it's kind of addictive. So that caused other fights and splits. It was all pretty intense. But now, with the group I work with, all that stuff is in the past. We've had to move on, and the guys you'll meet are really terrific, I mean really. It's they who'll teach you, not me, because what you've got to do is truly challenging. Not a lot of men can take it, and you may find it real hard to cope with at first, but I've got high hopes for you, Nick, I really have.'

'Fucking hell,' said Nick. He pressed the button on the side of his seat and leaned back. 'Hope I don't let you down.'

One thing Nick had always done on long hauls, especially to America, was have lurid sexual fantasies and try to keep an erection for a thousand miles. Or two hours. This would involve absolutely no physical stimulation, just mental imaging of previous lovers, or pornographic images of particular intensity, or memories of lovemaking episodes. He wanted to do this now. He felt like sleeping and he felt like nodding off to sleep with a bone on under his thin British Airways blanket. But now, sitting next to Tara Kennedy, this strange, beautiful American woman who seemed completely fixated on her job and who had not, not for one merest glimmer of a second, given him any reason to think she was interested in him, it would be all wrong to have an erection. There had been times in the past when he could fantasise about getting the woman on the plane next to him to give head as everyone was watching the movie. He couldn't conjure this up; it just so much wasn't going to happen that even a private fantasy about it was impossible. And yet she was quite affectionate – the way she spoke to him was warm and somehow embracing. He felt she really wanted him there, but she wanted him to have the shit kicked out of him by a load of irate, bitter women who hated men.

Really he was going to San Francisco to fuck the living daylights out of Tiffany; that thought immediately caused a surge in his groin. Tiffany had promised she would meet him at the airport. He had really missed her and this opportunity had just popped up out of the blue. How could such a good-luck piece of fate be tangled up with all this women's self-defence shit.

As he lay in silence with his British Airways eye pads over his eyes, his own earplugs in his ears, he pondered on ways of extricating himself from the whole thing as soon as he got there. He had nearly a hundred quid in his pocket; he could stay with Tiff for a couple of weeks until they'd fucked themselves stupid, and then quietly fly back home.

Chapter Twelve

Alice drove her VW Golf through the Cotswold countryside towards her parents' home in Tewkesbury. She hadn't visited for many months and pressure had been building. Her mother wasn't well – she had suffered a minor stroke which had made her left hand almost completely useless. Her father had recently retired and spent his days working with the choir in the beautiful abbey or maintaining their immensely colourful garden.

Tewkesbury had changed a great deal since she was a girl. Their old house had once been on the very edge of the town; now it was tucked well inside. Huge housing estates had been built on the flood meadows which surrounded the ancient abbey. However, the centre of the town retained much of its Tudor quaintness.

She passed her old school, an all-girls high school in her day, now a mixed comprehensive. Passed the old houses of friends she had grown up with and, finally pulling into the tranquil abbey courtyard, her parents' house down a little alley to one side.

She was greeted warmly, the smell of Sunday lunch filling the house. Alice always felt a great weight of responsibility fall off her when she visited home. She eyed her mother anxiously, but the old lady seemed very well. The house was the same as it had always been – charming, low ceilings and inconceivably old. Originally it had been three monks' dwellings knocked into one small house in the 1800s, thick oak beams and spiral stone staircases making it wonderfully picturesque, damp walls, packed mud floors and occasional flooding making it less than perfect for habitation.

Alice was also very glad to be somewhere Peter Welbeck didn't know about. She had become more and more ambiguous about her feelings for him. She had tried gently to wind the whole affair down – she didn't want a big, messy trauma, she wanted it to be a civilised parting. The more she pulled away, of course, the more he seemed to take an interest. He had never called her as much when she wanted him to, had never sent as many flowers and little cards, often depicting naked men with their erections barely covered by a towel. His taste was distinctly vulgar, his turns of phrase totally clichéd. She was convinced he'd never said anything original in his entire life. His response to this was not to shy away or try to defend himself against her spiky criticisms of virtually everything he did. He merely laughed and seemed to like her more, and that was the problem. Alice found it was actually rather pleasing to be truly unpleasant to someone and for them to enjoy it, to come back for more.

She truly didn't know what to do. They had almost stopped having sex because she found the prospect of it too annoying. If it ever did happen it was rather good and she enjoyed it, but then looked at him when it was over and found him unspeakably thick.

'How's things, then, darling?' her father asked once they had reached the wide open space of Tewkesbury Ham. He walked the old dog here every day and it was one of Alice's treats to join him.

'Good, thanks. Got a raise last month, which is great, but I've been overlooked for promotion again. They promoted a man which was a huge surprise. Not.'

'Oh dear. But you seem to be doing so well already. Lovely car and flat and everything.'

'I'm not complaining. It's just that I got to where I am so

quickly and I don't seem to be able to get any further. I feel sort of stuck and stagnant. I don't know what to do, Dad.'

'Oh. I see. You don't think it's your age?'

'What's that supposed to mean?'

'Well, husbands, babies, all that sort of thing.'

'Heavens above, Dad, I'm only twenty-nine. Give me a break.'

'Well, I know, darling. But you never mention anything about your courting.'

'Courting? Daddy, you are so sweet. People don't go courting these days, they have relationships.'

'I know, but you never mention those either.'

Alice had once sat down and added up how many lovers she'd had. Including Peter Welbeck there had been nine. She lost her virginity to a boy from Cheltenham when she was just eighteen, after a disco. She enjoyed sex but found most men, not including her father, very hard to understand. She had once discussed being in love with her women friends and decided she had never experienced it. She had been infatuated, thrilled, horny and sometimes quite slushy, but she didn't think she had ever experienced anything so all-encompassing as love. Maybe it was the men she was attracted to. Peter Welbeck fitted the bill being so large and strong and slightly stupid. Most of the men she'd been with were loosely in that canon. She had been on social dates with more complex, more lightly built, sensitive men and found them even more annoying than the big bruisers. At least, she felt, she knew where she stood with them. But as for the prospect of getting involved with any of the men she'd known on a permanent basis, it was just too absurd.

'Okay,' she said after considering the consequences of revealing her private life to her father, and therefore her mother, 'I'm having a relationship with a man called Peter Welbeck, who works for Victoria Life, loves playing rugby and has mag-alloy wheels on his Ford Mondeo.'

'Sounds like a nice enough chap.'

'He's awful, Dad. He's so boring,' said Alice. She threw a stick for the old dog, who ignored it.

'Well, why are you with him, then?'

'I don't know. Because there's nothing else on the horizon.'

'That's a very poor reason.'

'I know.'

'You should end it, then.'

'Should I?'

'Of course. It's unreasonable not to.'

Alice sighed and walked along beside her lanky old dad. Her father was right, of course, she knew he was. He always had been.

She felt very confident of the soundness of his advice. Her father had always given her good guidance; he was a very deep-thinking man. He'd been in the pioneering computer modelling team at Smiths Industries in the days when a computer still filled a whole room. He thought things through without forgetting any of the input data and came up with solutions.

'You're right,' said Alice. 'I'll finish it as soon as I get home.'

Chapter Thirteen

Tara waited outside the customs area door at San Francisco International Airport for Nick Gardener to join her. She had last seen him joining a very long queue at the immigration desks. He was travelling on a visitor's visa, so she was hoping there wouldn't be any problems. Her car was in long-term parking, hopefully not stolen. It was a late-model Jeep Cherokee. Her stepfather had helped her buy it during his previous visit, although she had barely driven the thing. A beautiful shiny black car, the newest and most expensive thing she had ever owned.

Nick appeared after a short while. Tara smiled and picked up her bag and walked towards him. Suddenly a young woman rushed past her and jumped on to Nick. For a moment Tara flashed on this being an assault and automatically started to move to his aid, but managed to stop herself before it became embarrassing. Nick was embracing the young woman with equal passion. She could only have been half his size, and getting on for half his age. She was wearing silver cowboy boots, her strong, suntanned legs bare, a small ra-ra miniskirt and a tiny skin-tight, revealing top barely covering her breasts. She also sported a massive half-finished tattoo over her back, a coiled snake perhaps, or a dragon – it wasn't completely clear. The woman looked so young, a daughter perhaps. She noticed one of Nick's hands cradling and squeezing the young woman's ass. They kissed each other on the lips in such a gross, hungry, all-engulfing way she had to turn around. She noticed a man watching the couple. He smiled at Tara and shrugged, as if to say 'if only'. Tara frowned. This was not what she had been expecting.

'Tara, this is Tiffany,' said Nick. Tara turned to face him. 'She's my San Francisco barely legal babe.' He was grinning from ear to ear. He must have known this woman was going to be here. Tara was angry, really angry.

'Hi, Tara,' said the young woman. 'Sorry about that. It's just been a long time.'

'Too fucking long,' said Nick.

'Hey, I oughta thank you,' said Tiffany. 'You brought this dumb ass out here. He was too dumb or too idle to do it on his own.'

'I didn't know you were being met at the airport, Nick,' said Tara as calmly as her anger would allow.

'You asshole!' squealed Tiffany, shoulder-barging Nick like a playful colt. 'You didn't tell her about me!'

'I said I was staying with friends,' said Nick. 'I've known Tiffany for a while now, met her when I was here last time.'

'I see,' said Tara, feeling duped and embarrassed.

'Is it a problem?' asked Nick, with what she took to be a pinch of defensive aggression.

'Why should it be a problem, Nick?'

'I dunno. You look a bit pissed off.'

'Well, I guess I would have liked to have known about this, but you know. Whatever.'

'Well, you know where I am. That address I gave you is Tiff's gaff. That's where I'll be staying, and I'll come and see you tomorrow, like we arranged. Is that okay?'

'That's fine,' said Tara.

'Okay, see you, then,' said Nick. He shouldered his bag and walked away, arm in arm with Tiffany.

Tara stood watching them go with nothing other than a feeling of tired depression for company. She had been expecting to take Nick into the city and drop him off, maybe even meeting his friends and arranging their future meetings over coffee in some previously unvisited kitchen. She did not expect an over-sexed, tattooed schoolgirl to throw herself at him as soon as he got off the plane.

'Hi, Tara,' said an incredibly familiar voice. 'I need a lift home.'

Adrian stood in front of her, looking great — healthy, tanned and wonderful. They embraced. Tara felt like crying but managed not to.

'Boy, am I glad to see you,' she said.

'That's mutual,' said Adrian. 'I just got in from Reno. Conference on particle physics assessment using UNIX programs. You'd have loved it. Dull city. I rang your office, they said you were due in about now, so I had a coffee and hung out for you.'

'Oh, Adrian,' said Tara. 'Where are you going?'

'How about your place? I could do with a shower and you have a real nice one. And I want to see your new car.'

Tara felt completely thrown by Adrian's response, in fact by his very appearance at the airport. He was the very last person she had expected to see there. It was possibly to do with jet-lag, although she was feeling good and the flight from London was never as bad as the flight there. She hadn't seen Adrian in something like two months. He'd been working away before she left for England.

'Nice car,' he said as Tara pressed the little red button on the key fob and the Cherokee bleeped its greeting and popped its locks. They stood on either side of the vehicle in the huge multistorey parking lot, thankfully out of the hot midday sun.

'Stepfather,' said Tara.

'Hey, they got married!' said Adrian. 'Wait a minute. Which one is this?'

'The Australian one,' said Tara.

'Not the Russian, then.'

'No, that didn't work out.'

'What does the Australian do, run a gold mine?'

'No. He's called Gordon Maquarie, Professor. An academic like you. Only he developed some polymer stuff, you'd know all about it. Supposed to make rubber redundant in ten years. They make condoms out of it already.'

'How appropriate,' said Adrian.

'Sorry?'

'Just what we need, a supply of free condoms. Not,' said Adrian jauntily. Tara looked at him and smiled. He was the nicest man she had ever met.

'Anyway, he came here while you were away to deliver a paper at Stanford and he helped me buy it. I was just going to buy a compact, but I can get all my mats and padding in the back of this if I have to.'

'Very sensible, and very classy, and if I dare comment, kind of sexy.'

'Really,' said Tara, her stomach responding with a delightful thrill. Adrian went to the back of the car and loaded his bags inside.

'Wanna ride, bitch?' shouted a vulgar male voice. Tara raised one eyebrow slightly as a Ford Bronco four-wheel-drive pick-up pulled up in front of her car. A young white man with hair cropped short at the front and running long down his back leered at her out of the passenger side window.

'No thank you. Not today,' said Tara, throwing her bag as gracefully as she could on to the back seat.

'Well, fuck you,' said the man almost by rote. 'I was only being friendly.'

'Okay,' said Tara. Adrian appeared by her side. The same height as Tara but a lighter build, he was the perfect example of the computer nerd. Thin, frail and droopy-looking with thick glasses.

'Oh, man, is that what you got? Baby, you don't know what you're missing!' shouted the man. He laughed at his own humour and looked at the driver, who was staring with insane psychotic intensity at her.

'Tell you what, why don't I beat the shit out of your boyfriend there and then me and my buddy take turns at your ass. Know what I mean?'

Adrian stood slightly behind her.

'What d'you think I should do?' he said calmly.

'Get in the car. Gently.'

Tara climbed into the driver's seat and smoothly shut the door. Without taking her eyes off the men in the Ford Bronco, she pressed the central locking button and started the Cherokee. The engine burst into life immediately. They couldn't go anywhere as the men's car was completely blocking them in.

'Don't say anything, just keep watching them,' said Tara.

'Maybe I should have done that men's course last fall,' said Adrian.

'He can't stay there all day.'

They watched as the two men glowered at them. Tara could see that they were talking to each other. She cast a quick glance behind the pick-up. A man was sitting in a large sedan, trying to look around to see what the problem was. He honked his horn. Immediately the young man who had spoken to them leaned out of the window and gave the offending driver the finger.

'He's pretty disturbed,' said Adrian.

'Very unbalanced,' said Tara, her hand holding the auto-shift lever, ready to roll.

The Ford Bronco started to move off, the driver obviously thinking he'd rather be out of the situation, the passenger clearly disagreeing with him. He leaned out of the window again and pointed directly at Tara, punctuating his speech with penetrative little jabs.

'I'm gonna fuck you one day, lady, like it or not. I got your fucking number,' he shouted, and threw his head back, laughing.

'Okay,' said Tara quietly, and without hesitation pulled out behind the pick-up truck. This meant she pulled in front of the man in the sedan, who now completely lost his temper and started honking his horn as he followed them.

'Get the number,' ordered Tara, her eyes fixed on the slow-moving toy-like truck in front of them.

'Better, I'll get a picture,' said Adrian as he held down the shutter on his digital camera. The camera flashed three times as the Ford Bronco turned violently up a ramp to a higher level of the parking lot. Tara didn't follow, but turned on to the down ramp and eventually pulled up at the attendant's hut.

The woman inside was black and very large. Tara handed her the long-term ticket and a fifty-dollar bill.

'Excuse me, ma'am,' she said. 'There are two men in the parking lot in a red Ford Bronco pick-up who are sexually threatening female drivers. They used very violent language and threatened to rape me and assault my friend. We are about to contact the police regarding this, but if you have any security people who can get on the scene faster, the men in question were last seen heading for the fifth level. Here's my card so you know who I am.'

The black woman took the card and read it carefully. 'I heard of you,' she said. 'You do a good job. I got a couple of guys I can call who'll go up there and kick their butts.' The woman gave the fifty-dollar bill back to Tara. 'You keep that, honey — have this one on the house.'

'Why, thank you very much,' said Tara. She shook hands with the woman out of the window and slowly pulled out into the road. She clipped her mobile into its housing and pressed two buttons. A voice came on the speakerphone.

'Hello, San Francisco Police, Public Safety Department. Can I help you?'

'Hi, yeah, this is Tara Kennedy. I'd like to talk to Detective Benson, please.'

'One moment, please.'

'You never stop,' said Adrian.

'Hey, I just stopped for three weeks while I've been in England. I get back here and it starts all over again.'

Chapter Fourteen

Tiffany Smooth lived in her mother's apartment at 1457 Page Street, a tree-lined road that ran parallel to the famous Haight Street, only a couple of blocks from the even more famous Haight–Ashbury intersection – the epicentre of the hippie movement which Nick only knew about because it was taking place just after he was born and his mum and dad had gone on about it endlessly.

Nick's mother and father had both been hippies in their youth; at least they were weekend hippies. They always wanted to hitch west to San Francisco; they never made it past Weston-super-Mare.

Pictures of his mum and dad with long hair and grubby-looking clothes were in the family photo album. There was still a sculpture made from wool and old twigs hanging above the fireplace in their cramped house in Headington.

Tiffany explained to him about where she was living as they lay wriggling in each other's arms and legs in the back of the taxi.

'With your mum?' said Nick, pulling away from her so he could see her clearly. 'What d'you mean you're living with your mum?'

'Oh, baby, she's not like "a mum",' said Tiffany. Nick was showered with kisses again. 'She's cool. She was a babe in the Sixties.'

'Yeah, I'm sure she was, but it's a bit embarrassing. I mean, shit, have I got to be polite to your mom and sleep in the spare room and everything?' Nick pulled away again. He couldn't help grinning, he couldn't help feeling unimaginably horny, but there was a streak of fear running through the moment. He didn't really know this girl after all; she was pretty weird and she looked even younger than he'd remembered. She also looked smaller and bustier. She looked like someone in a porn film, the sort of woman you don't actually meet, just look at and beat your meat over. It was all a bit too much.

'But you had your own place.'

'Oh, man, remember my room-mate? Turned out to be a nightmare. I think she was a serial killer on a break. You know, she was totally psychotic and I was, like, aaaah. And then me and Mom made up 'cos we really fell out over me working at the Crazy Horse, but now I've stopped all that shit and I'm back at college.'

'You've stopped working there?' said Nick, burying his disappointment. Although he had hated seeing her work there initially, as time had passed the notion of her exposed body being ogled by men began to turn into something very erotic for him. It had certainly entertained him as he dozed on the flight.

'Yeah. It was a kind of reaction thing to my mom. And anyway, Mom's great, you'll love her, everyone does. Don't worry, you're not going to get busted for statutory rape when you rivet me to the mattress with your glorious cock!' She lunged on top of him again, ground her groin into his stomach, grabbed his hair in both hands and pushed his head between her breasts. 'I'm twenty-two,' she said. 'I can show you my birth certificate if it makes you feel better. I just look kinda young, okay!'

The taxi finally pulled up outside a tall, terraced house with a big bay window.

'It's all made of wood,' said Nick, looking at the house on Page Street as he climbed out of the taxi with Tiffany still wrapped around him like a growth of ivy. He paid the driver, which used all the dollars he was carrying. The taxi pulled away and they stood on the sidewalk hugging each other.

'It's kind of old, but I forget quite how old,' said Tiffany. 'Not old for you guys with all your castles and thatched cottages, I guess.'

'Oh yeah, thatch, we've got loads of that where I come from . . . not,' said Nick, and tickled the taut skin around her sides. They both laughed so much he could barely breathe; it was utterly intoxicating being in her company.

The basement of the building had been converted into a garage and the sidewalk had been shaped slightly to take a car under the house. Nick stepped back from the kerb and almost fell over as his jet-lagged balance bones failed to compensate for the slope.

Five steps led up to a large gate which covered the front doors. The house had been painted white many years before, but the paint had long since faded and begun to peel. It was mottled in appearance owing to the trees that grew on Page Street. It looked rich but run-down, safe but wild. Nick could see people walking their dogs, pushing strollers with kids trotting beside them. In his jet-lagged haze, it all looked great, like the picture on the cover of one of the old progressive rock albums that his mum and dad had so many of. They kept them stuffed in a cupboard under the tropical fish tank.

'I want you so much,' said Tiffany, rewrapping herself around him.

'Mutual,' said Nick. 'I am fucking rock hard, have been all the way from Heathrow.'

'Oh, baby,' said Tiffany, allowing her hand to wander down to the front of his jeans. 'Rock hard all the way from Heathrow,' she added, trying to imitate his English accent.

'Is your mum here now?' asked Nick, glancing up at the window, half expecting to see a disapproving face peeking from behind the lace curtains.

'No. She's on her retreat at San Luis Obispo. She gets back tomorrow.'

'You mean we've got the place to ourselves?'

'We can fuck till we drop, baby,' said Tiffany with a giggle.

'I just cannot believe you. You are fucking unreal,' said Nick.

'God, I love your voice,' responded Tiffany, gently touching his face.

He followed her up the steps to the front door and walked into the wood-panelled apartment. It was dark and cool, quiet and still. He was surprised at how pleasant the place was. He had been half dreading finding it a desolate mess. It had crossed his mind that Tiffany's mother could be a junkie tragedy, and they could be living in a drug-softened poverty pit. It was clearly not so. The apartment was clean and smelled of polish and incense. It was a long, dark collection of rooms with peculiar windows looking out on tiny courtyards. Everything was strangely familiar and yet completely peculiar. He knew about the whole San Francisco hippie hangover from previous visits, but he had always seen it from a distance. It didn't really make sense to him. But this house was so aesthetically pleasing that he started to feel he understood what it was about. Something to do with being peaceful, being calm and restful, aware of the world but not troubled by it. It was what his parents had tried and failed to do so miserably. This house had such a serene quality and yet it was rooted, not fake and manufactured. It was old and well worn, it had the patina of thirty years of dope smoke on the ceilings. It was wealthy without being pretentious, comfortable without trying, and it felt so important. Like he was walking through somewhere that counted, that mattered to a lot of people. It was definitely at the very heart of the whole hippie thing.

'I want you so bad,' said Tiffany, pulling him by the arm into a black-painted bedroom. He smiled at her, but as he entered he couldn't stop his eyes wandering around the walls.

' 'S this your room?' he asked, looking at the strange posters on the walls: vampires and vixens, kitsch pictures of skulls with rats crawling through the empty eye sockets. There was a very full bookcase with hundreds of paperback books which all looked to be of one genre, gothic horror – blood-curdling, vampire-ridden, blood-sucking nightmares.

'Nice,' said Nick.

'Check this out too,' said Tiffany, turning her back on him and pulling off her top. Her whole back was covered with a tattoo of a curled-up multi-fanged viper. Nick couldn't believe his eyes. It must have taken hours to do and been incredibly painful. 'What d'you think?' she asked.

'Jesus H. fucking Christ almighty. What the fuck is that?' he asked.

'My project. It's not like completely finished yet. I didn't want to have scar tissue there when you came so I delayed the colouring. Still another five sessions to go. But it's something, isn't it?' She turned and smiled. He glanced at her perfect breasts – not a tattoo in sight, and he found himself relieved.

'You are the weirdest, sexiest woman I have ever fucking met,' he said as he dropped his bag. Then Nick Gardener, thirty-five, almost thirty-six, and Tiffany Smooth, just turned twenty-two, started ripping each other's clothes off in a disgusting, hysterical, giggling frenzy of lust and debauchery before they indulged in a five-hour, sex-juice-soaked fuck-fest which unfortunately for Nick, in his jet-lagged haze, he would hardly ever be able to remember.

Chapter Fifteen

Peter Welbeck was not essentially a bad man. He hadn't done a great number of bad things in his life and was not burdened by guilt. He lived by a fairly rigid code of ethics – he didn't steal anything and he tried not to lie too much, although he was encouraged to expand upon the truth to a degree in his line of work.

But as Alice Moreton's head banged against the car door repeatedly in response to his extremely violent thrusts, she decided he was capable of badness.

Alice had returned to London after her visit to Tewkesbury feeling much better about everything. She rang Peter, expecting to leave a 'dear John' message on his answer service. He was never at home. This time he answered the phone on the first ring, almost as if he were waiting for a call.

'Hi, it's Alice.'

'I know. How you feeling?'

'Okay. Look, Peter . . .'

'Uh-oh. The old heave-ho coming. I can tell.'

'I'm sorry.'

'So am I. You really are something, Alice.'

'But it's not working, is it?'

'Is for me.'

'No it isn't. You don't like anything I do, and I hate everything you love.'

'Had a good match this afternoon. We won again.'

'There you go.'

'I'd love to see you.'

'Well, I don't think we should any more.'

'Oh, come on, Alice. I mean, it's not as if we're married. What is there to finish? We don't see each other more than a couple of times a month. Why don't I come around and see you? I'll bring a bottle of bubbly. I've got to be in town in the morning anyway.'

'No, I don't want to see you tonight,' she said without thinking.

'Tomorrow, then?' he said, seeming very cheerful and clearly not taking no for an answer.

'No, I really think we should leave it.'

'We can't just leave it, we've got something going here, Alice, we really have.'

For the following two days Alice received calls on her mobile from Peter, doing the hard sell, suggesting trips to Paris, Rome, New York. He had never rung her so much before. Previously weeks had sometimes passed between his calls. Now, as soon as she had suggested they call the whole thing off, he was like a butcher's dog.

She was inspecting the damage caused by a thirty-mile-an-hour side-impact collision at the Heaton Common vehicle facility in Surrey when Peter suddenly showed up. The car she was crawling through was a soon-to-be-introduced electric-diesel lightweight passenger vehicle built by Mercedes Benz. Owing to the chemicals contained in the nicad batteries and all the adjacent new technology, the insurance industry wanted a fresh look at the risk factors. Modern petrol tanks had been manufactured to withstand astonishing amounts of stress; battery packs were a whole new dimension. The chances of fire, chemical burns or electrocution were still 'at the edge of knowledge'. Risk assessment-speak for unknown.

'Hi there. Bit of a mess you made of this one,' said Peter.

Alice was on all fours in the passenger compartment looking for damage to the battery bays which were what the floor of the passenger compartment was actually constructed of. She felt slightly exposed. Although covered in one-piece blue overalls, her arse was sticking out of the crumpled and twisted vehicle. She clambered out backwards and stood up in front of Peter.

'What are you doing here?' she asked.

'It's not far from my head office. Thought I'd drop in and see how you were.'

'I've got a pension,' she said rather cruelly.

'I know, although you do have room to up your contributions within the current tax framework,' he responded without malice. 'I've missed you,' he added, looking soft. He did have very nice eyes.

'I don't know how you got in here. This is supposed to be a secure facility,' said Alice.

'Look, don't worry, I just told them I was working with you, told them I was from the Victoria Life risk assessment department.'

'There isn't one,' said Alice.

'They don't know that,' smiled Peter. 'I thought you might like a break. There's a brilliant Italian restaurant just down by the river. They have a terrace with tables and vines and an excellent wine list. Please, Alice, I'd really like to see you, to talk to you again. I really have missed you.'

He reached out for her hand. She was holding a clipboard in one hand and a large screwdriver in the other. She sighed and smiled.

'This really is awkward, Peter. I'm very busy. I simply have to get a report done on this thing by the morning.'

'Of course. It's amazing to see you at work, it makes you even sexier. I mean, I wouldn't know where to start, looking at a wreck like that. How can you tell what's safe and what's a killer?'

She started to explain. She knew about sheer stress fractures and crumple zones, she had seen what damage sudden impact could do to a human body, she had witnessed autopsies on road traffic accident victims. She noticed as she described the differences in design in an electric vehicle and the dangers of battery acid leakage that Peter wasn't listening, just eyeing her up and down. In other circumstances this might have been an attractive thing to do, even mildly exciting, but at that moment it was just annoying. She felt duped that he had used a sales technique to get her to talk about herself or her work which would then lower her guard. On the other hand, he had travelled all this way to see her. And she was hungry and it was a long train ride back into town.

'Okay, I'll come for dinner, but that's all. I want to make that absolutely clear, Peter. I do not want to fuck you. Am I making myself plain?'

'That is a fairly unequivocal statement and I will file it away under very important, no fucking,' said Peter. 'What time do you get off?'

Alice checked her watch. 'Go and sit in your dreadful car and listen to your Simply Red CD for half an hour. I've got a few more things to check on this and then I'll join you.'

An hour later they sat facing each other on the delightful, sun-dappled terrace of the Casa Carlotta overlooking the River Thames just outside Goring. Peter kept the conversation going, never once mentioning golf or rugby, instead talking either business or books. Alice enjoyed his company but had a feeling of dread in the pit of her stomach. She was annoyed with herself for giving in and seeing him again, but nothing that had happened had changed her mind – she was going to dump him.

'I'll drive you home,' he said when they walked into the carpark. His Ford Mondeo bleeped quietly as he pressed the remote. Alice pursed her lips.

'No, the station will be all right, Peter. The last train leaves in about twenty minutes.'

She sat in the passenger seat. He sat beside her and rubbed his face with both hands. 'Don't do this to me, Alice.'

'What?' she asked.

'Well, lead me on then give me the big flick. It's really unfair.'

'I haven't led you on,' she said indignantly, having felt almost embarrassed at times during the meal that she was being unnecessarily sour-faced.

'Oh, come on, you have. You've been looking at me in that way,' said Peter. 'It's all a game to you, I know, but I've got feelings. I really, really like you, Alice. You turn me on something rotten and you, well, you drive me crazy.'

'I'll get a taxi,' said Alice, and without hesitation she opened the door and started to move.

'No, wait,' he said sternly. 'That's really unfair. Come on, we know each other well enough. Christ, Alice. You're the most special woman I've ever met. I know you get through men like the rest of us get through – God, I don't know – umbrellas, but to me you're really special.'

'I do not get through men.'

'Fucking hell! Well, for someone who is all pure and innocent you're pretty fucking raunchy. I've never had sex with anyone so horny as you. You're positively pornographic.'

'I'll get a taxi,' said Alice again, and this time managed to get out of the car. Faster than she could have imagined possible, Peter's arm shot out and grabbed her dress. He pulled her roughly back into the car, grabbed her head with both hands and started kissing her. Her arms were limp beside her, so great was the shock of this sudden, uncalled-for intrusion. Peter's tongue delved brutally inside her mouth. The smell of alcohol and garlic was overpoweringly strong. 'I want to show you how much I love you,' he said. He was breathing hard now; he was hot, strong and incredibly insistent in his movements. He took her limp hand and pushed it towards the mountainous bulge in his lightweight suit trousers. She recoiled, which seemed to make him more enthusiastic.

'Oh yes,' he said hotly in her ear. 'That's right, Alice. Yes.'

'I want you to stop right now,' said Alice as flatly as she

could, considering that she was pinned to the cloth seats of a small saloon car with her head at a very violent angle to the rest of her body.

'Oh yes, I'll show you how much I fucking love you,' said Peter as though he hadn't heard her. His right hand went straight for her crotch, and with a single, violent wrench he removed her panties. The departing material burnt her outer thighs. Peter was so strong, she could feel the bulge of his bicep in her back as his left arm held her rigidly in place. Still her body did nothing to resist. She had become a rag doll, a wet lettuce. It seemed that within seconds of the initial grab, Peter was on top of her, his sizeable penis was inside her and the handbrake of the car was digging agonisingly into her lower back.

'I want to fuck you so much,' he said as he pounded up and down. 'And you want to fuck me, I can tell, you're so fucking wet.'

It was true, her body did respond physiologically to his ministrations, but nothing inside her head told her she was having fun. She felt completely removed from the experience, as though she were watching from the outside. His breath on her ear brought her back into her body, together with the great discomfort of the handbrake in her back, the fact that she was almost bent into an L shape in order to fit into the car, her feet somehow pushed against the roof, his hands holding her legs as he watched his penis enter her, illuminated by the little interior light. His door must be open, she thought, it's the only way they could fit. She could scream.

He came inside her, very quickly and with three explosive and ugly-sounding breaths. The whole event lasted only a few seconds, maybe a minute.

'Oh Christ, Alice,' he said as he crawled out of the car very much in the way she had when he arrived in the afternoon. 'I wish we could get on.'

She lay in the position she had been forced into for a while, until finally her body was in such pain she had to move. It was very awkward but finally she managed to shift around in the passenger seat until she was staring straight ahead through the windscreen at the rows of parked cars in front of her. Everything seemed to be heightened, the colours more intense, the lighting more subtle. She pulled her shirt down, realised her breasts had been mauled out of her bra and adjusted them back in. Her panties, or what remained of them, were drooped over the steering wheel. She picked them up and put them delicately in her bag. She patted it and felt by the weight that her laptop was there with her, along with her mobile phone. She eventually looked over to where Peter was standing outside the car. His trousers were around his knees and he was urinating in a bush. He farted quite loudly, cleared his throat and spat. The phlegm arced through the low lighting and hit the leaf of a laurel bush, making it judder slightly. Alice felt herself dry-retch and put her hand to her mouth. It smelt of sperm and sex so she moved it away just as fast. She turned and looked out of the passenger window. A middle-aged woman was looking in at her.

'You all right, love?' she asked, her old, heavily made-up face drawn with concern. Alice nodded and smiled weakly. The woman stood up and looked at Peter, still not sure what to think.

'Evening,' she heard Peter say over the roof of the car. 'Lovely night.'

The woman walked away, joining a group of middle-aged people wearing what Alice took to be smart-casual golfing outfits. They walked into the restaurant arm in arm, men and women, having been together for years, probably with grown-up kids. And what was she doing, sitting in a car belonging to a man she despised who had just fucked her when she didn't want him to. There was really something wrong with her life. There must be.

'I'll drive you home,' said Peter as he sat in the car and started it up. 'Least I can do.'

Chapter Sixteen

Nick woke up from a very deep sleep to see no fewer than three women looking at him. He pulled himself up as best he could and rubbed his eyes. When he opened them again he could see that he wasn't mistaken. He was being stared at by three women. Tiffany, smiling all over her beautiful face, Tara Kennedy, with a recognisable but subtle smile, and another, slightly older but very attractive woman, who was also smiling and nodding slowly. Nick tried to smile but was worried that this might be the wrong response. Tiffany dived on him. She was wearing only a kimono and her warm flesh touched him in places that made the moment even more confusing.

'Poor little puppy!' she said. 'He doesn't know what's going on.'

'Good morning, Nick,' said Tara. 'Sleep well?'

'Yeah, thanks,' said Nick.

'Aren't you going to introduce us, Tiff?' said the woman he'd never seen before. Her voice was deep and American and slightly sexy.

'Nick, this is my mom. Mom, this is Nick Gardener, a stud from over the pond and a really, really nice guy. I mean really nice. Isn't he just the cutest thing you ever saw?'

'Good to meet you, Nick,' said Tiffany's mother. 'I have, as you can imagine from knowing my daughter, heard a great deal about you. My name is Grace, by the way. You don't have to call me Mom.'

'Oh, right,' said Nick. 'Hi, Grace.'

'Tara has come to take you away from us,' said Tiffany in a squeaky little-girl voice.

'Oh, right,' said Nick, his heart sinking as he remembered he was faced with the prospect of explaining to Tara that he didn't want to go through with the whole self-defence thing.

'It's okay,' said Tara. 'Take your time. Take a shower. I got here early.'

'Oh, right,' said Nick. Tara and Grace left the room and Tiffany stood up, the front of her kimono falling open, revealing her highly desirable body.

'Oh my fucking God. What a wake-up call,' said Nick, burying his head in the pillow. He had managed three orgasms with Tiffany the night before. He was so completely shattered the last thing he needed was to have the shit kicked out of him by some fat lezzo. How come such totally top-quality nookie had to be paid for in such a fucking awful way?

'I don't want to go,' he said, turning and looking at Tiffany.

'Oh, baby. You've got to go. Tara is totally excellent. I didn't hardly notice her yesterday at the airport, but Mom and I have been talking with her this morning. As soon as I finish this term I'm gonna do the course. It's awesome. It's fantastic what you're doing. I'm so, so proud of you, baby.'

'You are?' said Nick. He scratched his head – things were making less and less sense. 'But you said you thought it was all hippie shit when I told you about it on the phone.' They had managed to spend nine hours in each other's company the day before without communicating verbally. Nick cast his mind back and marvelled at how it was possible not to even think about the reason he was in San Francisco. It was amazing what you could forget when you were having so much sex and ice cream.

'Sure. I forgot all about this stuff but my mom did the course when I was about twelve. I hated all that shit then. You know what I was like. Anything my mom and dad did was crazy and fucked-up as far as I was concerned. You know what I was like when I met you. I was doing everything I could to get my mom pissed. I mean, working as a pole dancer at the fucking Crazy Horse, it was like taking a leak in your mom's coffee.'

'Shit, I can't keep up,' said Nick.

'Nick, it's really great what Tara teaches. It proves what a wonderful, amazing guy you really are that you'd even consider doing it. Most men would either be too shit scared or too fucked-up to even attempt it. I'm so proud of you.' Tiffany dropped the kimono from her shoulders and fell on Nick. He couldn't help but embrace her, feeling her taut body thrashing around on top of him, her buttocks like twin love-grabs. Nothing could help him resist holding them.

When he had showered and changed into the loose clothing Tara had specified, he found his Ray Ban dark glasses, rubbed some Californian poppy oil he found in the bathroom cabinet into his hair, and went into the kitchen. Grace and Tara were getting on like a house on fire, laughing and joking with each other. They seemed to sober up a little when he entered the room.

'Hi. Ready to go? 'Cos now we're running late,' said Tara.

'Sure,' said Nick. 'Any chance of a coffee?'

'I'll pick one up on the way.' Tara stood up, rattling her keys.

'Have a good day,' said Grace. She smiled at him. She was really beautiful, a little like Tiffany only smarter-looking. The eyes. It was always in the eyes – he knew that. He had just been looking at his own eyes in the bathroom mirror. They didn't look too intelligent to him. She could probably see that.

'Thanks,' he said to Grace, and followed Tara down the pleasant-smelling corridor and out of the front door.

'Nice car,' he said as he sat back in the passenger seat of the Cherokee.

'My stepfather bought it,' said Tara. 'Don't get the wrong idea. I don't make this kind of money teaching at Winning Strategy.'

They pulled away and Tara touched a button on her mobile.

'Hi, SF women's self-defence, can I help you?' said a voice over the speakerphone.

'Rene, it's Tara. I've got Nick on board and we're on our way.'

'Okay, fine,' said Rene, her voice louder than Nick thought possible. It was all so techno-flash.

'We may be a little late. Can you tell Tim to stay in the changing room until I get there?'

'Sure. He's there already, don't worry. Oh, and Detective Benson rang. He says they apprehended two men in that carpark at the airport.'

'Is that right?' said Tara. Nick saw her smile broadly as she punched the steering wheel.

'Yeah, sounds like just in time. They were intimidating some poor woman in a car with her baby. One of them was on parole, so he's back inside, the other one claimed he was the victim of a feminist conspiracy. They had to let him go but they're keeping an eye on him.'

'Great. I'll call Detective Benson when I get a chance. See you in a while,' said Tara. She touched a key and the phone went dead. They had pulled up at an intersection. As Tara scanned the street for an opportunity to move into a steady stream of traffic, she started talking. Nick was feeling pretty bleary but he put his best attentive face on.

'Okay, what you are going to see this afternoon is an introduction to a basics class. The guy I'm working with is called Tim Renaldo and he's been a padded assailant for longer than virtually anyone. He's a really nice guy and I know you're going to get along with him.'

Nick flashed on how this Tim would probably turn out to be a right tosser.

'There're going to be fourteen women in the class. I will have two assistants who've done a basics course but they are there just to help keep everything running smoothly. Okay. Now, I have warned all the women that you're going to be there. I know some of them are a little apprehensive. Two of them were really unhappy about it so I had to work quite hard to assure them that you were there for the right reasons. When we start the class we have what we call an opening circle. We all sit around on the mat and say just a short introduction, like your name, why you're there and stuff like that. Now, I just want you to keep it real brief if that's okay, Nick, like just say you're from Britain, you're here to observe because we're starting classes in your country. Something like that. Is that okay?'

'There's a Starbucks!' Nick said. 'Sorry, Tara, I heard everything you said, but I'm fucking desperate.'

He had been sitting listening to Tara, but all the time his mind had been on coffee. He had been scanning the street for a suitable store. Tara pulled the car over quite violently. 'Get your coffee, then we talk,' she said flatly.

'Okay, okay. Sorry, but you promised me coffee. I feel like shit.' He jumped out and trotted the short distance back to the coffee shop.

'Better now?' enquired Tara as he sat back in the car with a large brown paper bag full of pastries, muffins and a very large extra mocha double latte espresso cappuccino whatever. It was big and hot and very strong.

'Sorry about that,' said Nick. He felt uncomfortable about upsetting Tara, but kept reminding himself he owed her nothing, other than an air fare. The coffee kicked in pretty fast. Tara drove fast and spoke fast. They joined the Bay Bridge and started out across the water. Nick craned around and looked at the downtown skyline. He really was in San Francisco, he really was drinking a giant Starbucks coffee and eating a sugary Danish, sitting in a Jeep Cherokee with an uptight but beautiful woman, burning across the Bay Bridge on his way to Berkeley.

'All I want you to do is watch Tim. Okay? Watch how he works, when he speaks, how he responds to the students. In the breaks he'll sit with you and explain what's going on. You don't have to do anything. When we get there, you go in the men's changing area and I'll introduce you to the whole group. Okay?'

'Yeah. I'm cool,' said Nick.

'I know, but it's a very sensitive time for a lot of the students. I want you to be extra cool.'

'Okay, I'll be super-cool,' said Nick through a mouthful of Danish.

By the time he had finished his breakfast, Tara had pulled the car up in a small parking lot behind a new-looking concrete building. Large glass doors were hung with blue Venetian blinds. The logo Winning Strategy! was painted on the glass. However, Nick thought, it was all very discreet for America. No neon sign, no hard sell.

'I have to hit the ground running,' said Tara as they entered the building. He followed her into a tidy office where he was introduced to Rene, the woman she had spoken to on the phone. She was sitting in front of a desk supporting a large Apple computer. Tara then opened another door and walked through a slightly less tidy storeroom. Nick noticed a pile of enormous-looking helmets high up on a shelf. They were the size and shape of small dustbins. Battered and repeatedly repaired with silver gaffer tape, they looked like they'd been through a lot of history. A wet nose brushed Nick's hand. He looked down to see a friendly dog looking up at him, a large, nondescript brown-grey hound.

'She's okay, don't be alarmed,' said a male voice. Nick looked up and saw a man in a vest and jogging pants standing in a doorway. 'Hi, I'm Tim. And that's Bonnie,' he said, and held out his hand.

'Nick. Pleased to meet you.' They shook hands. 'Hello, Bonnie,' Nick said to the dog, which responded by barging against his leg and wagging her tail.

Tim was shorter than Nick, looked a lot older. He had long grey hair tied in a neat ponytail, a small goatee beard that was also greying, but Nick could tell from his shoulders and posture that the man was fit.

'I gotta go. See you in five, guys,' said Tara.

'It's great that you made it, Nick,' said Tim when they closed the door. The men's changing room was fairly small. Artificial light came from a fitting on the ceiling, and there were two vacuum cleaners against the wall and many boxes of leaflets piled in the corner. Hanging on a row of pegs above a long bench was an extraordinary collection of what looked like parts of a blue suit of armour. Although Nick had read the story of the impact suit's development in the book Tara had shown him on the plane, the real thing was still an intriguing sight.

'Tara's told you we've got a beginners' class here today?' Tim asked.

'Yeah, she's sort of told me what to expect.'

'Right. And you've done martial arts training?'

'Not much, and not for ages,' said Nick. 'I did a bit of Shotokan karate when I was kid. Well, teenager.'

'Okay, no, that's cool. Not all the guys have done any traditional training. I did a lot of judo at college, but some guys have done nothing.'

'Shit, that looks serious,' said Nick, feeling the padding on what he took to be the groin section of the suit.

'It *is* serious,' said Tim. He was smiling. 'It's serious but we have a gas.'

Nick waited with Tim for quite a while, getting to know him. He was almost annoyed by the fact that he did get on well with this man, just as Tara had predicted. There was a side of him that wanted to prove her wrong. She was so bloody confident.

Eventually there was a knock on the door and a young woman with many earrings and her hair tied up in a knot put her head around.

'Hi, guys, d'you wanna come in?' she said.

Nick followed Tim through the storeroom again, this time feeling distinctly nervous. He had no idea what to expect and wondered if this was what actors felt like when they got ready to go on stage.

They entered a large, brightly lit room, with a high ceiling. It looked more like a converted industrial space, as if it was meant to be a warehouse. The floor was completely covered in bright blue crash matting; the colour of the walls was subdued, a soft pastel shade of yellow-brown. Scattered about the room were seventeen women, of all ages, shapes, sizes and skin colours. A small blonde woman smiled at Nick as soon as she saw him. He smiled back, but felt the tension in his buttocks. He was really uncomfortable and, without any doubt, not having a good time.

'Okay, everyone,' said Tara. 'Can we all find a seat. Sit next to someone you don't know.' She smiled at Nick and gave him a sticker with his name written on it. Nick noticed that everyone was wearing their name on their shirt. He applied the sticker.

In the middle of the matted area a small circle of wire-frame chairs was already laid out, each with just a cushion and a low back. Tim guided Nick to a chair and he sat down – it was surprisingly comfortable. Slowly all the seats were taken up. Some of the women were talking amongst themselves, some sitting quietly, a few looking very unhappy.

Tara took a deep breath and everyone went quiet. Nick looked at her as she sat upright, her back straight, her arms and hands relaxed on her long thighs.

'Hi, everyone. My name is Tara Kennedy and I'm the teacher today. I want to welcome you all to the class and quickly explain that this is a very special place. I want us all to agree right now, right at the beginning, that anything we hear in this room, in this circle, stays in this circle. This is a sacred space, sacred to the people here now, and I want everyone to agree to keep it that way. Is that agreed?'

All the women said yes. Tara turned to Nick and Tim. Tim smiled and said yes, Nick followed suit. His heart rate was up; he was sweating and he felt big and cumbersome, sitting on the tiny chair. The women all seemed so small, they all looked so frail. What was all this about?

Tara picked up a tissue box that was on the mat in front of

her. 'Okay, first we introduce ourselves, then Tim
go off, Tim will get changed, then we start the
introduce ourselves, we have the tissue box. It's li
stick, okay? When you've got this, no one else ta
with me?'

There was general consent around the circle, s
smiling, some still looking faintly alarmed. Nick trie
expression, but he could feel a bead of sweat runnin
left temple.

'Okay, like I said, I'm Tara, I've been teaching a
Strategy for six years now. I did my basics class with
when I first saw him I thought he must be a certifiabl

The women laughed, Tim shrugged and smiled. Ni
and snorted through his nose. It was all so intense. H
back at Tara; she glanced at him and smiled. She really
tasty, he thought. Lovely neck, but just a bit fierce.

Tara took a deep breath. 'Okay, the reason I did the cl
because eight years ago I was on holiday on my own in n
Brazil and I was beaten and raped by three men.'

A woman sitting two along from Nick let out a sob.

'They had followed me through a small fishing villag
guess they followed me, I had no awareness – and they all s
me at once. However, I survived and made it back home. I
incredibly well looked after by my friends, I spent a lot of tim
counselling, and through one of those contacts I heard ab
Winning Strategy. I did this course, the same one you are do
today. Okay, so the first time Tim took me down on the mat
have to tell you, it was real hard.'

Nick swallowed. He felt dizzy with the knowledge. He ha
sat next to her on the plane for nearly twelve hours. Big an
horny, nursing a hard-on, probably sweating and smelling lik
the men who had attacked her. How could she handle it? He
noticed he was blinking a lot; he couldn't stop himself. He could
see a tear welling in Tara's eye. He couldn't believe what he'd just
heard. She was so beautiful. How could she be like this after

at she'd been through? How could anyone do that? Three
okes! Fucking bastards.

'Now, I want you to know that a lot of women have been
rough what you're going to go through in the next five weeks,
d they have had the same fears and apprehensions, and that's
ood. We don't want you to pretend to be brave – fear is your
riend. Be frightened. When Tim has his helmet on, you need to
e frightened of him, because he wants to hurt you. He is the
nemy, and that's what he's here for.'

Jesus, thought Nick. Poor bloke, having to sit there and have
this said about him. He glanced at Tim, who was still sitting in
the same position, not smiling, just looking around at the circle
of now uniformly uneasy faces.

'A really important thing to remember about Tim, okay?
This is like rule one of the class. When he doesn't have the
helmet on, he's the most trustworthy man I have ever met, and I
may call upon Tim every now and then to help you understand
the best way to use your body when it comes to specific moves.
But with the helmet on, don't trust him. Okay? Thank you. Over
to you, Tim.'

Tara took a tissue from the box and blew her nose. She
passed the box to Tim. Nick found himself looking at her in a
completely different way. He still fancied her, she was still
beautiful, but she was so sort of . . . unneedy. She didn't need
him to protect her. That was what it was. She didn't need him at
all. For anything.

'Hi there, my name's Tim Renaldo, I've been a padded
assailant for eight years now. I have a background in martial
arts teaching and a great interest in Eastern philosophy. I have
a triple-dan black belt in Judo, black belts in both karate and
tae kwon do. I have found this training to be supremely
effective, particularly for women, and it is so incredibly
rewarding that I always want to thank you women for letting
me be involved in teaching you. Really, I mean that. This job
is an honour. You guys, just by being here today, are real

brave. I think we're going to have a great day here today and really learn a lot. Okay.'

Tim smiled and nodded to the women in the circle and handed the box to Nick.

Fucking hell, thought Nick. What do I say? He swallowed and looked around at all the women. He had never sat in a circle of any sort before, and certainly not with a load of women who all looked as if they hated men for very good reasons he couldn't argue with. They were all, bar none, staring at him. There was, quite literally, nowhere to hide. He looked back down at the tissue box, his fingers folding the corner of a tissue nervously.

'Hello, my name's Nick. I'm from England.' A few of the women in the group laughed and smiled at him. 'Huh, s'pose that's obvious.' American women were so cool, he thought.

'Um, I have a little bit of experience in martial arts, a lot of experience of actual violence either on the street or in clubs and that. I have been a security guard, a swimming instructor, a fitness trainer and a lazy bastard most of my life.' Another laugh, more women this time, and seemingly more friendly.

'Tara, um, well, she asked me to come along and, like, watch and learn, so thank you for letting me. I don't really know what I'm going to see.'

Nick smiled and handed the tissue box to the woman sitting next to him. She took it, took a tissue out of it and wiped her eye. Nick felt his pulse as discreetly as he could. It was through the roof. He was very hot and uncomfortable; he really wasn't used to public speaking. He couldn't look at any of the women when he was talking. Half of them looked as if they hated his guts, but the blonde one who smiled at him when he walked in was still smiling.

'My father raped me for the first time when I was twelve,' said the woman sitting next to Nick. He could see only the side of her face. She didn't seem to be crying but she blew her nose repeatedly. She was about thirty-five, Nick guessed, pretty out of condition. Pretty depressed-looking. Not surprising. He wondered if this was going to be the case with all the women. Maybe they were all rape victims. Tara hadn't said anything about this, but it made sense – they all wanted to kick the shit out of men. It was all pretty weird. He had never known a woman who had actually been raped before. He'd read about it endlessly in the papers at home, but it never sounded very realistic. This was really different.

The woman next to him explained her life story, explained why she had decided to do the course and told everyone that she was very scared, particularly of Tim and the English man. Nick glanced at Tim again. He was nodding, showing he understood. Nick didn't nod; he didn't feel he understood anything.

The tissue box was passed around the circle. Now it seemed that only Tara and the woman sitting next to Nick had actually been raped. All the other women said they had always been scared but had no history of sexual assault. The tissue box was passed to the woman with the blonde hair who had smiled at Nick.

'Hi, my name's Mindy, um, I was . . .' She started to cry. She sat cross-legged and sobbed, tears dropping on to the tightly clutched tissue she had extracted from the box. 'I was raped last year by my ex-boyfriend. Um, I find it really hard to be here. I really don't want to do this, but I am so scared to even go out. It took really a lot to come here today. I just wanted to stay in bed, or to die. I just don't understand why men hate me so much. Or hate women so much that they want to hurt them. I really don't believe I can defend myself but I guess I've got to try.'

For possibly the first time in his life Nick felt an enormous wave of empathy. He could really feel her pain, and when he put that feeling into words in his head, 'feel her pain', although it sounded naff and Californian he could still feel it. He also wanted so much to help this woman, to embrace her and protect her. Although she was tasty, he didn't want to have sex with her, just assure her she was all right and he would fucking kill anyone who even touched her. He wanted to be the hunchback to her

Esmeralda. She was so frail – how could any bastard do that to her? He felt his hands grip each other tightly.

The tissue box continued on its journey around the circle until it was passed back to Tara.

'Okay, that was really good, thank you all for being so honest. Thank you for knowing you are somewhere safe. Here you are allowed to fail. That's how we learn, by failing. Here you are allowed to be scared. Fear is your friend, fear will protect you. This class is about being scared and strong. About making yourself safe. Okay, Tim and Nick will disappear now. We're going to do a gentle warm-up.'

'Fucking hell,' said Nick when he and Tim returned to the safety of the cluttered changing room. 'This is all too weird.'

'Pretty intense, huh?' said Tim, stripping off his clothes.

'I couldn't believe that about Tara. Fucking hell. She's amazing, isn't she? I mean, to have got over that.'

'She didn't get over it, Nick, she got through it. That's one of our sayings here, you'll hear Tara use it. The way out is through.'

'Oh, right,' said Nick, feeling admonished. 'Yeah, but then the other two women, d'you think they ever make it up? You know, just to sound, I don't know . . .'

'No, I don't think they make it up. What would they make it up for?'

'So they sound more, I don't know, important,' said Nick. 'I mean, I found that really uncomfortable.'

'What?'

'The circle thing,' said Nick. 'I never knew there was so much of this shit going on, but I was worried too.'

'Sure, it's very worrying.'

'No, but I mean it was sort of encouraging them to say that they had been raped. You know what I mean. Shit. I know it's not politically correct and everything, but how do we know?'

'How do we know they are telling the truth?'

'Yeah. Especially there, in that circle. It's almost a competition. It was like, Huh, you think you were raped, you should hear what happened to me! I mean, where do you draw the line?'

'Something tells me they're not making it up, Nick. Did you really think they were?'

'No, I s'pose not . . . but . . .'

'That's what all this is about,' said Tim. 'The only person who can really draw the line as you said is a woman. That's what we're trying to do here, teach women to draw a line that no man can ignore.' By this point Tim had a sports jock on and was adjusting a steel cricket box. He pulled on a pair of leggings fitted with extensive pads on the thighs and shins, then stepped into the vast groin protection pad which was held in place with two straps over his shoulders.

'I suppose so,' said Nick. 'But it still worries me. I mean, I've never raped anyone, I've never even got close. But many's the time I've been well fucked over by women. It's like, well, do they need all this encouragement to be victims? Let's all sit around and feel sorry for each other.' Tim smiled. Nick continued, 'I know Tara must have had a bad time, but I've been beaten up by groups of blokes, I've had me head kicked in more times than I can remember by some drunk twat in a pub. I don't get the whole fuss that's being made over these women. Is it worse to be punched in the face or to be raped?'

Tim smiled as he slipped his head through some enormous shoulder pads. He started doing up the Velcro strapping at the sides.

'Listen, Nick, most of the time when a woman is raped she is also punched in the face, sometimes killed afterwards. Sure, statistically, you are far more likely to be attacked by a stranger than any woman in that room.'

'There you go, then.'

'But listen to those stories – ex-boyfriend, father. I've heard about brothers, neighbours, uncles, teachers. Statistically it is very rare for a woman to be attacked like Tara was. It's mostly domestic, in the home or the workplace by someone the woman knows and may trust. There is nowhere safe for some of the women who come here. They have no boundaries. That's what they're here to learn to say . . .'

Suddenly an unearthly sound shattered their whispered conversation, making the dog jump. It was the word 'No!' shouted at full volume by seventeen women.

'Right on cue,' said Tim with utter delight. 'They're here to say no! That's all. When they say yes is up to them, but if they want to say no, normally, no one listens. What we teach them no one can ignore. Right.' He pulled on an old pair of dungarees which had been let out in the front with a strip of red material. With the shoulder pads on, his movements were somewhat restricted, and he struggled with the trousers before looking at Nick. 'Could you like give me a hand with these?' he asked, holding up the dungaree braces.

'Sure,' said Nick. The two men stood close, Nick moving the straps until they were over the huge extended padding around Tim's shoulders. It reminded him a little of dressing Barney when he was four years old, only on a vaster scale. But it was an intimate moment. Helping someone put their clothes on was only one step from helping them take them off. Nick felt uncomfortable, and yet very at ease with this grey-haired old hippie.

'Fucking hell,' he said. 'It's all so weird. I mean, you're going in there knowing that these women hate you, and you're going to let them punch and kick the shit out of you. I mean, even with this on it must hurt.'

Tim swigged from a bottle of water and shook his head as he rinsed his mouth and swallowed. 'No, it doesn't hurt. You can feel it, sure, you can like register the power of the blow, but we're real careful. You couldn't do it if it hurt.'

Tim pulled on some arm protectors and a pair of jogging shoes which had huge padded tops. 'D'you wanna try?' he asked.

'What?' said Nick.

'Well, try giving me a blow, reverse elbow to the solar plexus. You right-handed?'

'Yes,' said Nick. Tim gently took hold of his upper arms and guided him around. He was directly behind him — again that strangely relaxing feeling of closeness. 'Okay, right here,' said Tim, pointing with his gloved hand to an area about three inches above his navel. 'Full force.'

'No way,' said Nick.

'Why not?' asked Tim.

'Well, I don't want to hurt you for one thing. It's got to be well dangerous.'

'Sure, if you hit me in the head, but if you hit me just there, honestly, I'll be fine. Try it.'

'Why?'

'Because you'll never believe me, you'll only believe your body. Don't pull your punch. Full impact.'

'Fucking hell,' said Nick. He sighed and turned to look at where Tim was standing.

'That's it, line it up and go for it.'

'I really don't want to do this. You really want me to do it as hard as I can?'

'Sure,' said Tim with a charming smile, almost a laugh.

'But I'm, well, I don't want to be macho, but I'm a bit heavier built than the ladies.'

'Sure, but I teach men too. I can take it, believe me.'

Nick grimaced, extended his right arm as he remembered from his karate classes. Then, with a sudden chopping movement, he pulled his elbow back. The impact was astounding. It really hurt his elbow as he made contact — he felt the weight of Tim's body. Tim seemed to take off and slam into the wall behind him.

'Good one!' he said with a big grin.

'Are you okay?' asked Nick. Tim did seem to be slightly slumped, but he soon righted himself.

'I'm fine. I'm not winded. Listen to my breathing. I'm honestly okay. Now if I didn't have the impact suit on you'd have caved in my ribcage and possibly killed me. You hit real hard, Nick.'

'Sorry, mate,' said Nick. 'Fucking hell. That's incredible.'

'Feminism and hard plastic, man,' said Tim, picking up his massive helmet. 'That's what's made all this possible. The impact of your blow was spread out over the whole of my torso. I felt it all right. Boom. But no pain. Great force, Nick.'

'But you must get injured.'

'Usually hands, like if my hand is between, say, a foot and the suit, yeah, that can smart, but generally, nada.'

'Fucking amazing.'

'We'd better go in. I reckon they're waiting for us. Can you carry my water? I'll need a lot of that.'

'Sure,' said Nick. He picked up the water and followed the comically wide-looking padded assailant into the training room.

Chapter Seventeen

Tim stood behind Tara with his arms encircling her chest. Her hands were up protecting her face. Tim was gripping hard; she could feel his strength. 'No!' she bellowed. She raised her right foot, looked down, saw his foot and brought her heel down on his instep with all her might. Tim's grip relaxed as he howled in pain. She pulled up her arms, using the same movement she would use to take off a T-shirt, waiting until Tim's forearm was next to her mouth. 'Bite!' she shouted, and Tim released his grip. With her now liberated right arm she performed a swift elbow punch, sending Tim backwards, but he was still standing. She turned swiftly and eye-jabbed him, fingers and thumbs squeezed into a blunt stabbing weapon. His head went forward. She heel-palmed him under the chin, snapping his head back. He fell to the floor but he was still almost there, groggy, but unbowed. She then used her knee, aiming for the back of his head and slamming it home with all her strength. Tim's body flipped over and his arms went up, protecting either side of his head.

Jeanna, the assistant, blew her whistle. Tara stood up beside Tim's head, just out of reach of his arms. She continued to hold her hands up in the protective stance, looking at him. He was still.

'Look,' she shouted. Then she looked all around her. 'Assess,' she shouted, this time joined by many of the women who were watching her. 'No!' she bellowed, enforcing the statement with a stamp of her right foot. Only then did she run off the mat, joining the end of the long line of women. 'Call nine one one!' she shouted. This time the entire group of women joined in.

'Call nine one one,' said Tara again, only slightly out of breath. 'That is how we signify the end of the fight. That is how we say it's over, get help. Call nine one one. Find somewhere safe where you can get help. You have survived the primary assault, now you need to get help. Don't just walk away like a cowboy, swaggering. You have been assaulted, you have left an individual lying on the floor. But he is dangerous, maybe not to you, but possibly to other women. Call the police, they are on your side. Okay?'

Tara turned to look at Tim. He was still lying on the floor in the unconscious posture. 'Now look at Tim. You see how he's lying? When his arms are up like that, it means he's unconscious, he's not getting up. You may think you've put him down, but until he lies like that, he's telling you, you haven't done it. He'll get up again until he registers a blow he knows no one could survive. Okay, Tim.'

Tim back-flipped and sprang to his feet. Tara noticed the familiar look of confused horror and amazement on the students' faces. They had just witnessed a woman really fighting back effectively. Possibly they had never seen anything remotely like it before. As Tim took off his helmet and spat out his gumshield, he could see some of the women watching breathe a sigh of relief.

'Okay, now you can see that Tim is unhurt, and let me tell you, every one of those blows I applied to him was at absolutely full force, full impact. I did not pull my punches, Tim did not fake a reaction. Am I right, Tim?'

'Absolutely. This is the primary thing to learn today,' he said. 'This armour has been twenty-plus years in development. As long as you hit me in the target zones, the feet, the crotch, the stomach and the head, you won't hurt me. I can feel it, believe me. Tara hits real hard, and I can judge if what you did would have any real impact on an unpadded individual. That's what I'm trained to do. So don't pull your punches. Go for full impact.'

Tara glanced at Nick, who was sitting on a pile of cushions in the corner, completely engrossed. She smiled at him but he didn't seem to notice.

'Okay, let's go, then. Who's first?'

One by one Tara worked through the group. She and Tim had worked together long enough that half of their communication was effected with a look; they didn't have to talk that much. They worked slowly and methodically, Tara staying with each terror-struck woman. Nearly all of them initially froze when they felt the weight and strength of Tim's grip. He was very careful not to injure them, but he held them hard. Halfway through the second run, when most of them were beginning to find their way through the routine with less hands-on encouragement from Tara, one of the women, an older one who certainly had trouble hitting Tim without apologising, said, 'But what if he pulls your hair instead of grabbing you?'

It was the start of the 'what if' spiral. It always happened at some point in every class, although not normally so early on. The students on either side of the older woman nodded in agreement, then another added, 'What if he just pushes you down and climbs on top of you?'

'Okay,' said Tara, but before she could say more a third woman asked, 'What if he grabs you by the throat?'

In early classes, before Tara took the course, these 'what if' spirals would sometimes hold the class up for an entire session, and everyone would lose heart, morale would plummet, and the teachers would have their work cut out trying to raise it again in the following session.

'Okay, Tim, the "what if" work-out!' she shouted. Tim came up behind her and grabbed her hair, pulled her backwards and shouted at her, 'You're gonna get it, bitch!' Tara elbow-punched his unprotected mid-section, his grip loosened and he doubled over as she turned on one foot and kneed him in the face. He was down. He sprang back up again, this time grabbing her around the throat. 'Do as I say or I'll fucking kill you,' he shouted. Tara stamped on his foot which broke the grip; she heel-palmed him, eye-jabbed him, then fell on the floor and crotch-kicked him. He went down on his knees and she gave him a roundhouse kick to the temple. He spun on an axis and adopted the unconscious position. He sprang up again and pinned her to the floor, her arms trapped by his weight. He was straddling her. He said, 'Suck on this, you dirty little whore!'

Tara turned to the ashen-faced students. 'Okay, he's got me pinned down. What am I going to do?'

The women looked at her, their faces displaying a heady mix of excitement and horror. There was no response. 'Okay, here's what I do,' she said. 'Nothing.' Tim maintained the position. After a while he said, 'I really am gonna make you suck my fuckin' dick, you bitch!'

Tim dithered for a moment then moved one of his hands to mime undoing his flies. Immediately Tara heel-palmed his chin, twisted her body to tip him off, span around on the floor and kicked him in the face with such force that his body was sent spinning off and away from her.

Again she stood up and again Tim sprang to his feet.

'I don't want to fuck you, you slimy little cunt, I'm gonna kill you!' he said, taking a swipe at her. She dropped on to the floor, landing Tim a massive blow to the groin as he approached. He collapsed on top of her but she had a leg raised for her protection; she smashed it into his face and he span off, lying in the unconscious position again. This time he didn't move.

Tara stood up, looked down at Tim, looked around, shouted, 'Look, assess!', and as she stamped the floor, she bellowed 'No!' The students went wild. They clapped and cheered. Tara glanced around at Nick, sitting ashen-faced and spaced-out in the corner. However, he was clapping too.

'Right, well, what you saw there,' said Tara, when she had regained her composure, 'were some moves which we will learn later in the course, but I just wanted to show you that you are in the strong position. Your assailant has, by the very nature of biology, to open himself up as a target. You saw when he had me pinned to the floor, there was nothing I could do. He had superior strength, he had the advantage. I could do nothing. But neither could he.' She made a great deal of the last phrase, looking each woman in the eye as she walked along the line. 'Neither could he,' she repeated. 'He had to make a move in order to be able to rape me, and when he makes a move, what does he do?'

'Opens up a target,' said the blonde, smiling woman who had been crying.

'That's right!' said Tara, delighted and always amazed by how fast students picked up on what she was showing them. Teaching was usually a downhill run, with the students learning moves and the reasoning behind moves as fast as she could teach them. 'He has to move in order to do anything, and when he moves he opens himself up as a target. So the rules are very simple. Breathe, wait, assess, react fast, deliver the blow with total intention, maximum power, full impact. Okay, let's take five.'

The women dispersed and lay down, sat or flopped on chairs in the seating area. They drank copious amounts of water from plastic bottles and ate fruit, mainly bananas. They had been on their feet and active for an hour and a half and looked pretty tired. Tara walked over to where Nick was sitting and pulled a large bottle of mineral water from her cooler bag.

'You okay?' she asked quietly.

'I s'pose so. It's all a bit much, though. I still don't know what I think.'

'Okay, well, after the session, we'll talk about it. We always have a little circle then, just for staff.'

Nick nodded without saying anything. Tim sat down next to him and put his arm around him.

'How you doing, buddy?' he asked, with a voice so full of kindness it was impossible to misinterpret.

'Okay,' said Nick. Tara and Tim exchanged glances.

'Tim, I didn't get a chance to tell you, but Mindy — remember, the blonde woman with the history? — she wants to do a re-enactment.'

'Okay, that's cool.' Tim nodded.

'What's that?' asked Nick.

'Um, a re-enactment, well, we kind of replay the events of her assault,' said Tara discreetly. 'You remember Mindy, the woman with the blond hair?'

'Oh yeah,' said Nick.

'Well, she wants to go through that attack again. She asked me about it this morning while Tim was changing. It's like part of the healing process. You'll see it all in a while, but Tim will play her ex-boyfriend, the guy who raped her, and she'll try and deal with the situation differently.'

'You're kidding,' said Nick. 'It's a bit sick, isn't it?'

'Why d'you say that?' asked Tara, still intrigued by this Englishman's reactions. She could tell he wasn't happy, was clearly uncomfortable when confronted with such open displays of women's strength.

'Well, you'd think . . . I'd have thought she'd just want to get over it. You know, put it behind her, not bloody well act it all out again. Blimey.'

'I think the problem is,' said Tara quietly, 'that she is finding it very difficult to put it out of her mind. You see, what tends to happen is the event plays over and over like a tape loop, endlessly repeating itself. Driving her crazy. If she re-enacts the situation, she'll probably have the first good night's sleep since the incident took place.'

'Blimey. I don't know. It's all a bit weird,' said Nick. 'Is Tim really going to pretend to be her boyfriend?'

'Sure,' said Tim. 'It's amazing what happens.'

Tara and Tim left Nick and discussed the shape of the rest of the session as they drained their water bottles. It was hot work but both of them were buzzing. They agreed it was a good group and all the problems they were confronting were solvable.

Tim replaced his helmet and Tara walked to the centre of the mat. The class resumed with renewed vigour, the women seemingly charged by the events that were taking place, their faces displaying their enthusiasm. They were learning fast, and as Tara explained to them, their body memory was being rein-forced. They didn't have to intellectualise what they were doing, it would just come to them when they needed it, and they would know it was there, ready.

After they had been through the entire group of students teaching them another move, in which Tim pulled them down on the floor and rolled them over, Tara asked them all to stand in a circle. They all put their arms around each other and pulled in close.

Tara noticed Tim join Nick by the side of the mat as she started speaking very softly. 'Okay, now, we've been having a really good class, we've all really learned a lot. I'm really impressed with what you guys have done today. One thing we can do is re-enactments. You may have heard people talk about this aspect of the training, okay? This is like really up to you, as individuals, but we do know it has a profound psycho-logical and emotional effect. So if anyone wants Tim to portray an individual from your past, we'll tell him what to do. I'll be there with you all the way. Okay?'

'I want to,' said Mindy. The other women all looked at her. Some smiled, some choked back a tear, some looked horrified.

'Okay, Mindy,' said Tara, knowing this was going to happen. 'That's good.'

'I'm real scared, though,' said Mindy, now crying freely.

'That's okay, we're all here with you,' said Tara. The rest of the circle nodded and muttered encouragement. Tara went through the ritual of the closed circle with the women. They were encouraged to express their hopes for the world, and their determination to halt violence against women. They ended with an exultant 'No!' as they all pounded their feet into the crash mats.

'Mindy is ready,' said Tara after a little time spent counselling her. 'What d'you want Tim to do, to say?'

'I don't know,' said Mindy, now weeping hopelessly.

'Okay, well, what's your ex-boyfriend's name?'

'William.'

'Okay, your name is William,' said Tara to Tim, who was standing on the far end of the mat holding his helmet. He nodded.

'What did he say to you?' asked Tara.

'He like . . . he said he loved me,' said Mindy finally, wiping her eye with a soggy tissue. 'But he said if I didn't do what he wanted he was going to hurt me.'

'Okay,' said Tara. 'You ready, Tim?'

Tim nodded and attached his helmet. He walked up to the terrified Mindy. Tara stood right by her side. The woman was now sobbing uncontrollably. As Tim got closer Tara could sense the woman's strength leaving her body. She was caving in, collapsing, all her boundaries were down.

'Hey, Mindy, I love you, okay? Don't you believe me?' said Tim. 'I fucking love you. But you make me so mad.'

Mindy turned towards Tara and fell into her arms. 'That's just what he said,' she sobbed. Tim's arms dropped down by his side. He went 'neutral'. He didn't move at all. Tim really was the best, thought Tara.

'Okay, now, tell William to stop where he is,' said Tara gently. 'Take up the protective stance we learned today, and tell him no. No further.'

'I can't,' said Mindy.

'I saw you do it,' said Tara quietly. 'I know you can.'

Tara embraced Mindy for a full three minutes until the sobbing subsided. The room was completely silent, everyone focused on this single event.

'Okay, I'll try,' said Mindy finally.

'Mindy is ready,' said Tara. Tim immediately sprang back to life.

'Hey, Mindy, don't fuck me around. You make me so horny. What d'you expect?' he said as he walked towards her. 'Dressed like that. I love you, don't do this to me, you're making me real mad!'

'No,' said Mindy, loud and clear, but with an element of pleading in her voice. Tim stopped his approach.

'Don't ask him no. Tell him no,' said Tara.

'No!' shouted Mindy, this time getting some positive feed-back from her fellow students.

'What d'you mean no?' said Tim from inside his helmet. 'You don't say no to me, baby. No way. I'm William, you know. Come here.' He made a grab for her arm. Mindy was digging in, her eyes fixed on the absurdly shaped helmet on Tim's head. Although Tara had seen this sequence of events countless times before, the intensity of the moment was in no way diminished for her. Tara was with this girl, this girl who had been punched, kicked and brutally raped by her so-called boyfriend. She was there too. It wasn't Tim standing in front of her, it was this asshole William. Mindy adopted the stance, moving back slightly to keep her distance from the threat.

'Stand your ground,' said Tara sharply. 'Don't move back. If you move back you're inviting him to come forward. Again, tell him to go.'

'Go away, leave me alone now!' shouted Mindy, her red, tear-stained face twisted by fury. Tara knew she had broken through. Mindy had found it, what was there in all women, the deep, deep well of fury.

'Hey, don't tell me what to do, bitch. I've had it up to here with being told what to fucking do. You do what I say or so fucking help me, Mindy, I'm gonna hurt you bad.'

Tim approached her again, grabbing her by the shoulders.

'No,' shouted Mindy in a voice Tara knew no one in the room would recognise as her own. This was not the polite voice they had heard earlier. It was from the gut, from the spleen and womb, the most dark, powerful source of human experience. 'No.'

The blows came thick and fast, some unfocused, some panicky, but all of them delivered with enormous force and one hundred and ten per cent commitment.

Tim made very loud pain reaction noises, not something he'd done in the class previously. He had clearly judged that it would be appropriate and it didn't seem to stall Mindy's defence. Tara assessed what she was doing. She heel-palmed him first, not a good move, then she eye-poked him, propelled her knee into his groin with very good accuracy and power, enough to rupture a testicle and put any man on the floor. Tim collapsed with a low groan, and before even Tara expected, Mindy landed her knee in Tim's, or William's, face. Tim rolled over, then started to get up again. Mindy lost it – she started to kick out pointlessly, so desperate was her need to destroy this demon. Tara stopped her, grabbing her by the shoulders but not blocking her view of Tim lying on the floor.

'Think what you're doing. Don't waste your energy with pointless kicks. Get down on the floor, that's where you're strongest.'

Mindy threw herself on the floor like a woman possessed, lined herself up beautifully and screamed, 'No, William, you fucking asshole, I said no!'

The kick was devastating, sending Tim spinning across the mat. He adopted the unconscious position and the students' cheer went through the roof. Tara and Mindy embraced. Tara could feel her student shaking, but the tears were gone; she felt hard and strong.

'Well done, baby,' said Tara softly into her ear.

'Thank you so much,' said Mindy, tears now returning. 'Thank you so, so much.'

Tara briefly turned to see where Nick was sitting. He had disappeared.

Chapter Eighteen

Alice was not concentrating as she stepped out of the lift on the thirty-third floor. It wasn't a standard lift, it was a builders' hoist, a metal cage attached, supposedly securely, to the outside of a gutted office structure, a massive repair job as a result of the Canary Wharf bomb. The toe of her ankle boot caught on the lip between the lift floor and the scaffolding and she stumbled slightly.

There had been six separate claims for work injuries on the site, and Alice had been asked by the insurance company to have a look at the procedures and building practices to see if there was any way to improve standards.

It was mainly a cosmetic job, everyone knew that. There was something in a builder's mentality that could override any safety system, no matter how clear the dangers. She had visited another site where a lever that operated a safety guard on a lift similar to the one in which she had just travelled was permanently secured in the Up position. This meant that the men or piles of bricks going up four hundred feet in the lift could easily fall out. Which was exactly what had happened. Luckily it was bricks and not people, and luckily they only fell on the foreman's van, destroying the vehicle. This site was in far better shape, but building high structures was always a risky business.

'You all right, miss?' asked one of the burly but friendly-looking lads who stood around the lift as she stepped out.

'Fine, thanks,' said Alice. 'How are you all getting on?'

'We're all dandy,' said the man in a delightful Irish brogue.

'Are you the safety officer, miss?' asked another Irishman.

'No, I'm a risk assessor,' said Alice. She had to speak up – the wind was very strong and the sound of the wet cement vibrators being used on the floor above was intense. 'But it's the same ball park. I'm just having a look around, to see what you're all doing. I'm basically here to try and make sure you lot live long enough to collect your pensions.'

'Not much chance of that with the amount Michael drinks, miss,' said the first man. There was a great deal of mirth at this. Alice smiled. She was here, high up on this building site, but she felt miles away. There was something so huge missing inside that she couldn't be sure where her body was. She was looking at the world through a long tunnel. She could still function perfectly well – she hadn't missed any days off work, she still got up in the morning and had a shower, drove to work, went home, did the shopping and laundry. But she had burned the clothes she had been wearing the night she went out with Peter. She hadn't cried much. Once she noticed the phone number of the Samaritans on the back of a bus when she was in a traffic jam. She almost considered writing it down but never got round to it.

Peter had rung about three times since it had happened, although she didn't know what exactly 'it' was. He had left fairly cursory messages on her answer service. She hadn't been answering the phone. He didn't seem to want to see her again. She had rung May again – she'd wanted to talk but the baby was crying in the background. May begged her to visit; she claimed she was going crazy and needed to see an intelligent adult. Alice promised she would, but knew that any visit was going to entail a one-way sympathy transaction. Sleepless nights, soiled nappies and an irate and annoying partner were enough for May to cope with.

Alice walked to the edge of the concrete platform which would one day be the floor of an air-conditioned office space. The drop was considerable, even for someone used to clambering about on dangerous structures. Thirty floors down to a pile of scaffold poles and three Portaloos. She stepped back and her hand automatically went to her chest.

'Bit of a drop there, miss,' said the first Irishman. 'You get used to it after a while.'

'Surely there's supposed to be a safety rail there,' said Alice, her hair blowing across her face.

'There is too,' said the Irishman. 'I think the bloody thing blew off this morning. It is terrible windy up here.'

Alice made a mental note and looked up. She climbed a ladder and emerged on the very top of the structure. The view was wonderful. To her right the even greater height of the Canada Tower, its massive glass bulk towering above her. Directly in front, stretching into the distance, the River Thames curved its way towards Tower Bridge and the City. Slightly behind her and to her left the Greenwich Observatory, the Cutty Sark in its riverside home, the Royal Seamen's Hospital and the Millenium Dome.

Alice breathed deeply. The wind thundered in her ears; her hair, long and dark, whipped about her head in a frenzy. She felt good for the first time since . . . When? she wondered. Since Peter in the car. It was never far away, and yet she still wasn't sure what had happened. Basically rape sounded wrong – it didn't seem like a rape, he hadn't really hurt her, there were no injuries except for some bruising where she had been lying on the handbrake. He did come inside her but she'd had her period since so she wasn't pregnant. What was she supposed to do? It was just one of those things. She didn't like Peter very much so she wasn't upset at the thought of not seeing him again.

She just couldn't seem to start her life again. Something had stopped that night, some spark had died – that was the only way she could think of it. It was whatever made her funny at a dinner

·party, whatever made her able to come back with a witty retort to a man's posturing, or a woman's emotional outpourings. She hadn't even known she had it before, but now it was gone, whatever it was, there seemed to be nothing left.

The crane which towered above Alice's head started to move; the large electric motor that powered it was right beside her. The sudden noise made her jump. She looked up. The huge steel arm of the crane swung around; she felt a little dizzy. She could see the operator in his little cabin, wearing headphones, in contact with the site foreman on the ground, nearly five hundred feet below him. What a peculiar job, thought Alice, secluded in that little box all day, swinging around and around as the building below him slowly took shape. She quite fancied it, she decided. She felt she wanted to be in a little box, removed from everyone.

She had spent a great deal of time in her flat. She had changed all the locks as she wasn't sure if Peter had a key. So she must have thought he had done something wrong because she didn't want him to do it again. Maybe he did rape her. How could she tell? She hadn't given it a great deal of thought. Not that she was unaware, but it had never been something she had confronted before. She had been scared on the street numerous times in her life when some strange man had lunged towards her, but it had usually been quite comical and she had always been able to say something rude and spiteful to make the man feel small. That was what she felt had gone – her spikiness. Her mother had always criticised her for it. Maybe it was no bad thing. Maybe she would find a husband now, instead of some bloke who wanted to fuck her in the back of a car when she didn't really want him to.

The crane creaked as it took the weight of another bucket of ready-mixed cement all that way below.

'I'll have to ask you to move now, miss,' said yet another Irishman. 'We'll be pouring up here in a moment. There's not really enough room for you to watch.'

'That's fine,' said Alice. 'I've seen enough.'

Chapter Nineteen

It was such a relief to get out of that room. The last twenty minutes had been hell. He found a taxi on a street a couple of blocks from the training centre. The driver was the same age as him, with tattoos, a small goatee beard and a shaved head.

'You from England?'

'Yeah, London, mate.'

'Hey, you like it here?'

'Brilliant, love it,' said Nick, finding it hard to be jovial.

'It's a piece-of-shit town. For straight guys. You gay?'

'No, mate.'

'Me either. I don't mind gays, be a hard town to live in if you did. You married?'

'Nah.'

'Divorced?'

'Nah, never did it, mate.'

'I did, man, and I'm still bleeding.'

'Oh yeah,' said Nick, looking out at the less than glamorous streets of Oakland. This was one friendly taxi driver.

'I married a beautiful, intelligent, successful woman.'

'Sounds all right,' said Nick after a moment's silence.

'You'd think so,' said the driver as they started up the gradient towards the Bay Bridge. 'She dumped on me. Big-time, every fucking day. All her stress and tension from work, all my fault. All her fuck-ups, all my fault. Didn't matter what happened, all my fault. Everything that went wrong was because I was a dumb ass. She could never accept responsibility for her own failings. You know what I'm saying?'

'Yeah, mate,' said Nick.

'She cheated on me. She fucked anything she could, on the desk at work. You understand me? Guys who worked under her, they fucked under her. She was always on top.'

Nick was starting to have erotic images of this woman screwing men on her desk in a high-rise office.

'Bitch gave me herpes, fucking dirty bitch gave me herpes.'

'You're kidding.'

'No, man, this is all true, believe me. I never cheated on her, dumb ass that I was. I fucking loved the bitch. She got herpes and gave it to me. Then she had the gall to blame me. Tried to sue me. D'you know what I did, man?'

'No, what happened?'

'I sued her ass. I went to court, accused her of infidelity, of giving me an incurable disease. Herpes simplex is incurable. Did you know that, man?'

'I'd heard, yeah.'

'You got it?'

'Uh, no. No, I haven't.'

'Don't get it, believe me. Anyhow, I sued her ass. I got the house and the car and she has to give me maintenance, like she earns top dollar, you know what I'm saying? She is mad as all hell and doing everything she can to stop paying me. And we had a lady judge. I tell you, the bitches will walk all over you if you let them. It's a fucking war out there, man. We've got to stick together.'

'Who?' asked Nick, feeling he'd missed something.

'Men. We've got to back each other up. Women have taken over this town, man. They run the place, they own the place. All me and you are good for is fixing the washing machine and the car, and what's in our balls. That's all they want from us, they don't need us for anything else. We're over, man, finished. Game over, you know what I'm saying?'

'Yeah, I do, mate, I fucking do,' said Nick. It made sense, it really did.

'Look at that, isn't that fucking beautiful?' said the driver. He was gesturing towards the approaching skyline of San Francisco. 'Built by men, you know what I'm saying? Built by men, designed by men, created and dreamed up by men. We did that, not fucking women. They say we're destructive and violent. Bullshit, man. Look what we done. We made this fucking place. We build and create, we design and dream and stretch ourselves. We build bridges and boats and planes. Women use them and criticise them and trash everything we do. The tables are gonna turn, my friend, they're gonna fucking turn.'

'How d'you mean?' asked Nick.

'I don't mean women back in the kitchen, having ten kids. I mean, men are going to back off, start having more fun, work less, you know, go fishing. Fuck work and career, let the women do it. They're welcome to all that shit. Keep it.'

He leant out of his window as an open-top Mercedes sports car overtook the taxi. It was being driven by a glamorous-looking young woman. 'Live in the fast lane, you fucking moron,' he shouted, and then laughed. 'You'll die young and have a shit life.'

Nick got the taxi to drop him outside the Moscone convention centre on 4th and Mission. There was no reason behind this other than the fact that the meter had been approaching a sum that almost ate up the last of his reserves.

He rang Tiffany from a call-box and breathed a sigh of relief when she answered. She sounded worried when she heard his resume of what had taken place but he decided to ignore her, he just kept on insisting she drop everything and get a bus downtown.

While he waited Nick went to a bar across the street and bought a soft-pack of Camel untipped cigarettes and lit one up. He hadn't smoked for nearly a year. No one seemed to smoke on

the streets of San Francisco any more – he felt mildly embarrassed as he sat under the portico of the convention centre
puffing away. However, the effect was brilliant. He felt his
buttocks relax a little for the first time that day.

After a while he saw Tiffany walking quickly towards him
across the tree-shaded walkway.

'You okay, hon?' she asked, her face clearly showing concern.
American women were so easy to understand.

'Let's go for a drink,' said Nick when he had finished holding
her. 'I'm bloody parched.'

'Okay, baby, where d'you want to go?' she asked, sympathetic
but keeping a safe distance. He knew his anger was showing; he
couldn't help it.

'The Circus,' he said, the idea suddenly popping into his
head. 'I want to go to the fucking Circus bar. Just as long as I can
have a cold one, you know. I've had a shit of a day.'

'The Circus? Are you sure?' asked Tiffany. The bar Nick had
worked in two years previously was not known for its highbrow
clientele, more as a meat market.

'Sure. Is big Mickey still there?'

'Hey, hon, I don't know. I'm a college girl now. I don't hang
out in places like that any more.'

'That class was totally weird,' Nick told her as they walked
along Market Street. His head was full of noise – the taxi driver
and the class, all this fighting, hatred, mistrust and lies. Cheating
and cruelty – it was all so fucked up. The sun was shining,
making dappled patterns through the trees on the couples who
walked along happily together beneath their shady bough. No
one was raping anyone or even threatening to. The world was
full of happy couples, men and women, getting along and mostly
having a good time. It was normal. 'I just walked out. I had to get
the fuck out of there, I couldn't take any more.'

'You didn't tell them for why?' asked Tiffany.

'No, I just legged it when they were in the middle of some
really weird stuff. I cannot handle it, Tiffs. I really can't. Maybe

it's me, maybe I'm really fucked up. But to me, the whole thing stinks of poncy, holier-than-thou, weird hippie shit. Everybody being caring and sharing and New Age when we all know they don't give a flying toss.'

'Oh, I don't know that's true,' said Tiffany.

'They're doing it for the fucking money. Come on. We all know that. I mean, those women have paid five hundred dollars to be molested by some bloke in a padded suit. Jesus. It's all so fucking pervy. I feel like I need a wash. You know what I mean?'

'Oh, baby,' said Tiffany sympathetically. She wasn't looking at him the way she normally did, however. She just stared at the sidewalk.

'I mean, sure,' said Nick, deciding to play safe. 'Some of the women there have been raped and, believe me, that really upset me when I heard that. It's not that, it's the pious nodding and all the "we care too" stuff. It made me want to puke.'

They entered the Circus bar, and sure enough there behind the long counter was big Mickey, the vast man who had employed Nick for six months.

'Hey, look who's back in town,' he said as they approached. Nick was flattered to be remembered and the two men shook hands. Mickey's hands were enormous, heavily ringed and hugely powerful. They sat at the bar as Mickey gave them both a beer. Nick took a hard swig and lit up another Camel.

'Babe, I didn't think you smoked,' said Tiffany, looking slightly put off.

'Believe me, after what I've had to sit through today, it's a wonder I'm not using a crack pipe.'

They sat side by side at the bar, sank a few beers and played with beer mats. Nick allowed the cold beer to trickle through him. He just wanted to wash away all the shit he had heard. It was all such a nightmare.

'It's a real shame you didn't get off on it, though,' said Tiffany after a long silence. Nick had been running over the events he'd seen. The re-enactment had been what finally sent him scuttling from the room.

'I'm glad I didn't get off on it. What sort of a perv would want to do that?'

'I don't know, Nicky, but, shit, I was real proud of you doing the course.'

'Have you actually seen what they do?' He could feel the tension in his scalp. People had told him he looked scary when he was like that. Tiffany shook her head. 'They, like, they re-enact a rape, like some woman in the class said she had been raped by her boyfriend. Anyway, then Tara got the bloke in the suit to attack her again, only this time she fought back.'

'That sounds great, though.'

'Yeah, but it's all fake. It's tricking these poor women into believing they could fight back. It's shit. That's what got on my tits. In a real-life struggle she wouldn't stand a fucking chance.' He threw his matchbook down on the bar. 'Oh, fuck it, I really don't want to talk about it. That's just what they do. Talk it all through and work it all out and understand each other, when really it's all bollocks. The women don't stand an earthly and it's all a crude way to make money out of other people's suffering. It's like Oprah and all that caring, sharing crap that you fall for over here. Let's get something to eat.'

Nick stood up to leave. Tiffany excused herself and went to the ladies' room. Big Mickey joined Nick, leaning over the bar, wiping a glass as he spoke.

'Nice piece of tush,' he said, his gold tooth glinting.

'Tiffany, yeah, she's great. I met her here. Don't you remember?'

'I remember you were drowning in pussy all the time you worked here, man,' said Mickey with a lascivious chuckle.

'I'm staying with her and her mum over on the Haight.'

'Stayin' with her mom! Sounds serious.'

'I dunno. I am a bit serious about her.'

'Okay, don't say I didn't warn you, man,' said Mickey,

taking a step back and placing a polished glass on the shelf behind him.

'You never warned me about anything, Mickey. What you on, mate?' asked Nick.

'You wanna know what I know?' asked Mickey, glancing around the bar to see if he was being overheard.

'Yeah, all right, what d'you know?'

'If I'm not mistaken she's a ten-dollar whore, Nick. Used to work up at the Crazy Horse. Blowjob on the roof for fifty bucks. Takes it up the ass for a C note.'

Nick chewed his lip. He felt a surge of anger race through him. He scratched his head; his scalp had gone tight. According to Mickey, any woman who came into the bar was a whore and therefore worthless and deserving of no respect.

'I know for a fact that's bullshit,' he said as heartily as he could. 'She was a dancer, yeah. That's all. She's at college now, Mickey, gave all that shit up a long time ago. We've got a thing going.'

'Hey, respect, Nick. Respect,' said big Mickey. 'But you know what they say, you can take a whore to culture, but you can't make her think.' He burst out laughing and put a friendly hand on Nick's upper arm. He patted him and said, 'Way to go, boy. Don't leave it so long next time.'

Nick smiled. It seemed the best thing to do. He didn't want to lay the nut on big Mickey, he wasn't worth it. The man was a bore anyway. They shook hands and promised to stay in touch. As they walked out of the noisy bar Nick noticed Mickey give Tiffany a lecherous wink.

It was still light out on the street. The place was buzzing. Nick thought of asking Tiffany what else she had done when she was working at the Crazy Horse. He flashed on the idea of giving her money, taking her into an off-street carpark and ramming his cock in her mouth.

He felt horny. He looked at Tiffany's neck and he wanted to bite it. He wanted her, but he wanted her dirty. He felt a thrill of excitement as he imagined the ways he could bring up the subject of a shag. Saying nothing to her was almost more exciting; just being with her and thinking of dirty things to do to her without saying anything was more of a thrill. That's what he needed after a crap day like the one he'd had. A thrill.

'I need something hot, like a fucking curry,' he said. 'There's never any decent curry in America.'

'We could go to that Thai place off Anderson Street,' said Tiffany. At last Nick started to have a good time again. He delighted in the tense feeling in his stomach. He wanted to be so dirty with this girl, and she was the one girl he had ever met who seemed willing to do anything.

They held hands over the table in the Thai restaurant and kissed each other gently on the lips.

'D'you know what I really want to do?' said Nick.

'No. What d'you really want to do, baby?' asked Tiffany softly.

'See you naked.'

'Oh, baby.'

'Buck naked, legs spread, on stage at the Crazy Horse.'

'Honey!' said Tiffany with a broad smile. 'You are so totally kinky.'

'Tell me about it,' said Nick. They looked at each other softly for a moment. Nick felt electrically alive. 'You'll do it, then?' he asked.

'You serious?'

'Sure. Why not.'

'I don't do that shit any more, Nick. I told you for why. And my mom would die if she found out.'

'I won't tell her.'

'You really want me to go back there? I thought you hated it.'

'I do, but I just want to have a good time, and you make me so fucking horny, Tiff. I can't tell you. The idea of seeing you being ogled at by all those pervy blokes, I dunno, it just makes me well horny, that's all.'

'Baby,' said Tiffany, clearly trying to decide what to do.

'Oh, come on, Tiff, you're so good at it. Like a double dose of Viagra. Drives me insane, makes me rock hard for life.'

'Baby!' said Tiffany. She looked shocked. He stopped the thrill rush for a minute, worried he might have pushed it too far. Her brow was furrowed; she stared at him. Then she changed her expression, raised her beautiful eyebrows and said, 'Okay.'

'Brilliant!' said Nick. 'Oh, baby, you are so horny, I can't tell you.'

'Yeah, so you keep telling me.'

They split the bill between them. Nick was now down to his last few dollars. He'd spent money like water in the three days he'd been there, buying stupid gifts for Tiffany, taking taxis everywhere, eating out in classy restaurants. He didn't want to think about what he was going to do about it. He walked arm in arm with Tiffany back down on to Market Street and along to the Crazy Horse.

The lighting in the entrance was garish and unforgiving. Massive gaudily coloured posters showed women with too much make-up striking 'sexy' poses on the stage. 'World Famous Live Revue Bar', said the flashing neon sign. Tiffany was welcomed with a big hug by the girl on the door. The enormous bouncer checked Nick out and ushered them both inside.

He breathed in the fetid, smoky air. He wanted to be there so badly and he wasn't disappointed. He wanted something this garish to burn out the memory of the class he'd seen. He wanted to look at chicks and get horny. The place was hopping – hundreds of punters and a girl on stage wearing a ripped vest which easily revealed oversized, surgically enhanced breasts, completely out of proportion with the rest of her long, skinny body.

Nick looked at Tiffany, who was working her way to the bar at the rear of the room as fast as she could. Many of the businessmen sitting at tables clearly recognised her. They smiled when they saw her and patted her arse as she passed. Some of them waved ten-dollar bills in her direction, folded along their length. This was to indicate that they'd like to see her strip. They would then tuck the bills in her garter belt or panties as she squatted down on the edge of the stage to talk to them.

He followed her slowly towards the bar, where two barmen in white shirts were putting drinks on trays which were delivered by women wearing see-through vests and butt-floss panties.

Nick sat on a bar stool next to Tiffany, shook hands with someone, presumably a barman, accepted a drink and lit up a Camel. The sound system was very powerful. They were playing 'Roll with it' by Oasis as the girl on stage, now completely naked except for minute panties, writhed around on the floor with her legs as wide apart as human anatomy would allow. She held on to the steel pole in the centre of the stage and pulled herself up and hung on to the bar so that her arms were high above her head. Her breasts now became ludicrous spectacles of non-flesh. No life form had previously conformed to the type of tissue engineering on display. She pouted through the tangled mop of her dyed-blond hair and then, in time with the music, started to make moves as though she were being slapped across the face. The crowd cheered as slowly her legs parted and she lifted them into the air. She had good stomach muscles, Nick noted, as she started to judder as though she were copulating, her head thrown back in mock ecstasy. Nick raised his eyebrows and took a puff on his Camel. He sighed and looked at Tiffany, who was cheering the girl on stage.

'That's Kirsten,' she shouted in Nick's ear. 'She's just had her breasts done again. Don't they look fantastic?'

'I prefer yours, babe,' said Nick, and kissed her on the cheek. She smiled at him and patted his thigh. He looked down at her hand; every finger had rings on it. Even her thumb sported a thin silver band. Nick knew what was coming before it hit him. He had felt lonely in places like this before. He suddenly didn't know why he was there. When Tiffany touched his leg with such tenderness, it went against the lust-hard grain. He suddenly felt he wanted to leave. It was all a mistake, he didn't really want to watch her strip, he just wanted to be safe and warm somewhere. He leant over to talk to her. He didn't feel he could just change his mind, suddenly ask her to leave. Everything was such a mess inside his head; he didn't know what he wanted. Tiffany turned to him before he could say anything.

'I just spoke with Elliot. He's the floor manager over there.' She pointed to a man with a dark beard and neatly tied-back ponytail who had been standing near them. 'He said I could do my old act. They'll even pay me three hundred bucks.'

'Jesus!' said Nick.

'Only one thing. Please, please don't tell my mom.'

'Okay, whatever,' said Nick.

Tiffany threw her arms around him and kissed him passionately. 'I'm only doing this for you, baby. You know that. Don't hate me.'

'How could I hate you? Fucking hell, my only worry is I'm gonna come before I can get you home.'

'Please don't hate me,' she said again as she walked away. He smiled at her, returning her blown kisses. She disappeared through a door and someone tapped him gently on the shoulder. It was a tall barman. He was offering Nick another beer. Nick shrugged and mouthed that he didn't have any money. The barman nodded and mouthed that it was 'on the house'.

Kirsten, the girl with the unfeasible breasts, had finally solo-shagged herself into oblivion on the floor. She sprang to her white high-heeled feet, picked up her torn costume and shimmied around the edge of the stage, receiving more and more ten- and twenty-dollar bills from an adoring public. They tucked them gingerly into her minute G-string, all pulling it a little further than necessary to insert their cash. Finally Kirsten stood up and bowed. She received a round of applause such as was normally reserved for opera divas on the opening night of *Tosca* in La Scala, Milan. Tumultuous and loud enough to give the sound system a challenge.

The men in the audience talked among themselves as a video started playing on the hundreds of monitors that littered the ceiling – more naked women cavorting in more Crazy Horse bars all over America. It was the corporate video for the Crazy Horse chain. It made Nick laugh. It was the McDonald's of nude dancing, the KFC of the jiggle industry.

The screens returned to the corporate logo and another heavy rock song burst through the room. Nick had heard it a thousand times, working in bars and clubs. He couldn't place it but knew Run DMC had something to do with it. 'Walk This Way!' screamed David Lee Roth, and Nick's heart skipped a beat as Tiffany appeared on the stage wearing a white miniskirt which barely passed her crotch. She danced around the stage, occasionally stopping for a raunchy knee bend, and right in front of some very delighted-looking Japanese punters, bending over double, the thin line of her panties flashing out from between her long thighs.

Nick smiled. She danced with such joy and enthusiasm, such honesty. He wanted to masturbate as he watched her. She was so horny he just wanted to lose it. She blew kisses to the punters, threw her head back, danced like a banshee and clung to the central bar as she sailed around, legs in the air, giving everyone a glimpse of her panties.

'She is one fucking hot little piece of ass,' said a fat man who was standing next to Nick.

'Yeah, she's fucking brilliant, isn't she,' said Nick proudly. He wanted to add, 'I love her, she loves me too and we fuck like donkeys every night'. He said nothing.

Tiffany spun around in the miniskirt, looking left and right provocatively. The crowd cheered as she delicately took hold of the hem of her dress. Everyone knew she was going to take the dress off but still the tension she managed to create by delaying the moment was electrifying. Nick found himself very excited by the prospect of this upcoming display, the woman with whom he had spent exhausting hours of intimacy showing herself in this manner. He wanted her to take the dress off. He wanted to join in the shouts of encouragement and whistles coming from the floor.

'Go on, Tiff!' he yelled, immediately feeling embarrassed. He glanced around and realised that no one had looked at him or even noticed. Hundreds of men were shouting out at her, hundreds living the moment when a woman takes her clothes off in front of a man. When he finally gets to see it all.

Slowly she pulled the dress up so that her panties were revealed. She writhed her groin around expertly, then slowly pulled the hem higher and higher. Her pierced navel and taut stomach were now clearly visible. She was gorgeous, thought Nick, absolutely fucking gorgeous. Then, as her face disappeared behind the thin fabric, her breasts appeared, the moment the crowd had been waiting for.

Her breasts, Tiffany's, the girl he had watched sleeping, her small, round, perfectly formed breasts which he had held and brushed and kissed. Nick felt himself almost cry with the pleasure the sight gave him. He was crazy about this crazy girl – she was the ultimate, the best, the bravest and the most sexy woman he'd ever known. At that point he could have died happy. If there was one thing Tiffany knew how to do, it was how to have a good time. She swung the dress around her head as the cheer went up. The punters loved her. She was so much more natural than the girl who had gone before – very little make-up, shorter hair, no breast enhancement, just a beautiful, lithe young body.

'I'll tell you what I'd like to do,' said the fat man standing next to him. He had grabbed Nick's arm and pulled on it slightly, not aggressively but insensitively. 'I'd like to nail that bitch to my workbench and fuck her ass, you know, real hard. Make the little pussy squeal.' The man laughed and his eyes twinkled. He looked like a perverted Father Christmas, the sort who could be found happily shagging his reindeer, making the little pussy squeal.

Nick chewed his thumbnail. He looked around again. Hundreds of men in business shirts were looking at Tiffany, naked on a stage in front of them. They weren't using their brains, they were using their dicks to think with. They all wanted to do something to Tiffany, and in an environment like the Crazy Horse it now seemed to Nick that they all wanted to hurt her. They wanted to watch her suffer. Nick remembered the response the girl with big breasts had received when she pretended to be slapped. They loved it. Nick loved it too, he knew he did, but it worried him for the first time. He was torn between caring for this girl and wanting to join in with all the other guys and mentally shag her to death. Was that what he really wanted? Underneath all the good-time stuff was he just another violent man who wanted to hurt women? Did he want to destroy that joyous youthful energy displaying itself so wantonly on the stage before him? Bollocks. That was the sort of thought he was meant to have, the sort bitches like Tara imagined men had. He didn't want to hurt Tiffany, he wanted to shag her and have a good time. It was different.

He wasn't depressed any more, he was riven with fifteen different feelings. He wanted to love Tiffany, he wanted to see her in a virginal white wedding dress, but he also wanted to shag her in a dirty pornographic way with the lights on. He wanted to spend time just talking and holding her gently, but he also wanted to tie her up and taunt her fragile beauty. He was so much stronger than her, so much heavier and bigger. It was all so fucked up. She needed him to protect her. But how brave she was being, standing naked and in control in front of five hundred men.

He looked at her face as she danced. She was looking at him, directly at him. She was smiling — such a sexy, beautiful smile. She wanted him, she had said so, she wanted him so bad. He was the luckiest man in the room. Any one of the men around him would have paid top dollar to be in his position, and they still wouldn't be in his actual position because Tiffany loved him. She didn't do it with him for any other reason than she loved him. And yet he was riven. Utterly riven. He really needed to get out. He'd left this club before, the first time he'd seen her there, and he'd left the class in the afternoon. He'd always run out of places when it got too weird. Sally's parents' house after Barney was born. He could still remember walking away, down St Margaret's Road in the cold night air, just wanting to get as far away from them all as possible. Maybe after all these years he was realising he was a coward, that for all his size and strength and his seeming happy-go-lucky attitude to the world, he was terrified. Maybe all that New Age therapy shit he'd seen in the afternoon was right, maybe that smarmy fucker Tim was right. Maybe Tim really was happy and he, Nick, was fucked up. Maybe Tim never wanted to pin a woman down and really fuck her like the fat bloke with the beard, who was still leering at Tiffany. Maybe they were right and he was a mess inside and he needed to do all that therapy shit and get reborn. But then he'd just be a hippie airhead like them, and he'd always have to share all his feelings when half the time he didn't have any fucking feelings. It was all too fucked up.

Tiffany bowed when the last chord was played at a deafening level over the massive sound system. She stood back up, her arms over her head in triumph. The crowd loved her, adored her, and wanted to take turns fucking her. It was completely honest and real. There was no pretence at caring what she thought or felt, there was just a communal desire among all the men there to get their rocks off. Nick knew that was what it was. They didn't really fuck her, they just wanted to, and uptight bitches like Tara would never understand that. Never.

Chapter Twenty

'I don't know what happened. I didn't see him go,' said Tim. He took another swig from a water bottle. 'He seemed fine during the break, a little freaked but then we know that happens. But I don't ever remember a guy like, walking out like that. That was real strange.'

Tara, Tim and the two assistants sat on chairs by the side of the mats, mulling over the class.

'I'm so embarrassed about the whole goddamn thing,' said Tara. 'I shouldn't have brought him.'

'Come on now,' said Tim, putting a gentle hand on her forearm. 'You did the right thing. It's real hard finding a guy who can do this crazy job. We all know that. And especially finding one in a strange country.'

'It's not that strange. I lived there for three years,' said Tara.

'Did you? Where did you live?' asked Jeanna, the assistant Tara was training to be a teacher.

'I was a student, at Sussex University. My mom moved there after my dad died. She still lives in Cambridge.'

'Wow. I've never been out of California,' said Jeanna morosely.

'You need to find someone, so it like stands to reason you've got to start somewhere,' said Tim.

'He seemed like a really nice guy who was just a bit

overwhelmed,' said Jeanna. 'You know, it's tough the first time you see what we do, especially for a guy. I thought he was cute.'

Tim laughed. 'Oh dear, Jeanna thought he was cute. Two of the students asked me where the cute English guy had gone. What is it with you guys? How come I'm never the cute one?'

'Oh, you're cute, like a kind of old uncle sitting on the porch, that kind of cute,' said Jeanna. The three women sitting around the table laughed at Tim as his face dropped.

'Oh, that's real smart,' said Tim. 'That's real good. Thank you.'

'Anyway, other than the disappearing limey, how did we feel the class went?' asked Tara, trying to stick to the agreed format of after-class sessions. It was a period of the day she really looked forward to. The students had left, the mats had been swept and mopped down, Bonnie the dog was allowed out and rubbed against everyone's legs in delight.

Tara looked at the notes that Jeanna had kept on each student, reminding herself of their names, their strengths, weaknesses and the difficulties they had experienced in the session. 'Tim, d'you want to start?' she asked as she put the clipboard down on her lap.

'No. I think you should start, Tara. You've got jet-lag and you did a real good class.' The two assistants nodded their agreement.

'Thank you, Tim,' said Tara. She smiled at him. He was such a wonderful man. Why couldn't they all be like that? As far as Tara was concerned Tim's very existence invalidated all the excuses men might make for their negative and dangerous behaviour. He was a heterosexual man who was so at peace with himself.

'I thought it was a great class, a really good bunch of students and you guys were great,' she said, touching the two women on either side of her. 'I think we make a great team. I think you, Tim, as usual, really are the best padded assailant there's ever been, but don't tell any of the other guys I said that.'

'I may just keep that compliment in my back pocket for a bad day,' said Tim. Bonnie the dog looked up at him lovingly and wagged her tail.

'It's true I am a bit tired, I sure will sleep tonight, but I'm real glad I did the class. I almost pulled out and asked Mary to do it, but a tough class really is a great way to beat jet-lag. I had a great time in England – they're real keen to set up a programme there. I had hoped Nick would be here with us, but who knows? Anyway, a great class. There's no one I thought was, like, a real problem. I would predict we'll have another history come out at next week's opening circle.'

'Marsha,' said Jeanna.

'Yep,' said Tim.

'I think so,' Tara agreed. 'She's real good at fighting, but you don't get that kind of anger from having your ass pinched in the office.'

Marsha was a small, wiry, black-haired woman who had told the opening circle she had no history of sexual abuse or assault. By the end of the class Tara knew she did have something in her past. She just didn't want to talk about it. They never encouraged women to say anything. They had learned from experience that it always came out at some point. One of the exercises would trigger some reaction eventually. They merely discussed it so that when the time came they would all be ready, all knowing that everyone else on the teaching side knew.

Tara looked at Jeanna. She said her piece, basically that she really enjoyed assisting and she hoped one day to be in a position to teach. And she really did think the English guy was cute and she was mad at him for leaving.

Then Iris, the assistant with the multiple earrings and crazy hairstyle, had her say. Much the same as Jeanna, although she could live without the English dude. She thought the class went well, and particularly the re-enactment with Mindy. That really raised the spirits of the whole class and she thought they'd start on a high the following week.

'Tim,' said Tara. 'Your turn.'

'Well, it was great. It always is. It's always real hard work, but they are great students and you guys were real great.'

'You've got to find a better word than great,' said Jeanna with a giggle.

'Oh, you guys are so smart,' said Tim. 'Okay, it was exuberantly fulfilling. I get so much out of a class like this. I'll be on a high tonight and I'm cooking a weird Hawaiian fish thing for a whole bunch of people from my neighbourhood. They are lucky people because it's going to be cooked with such positive energy. I can feel it. Ooeee oooeee.' He waggled his arms around his head and made a spiritual 'at one with himself' face. 'Even though I'm nothing more than an uncle sitting on the porch, I can still just about prepare dinner.'

'Oh, Timmy,' said Jeanna.

'As for our English friend, he's a really nice guy. I liked him a lot. He's really uncomplicated without being dumb, you know. He's very clear, and he's just confused about us. That's all. I guess what he saw brought up a lot of stuff from his past, who knows what. We know nothing about his history – well, not much. I think we'll see him again. In fact, I quite fancy a breakfast out in the morning. Maybe down the Haight. Haven't been there in years. Hear it's looking quite smart.'

'Would you?' asked Tara. 'I guess we should try one more time.'

'Sure.'

'He's staying with . . . well, he's having a thing with Grace Smooth's daughter.'

'When you say Grace Smooth, you don't mean Grace Smooth,' said Tim.

'Oh my God!' said Jeanna.

'Who's Grace Smooth?' asked Iris.

'That's like saying "Who's Joni Mitchell, or who's Jerry Garcia",' said Tim.

'Who's Jerry Garcia?' asked Iris.

'You're not . . .'

'I know who Jerry is,' said Iris. 'I never heard of Grace whatever.'

'She was a singer in the sixties and seventies,' said Tara. 'With Matheson Cowpie.'

'Oh, I heard of them. Like a hippie band.'

'Progressive acid rock to be precise, yeah,' said Tim. 'In fact I believe I still have an old copy of *Rolling Stone* in which she features, semi-naked I believe. She was a very beautiful lady in her prime.'

'She's not so bad in her dotage,' said Tara. 'Really supportive of what we're doing.'

'Wait, you met her!' squealed Jeanna.

'Yeah. Nick is staying in her house, on Page Street.'

'He's staying in Grace Smooth's house? Oh my God!' Jeanna said, staring at the heavens.

'I never heard of her. How can you get so excited?' asked Iris.

'Imagine if someone you knew was staying in Sheryl Crow's house.'

'Maybe k.d. lang's place and I could get excited.'

'Okay, well, Grace Smooth is the k.d. lang of her generation. Well, not quite,' said Jeanna, realising her mistake. 'But you know what I'm saying. She was so cool.'

'My God, you haven't heard of her,' said Tim, looking at Iris. 'That makes me feel even older. Maybe I should be a grandpa on the stoop.'

He got up and walked around as if he was a half-crippled old man. 'Time to go, old doggie,' he said in a toothless Southern drawl. Bonnie stood up, yawned and stretched, then lay back down again.

'Sheeeit,' said Tim.

Chapter Twenty-One

There was a large, old stained mirror leaning up against Tiffany's black-painted wall. Twenty candles lit the room and made the air dry. Nick had mounted Tiffany from behind. Her panties were pulled roughly to one side, her shirt hoisted up to her shoulder. His large left hand held her in place; it made her shoulders seem even smaller. His fingers almost spanned the width of her back. She juddered and moaned with each thrust, her hair obscuring her face, her body glistening with oil and sweat. Nick watched himself, half crouching over her, his thrusts sudden and savage. His face was red and flushed; he felt so angry and hard. As he looked down at her stretched perineum his penis seemed bigger than usual. Angry hard, that's how it felt. He was fucking Tiffany as he had told her he would on the way home in the cab. He had told her lovemaking was for another day – tonight he was going to fuck her. She nodded in compliance and offered to start sucking him there and then. He laughed, too embarrassed to allow her, shocked again that she was always prepared to go further than he dared even think. He didn't want any more men watching her perform, only him.

'You can do anything you want,' she said as he pushed her down on the bed and started roughly removing her clothes. He ripped the bathrobe off the hook on the door and used the waistband to bind her hands together.

'Oh Christ, baby . . .' said Tiffany, but if she'd meant to say more she couldn't. Nick stuffed his erection into her mouth. He held her hair, knelt over her and fucked her head. It took everything in his power and experience not to come there and then, but he managed. He lay on top of her heavily, using her body for his pleasure, kissing her obscenely, forcing her legs apart and feeling her wetness. He was lost, he was gone, there was none of Nick there, just an animal who needed something. Tiffany's body reacted strongly to his crude demands – she writhed and opened, engulfed and withstood an hour of repo-sitioning, re-entry, repeated thrusting.

The mirror, against all his expectations, was his undoing – seeing himself on top of this small woman, seeing the arched and painful-looking position she was in, his huge hands controlling everything she did, her wrists tied together. He tried to ignore it, to feel again the intense pleasure her tightness afforded him, but it was all slipping away. He slowly became aware of a lump in his throat. Tears stung his eyes, his mouth felt hollow and dry. He hadn't felt like this since he was . . . He couldn't even remember – since he was a child. He looked at his face. His mouth had changed shape without him doing anything; it was open but hung down at the edges. Tears started to pour down his cheeks. He looked down – his erection had almost completely dis-appeared. He slid out of Tiffany; she fell to one side, still tied at the wrists. She pushed her hair to one side with her upper arm.

'What's up, baby?' she whispered.

Nick knelt back, his hands and penis limp in front of him. The sobs racked his body. He heaved in a breath like a fisherman pulling in a full net. It was so hard to do; his throat was almost unbearably tight. He didn't know what was happening because behind all these huge sobs and uncontrollable wails, he was still having thoughts, quite coherent thoughts about the guy in the taxi, his mum, the plane ride home, where his ticket was, how much money he had left.

'Baby, what's the matter?' asked the ravished-looking Tiffany.

He leant forward suddenly and saw her flinch. That made him cry more. She thought he was going to hurt her. He was going to undo the stupid towelling strip that tied her lovely wrists. He pulled at the knot with his teeth and undid the bonds. He held her wrists gently and kissed them.

'I'm sorry, I'm so, so sorry,' he managed to utter between sobs. 'I don't know, I just don't know what it is.'

He stayed kneeling, now really lost in a red universe of misery and regret.

'Nicky. Baby, it's okay,' said Tiffany. She sat up in front of him, her clothes wrenched and torn, her breasts exposed in the soft candlelight. She pulled back her thick hair with both hands and then softly caressed his shoulders.

'What's up, baby? Did I do something wrong?'

This made Nick wail louder. He embraced Tiffany as softly as he could, slowly but gently pulling her closer. He put his forehead on her shoulder – he didn't want her to see his face.

'I'm so embarrassed,' he said when the sobbing finally started to recede. 'I don't know what it is. I think it's Mindy.'

'Who's she?' asked Tiffany, with more than a pinch of alarm in her voice.

'She was one of the girls in the class today,' said Nick, his head still buried in her shoulder. He could just see her left nipple and a faint hint of pubic hair emerging from one side of her panties. What was all this about? Sex was supposed to be fun, not this heavy shit. What had those women done? Then he remembered the girl in the class and the feelings came rushing back.

'She was so sweet, such a nice woman, you know. I could tell, and her fucking boyfriend had raped her, and I just couldn't take it. She kept smiling at me, you know, she just wanted to be loved. That's what's making me cry. She wanted men to like her, not hurt her. She was so confused about what happened, she didn't understand why a man would want to hurt her so much. She was so like you, Tiff, a girl, just like you . . .' The sobs welled up again and the tears gushed afresh.

'Oh, baby, it's all been too much,' said Tiffany. She pushed him back on to a pillow. He buried his head beneath the crumpled duvet and sobbed and sobbed. He felt Tiffany stroke his back gently, felt the tension drop from his shoulders.

That was it. He must have fallen asleep because the next thing he knew he was lying in the bed alone and the sun was starting to blaze in through the large bay window.

His eyes felt raw, his throat felt worse and his chest ached. The previous day swam back into his head and he didn't want to know. He'd got drunk, smoked cigarettes and blown it during a session with Tiff. She must have got pissed off and left him. He had about twelve dollars and a return ticket to London; he had no work lined up other than running the door at Trash. He had a teenage kid who wanted to live with him and nothing but humiliation to show for his troubles. Life was completely and utterly shit. He had totally blown it again and could think only of how to get out of the house without Tiffany or her mum seeing him. He slid out of bed and crept towards the window. The house was built on a hill, of course – the back garden seemed as if it were sixty feet below, even though at the front of the house the room was virtually at street level.

He looked at his bag in the corner – quite tidy, it would only take a minute to pack, get dressed and be gone. Maybe they'd gone out shopping or something. He started pulling on the clothes he'd worn the day before but they stank of stale cigarette smoke. He folded them up and found a clean set in his holdall. As he dressed himself he got a glimpse of his reflection in the mirror. He was thirty-five, broke, useless, stupid, hopeless. He had nothing to offer except his good looks, and they weren't much to shout about. He'd never achieved anything, never stuck at anything. His arms felt weak and bloated, helpless. He was seven thousand miles from home but home was shit anyway. What was he supposed to do? The taxi driver from the evening before came back to him. He was right, the women were doing everything. Nick had never actually known a man who did anything. You couldn't call being a security guard or a bouncer a career – it was a time-filler, a way to scrape together a few bob until the weekend. He had no aim in his life, nothing to do except exist, and what for? To breed. He'd done that and fucked up. He hadn't built anything, hadn't designed anything, hadn't even had a good idea. He'd never had an idea in his life. Maybe a better way of doing a stomach exercise, or his little habit of always keeping a clean towel at the gym in case he forgot to take one.

He quickly pulled on his huge lace-up boots and found his leather jacket. As he picked up his bag the door opened slowly and Tiffany stood there in her kimono, carrying two mugs of coffee.

'Hi,' she said.

'Hi,' he replied, immediately feeling like a louse for even thinking of legging it away from such a wonderfully honest, open face.

'You off someplace?' she asked, the edges of her eyes giving the lie to her smile. She was hurting. He pulled off the leather jacket and threw it on the ground.

'Sorry. Sorry, Tiff. I'm so sorry about last night.'

'I made you a coffee,' she said, kneeling down beside him. 'And what happened last night was the nicest thing that has ever happened to me. Ever, okay? With any guy, ever. I really mean it. It was beautiful and touching and it's made me fall completely in love with you. Okay? So don't apologise.'

He sipped the coffee she had made for him and sat in an armchair which was covered in clothes and books. 'Fucking hell. Have I gone bonkers or what?' he said. He stared into his mug. He had never felt like a bigger, more awkward kid. He had woken hating himself for the first time in his life.

'You're so cute,' she said, and knelt down between his legs. She looked small, nursing her coffee cup and looking up at him. 'I watched you sleeping this morning for hours,' she said. 'When people sleep, you see the real person, and you're so clear, so beautiful. Really, Nicky, what happened last night was great. You admitted you got hurt by seeing that class yesterday, that's all.'

'Oh God. I don't know what's going on, Tiff. I'm fucked. I haven't got any money, my life in England's a total pile of shite. My boy wants to live with me. I can't afford to look after myself, let alone him. Now I've come all the way here, and I've seen you again which has made me fall in love all over again. And I'm here to learn how to be punched by angry women I haven't raped so they get to feel better because they have been raped by someone else. It's all so weird.'

'Tiff, someone to see Nick!' shouted Grace Smooth from down the hall.

'Oh, fuck. I bet that's Tara,' said Nick. 'What the fuck do I do?'

'Wait here,' said Tiffany. 'Don't worry. Wait here.'

Nick paced around the room. He felt dizzy. He felt himself being pushed into something he didn't want to do, but which somehow still felt inevitable. He looked out of the window again. He could just jump out, try to land head first on the concrete path in the little garden, finish it all quickly. Leave the fucking stupid world. He'd got no money, he was pretty crap at everything he did. His Triumph Stag was broken, a heap. Supposedly it was a classic V8 sports car, but he couldn't even make it start. Only Barney, little Barney, who was now so big and gormless, stopped him diving through the glass.

'Hey, man, how's it hanging?' Nick turned to see Tim standing in the door. 'You hungry?' he asked.

They walked the short distance around the block to a large café on Haight Street. Bonnie the dog trotted along beside them, greeting the myriad homeless people sitting on the sidewalk. The café was spacious, busy but friendly. Nick had never been there before.

'Used to come here a lot,' said Tim. 'They do great breakfasts.'

The two men ordered their food and found a table near the window. Tim sat facing Nick, Bonnie sat obediently outside the door, accepting pats and strokes from passing strangers.

'It's so much nicer round here than it used to be,' said Tim. 'It got really fucked up in the eighties. I guess I haven't been here in a long while.'

Nick smiled. He was damned if he was going to say anything. There was a silence which didn't seem to bother Tim. Nick watched him stir his coffee. He was surprised Tim drank coffee. He would have expected him to take camomile tea or some other noxious herb concoction.

'So, you hated the class, you thought we were all perverse weirdos and you thought the women were making it all up anyway,' said Tim suddenly. Nick looked at him, frowned and shrugged. 'And you think the women wouldn't stand a chance in a real fight against a real angry guy with a knife who wanted to fuck her.'

'Getting closer,' admitted Nick.

'Could be right,' said Tim. 'Could be right.' He sipped his coffee and looked out at the street. 'On the other hand, imagine if you heard that Tiffany had been attacked by some guy and she'd stopped him. Knocked him out cold. That'd be pretty good, wouldn't it?'

'I suppose so, yeah. If it happened.'

'Okay, so you don't think it happens much.'

'What?'

'Men raping women.'

'Yeah, it happens. I'm sure it happens, but, well, not that often.'

'I don't want to be boring but statistically it happens about once every six seconds, in the US alone. Honestly, Nick, it happens. Even if you throw all caution to the winds and say half those women are lying, vindictive bitches and they're making it up to get at ex-boyfriends or fathers who wouldn't buy them a white T bird, then that goes to one every twelve seconds. It happens and it happens a lot.'

'Well, I don't fucking do it.'

'Okay. Well, bully for you, as they say in England.' Tim smiled again.

'Look, I don't know what I think. I know the women in the class were really raped, I'm not saying that. I just didn't like the way you and Tara sort of responded to the whole thing.'

'Okay,' said Tim. That was all he said. Nick was expecting him to respond in some clever way, but he didn't. He just sat there looking out of the window, occasionally glancing at Nick.

'It was like you knew all about rape and were just going through the motions,' said Nick eventually. 'It wasn't to do with fact, not, like, what you were doing, it was to do with, like, the style. It was the know-all, holier-than-thou style of the whole thing that got on my tits, if you want to know. I'm sorry, mate, but all this hippie bullshit, this New Age therapy-speak shit. Really, I'm not into that. "This is a sacred circle, nothing you hear inside this circle must ever go outside." I felt like I was back at primary school or something. And they all bought it. They all sat there and lapped it up. I felt you trapped those poor women in that class, convinced them you had the answer to all their problems, their fucking awful boyfriends and fathers and uncles. I'd be the first to admit that it was bloody awful, what they went through, but then you and Tara sat there smiling. And she's, you know, what happened to her, I don't know. Oh, shit.'

Nick could feel tears welling in his eyes, could feel his throat tightening again as he spoke. He didn't know why it all upset him so much. He just wanted to forget the whole thing and be back on the door of Trash every night with nothing to worry about but the rent.

Tim sat facing him without smiling. His face was blank; he was just sitting waiting. It annoyed Nick to think that this man seemed to know what was going to come next. He seemed to know that if Nick spoke, Nick would cry, so maybe he thought if he could get Nick to cry then he would 'open up emotionally' and become more malleable. Well, thought Nick, fuck that for a game of marbles. He decided he would not cry and would say no more just to fuck up the system.

A happy Italian-looking waiter brought them both huge plates of breakfast – eggs over easy, hash browns, bacon, toast, mushrooms, tomatoes.

'Enjoy,' he said cheerily.

'Thanks,' said Tim, and started eating. Nick stared at him in disbelief. Maybe he knew Nick was going to be quiet after his little outburst, and the New Age system said 'hold your ground, let them come unto you', or some other spiritual crap. Like those posters with a Red Indian sitting on a horse looking majestic. Nick shook his head and started eating. He was ravenously hungry and hadn't liked to mention that he didn't have enough money to pay for the breakfast.

'So, why did you come?' asked Tim without a hint of malice.

'You mean why did I come to San Francisco?' said Nick through a mouthful of egg and hash browns. Tim nodded. ' 'Cos Tara asked me and I thought she was a bit tasty, and I thought I could see Tiff, and I dunno. I liked it when I was here last and it's always nice to get out of England.'

'But you knew Tara was looking for someone to train.'

'Yeah, yeah, she went on about it a lot.'

'And you were interested?'

'Yeah, I was interested. Until I saw what you do. I thought it was like a self-defence class, not a therapy session.'

'It is a self-defence class, one designed specifically for women.'

'I know, I read the book.'

'What book?'

'The one Tara had. The history of how it all got started.'

'Oh, right. And why d'you think Tara asked you?'

'Oh, fucking hell, I don't know,' said Nick. He took a swig of coffee and tucked into his breakfast. 'I know you'll have a weird, hippy-drippy reason. Some fuck-awful spiritual thing. It's bol-locks basically. Look, as far as I can tell Tara could see that I could handle myself and not lose my temper in a rumble. That's all.'

'I'll tell you,' said Tim. 'She asked you because she was fucking desperate. I'm not going to flatter you, man, you were bottom of the list. She needed to find a man in England to do this crazy fucking job, and there aren't any, Nick. You hear what I'm saying? This is a brilliant system of self-defence which will only work if someone, some man, is prepared to do what I do. What man in his right mind would want to do it? Eh? You'd have to be fucking crazy. Am I right?'

'Yeah,' said Nick. 'And you don't have to swear to communicate with me. Okay?'

'I swear because that's how I talk, Nick,' said Tim with a flash of anger. 'Don't be so fucking paranoid. Jesus H. Okay, here's how it is. You remember the girl on the far side of the opening circle from us? Blond hair. Mindy.'

'Yeah, of course I remember her,' said Nick.

'Well, okay, I'll be straight with you now. No talking out of school, but I'd like to fuck her real bad.'

'You what?' Nick squeaked.

'I'd like to watch her take her clothes off and I'd like to fuck her. I'd like to hold those two beautiful hips of hers as I screwed her from behind, you hear what I'm saying? Those dreamy buns are so hot, I'd like to look at them for about a year. Okay? With her permission, of course. I don't want to rape her, Nick. Not at all, but I would love to fuck with that beautiful girl until my dick dropped off. She had the most amazing ass I've ever seen, and believe me, when you get to my age you've seen a few.'

'How can you say that about her? For fuck's sake, the poor woman had been raped,' said Nick, feeling the hot, burning sensation in his throat again.

'So that means she never wants to have sex again with someone she likes?'

'I don't know,' said Nick.

'Or does it mean she's like soiled? You wouldn't want to go near that pussy because it's been defiled?'

'Steady,' said Nick. He paused for a moment, looked at Tim. Was this part of the clever New Age stuff or was this bloke for real? It didn't sound like hippie shit. 'It just feels wrong to talk about her like that. Like, not respecting her, after what she's been through.'

'So we should like put all raped women on a pedestal and worship them? "You have been defiled and we therefore cannot discuss the merits of thy beautiful ass." '

'I don't know,' said Nick.

'She's just a woman like any other, Nick. I won't differentiate. I took a shine to her because she was beautiful, not because she'd been raped.'

'She was well tasty,' said Nick.

'Yes, that is a good description, she was well tasty,' said Tim with a broad smile.

Nick remembered Mindy's face very clearly. Had wanted to cry when he heard her speak about being raped by her boyfriend. He remembered swallowing hard and trying not to sob. Her face was so beautiful and fragile and showed her pain so well. Then when she had done her 're-enactment' it was just too much. Then he could see how badly she was hurt, and it all started to make him feel sick. Making her go through it again. Why would anyone want to do that? He couldn't imagine what it would take to make someone actively want to relive something like that. But then he'd never really been beaten in a fight. Not since he was a kid, a little kid. That's where the feelings came from. The lump in the throat, the stinging eyes. The feelings were the same ones that had happened to him in the playground, all those years ago in Headington. Vincent Pickering tripping him over and punching him. Calling him a sissy and there being nothing he could do. The other kids watching and laughing, no one helping him. Vincent Pickering was three times bigger and stronger, older and taller. He could do anything he wanted to Nick, and he did.

Nick complained to his mum, and his mum talked to a teacher who talked to Vincent's mum which made Vincent behave even worse when no one was looking. Now Nick was a snitch, which was worse than being a sissy and therefore deserved more vicious punishment.

Nick had lived in terror of Vincent Pickering for years, until he left the school. Once he had grown up he thought about looking Vincent up and laying the nut on him. Giving him a right good pasting. He'd probably be a fat bastard driving a Ford Granada with rusting wheel arches. The sort of bloke who used to cut him up on the Westway when he drove his Triumph Stag.

'Okay, I get it,' said Nick. 'I sort of get it.'

'You get it?' asked Tim.

'Yeah. Look, it was the re-enactment bit that really got me. It's like, well, I can understand it a bit better now. If I could have a go at the kid who bullied me at school, if I could get to smack him about a bit now, it would be good.'

'You had a kid bully you at school?' asked Tim, with lavishly displayed concern.

'Yeah,' said Nick with a laugh. 'But I don't need to talk about it and share it. It was twenty-five years ago, for fuck's sake. What are we going to do, invite all the punters in here to join us in a sacred circle so I can share my pain?'

'Okay,' said Tim, putting his hands up in surrender.

'I mean, what's hard for me to understand is the sort of . . . the anger that the women feel. You know, and that's all pouring at you, and you have to take all that and not take your helmet off and say, "Wait a minute, you stupid fucking cow, it wasn't me!" '

'Sure.'

'What, you want to say that sometimes?'

'Sure.'

'Nah, you're too holy.'

'I am not holy. Sure I want to sometimes. But you're forgetting the real charge. You haven't seen what's really happening yet.'

'Oh, right, you mean if I'd stayed it would all've been clear.'

'No, you didn't see it because you weren't watching. It was all happening there in front of you and you couldn't see it because of all your prejudices. I come out of a class feeling incredible. Seriously. I feel tired and a little bruised sometimes, but I feel incredibly happy and high. The energy I get off these women is unimaginable. It's not hippie shit, Nick. I have no fear in stating that if you wore the suit and did a class you'd feel it. There're guys I know that do padded assailant training that are the most unhippie-type guys you could meet. A grounded airline pilot, computer programmers, shopfitters, clothes designers, an ex-Marine. They all get it too. It's a charge because you are the doorway that releases thousands of years of fear, and it doesn't leak inside the suit. The suit protects you in more ways than just the physical. It's like, and brace yourself for some hippie shit, it's like a psychic suit as well. You, Nick, the guy sitting there, are really safe in that suit. It's you that makes the outside into the most shit guy on earth. Inside is just Nick, and you'll know that. You'll never think, "Oh, they don't like me, they hate me and think I'm a pervert." '

'Okay, okay,' said Nick. 'So it's like therapy and self-defence. Really groovy, man,' he said, impersonating a doped-up hippie. 'But it's the self-defence bit that worries me too. You're telling these women that they can win a fight against a bloke? Okay, some blokes are pathetic, but a really mean guy who wants something, no fancy heel-palm punch is going to stop him.'

'There've been so many cases where it did.'

'Yeah, but come on. This is the difficult bit. Look, if we're being honest with each other, I know I could beat the shit out of any of those women. It would be so easy. I mean, even the idea of it is sick, because it's just, well, it wouldn't be a fight, it wouldn't even be bullying. I s'pose it would just be assault, plain and simple GBH. They couldn't do squit to stop me.'

'You don't know that.'

'I do. I know what I saw.'

'Sure, you saw a bunch of scared women who for the first time in their lives got a taste of fighting back. Those women yesterday couldn't fight you, but come back in six weeks' time when they've finished their basics course and they'd give you a run for your money.'

'They couldn't, Tim. That's what I'm saying. It's a dangerous con.'

'They could, Nick. What you're saying is a dangerous mis-conception. I'll tell you how I know. For a start, yesterday I wasn't even trying. I was real gentle with them. Slow, step by step. It's like teaching someone to swim. You gotta let them get over the fear of the water so they know they can just float out there, held up. What we are saying is be scared, but know you can defend yourself. After a few weeks I attack them a little harder, and a little harder, until by the time they do an advanced course I don't hold back, I charge at them with full force, my grips are as tight as I can make them. I make sounds when I'm hit, I shout at them more, right in their faces. By the end of an advanced course you're looking at women with more experience of unarmed fighting than most men get in a lifetime. I am telling you, Nick, as a man who knows, they've only got to kick you in the balls once and you are down. Those kicks have power, and if they catch you with a roundhouse to the temple, you are in hospital, man.'

'I just don't believe it. In a real fight situation it's so messy and ugly. There's no style to it, just get stuck in and make sure when you punch someone you really hit 'em.'

'That's what we teach.'

'Yeah, but look at my arm,' said Nick, pulling his T-shirt up and revealing the bulk of muscle. 'My upper body strength is just so much greater than any woman's.'

'That is an impressive arm, Nick, if that's what you're into. But all that muscle slows you down. Plus, a woman's legs are much longer and stronger than your arms. That's why we teach them to get on the floor. You saw how much floor work we incorporate.'

Nick scratched his head. It almost sounded plausible. Then he remembered Mindy again. Her face when she hit the mat. It was like seeing a baby being ravaged by a dog. Nick just wanted to wade in there and kill the dog, tear its head off and stamp on it. He suddenly remembered he wasn't the only one who remembered Mindy.

'And then you fancy them as well, which is just too kinky.'

'Why is that kinky?'

'Well, 'cos you're so powerful in the class. And you get to grab them and throw them on the ground. Jesus. And even though they looked like they hated you at the beginning, I saw the way they all looked at you after the break. They were all in love a bit, some of them a lot.'

'Sure, that's a difficult side. It's called transference.'

'Oh God, here we go.'

'That's not a hippie word, Nick, back down. It's a Freudian term.'

'Oh, for fuck's sake. As if that makes it better,' said Nick with a laugh.

'Okay, well, that's something that happens in the class. The women are so overwhelmed by the emotions released by the experience of actually fighting off a man they think that Tara and I have some kind of magical power which enabled them to do it. They find it hard to accept that this ability is inside them, so they transfer that feeling, that knowledge of power, on to us. And that's a real dangerous time if you find that person attractive. It's very tempting.'

'Like Mindy.'

'Like Mindy. She's a cute kid and real trusting. It would be very easy to make a move, so we've made it a primary ruling in the training – no socialisation for one year after the end of a class.'

'So you can shag, you just can't talk,' said Nick, chuckling.

'No, Nick, no socialising means no contact.'

'Sorry I asked,' said Nick with a mock pout.

'Oh, you English guys are so clever,' said Tim, realising he had been joking.

'A year,' said Nick.

'A year.'

'Fucking hell. That's a bit harsh.'

'It seemed like a good period of time. We guessed it would show that there was something deeper, you know, not just the initial frisson.'

'So, have you ever gone out with a girl from a class?'

'Sure. The mother of my eldest kid was a student.'

'Really?'

'Sure.'

'You still with her?'

'No, I'm with another student.'

'Blimey, so you've had two of them?'

'I don't like to think of myself as having "had" any of them, but I have dated students, yes.'

'How many?' asked Nick, his smile broadening by the moment. He had noticed for the first time that Tim looked a little embarrassed. It was so hard to embarrass an American that he took great pleasure in doing so when the opportunity arose.

'Five. I guess,' said Tim, looking out of the window.

'Five!' said Nick loud enough for people to cast them a glance. 'You've been out with five! But you're a holy man. You're a New Age guru, for crying out loud. All you do is put the helmet on, maul young girls until they fall for you and then shag them.'

'Jesus, you guys are so smart. Not. You have just made my entire life seem like a shoddy, perverted lecherous romp. Like one of those "Carry On" films you guys are so good at making.'

'Five!' said Nick again. 'You've shagged five women from the class. That's disgusting!'

'Okay, keep it down, there could be someone in here who knows me.'

'You should be banned, mate. You're a fucking liability. Blimey, does Tara know about this?'

'Yes, of course she does. She knows about Orla, that's the woman I'm with now. She knows about it. Not all of them. I mean, I'm entitled to my private life.'

'She doesn't know!' said Nick, leaning back in his chair. 'I don't believe it. Jesus. This is brilliant, Tim. I love you, mate.'

He leant across the table and gave Tim a kiss on the forehead. Tim smiled, slightly flushed. 'I'll tell you something, though,' said Nick. 'I promise not to tell Tara if you'll pay for breakfast. I'm totally fucking boracic, mate.'

'I am guessing that means you're short of cash.'

'Yeah, short as in "I haven't got a penny to my name." '

'Cool,' said Tim, extracting his billfold.

Chapter Twenty-Two

Alice sat at her desk and did nothing. Her hand was over her mouth as she stared out at the flat, grey London skyline. Her office, on the eighth floor of a block just off Gray's Inn Road, faced east. She had a view of the tower blocks of the City, and in the far distance, just visible through the pollution, she could see the crane she had stood beside on top of the Canary Wharf extension building.

She had a classified government CD on her desk containing information on bomb blast damage from the Canary Wharf and City of London IRA bombs. She had a report an inch thick waiting to be proof-read on the implications of a Terminal 5 at London's Heathrow airport. Although it had never happened, a 636 coming down in a densely populated area was something that had been considered. With the last five miles of the easterly approach right across the rooftops of south and west London, with variable weather conditions and more and more air traffic, the risks could only increase. Her report painted a gloomy picture, with data taken from Lockerbie and the tragedy of Flight 800 off Long Island in America.

Then there was the issue of the manufacturers buying back that ageing fleet to take them out of circulation. They didn't want thirty-five-year-old 636s and 626s taking off, period. However, some of the smaller airlines were becoming reluctant to part with their machines, the cost of replacement being prohibitive.

Once she had sifted through all the information, she couldn't help but wonder if flying in civil airliners was such a good idea.

All these reports were highly contentious and very confidential. Leaks from her office could jeopardise a company's performance, or cause unnecessary anxiety amongst the population, but the risks needed to be known.

All these reports and more were on her office computer, not connected to the Net or even the intranet in the office to reduce the risk of hacking. Her screen was waiting for her to enter her three-level password; it had been waiting for an hour. Eventually even other people in the office noticed that Alice wasn't behaving normally.

'Are you okay, Alice?' asked Richard Smith, another risk assessor whose desk faced hers on the other side of the office's central corridor.

'Sorry?' said Alice eventually.

'Not your usual highly efficient self. You're even making me look like a workaholic which is going some, believe me.'

'Oh, right,' said Alice. She looked at her screen and was almost surprised to see her password dialogue box still in front of her. She tapped in the code. The computer beeped aggressively. An error; she had typed her code in wrongly. She ran her fingers through her hair and looked over at Richard Smith. He was already talking on the phone. She sighed and tried again. This time the computer started beeping loudly – an alarm signal. It gave the user only two chances and then set off an alarm system which was relayed to the security office on the ground floor. She panicked, looked around for help, got up and walked to the back of the computer where for some reason she had imagined she could unplug it and reboot. The cables were all secured – it was a sealed unit, like all the computers on the eighth floor. She knew that. How could she have been so stupid?

A security officer emerged from the lift and scanned the

room. He saw Alice immediately and came to her desk. He used her phone to ring down to the security office and the alarm stopped.

'What happened?' he asked without seeming to allocate blame.

'I must have typed my code in wrong. It's never happened before. I'm sorry,' said Alice.

'It's okay. I can override the reboot block,' said the man.

Alice suddenly noticed a tear drip on to her wrist. She was crying. She stood by her desk and cried as the security officer, a man with a bald patch on the crown of his head, gently tapped the keys of her keyboard.

'There you go,' he said as her entry code box appeared on the screen again. He looked up at her and his face registered genuine concern.

'What's wrong?' he asked.

'Nothing,' said Alice, fighting back the tears.

'Well, there must be something wrong. Everyone's typed in their security code wrongly at some time, I know I have. It's not that serious.'

'It's not that,' said Alice, realising too late that by saying this she had opened the door for him to ask another question.

'What is it, then?' he asked.

'I don't know. It's personal,' she said. The man nodded. Now he looked concerned in another way. He was assessing her from the point of view of her being a security risk. There were no military or defence secrets in the building, but there was information that could be catastrophic or invaluable if it got into the wrong hands. As anyone in the security industry knew, no matter how good the physical and technical safeguards were, the human element was always open to potential attack.

Three days later Alice was called into the office of her superior, Maureen Custance. Maureen had run a company at Lloyd's for many years before the crash. She managed to survive but got out and eventually found a management position at the

Risk Assessment office. She was a nice woman, as far as Alice was concerned – respectful of her minions' skills and attention to detail but stern enough to make sure they did the job.

'Alice, something's wrong and I'd like to know what it is,' she said bluntly as soon as pleasantries were over.

'I'm sorry,' said Alice, blowing her nose. She'd had a cold for ages and it wouldn't seem to shift. She'd lost weight and her hair had somehow gone flat. 'I'm a bit under the weather at the moment. I'll be as right as rain before long.'

'This is more than a common cold. We're concerned about the security aspect, you know that. You're getting seriously behind in your work. People are starting to ask questions, Alice. It's so unlike you – you've always been exemplary when it comes to deadlines. You can't wonder why we're worried.'

'It's got nothing to do with work,' said Alice, the bags under her eyes giving testament to the little sleep she was managing to get. 'I'm just a bit run-down.'

'Why? What's wrong?'

'I don't know,' said Alice, starting to cry again. 'Everything.'

'What d'you mean?' asked Maureen. She got up from behind her desk and squatted down beside Alice, offering a tissue.

'It's my boyfriend. Well, he was my boyfriend.'

'Oh dear,' said Maureen. She sighed and put a gentle hand on Alice's shoulder. 'You'll get over it. You're young. I know that's easy to say, but you will get over it.'

'There's nothing to get over. I hated him anyway,' said Alice, pushing her hair away from her face and blowing her nose noisily. 'He was a total bastard.'

'That's the spirit. They all are, dear. My husband was unspeakable, dirty old sod. Went off with a woman only a year older than our son. Good riddance, I say. I don't miss him farting in bed, I can tell you.'

Alice smiled up at Maureen Custance. She wanted to say something about what had happened to her in the Ford Mondeo in the carpark, but she didn't know how to say it. If she said the rape word, she was worried that the whole edifice of her life might tumble down. She could cope, she had to. Somehow.

'I'm so sorry I've been a worry,' she said. 'I really think I've turned a corner. Honestly. I'll really put in some overtime and catch up. I love the work, Maureen, I really don't want to jeopardise my position here. Just sometimes your private life gets a bit . . . well . . .'

'I know what you mean, dear. Don't you worry, and if you ever want to talk . . . Really, I mean it, woman to woman. My door has no lock. You hear me?'

Alice nodded and went back to her desk. Richard Smith watched her every step of the way, as normal.

'Everything all right?' he asked jauntily.

'Until you spoke, you little prick,' she said quietly.

'Ah, back to normal,' said Richard Smith. 'Jolly good. Jolly good.'

Chapter Twenty-Three

'This is going to be one tough day,' said Tara as she poured her breakfast cereal. Adrian briefly looked up from a thick bound pile of paper which was covered in minute computer print-out.

'It is?' he asked.

'Sure. We're starting three weeks of training with the new padded assailants.'

'That must be tough,' said Adrian. He held a hand out to her – such a clever hand, a hand that knew so much weird stuff about the world, the universe. Tara was happy that Adrian had stayed over. It was the third time in a week and it seemed good. He was so quiet in terms of talking, he never said a lot, but he was thinking so much you could almost hear him hum. It was as though so many thoughts and such a level of concentration could make the air around him vibrate.

'I feel good about it, though,' said Tara, trying to make the conversation work again. She had left it too long; Adrian was back inside his world of numbers again. Just like her father, Tara realised. This attempt to get someone to talk was a feature of her entire life. Being a non-academic child of two academic parents was never easy. She wanted to play and talk and roll around; they wanted to read and sit and think. Her father had been a molecular biologist at Palo Alto. He died when Tara was twelve and left a hole in her life the size of an open-cast mine she'd seen on her fateful trip to Brazil. She had a large collection of photographs of her with her father from their short and rare holidays together. Sailing boats, fishing, climbing mountains. She was their only child and adored beyond reason. Tara remembered little about his death. She was kept away from the hospital where he was slowly drowning. She learned later that lung cancer wasn't a pleasant way to die.

She could still cry about him if she thought about him too much, and now she had grown into a woman, she realised that at fifty-six he was very young to die. He smoked all the time, and strangely, even to her, she still had affection for the smell of tobacco, although she had never allowed a cigarette to touch her lips.

Her mother's new husband, Professor Gordon Maquarie, was a charming, loquacious Australian. He was teaching at Cambridge, anthropology, mainly studying northern European and Caucasian blood-lines. Tara's mother, also an anthropologist, seemed the obvious choice for him. They both had grown up children, they had both been widowed, and they both needed to get away from where they had lived with their previous spouses.

Tara had never felt like an academic; she really only felt at home on the squash court or in the swimming pool. She was a competent student but nothing amazing. However, she was hugely impressed by and attracted to people who excelled academically. She could tell at a glance that Adrian was brilliant – having been brought up in a heady environment, it was second nature to her.

Adrian's hand reached out for a piece of buttered toast Tara had prepared. The hand was operating completely autonomously from Adrian's head; he was still engrossed in his computer printout. It located the toast with a delicate movement Tara found close to downright erotic. She loved Adrian's hands more than anything else about him. They were so beautiful, like something Leonardo Da Vinci might have drawn. Always drooping, looking relaxed, so sensitive and careful. Adrian never knocked anything over.

'I have to go,' she said reluctantly. She would have liked to have stayed and enticed Adrian into bed, but she was already running late. They didn't kiss.

The drive from her apartment to the Winning Strategy training building took roughly three-quarters of an hour. She relished the journey, playing an old Matheson Cowpie tape she had found in a box under the spare bed. There was Grace Smooth's voice, so reminiscent of an era when her father was still alive, when Tara lived only three blocks from Embarcadero Street, where she was now sitting in a traffic jam.

Professorville was the local name given to this area of beautiful shingle-clad homes in shady tree-lined streets. Some of the greatest brains in America had lived and, she presumed, continued to live there, although property prices were so high she doubted that a mere academic could afford it any more.

However, it was home turf for Tara – it was where she knew who she was. It was where she had come after Brazil. She could have gone to her mother's in England but she didn't. She wanted to be home, to recover somewhere she felt safe. To scrape off the stain that the three men in the Brazilian dirt had put on her. She stayed with family friends, another academic family who took her in and made her feel safe. She was lucky; she knew so many women who had no one to turn to.

As she drove down University Avenue she glanced at the building on the corner of Waverly Street, where she had been seeing Pat, her cognitive therapist. Pat had really helped back then – she made the space for Tara to finally get angry and allow all the vileness out. And then she had gone to Winning Strategy and built herself back to capable again.

Brazil. How could that one event have changed her life so much? She wondered what would have happened if 'it' had never taken place. If she hadn't caught that bus, if she'd stayed at the hotel complex as that American boy with the blond beard had begged her.

She liked him, that was why she had left – she didn't want to find out what would happen if she allowed herself to get close to him. He was a brain, like Adrian. A computer boy from Microsoft, on holiday and painfully lonely. So gentle and sensitive – she felt if she shouted at him he would fold up and die. He wasn't nerdy and talked about his feelings and his life with great fluency. If she'd stayed there, maybe they'd be married and living in Seattle with two kids and a nice suburban house. She wondered what the kids would be called. As Matheson Cowpie played their famous song 'Settling', with its memorable lyrics 'There's no place left to roam so I'll make this house my home', she allowed herself to be transported to another life entirely. One of Christmas and birthdays and parents and family gatherings and sitting reading a story to children. She had never achieved it. Instead she fell in love with an even more frail and delicate brainy man who couldn't have children, who needed his own space and was always emotionally distant. He did manage to talk about his infertility a little; he felt he had shrunk in some way as a result of the discovery. Maybe now she never would have children. She wasn't looking for anyone else, couldn't imagine life without Adrian or, more to the point, with someone else.

One of the trainees was sitting outside the Winning Strategy building when she arrived. She had planned to get there early to check her e-mail and make sure everything was tidy before the four men arrived.

'Hi, I'm Tara,' she said.

'Hi, Jonas,' said the man. When he stood he was shorter than Tara. 'Everyone calls me Jo.' They shook hands.

'Hi, Jo. Sorry you had to hang around. The traffic was pretty bad over the Bay Bridge.'

'Don't worry about it,' said Jonas. He was cool. She had heard about him, of course. He had a brown belt in tae kwon do, came originally from Vancouver, was heterosexual, single, with no children, fairly flexible in his time. He came into contact with the group through a man who made body armour in Oregon,

Haines McCullough. Jonas was of Scandinavian descent and had earned his living as a carpenter, building log houses and hot tubs all over the Pacific Northwest. He had built Haines an extension to his workshop and asked about the suits he saw in various stages of construction. Haines, who had once been a padded assailant himself, had talked to the man and suggested he try becoming one.

That was two years ago. Tara never ceased to marvel at the excuses men would come up with after they had initially agreed to take part. Delay and indecision seemed to be part of the process.

They entered the building together. Jonas had been there before, as an observer had witnessed two complete courses. The lonely man just sitting at the side of the blue mat. Tara hadn't taken these courses, but she heard that Jonas had been very positive, quite open with his emotions – although he never cried in the class he was very happy to talk about his feelings. This was considered a big bonus, as many of the candidates, although suitable physically, seemed entirely unprepared for the emotional strains of padded assailant-hood. However, Jonas was cool, and some of the other staff felt that might be a defensive thing, covering a real fear which could erupt during a class.

'I've just got a few things to check in the office,' said Tara. 'Can you like make yourself at home? You know where all the coffee and everything is, right?'

'Sure,' said Jonas. He walked on to the blue mat, dumped his bag and started stretching.

Tara checked her e-mail, mostly applications to join the course in America, but one from Yolanda in England.

Tara. Miss you so much! Had so many calls, about 350 so far. I have been sending out forms and licking envelopes! The phone never stops. Great work.
    love as always Yolanda

Tara smiled and wrote back as encouraging and witty a letter as she could. She heard male voices from the training room. She switched off her machine and walked in. Jonas was now on the floor going through a stretch routine. Another man was there, big, black, still carrying a large bag.

'Yo, I'm Corville,' said the man, holding out his hand.

'Hi. Tara.'

'Great place you got here,' said Corville.

'Yeah, it's a good space to work in,' said Tara, looking up at the steel rafters under which she had found her salvation. 'I'm glad you came, Corville, really glad.'

'Hey,' he said, shrugging. He dropped his bag. 'It's a privilege.'

Corville was gay. He had come to their attention through the gay self-defence movement centred in the Castro district of San Francisco. He had a magnificent body, absolutely no hair on his head and an implicit understanding of what they were trying to do. He was the great black hope for the impact group.

'How many more guys are on this course?' he asked, now making himself and Tara a cup of coffee. She didn't have to ask, he just knew. Why was it that gay guys always knew stuff like that and straight men never did? You had to ask them for coffee and then they made it for you like it was a big deal.

'There should be four altogether – you two, a guy from New Mexico called Raul Menendez, and a guy from England called Nick Gardener, but you know how it is. You two guys are actually here, so . . .' She smiled flatly.

'Wow, it's tough getting you straight boys to come in here,' said Corville. Jonas smiled and pulled his legs further apart in an impressive stretch. Corville raised his eyebrows as he watched, then glanced at Tara and burst out laughing. 'Girl!' he said, and that was all.

There was someone knocking on the door. It was wide open and the bright morning sunshine was pouring through. A figure filled the void.

'Come in,' said Tara, without being able to see who it was.

'Do I take my shoes off?' asked the man, who, with his American accent, was clearly not Nick Gardener.

'No, don't worry about it,' said Tara, walking towards him. 'You must be Raul. I'm Tara.'

'Hi there. Am I late?'

'No, you're fine, don't worry.' She introduced the men to each other, watched as they shook hands, the fleeting moment of eye contact and then away. Strange creatures, men, such strange creatures, but these particular ones seemed nice enough. She smiled to herself – three men in the room, not one of whom she'd met before, all from the USA. Her mission had been to find a man in England. It would appear, even though Tim had implied otherwise in his phone message, that she had completely failed.

'We're just waiting for Tim now. You've all met him, right?' The men nodded. 'But before he gets here I'd just like to say . . .'

'Hello,' said a flat-accented voice from the dazzling doorway. Tara's heart almost skipped a beat. He was there, carrying two kick pads and a heavy shoulder bag.

'Hi, Nick, you made it,' she said, doing everything she could to hide her delight.

'Yeah. I did,' he said. He shook hands with the other three, introducing himself. Bonnie the dog wandered in and introduced herself with wagging tail, followed by Tim, carrying a massive bag that contained his suit.

'Hi, everybody, sorry we're late. Bay Bridge.'

Tara walked to the corner and looked at her recruits from a distance – four different heights, three races, two colours and six months of unrelenting effort. Not bad considering finding any man to do this job was the hardest part of the whole business.

When everyone was settled with coffee and a few cookies which Nick had purchased on the way, which turned out to be the real reason they were late, Tara started her spiel.

'I want you to know that what you're doing is really great,

and that I know we're going to have a really great time learning. It's going to be tough. It is a physically demanding experience, but as any of the guys who've done this before will testify, it's hugely rewarding, although not financially.'

The men laughed. They all watched her with a keen intensity, even Nick, Tara noticed.

'We're going to start like we start a class, talking through our histories, why we're here, what we hope to gain from this, and what we hope to give. Because you know Tim, and because I'm the only woman here and you probably know about me, I won't speak, but if you have any questions, I'll answer them as best I can. Is everyone cool with that?' There seemed to be general agreement. 'Okay, Raul, d'you want to start?'

One by one the men recounted their tales, Raul with difficulty. He clearly wasn't used to speaking like this, even though he would have witnessed the opening and closing circles of classes he'd attended. Raul's family were originally from the Echo Park area of East Los Angeles. He had a respectable middle-class background – his father had been general manager of the Marriott hotel in downtown LA. Raul's fourteen-year-old sister had been raped by a gang in revenge for a slight his eldest brother was supposed to have made to one of them. It had devastated the entire family, and they had moved to New Mexico to try to extricate themselves from the downward spiral of the community they were living in. Raul agreed there was still bitterness inside him from what had happened to his sister, and he was very nervous about the training.

Jonas was really keen – he had seen the effect the training had on women and he wanted to be a part of it. It was in total contrast to his main job of carpentry, and he felt he could manage both. He had no knowledge of anyone who'd been sexually assaulted and was very depressed to see how many women in the classes had suffered. He still could not put himself in the shoes of a rapist, he couldn't understand what drove them to do it, and he wondered if he would be able to 'act' as one when called to do so.

Corville was very funny, but then very touching and honest when he described the beatings and rapes he had suffered as a young black man. All his assailants thought of themselves as straight – some were white and some were black but all of them were violent and abusive. He had been a thin and frail young man, and it was only when he came out and met other men in the same predicament that he started to gain self-respect and develop ways to really protect himself. He knew through his experiences with the gay self-defence movement which had started using a similar suit in its training that this was a system that worked. Although he had no desire to go to bed with women, that didn't mean he didn't like them. He was no gay misogynist – some of his best friends were girls.

Tara noticed all the men laughing at Corville, whose face was especially expressive. He was very prone to using his eyes and teeth, rolling the former and baring the latter as he underlined a point.

'Nick,' said Tara with a gentle smile.

'Yeah,' said Nick. He stretched his hands in front of him and sighed deeply. He then scratched the back of his head. 'Okay, well, I'll be straight with you. I didn't want to come. I think it's bloody daft and I can't stand all this I'll show you mine if you'll show me yours business.'

'Girl, you don't know what you're missing!' said Corville with his tongue literally in his cheek. Nick laughed.

'But I've agreed to try and do it, and try and join in. I dunno what to say. I'm from England, I'm thirty-five coming on thirty-six. I've got a fifteen-year-old son called Barney and I hate his mother. My mum and dad are still together. My dad is retired, used to be a manager in a car factory, and my mum works in a hospital. I've got an elder brother who lives in Australia. I live in London, I'm a bouncer – door security heavy – and I've done a bit of bodyguard work. I've been a swimming instructor, a tennis instructor, a lazy bastard and generally I like to have a good time, have a party, not get too stressed. I'm straight, I've got a few gay mates and I'm cool with that.'

Corville mopped his brow extravagantly. Another laugh.

'I've got a girlfriend here in San Francisco. I dunno where I live at the moment. I'm broke, I need something new to do, and this seemed like a good idea. That was until I saw a class. I found it really difficult. It's different where I come from, I dunno how to express it.' He was silent for a moment, looking at his hands. 'There's something in me, like an alarm bell, when people get all sincere and share their feelings in a kind of formalised way. I know English people are supposed to be uptight and repressed, but that's bollocks. We're just different, and it's the kind of therapy-session stuff that gets on my wick. I just found it really hard to sit here in this room when some poor woman was pouring her heart out for all and sundry to just nod their heads and, you know, "be sensitive". It rubbed me up the wrong way.' Another pause. Nick had looked at his hands all the way through the speech. Tara watched him. He was thawing; she could sense it. 'It was good to talk to Tim and, you know, just to find out he was a human being, not some fucking guru. I found it well confusing and, yeah, okay, he helped. Like, fancying a woman as I watched her being thrown on the floor and that, I don't mean I fancied her because she was thrown, I fancied her, and then she was thrown, and then when she kicked back, she really hated Tim. You could see it, she really hated him and that's hard to take. That makes me want to walk out the room. You know, I'd feel like saying, "Christ, if you hate me that much, I'm off, mate." And it looks so bloody painful. I can't believe it don't hurt. And I was thinking, am I going to do that? You know, when you actually see it for real, it's just, well, it's intense. That's a word I learned from you, Tara.' He glanced up at her and smiled, the first time he'd stopped looking at his fingers. 'So as I say I talked to Tim, and, you know, I felt, after I thought about it, maybe this is something I could do. I've never known anyone who was raped

— at least, I didn't know if they were. They've never told me. I'm the same as you, Jo, mate. Can't fucking understand it. You know, if I'm with a woman and she's a bit frosty I'm out of there. I might be angry 'cos she rejected me but I'm angry as I leave, not as I try and stay, you know what I mean?'

There was nodding around the small group.

'Bloody hell,' said Nick with a big smile. 'You've all just nodded at something I said and I don't mind. I've been in California too fucking long.'

Chapter Twenty-Four

'You want me to pinch your little pussy, you fucking whore, you want me to touch your dirty slimy cunt? Huh, is that what you want? Suck on that, you little dumb fuck. If you say anything, anything, I'm gonna open your throat with this fucking knife. You don't like it in the pussy, how d'you think you're gonna like it in the ass? Bit of back door, huh, you tight-assed little bitch. I'm gonna fuck you up big-time unless you do what Daddy says. Was that a little kid I saw in the next room? Huh, I like the look of your little girl, maybe I'll have her too, I like a bit of fresh pussy meat. If you don't do as I say I may make you watch as I fuck her asshole. If you don't seem scared I can't get it up, so I'm gonna hurt you, just cut off one of your titties, that'll help me,' said Detective Benson. 'I guess those are the ones I can remember off the top of my head. Not very nice things to have to remember, but there you go. That's my job, to like, know this kind of shit.'

Nick sat in shocked silence along with the rest of the trainees. It was the deadpan delivery, the chilling accuracy to the quotes, which hit him as hard as the words themselves. This stream of filth had come directly from the mouths of convicted rapists and the testimonies of their victims. Detective Benson, who worked closely with Winning Strategy, had investigated over three hundred and seventy rapes in the previous ten years and had built an impressive dossier on the methods and madness of sex offenders, from the one-off drunken lunge to the psychotic serial sex murderer. He had dealt with them all.

'It seems only to be the seriously deranged who need the pain or fear on the woman's face. Some guys keep asking if the victim is enjoying it, forcing them to play along as though they are great lovers and the woman is a willing partner. You need to be able to play a large number of roles, and from our experience of previous trainees, it's the more psychotic elements that padded assailants find harder to get a handle on, which is probably just as well.'

Detective Benson looked so well balanced. He smiled as he spoke and made plenty of eye contact with the men in front of him. He had short-cropped, slightly red hair and a nasty-looking scar on his left temple. He looked a bit like a cop from a TV show. He was well dressed and looked way too smart to be an English cop.

'A lot of the time these guys will use diminutive terms mixed in with the abuse – little snatch, little asshole, little titties. Even, I'm just gonna give you a little fucking, or, Give me a little smile, bitch, before I cut one on to your face. That kind of thing works well. It's up to you and it depends on the situation, but certainly if you know the woman has kids (you may have noticed I used one of those earlier) well, that's a great one to go for. The little bit of fresh pussy meat in the next room, you don't do as I say I'll go and try on your little daughter or son for size. That kind of thing is pretty much guaranteed to get a reaction. Any questions?'

Corville burst out laughing. 'Any questions! Girl, where you coming from! We can't even breathe after that shit, let alone ask you questions. Is this really the kind of shit we have to say?'

'Well, I'm just telling you what we know has been said in the past, to give you some idea of the ball park these guys work in. It's pretty whacked out, huh?'

'A little,' said Corville with another deep laugh.

'It's going to be hard to say this shit,' Tim interjected. Nick found it a relief to look at Tim all of a sudden. He was still trying to work out where the policeman got off. He said these incredible things so calmly. Nick had experienced no apprehension before meeting the detective. He knew he had heard everything a man could say; he wasn't prepared to be shocked. However, the sheer lunatic violence of the language, the utter horror of what he'd just heard, had riveted him to the blue mat.

'You have to remember that all you are doing is driving the suit, it's not you saying it, you're operating a puppet almost, making the character talk and react. You need to keep a distance from what you're saying while at the same time totally going for it so the student gets the full force of the attack. There's no point verbalising unless we can be as offensive as the real thing. The first time a lot of women hear this shit they just freeze up. We've got to help them break through that barrier.'

'Any of you guys want to talk to me,' said Detective Benson after another brief silence, 'they got my number in the office. I think it's really great what you're doing and all power to you. Okay, now I got a case I'm working on that needs a bit of attention. I have to go interview a guy who we suspect has raped nine little girls over the past couple of years. He's a pretty shitty individual, so believe me, I'd rather stay here and watch you guys.'

He stood and shook hands with each of the trainees before he left. Nick could never remember feeling more relaxed and more impressed with a police officer. Detective Benson was clearly, as Tara had said in her introduction, a very special policeman.

'What a fucking amazing guy,' Nick said when he'd left.

'Yeah, he's pretty cool,' said Tim. 'He's been real supportive ever since we started. Even helped us compile the list of students who've completed the course and successfully resisted an assault at a later date. Got us police reports from all over the country.'

'Way to go,' said Corville.

'Pretty daunting, though, huh?' said Jonas after another brief silence.

'It's tough the first time you feel what you're saying really make an impact,' said Tim, 'but when you get a really good fight out of a student, you know it was worth it.'

'I don't know if I could ever say that stuff to someone,' said Nick. 'Is that really what blokes have actually said?'

'I'm afraid so, Nicky boy,' said Tim. 'But that's just what they said. It's what they did that's real sick.'

'You know, sometimes I just hit this wall. Since I been doing this training, you know, I've learned so much about blokes. I s'pose I thought I was going to learn about women, you know, about what makes them able to defend themselves and everything, but what I've really learned is how sick blokes are, how sick we all are in a way. I am fucked by the whole thing.'

'Join the team, Nick,' said Jonas with a sad smile.

'There are days when I fall on my knees and thank the Lord I am not straight,' said Corville. 'Not to try and claim that there aren't some seriously sick gay individuals out there, but man oh man. We got pride and we can come out and we can scream. Straight guys, what a burden.'

'Tell me about it.'

'Sure,' said Tim. 'Every woman looks at you and thinks, "Shit, I bet he could, or I bet he has." You know what I'm saying.'

'Every day,' said Jonas.

'Fuck, yeah, it's true,' said Nick. 'I'm really aware of it at the moment. I just assume every woman I see thinks I want to rape and kill her. It's not a lot of fun.'

'It'll pass. And you're forgetting the suits,' said Tim, looking out of the window and grinning. 'The suits change everything.'

In that instant the door burst open and a man started to shoulder his way in, weighed down with two huge shoulder bags.

Haines McCullough had twice come down from Portland, Oregon and measured every last inch of the trainees. During the first two weeks of training Nick had lost a great deal of weight, nearly forty pounds. His exercise regime consisted of long runs around the Page Street neighbourhood, hundreds of crunch-ups every day, swimming dozens of lengths in the university pool at the Berkeley campus. He drank gallons of mineral water and sat for hours in the steam room dripping. Once the training started he found he very rarely had sex with young Tiffany Smooth. He had cut down on his alcohol consumption, drinking only a couple of bottles of chill-filtered beer each day. He had cut right back on fast food, although he did still sneak the occasional Big Mac in when no one was looking. They tasted so much better in America, not like the sad excuse for Big Macs you could buy on Oxford Street back home in London.

His neck was the first thing to shrink. He had bought an old denim shirt with him from England, a favourite, with pearl buttons and faded to near-rag-like conditions. He hadn't attempted to do the collar up for years, and now suddenly it fitted. It wasn't even tight. His arms seemed thinner, which he found a little disturbing – he had spent so many years of his life pumping them up to their glorious size that it seemed crazy to let them go down. However, his torso he was pleased with – he looked quite ripped. His stomach didn't feel as if it was going to burst his jeans any more – he even had to gouge another hole in his belt to keep his trousers up.

'You've shrunk,' said Haines as he was joined in the training room by his son Murphy. The two men were carrying three huge bags between them. They let them drop with a satisfying thump. Their arrival had been keenly awaited for weeks since they had had their measurements taken.

'The one in the red bag is yours, Nicky boy,' said Haines. 'The pink bag is yours, Corville. I thought that would be appropriate.'

'Way to go, girl!' said Corville.

'You get the tan one, Jonas. Kind of a woody feel to it.'

'Thanks, Haines,' said Jonas with a smile.

'It's like Christmas,' said Corville. 'I am so excited! What has Santa bought me!'

Nick unzipped his enormous bag and looked at the carapace inside. The suits, which came in many sections, were made of high-density foam covered in a very durable black nylon fabric. They could be washed down with hot soapy water after use, the foam interior completely protected from moisture.

The helmets were built using a standard American football helmet and face shield as foundation. Nick had tried on five to find one that fitted. It was comfortably tight so it didn't slide around. On to this helmet Haines had built a three-inch-thick high-density foam casing, reinforced with heavy-duty fabric bandage. The eye protectors were made of Kevlar webbing, a material used in the construction of bullet-proof vests. This allowed the wearer to see out and the students to practise full-force eye jabs without fear of injury to either party.

'Well, don't just look at them, try them on,' said Haines. 'Thigh pads first, that's the white pants, then crotch piece, then chest, arm and shin pads and the shoes.'

There were no women present so the men stripped off everything except their T-shirts. In the bag Nick found a new jockstrap still in a plastic bag. He slipped the steel cup, just like a cricket box, into the pocket of the jock strap and pulled it on. He made sure it was comfortable and tapped the outside. It was an odd feeling to put his hand where his cock was and feel only a steel cup. He punched himself a little harder and felt no pain. He smiled at the other men, who were all busy pulling on various bits of padding.

Nick pulled on the white leggings, which contained sub-stantial built-in thigh and shin pads. This section of the suit was fully machine washable, and he'd been assured it needed to be. They had overcome a lot of the problems with the suits, but heat was still a big issue. By the ninetieth fight a padded assailant was a very hot person.

He gingerly picked up the crotch protector. It seemed enormous, a great curved piece of black armour with a deep pocket for his wedding tackle. He slipped his legs through the retaining straps and pulled the thing up. It fitted very snugly, although it was a little how he imagined it would feel to wear a nappy.

Two straps went over the shoulders and clipped into position, holding the protector in place. The clips were kept from his body by carefully made soft padding.

He slipped the abdomen and chest protector over his head. This section also contained the large shoulder pads. These were partly to protect the collar bones, but their function was chiefly to support the helmet. The whole thing was bulky but not heavy. Tim had explained how the old armour had really weighed a lot, was incredibly hot to wear and would often start to fall apart halfway through a class. Haines McCullough's skill had greatly improved the comfort and agility of padded assailants.

Nick was impressed by how easy it was to move in the armour. He didn't feel weighed down by it, although he could immediately tell he was going to get hot. He pulled on the knee and shin protectors, followed by the upper and lower arm pads and the elbow pads. Finally he slipped on the shoes, which were standard trainers fitted with a huge protecting layer of high-density foam, making the wearer look like a character at Disneyland.

'Okay, looking good,' said Haines as he tugged at various parts of Nick's suit. 'How's it feel?'

'Feels good,' said Nick. 'Really comfortable.'

'You won't say that after fifty fights straight through, but it's nice to hear,' said Haines with a twinkle. 'Try a roll.'

Nick jumped around a bit then rolled backwards. It was extraordinary. The suit protected him, minimising the impact as he fell. He stood up again. This took some practice as the suit restricted his movements. It seemed that a half backward somersault on to the feet was the best method, if a little showy.

He rolled again, this time with less care, and after a few attempts he was literally throwing himself against the floor with barely a thought. Corville and Jonas were doing the same.

'Man, I wish Raul had stuck with it. He'd have got off on this,' said Jonas.

'Yeah, you're right,' said Corville. 'I knew these would be fun, but not this much fun. I can't wait to go clubbing in this.' He looked at the horrified expression on Haines's face, smiled, and then burst out in an extravagant, infectious laugh. 'Girl, as if!' he said, and pushed Haines gently. Nick noticed Haines's son Murphy looking at Corville in a way he recognised – a mixture of amazement, fascination and sexual excitement. It was clear to probably everyone except Haines which team Murphy was going to be batting for.

'Okay, guys, go all the way, try on your helmets,' said Haines. One by one the men inserted their gumshields and slipped their heads inside the huge, ungainly devices.

As the tightness and heat engulfed Nick, he felt an aura of seriousness descend along with them. He could see out fairly clearly but his hearing was severely impaired. He looked at the other people in the room. Two other men with dustbin heads like his. Haines, the smiling, grey-bearded hippie and his son Murphy. Tim, who was busy adjusting the straps on Jonas's helmet. He could see them and hear most of what they were saying; they couldn't see him. He snarled at them and mumbled 'You fucking bastards' under his breath. No one reacted – they had no idea what was going on inside the helmet. He suddenly became aware of his heart rate. It had gone up considerably.

He saw Tim walk towards him. 'Everything okay in there? How's it fit?' he asked.

'Okay. Good,' said Nick, not sure if he was shouting as he could only just hear his own voice. 'Bit hot, but it all fits okay.'

'That's good. Want to try it out?'

'Sure,' said Nick. 'What do I do?'

'Let's just go step by step through that basic routine we've done – grab from the rear, foot stamp, elbow, eye jab, heel palm, knee to the crotch and head.'

'Okay. But slow.'

'Sure. Real soft and gentle,' said Tim.

He turned around and Nick embraced him from the rear, feeling oddly distanced because of the suit. He could only just feel Tim. He registered an impact on his foot but only just; he moved a little as Tim lined up for a reverse elbow blow. Nick tensed his stomach muscles and gritted his teeth. The blow came, but it was like being hit with a huge sheet. He could feel the impact but it was spread evenly all over his torso. He stood motionless as Tim turned slowly and jabbed the helmet at the centre of the eye protection gauze.

'Heel palm next,' he heard Tim say. 'Keep your head up, not tense,' he reminded Nick. The blow came. His whole body moved backwards with the force of it. It felt as if Tim had hit him hard – he had to take two steps back to regain his balance.

'Fuck,' said Nick.

'You okay?' asked Tim, clearly anxious.

'Yeah, I'm fine, it's just all so weird.'

Tim smiled and then gestured towards his knee. Nick re-membered to make the thumbs-up sign. Tim came towards him and suddenly Nick was in the air. He didn't feel the impact, just the movement, but it knocked the wind out of him momentarily. When he landed again he could feel where the tightly fitting crotch piece had dug into his thighs and buttocks, but it had left his balls untouched. He stood regaining his equilibrium for a moment and then remembered to kneel down on the floor as though nursing two ruptured testicles. He let his head loll forward, trying at the same time to leave his neck relaxed. The blow came; he saw a flash of Tim's knee in his face. Again it seemed that the blow was spread across the whole of his upper body. The helmet was built in such a way that the impact was transported through to the shoulders, so the neck didn't suddenly snap back, avoiding the debilitating injury the blow was designed to cause.

Nick flopped on to the canvas and put his arms up on either side of his head in the gesture he'd learned. Knockout. Game over.

'That was amazing,' he said with relief as he took the helmet off. He spat his gumshield out and felt the top of his head. It was soaked with sweat. He could feel it running down his back.

'That really was amazing,' he said again, panting and looking at Tim.

'You okay?' Tim asked.

'Sure, I'm fine.'

'Okay. Only I always worry when I pop someone for the first time.'

'Honest, I was fine. The crotch blow caught me, but I'm not injured. I was a bit winded, that's all.'

'Nick, d'you know what I did?'

'No. What?' said Nick, not understanding Tim's concern.

'I went for broke, man. I went full impact. You just withstood blows ten times more powerful than you'd receive from most women. You took off, man.'

'You bastard,' said Nick, grinning across his sweaty face.

'It's the best way. There's no point me tapping you, you wouldn't feel it anyway. It's got to be all or nothing. Now you know you're okay. I can hit real hard, Nick. You know that.'

'I know that,' said Nick, who had held punch pads up for Tim to practise on one morning. His blows had a sudden impact which could never be predicted.

Nick sat down on the low bench that ran the length of the mat on one side. He took a swig of water from his Calistoga bottle and swilled his dry mouth out. He watched as Tim went through the same exercise first with Corville and then with Jonas. He could see the force of the blows Tim was delivering, massive and devastating in any other circumstances. Corville moved back when he was hit, Jonas took off and seemed to fly through the air. Both men were smiling when they took their helmets off.

Nick sat, quietly looking inside his helmet. This was the bit that worried him – they had discussed the issue of 'character' in the previous weeks. Each man needed a character to adopt when he put the helmet on, to psychologically enable him to be the attacker.

Nick thought of the characters in movies he'd seen who'd been pretty wild. Jack Nicholson in *The Shining* – bit obvious and American. Dennis Hopper in *Blue Velvet* – still an American. Then he remembered the Welsh bloke in *Silence of the Lambs*, Anthony Hopkins. What about Hannibal Lecter? He was pretty mean. He ate people – that was fairly aggressive and unpleasant. He also had a cult fear attached to him as the most repugnant, evil bastard that ever walked. Hannibal. Sounded good. Made him feel evil.

He pulled the helmet on again, then crouched a little, finding his balance. He scanned the room and started to move about. 'I can help you, Clarice,' he said, adopting as posh an accent as he could manage, hissing the words through his teeth. It felt good.

'People are going to think we are in love.'

He knew he must sound really evil. He had thought about cartoon superheroes and villains like Superman and Spiderman, but they just weren't mad enough, weren't dirty or grown-up enough. He understood finally that in the suit, in the helmet, he needed to exude evil, he needed to become Hannibal.

The transformation in his life during the course had been unnerving and fulfilling. He felt as if he were a different man; he felt parts of his body and mind come alive, as though they had always been there but had hitherto been left dormant, untouched. He had spent a lot of time with Corville and Jonas, the three of them eating out in a pasta bar in Berkeley after class, sometimes joined by Tiffany or Corville's partner Rudy, another self-defence teacher. Nick felt at home with them, being completely honest about himself, hiding nothing, not pretending he didn't care about things as he had done before.

The time he spent with Tiffany had become a lot calmer. They didn't immediately jump on each other's bones as soon as they came into contact. Owing to his packed training schedule he was rarely at the house, and when he was there he was sleeping off the exhaustion of his routine. Days would pass when he and Tiffany would only cuddle together in bed. She suffered from difficult periods and he found it delightful to rub her shoulders and back to ease the tension without getting an erection. Tiffany was, however, becoming increasingly unhappy about the situation because his coming graduation as a padded assailant meant only one thing – he would soon be returning to England.

He hadn't missed England or his life there. The only person he ever thought about with any regularity was Barney. He had spoken to him twice on the phone and had even written him a letter including some photos of him on the beach and sitting with his new buddies Corville, Tim and Jonas. He thought he looked good in the pictures and was proud to send them to his son. However, actually sitting down and writing a letter had proved to be very difficult. It was only when Tiffany came back from college and made him sit at the high kitchen table that he managed to fill three-quarters of a page.

'Your writing is pretty shit,' said Tiffany. 'You write like a kid.'

'Thank you,' said Nick, folding the letter rapidly without reading it over. He noticed she'd started to criticise him more regularly – nothing big, and she always apologised, but her sniping slowly began to make him feel uncomfortable. It was difficult, effectively living with someone when the arrangements were so informal. And there was Tiffany's mother.

Grace Smooth, as Nick had now discovered, had been very famous in the sixties. She still was a pretty big noise among the generation a few years older than Nick. He had heard of Matheson Cowpie and he found her name had a certain resonance in the city. She didn't talk to him much, but she had bothered to tell him that she thought what he was doing was good and that she was happy to support him. He could stay in her house as long as he needed to.

It had become slowly apparent to him that the huge journey every night back to Tiffany's was becoming less and less attractive. She would be in her room, surrounded by books, studying at her small desk, chain-smoking and slightly short-tempered. He would watch a small black-and-white TV set which rested on an empty pasta box on the kitchen floor and feel a little in the way. Tiffany was studying politics at San Francisco University and had, at the late age of twenty-two, decided to take it all terribly seriously.

During the last week of his course, Nick stayed at the boarding house Jonas was living in, which was a mere five blocks from the training centre. It was nearer the pool and the excellent gym facilities he had access to. He had agreed with Tiffany that as the course was so intensive it would be better for both of them if he were there. He also felt it wasn't right to be relying on her so much. She had her own life and needed time to study. All the usual excuses.

The move to the boarding house turned out to be a great relief. Although he wasn't earning much, Nick had enough cash to pay the rent with some to spare for eating out, which he did virtually every night. His room was spacious and airy, with its own little bathroom. He felt at home, actually unpacked his bags for the first time since he'd been in America. He got on well with Jonas the carpenter, who had an attic room at the top of the house. The two men spent most of their free time together.

Outside his room, Berkeley was buzzing with excitement. It was mid-June, and the sun was hot. Thousands of young people milling the streets each night reminded him of the atmosphere of Oxford in the early summer, except these students were far more approachable.

Halfway through the course Nick's birthday arrived. He had forgotten all about it until he woke up on the anniversary, opened the blinds and saw the bright Californian sun. 'Thirty fucking six,' he said out loud. 'You poor old sod.'

Somewhere, not very deep inside, there was still a nineteen-year-old having a good time, most of the time. He told Jonas it was his birthday as they jogged that morning. Jonas wished him a happy birthday and that was the end of the matter.

However, when he got to the training centre later that morning he was greeted by everyone he had ever met in California. Even Tiffany's mother had turned up, wearing a famous person's dark glasses.

Americans were so good at celebrating, he thought, as he blew out thirty-six candles on his cake, baked in the shape of an impact suit. Nick ate part of the head and drank strong coffee. Tara was there with a frail-looking but intense man Nick decided must be Adrian. Nick talked to him briefly about Oxford.

He was disappointed and relieved at the same time as he spoke to Adrian, who was very admiring of what Nick was doing. Nick had allowed himself more than a handful of fantasies about Tara since he'd met her, but they always ended up being complicated and painful.

Adrian had studied at Oxford at the same time Nick had been working in Browns café. It turned out he had been to Browns; it turned out he was pretty sure he could remember Nick working behind the bar. They talked about his son and Sally's parents. Adrian had heard of Sally's father. He explained what he was working on and Nick admitted he didn't understand a word.

Tiffany grabbed him and embraced him. She had taken time off college and driven with her mother. They hugged for a long time and she told him she missed him. He told her the same, but he knew he didn't really. Everything was so different.

Once everyone had finally left Nick found his birthday to be a bit of a let-down. It was back to the grind of learning moves with Tim and Tara, always Tim and Tara. He had got to know Tim really well, but Tara stayed distant – friendly, always on hand, but aloof. They had worked with a variety of volunteer students who sparred with them, usually on a Friday. This became a highlight for Nick, as it meant he actually saw some fresh faces, and some of the women he worked with were babes, no doubt about it.

He popped into Tara's office as the last people were leaving. Jonas and Corville were taking five outside. Tara was typing at her computer. She looked up.

'Nick,' she said.

'Yeah.'

'Oh, I thought you wanted something,' she said after a pause.

'Oh, well, no, not really.'

'Oh, right.'

'It's just . . . Well, I don't know what it is. It's just the way you run this place. It's weird. I mean, I understand it now, I know it's run by women and we just do a job here and all that's fine, but I feel kind of isolated. Socially. You know, I never see anyone except you and the guys. There're all these interesting people popping in and stuff, but we never get to meet them.'

'Which people?' asked Tara.

'I don't know. People. They pick up leaflets, they look at us like we're in a zoo. I feel like I haven't met anyone who's involved in the organisation, I don't know how you run the joint, nothing. I suppose I know I'm being excluded which I agree with but on a day-to-day basis it feels weird.'

'Okay,' said Tara. She sat back in her chair and looked at him. She smiled. 'You're a strange guy.'

'I'm not.'

'You are. It's just so weird to see you adjusting, 'cos I can see it hurts, not being in control, playing second fiddle and all. But that's what this place is all about. The students have to see women in control, that's what makes it work.'

Nick nodded at her, relishing this time when he could stare at her. She had grown more beautiful in his eyes the more time he spent with her. He didn't really feel lustful toward her, although he knew it wouldn't take much to start feeling so, but he was partially in love with her. She was the strongest, the most powerful and self-contained woman he'd ever met. If only. He couldn't imagine her nagging him, or hassling him. If only. He liked Adrian, although he was a bit of a wuss. He didn't want to do anything, it was out of the question, but if only. That was as far as it went. He did once imagine them walking together through a hot desert, both wearing only chamois leather loincloths, her all brown and Native American-like, ready to do it in the dust. He did imagine that, quite often. She had a bow and arrow and was tall and strong and independent in the fantasy. He didn't want her to be the little squaw, but she was more or less naked and desperate to shag him – that bit was important.

Tara, normally always at the training centre first, was the last person to arrive on the day that Haines McCullough delivered the suits.

'Hi, everybody,' she said as normal. Then she froze, her mouth wide open. Nick noticed her perfect white teeth, not a filling in view. There was no doubt in his mind that she was the most beautiful woman he'd ever seen.

'Look at you guys,' she said finally. 'I've got three new boys!'

'What d'you think? Isn't it just wild!' said Corville as he sashayed up and down the mat like a model on a catwalk, his posture absurd and hysterically funny in the cumbersome body armour.

'Fantastic, guys,' said Tara. 'I am so proud of you. You've made it. You've all made it.'

'Not quite all,' said Jonas. 'We were just saying how it's like a shame Raul isn't here today.'

'Sure,' said Tara. 'Sure. I'm still really upset about that, but as you all know, it's a tough call.'

Nick realised that what she had just said was true. It was tough. He had found the physical side easy – he was fit enough and in many ways he found that aspect relaxing. It was the emotional stuff that was difficult, too difficult for some.

Raul had broken down during a training session with two women from an advanced class, both with a history of sexual assault. He said the voices in his head were driving him crazy, he couldn't handle it. He was screaming with anger, and when he finally subsided, he said the anger was still inside, he couldn't seem to get it out. He kept remembering his sister as a little girl, running along Venice beach in the early morning, such a sweet little girl. Now she was, according to his description, just a hollow-eyed fat chick sitting in a trailer park in New Mexico.

Raul's inability to tell them what blocked him and made him so angry made him fear what he would do in a class. He had given up about a week into the course, which had left everyone involved feeling deflated. They all liked him and all wanted him to stay. Nick missed him particularly because of his anger. After Raul had left Nick felt he was 'the most angry boy in the group', a title he didn't relish. They 'workshopped' his anger, a session that he found made him more angry. Suddenly his anger felt like his own affair and he didn't need them to judge it, and yet as time wore on he could see they weren't judging it. He acknowledged that his anger came from feeling he was being judged by women, his slow realisation of the role he had played in the misty area between love and rape where most heterosexual men resided. He knew he'd never raped anyone, but also he knew that on many occasions he'd been sitting in groups of men, maybe outside a pub on a sunny day, and he'd done it. Sizing women up as they passed and, in doing so, intimidating those women in a way far more terrifying than he'd ever realised.

'Okay, let's do our exercises again, only this time for real,' said Tara. She had barely been there ten minutes and already she was ready to work. Nick was still amazed by how driven everyone was in America.

He inserted his gumshield and picked up his helmet, slipped it on over his head and did up the straps. Hannibal. That's who he was. Instantly and without effort – Hannibal, a horny fucker who wanted some screaming bitch meat to chew. He looked at Tara through the protective netting in front of his eyes. He sneered and made a lecherous face, his jutting chin tightening the retaining strap on the helmet. He looked at her in a completely different way – her long slender neck, the way her hair was cut short on the back of her head. She was fucking sexy, she was asking for it. He wanted to bite her neck and push her down on the floor and fuck her. Christ, she'd look sexy with a cock in her mouth. Fucking frigid little cock-teaser. Who did she think she was? She was so fucking smart, all the clever bullshit and holier-than-thou crap she dumped on him.

She was standing there with her back to him, her pert little buttocks under the loose-fitting training pants. He imagined her thin panties pulled up between those gorgeous buttocks, like some fucking calendar girl. Just waiting for it. How dare she say no?

He walked up behind her, grabbed her around the chest as he'd been taught. He felt her tits under his arms. Fucking hell, she was well horny.

'No!' she screamed. Nick was surprised. She pulled his arm up against his will; he tried to stop her but couldn't. He actually couldn't stop her.

'Bite!' she shouted, and automatically he pulled his arm away. She didn't bite him but he felt her lips on the unprotected area of his forearm. Then he felt the impact on his right foot, so fast, so strong. He started to step back but the blow came to his stomach before he could move. He began to bow over as he had learned in training, but before he could even do that she got an eye jab in, then a knee to the groin. He went down. Another knee to the head sent him spinning. He landed heavily and rolled on to his back, putting his arms up beside his head.

'Call nine one one!' shouted Tara triumphantly. 'You're a natural,' she added, and embraced Nick when he had removed his helmet.

'God, it's weird,' said Nick.

'You'll get used to it,' said Tim. But Nick wondered.

Being that close to a woman who really didn't want you there, feeling her breasts so clearly against his forearms. He couldn't help remember, but he didn't want to say anything to her. How could a comment like that be tolerated? He had to be so careful, all the time. Even when he wasn't in the training room he felt he was walking on eggs. He spent many hours sitting in on courses being run by Tara or one of the other teachers. Again and again he heard the terror in women's voices. Once they opened up and allowed themselves to think about it, it was clear that they all, without exception, saw most men as a potential threat. Some women's lives were so devastated by fear that they barely left their houses. Everywhere they went they were in fear for their dignity and their safety, if not their very lives. Again and again Nick wanted to remind them that he, and in particular Corville, were in much greater danger, statistically, of unprovoked assault by a stranger in a public place.

As Tim had told him, the statistics couldn't be more stark. Ninety-two per cent of street assaults were against men, not women, and of those, the vast majority were against black men. It didn't make any difference to the women he saw; he finally accepted that they were more scared than he was, more of the time and with good reason. An assault against a man by a stranger was usually a one-off, a chance thing, being outside the wrong bar with the wrong drunk at the wrong time. Women were more often stalked, hunted, invaded in their homes, raped and killed in a way no men ever were. There had been a serial rapist in the San José neighbourhood only three months previously. Tara acknowledged that unfortunately a series of attacks like that was good for business. The man had spied on his victims, waited until they were alone and then spent hours torturing and humiliating them at his leisure. He was captured by pure chance when an off-duty policeman who was returning home saw him leaving a neighbour's house suspiciously. He was arrested, and the police officer found his neighbour bound and gagged, hanging by the wrists from a rafter in the double garage.

It didn't matter how statistically rare these events were, still something like a one in ten million chance, the terror the attacks provoked in all the women Nick talked to was undeniable.

The statistics he'd discovered about unprovoked street attacks were completely reversed when it came to domestic violence. It was the men that women knew, lived with and trusted who were the most likely to attack and rape them, a piece of information Nick found particularly depressing. How did you legislate against that? No amount of street lighting or safe bus routes could remove that chance.

The only response to this terror, the only thing he saw that did any good at all, which made all the women take heart, breathe in and get back out on to the streets, was the Winning Strategy training course. The longer he spent watching and practising, the more he became converted.

At the end of the three-week period there was a graduation ceremony for the three new padded assailants to which the men could invite friends and family.

Nick wished his own mum and dad could come. They would be amazed to see him in the suit. He didn't think his dad would understand, but his mum would approve, he felt sure. He had sent them a postcard but found he couldn't begin to explain what he was doing in San Francisco except to say he'd finally, at the age of thirty-six, discovered what he really wanted to do.

The graduation ceremony consisted of each man doing a series of three short individual assaults and two multiple assailant assaults followed by a prolonged psycho session with a woman who had completed an advanced class. The psycho session was a fight where they played a man who felt no pain, someone laced out on PCP and capable of inhuman acts of aggression. The woman would have to fight long and hard and deliver twice the number of knockout blows as normal.

Nick and Jonas admitted to each other that they were nervous on the morning of the last day. They swam for an hour in the beautiful outdoor pool on the Berkeley campus. They were two very fit men, Nick now with far longer hair than when he'd arrived in America, sitting on the edge of the pool after their swim, minding their own business.

They were approached on three separate occasions by young female students. Nick was charming but uninterested. Something had happened to him during the three-week training period. He wasn't sure what. It wasn't bad – he felt more relaxed. The tension he used to feel at the possibility of 'missing out' on a potential shag had completely dissipated. When a very pretty blonde girl with a pierced belly button not unlike Tiffany's stood in front of them, Nick amazed himself by how he didn't, however briefly, imagine shagging her. She was nice – he spoke to her, he looked her in the eye, he laughed when she was funny, but he didn't want to shag her over the end of a sofa. It wasn't that he couldn't have found her attractive, it was simply that it wasn't appropriate. Nick Gardener had learned that he could contain his various lusts until the appropriate time without diminishing the pleasure he received from them when they were sated.

He felt much more at ease in the company of women, felt he understood a little more what they were about. He enjoyed their company without wondering what they would look like with his cock in their mouths.

They arrived at the training centre at around five in the afternoon. It was already busy. Rows of chairs had replaced the coffee-and-relaxation area to one side of the large blue mat – they were expecting over one hundred people. Nick hugged Corville and they both screamed.

'I'm so nervous, girl, I could die!' said Corville.

'Hey, me too, mate. But it's been great, hasn't it?'

'It's been wonderful,' said Corville. Nick had also been amazed by how he had got on with this man. Six foot three inches of black homosexual, so out and proud and so wise. He had tried to imagine how he would describe Corville to the men he used to work with outside Trash. The daydream always turned into a nightmare. He would be 'a big black bender' to them; out would come all the jokes about how you had to call a six-foot black poof with an axe 'sir'.

Corville did have a tendency to scream and camp it up at times, but when they were observing classes, Nick always checked him to see how to react when there was a particularly emotional scene taking place. It was as though, underneath the pizzazz of his street gayness, there was a man who understood suffering and allowed people room to suffer without judgment.

'It's great to see so many people here,' said Tara to the assembled crowd when they had all got settled. The room seemed to have shrunk – so many people were crammed in, half of them standing, craning their necks to try to get a view. Nick noticed Tiffany, wearing a white blouse with her hair tied back, so different to when he had first seen her. Grace Smooth was there too, in dark glasses naturally. He stood with Jonas and Corville, their backs against the wall, facing the crowd, nervous, and hoped it would all be over soon.

'I'm going to be brief so we're not here all night,' said Tara as she took her position at the centre of the blue mat. 'I guess all of you know what we do here in this room. But you may not know that still the single hardest aspect of what we do is finding men to help us. Well, we've found three – two Americans, Jonas and Corville, and an Englishman, Nick. He's going to be involved in the first Winning Strategy group in London, England.'

The entire crowd burst into spontaneous applause. Nick smiled and felt himself blush, while also not quite understanding why they were clapping.

'We are being helped tonight by some special women who have volunteered to be guinea-pigs for us. They will be attacked by our new padded assailants.' Tara gestured to three women standing along from Nick. 'We have Vicki, Robyn and Mindy.'

When Mindy had walked in earlier Nick's heart had sunk. She was the blonde woman who was in the first group he had ever watched, the woman Tim had said he fancied, the woman whose boyfriend had raped her. She was standing next to Nick, smiling at him.

As Corville and Jonas prepared for the first session, Nick moved off the mat to the small area by the office door. Mindy appeared by his side, discreetly turning her head away from the crowd. She touched him on his padded shoulder.

'Nick, can I tell you something?' she asked. Her voice had that ring to it that Nick had always loved – American, bright, sexy.

'Sure,' he said, this time looking at her and fighting fifteen different impulses. He found her highly attractive and wanted to bite her neck and pull her hair and kiss her and use a sofa in many unusual ways.

'I know we're not meant to socialise, but you're going back to England and I guess I'll never see you again, but I think you are the most beautiful man I have ever seen and if there is ever any way we could spend time together I would really appreciate it.'

'Fuck me,' muttered Nick, as an exultation rather than a suggestion.

'I'd love to,' said Mindy, taking the statement at face value with a flicker of a smile.

Nick buried his face in his hands, then took a peek at Mindy from between his fingers. He could feel that he was excited under the steel box of his groin padding. How could she say that to him? Now?

'I can't handle that,' he said.

'I'm sorry. I should've waited. It's just been so hard seeing you here again. I was so confused when you walked out during that first class. Really. But I found out that you were kind of really upset then and it really moved me, that there were men sensitive enough to like be affected that much. And now you've become a padded assailant. You'll never know how much you helped me.'

'Jesus, Mindy. You've really done my head in. You are the most tasty woman I've seen since I've been here, and now this.'

'I'm sorry,' she said.

Nick glanced up at Tara. She was looking at him. It was soon to be his turn to do an exercise. He nodded and put in his gumshield, pulled on his helmet and walked to the centre of the floor.

Mindy then walked on to the mat and stood with her back to him. Annoying little bitch, he thought as he walked up behind her.

He fought hard and long with Mindy, but she fought back harder and faster. It was only when he took his helmet off afterwards that he realised that not once, not even for a shaving of a second, did he have the slightest sexual feeling for her during the fights.

As he regained his breath after the bout, he marvelled at the soundness of his own mind.

For the rest of the night the fights were fast and furious. Nick had grown used to his helmet and barely thought about Hannibal when he didn't have it on. He was amazed, however, to discover how much having this little game with himself helped him when he was wearing the cumbersome thing.

Oddly for Nick, who was never normally short of words, one of the hardest parts of the evening was the vocalisation during the multiple assailants section. Two men would approach the woman together, talking to each other about what they would like to do to her.

'Hey, look at that little bitch,' Jonas would say in a very convincing street drawl.

'Well fucking tasty,' Nick would agree, adopting a cockney-influenced street parlance of his own. 'I could give that some serious shaggin'.'

However, the two accents didn't exactly meld, and some of the women who had been helping with the training actually burst out laughing when they heard Nick's accent. There had been a great deal of discussion about him adopting an American accent, but he had only had to attempt it once to convince everyone present that it wasn't a good idea.

During the build-up to the inauguration night it was decided that it would be best if Nick offered only responsive grunts, leaving the other two to set the pace.

He did his first multiple assault with Corville, who was an expert mimic and sounded nothing like the man Nick had grown to admire. Instead, a soupy-thick, low-brow, sloppy-mouthed-thug voice emerged from the enormity of his helmet. They walked up to Robyn, whom Nick had never met before.

'She's a fucking dirty-looking bitch,' said Corville.

'Mmuhh,' said Nick.

'I'll hold her, you fuck her slimy little cunt, man,' said Corville with a chilling laugh. Robyn responded, fighting one into unconsciousness then using his body to protect her from Nick. Try as he might to get closer, she kept her distance until she was ready, then boom! Her blows were well aimed and powerful, and it was only a matter of seconds before both men were on the floor adopting the unconscious position.

The crowd erupted in support for the woman, and when Nick stood up, he could sense that the applause was for him too. Totally weird, he thought, to be clapped for threatening to gang-rape a woman. How was this ever going to work in England?

Chapter Twenty-Five

Alice found her way to the Holborn Centre in Sandland Street and managed to get a legitimate parking space, on a meter, at ten o'clock on a Monday morning. It must be a good omen, she thought as she glanced at herself in the rear-view mirror: a bit haggard but it would have to do. She had been crying, she always seemed to be crying, and now she had more or less got used to it. She had this one quick assessment to do, then she had to get back to the office, put her report in and get a flight to Aberdeen. At least she had her work – that seemed to be holding together. She wanted to be away all the time. Her flat was so depressing; she just couldn't clean it. It was in a terrible mess, everything was untidy, dirty, there were so many broken things there, she didn't know how it had happened, but everything seemed to be broken.

She was going to Aberdeen to inspect an oil rig that had suffered five separate fires in two months. Looked like sabotage, but she couldn't be sure until she got there. A fat file of the rig's technical specifications was thrown into the boot next to the rotting shopping she never managed to clear out. Alice loved oil rigs – lonely islands of metal standing so solidly in the flat grey sea. She loved helicopters and the unspeakable dangers they represented. She even liked the all-male company on board a big rig, and had never felt intimidated by the men. She seemed to be given more room than normal and was always treated with respect. She was looking forward to the trip, which would see her out of London and her flat for three days.

She crossed the road and checked the address she had been given. It was an old Victorian school building, long since transformed into some sort of acting or community centre. The playground had become a carpark; a few tables and chairs were placed in the bright morning sunlight. A gaggle of scruffily dressed actors sat smoking and talking loudly, not seeming to see her as she entered the building.

'I'm looking for someone called Tara Kennedy,' said Alice when she reached a low reception desk.

The young woman behind the desk was eating a bacon roll. She smiled through the crumbs and pointed upward.

'Third floor,' she said eventually.

'Thank you,' said Alice.

She briskly climbed the wide stairs to the third floor and opened her file as she climbed. She was assessing a public liability risk for an insurance company in the City. It was some sort of martial arts thing which had become trendy in America – it was bound to be lethal and impossible to cover.

On the third floor she walked down a short corridor until she heard a strange sound to her left. She stopped and looked through a circular window in the bright blue-painted door. Inside, a man, at least she thought it was a man although it was hard to tell under his costume, was storming around the room. He looked like a giant bug, a ridiculous alien from a 1950s science fiction horror movie. He was grappling with a woman. It seemed he was trying to grab her breasts. The woman screamed at him and belted him in the stomach. The man collapsed on the floor, his huge head hanging, and then the woman kneed him in the face so hard the man spun across the floor and lay still.

The woman who had beaten the man senseless saw Alice through the window and bounded across, opening the door.

'Hi, I'm Tara Kennedy,' she said with an American accent. 'Are you Alice?'

'Yes,' said Alice, her pulse racing, feeling a little queasy. 'Alice Moreton from the risk assessment office.'

'Great. Please come in.'

Alice entered the room and immediately felt more uneasy. The floor was made of some sort of sponge rubber which gave way as she stood on it.

'Maybe you should kick your heels off,' said Tara kindly. 'Don't want to damage the floor. It's not ours, you see – we're just borrowing it for the time being.'

Alice complied, sliding the low-heeled pumps off her feet. Then the floor felt rather pleasant, soft and springy underfoot.

The giant bug-man seemed to roll to his feet, defying gravity as he did so. It was quite a disturbing sight, Alice found, almost like looking at a film of someone falling over in reverse.

'This is Nick,' said Tara. 'Nick Gardener. He's my assistant in the class and he's also the main reason you're here, I guess.'

The thing removed its helmet. There was a man underneath – sweaty hair cut short, dark eyebrows, peculiar-shaped mouth. He spat something out of his mouth – a plastic thing like boxers wore. Suddenly he was quite nice-looking.

'Hi, how d'you do,' said Nick with a pleasant smile. He offered her his hand. She shook it; he was very hot. She wanted to wash again, felt sick.

'How d'you do,' she said, hoping none of her feelings were showing to the outside world.

'Have you heard about our work here, then?' asked Tara.

'No, not really,' said Alice. She felt slightly nervous in the man's company; she wasn't sure where to look. The suit made him so big; she wasn't sure what was underneath. It was all a little disturbing. 'I read something about it, your letter to the insurance company. Eagle Star, was it?'

'Yes, that's right,' said Tara.

'Yes, so it's some sort of martial arts thing, is it?' asked Alice. She had put her briefcase on the floor and had started looking through its contents for the file on the case.

'Not quite,' said Tara. 'Nick is what's known as a padded assailant, a trained attacker, if you like. We teach a form of self-defence for women, specifically designed to teach women to defend themselves against assaults by men.'

'I see,' said Alice, her heart rate now uncomfortably high. She didn't trust this man, that was what it was. She didn't like him, the way he looked at her — she knew the look. It wasn't affectionate or even flirtatious, it was lustful and dangerous. It was the look she had seen before, in the carpark. She pushed the thought away; she didn't want to think about it any more.

She stood up and her vision started to blur. The sudden movement seemed to drain all the blood from her head. She should have tried to eat something for breakfast — she had lost so much weight her clothes just hung off her.

'Um, so what exactly does the work entail?' she asked.

'Well,' said Tara, 'the best thing to do is show you. Okay? Would you like to sit down?'

'Why do I need to sit down?' asked Alice, very confused.

'You don't have to, I just thought you might want to.'

'Oh, sorry,' said Alice. Tara motioned towards some low cushions at the side of the room. Alice then saw a woman sitting there whom she had not seen when she entered. The whole experience started to take on a surreal quality — people appearing out of nowhere, the man in the strange costume, this American woman who looked at her in such a chilling way. Who were these people? Where had she been sent? She wanted to curl up and sleep, she wanted to vomit, she wanted to be dead.

'This is Daisy. She's assisting us today.'

'Hello there, come and sit next to me,' said Daisy. She smiled and seemed quite harmless.

Alice sat down, somehow misjudging the distance and falling rather heavily.

'Sorry, sorry,' she heard herself saying.

'Okay,' said the tall woman with the short hair. 'Well, Nick and I will show you one of the exercises we do, okay? This first one is like a display thing we show students which gives you an idea. Afterwards I'll let Nick tell you about the suit, how it works and . . . well, we'll let you be the judge.'

Alice nodded and watched, feeling relieved that she was sitting and not about to fall over.

The man put his gumshield in and pulled on his helmet.

'Okay, Nick is going to be someone I know. Standard situation – we've been socialising and he wants to take it further.'

The man stood next to Tara and put his arm around her shoulder.

'Come on, baby. Just for old times' sake,' he said, his voice slightly muffled by the helmet. 'I want to show you how much I love you.'

'No, I don't want to,' said Tara, putting her hands up.

'Oh, come on, you're so fucking gorgeous. I'm dying for it. Christ, you came out with me, I bought your fucking dinner, it's the least you can do.'

'I said no!' said Tara, moving away a little. The bug-man moved closer again, his left hand on Tara's hip, the right hand moving towards her breast.

'But you've been flirting with me all night. You can't just turn around and say no. Come on, baby, I know you love it . . .'

'No!' said Tara, this time pushing the man away and standing with both hands up in front of her face. Alice was shaking; she could feel her whole body shaking. There was nothing she could do about it. She was holding a pen over her notepad and it was visibly quivering. She tried to stop it with her other hand but both her arms had started to shake. She pushed herself back against the wall in an attempt to get the shaking to stop. She did not take her eyes off Tara.

The bug-man moved towards her. 'Don't tell me to stop, baby. Never do that, d'you hear me? So help me, I'm fucking desperate. You can't tell me shit like that.'

The man grabbed Tara suddenly and his big, ugly bug-head bent down as if to kiss her. Tara screamed 'No!' so loudly that

Alice felt herself jump. She heard her own voice now, whimpering and vibrating with the shakes from her body.

Tara jabbed into the man's eyes with two clenched bunches of fingers. The man pulled his head back.

'You fucking bitch!' he screamed, but before he could do anything Tara had landed her knee in his crotch. He collapsed on to his knees, and before Alice thought it possible Tara had smashed her knee into his head. The man reeled backwards and collapsed on the floor. Tara stood close to him, watching him. Suddenly his arm whipped out and caught her ankle. He jerked it so hard that Tara fell to the ground. Alice screamed, her scream uncontrollable, a sudden burst of fear. She felt a hand on her arm and froze, feeling cold, almost dead, the world shrinking further away.

'You okay?' asked a concerned voice. Alice couldn't move or react. With sick fascination she was watching the drama unfold before her. Tara pulled her leg free and span on the floor, not attempting to get up or get out of the way. She used her legs to kick. As the man got up she landed her heel in his crotch again, as he fell she landed a devastating blow to his head. The man froze for a second before collapsing on to the floor with a grunt. His arms came up to the side of his massive, padded head.

'Look. Assess. No!' shouted Tara once she had stood up and looked around the room. She then ran to the bench where Alice was sitting and shouted, 'Dial nine nine nine.'

Alice sat still, watching the pen in her hand continue to shake. She was hoping they would all just go away and leave her. She could make it down to the car and drive home, crawl into her messy bed and just curl up.

'I think she's a bit upset,' said Daisy.

'Oh, sorry, are you okay?' asked Tara, slightly out of breath.

Alice looked up at Tara. How had they known? How had they known what had happened to her? It was like something out of *The Avengers*. She was Emma Peel, taken to some weird organisation that knew everything that had happened to you and re-enacted it right in front of you. But why? How could they have known almost the exact words Peter had used?

'Alice, are you okay?' asked Tara. She was kneeling down in front of her, holding her forearms gently.

'Who told you?' asked Alice, then immediately regretted it because it sounded so stupid. But it seemed the only logical explanation.

'Who told us what?'

Alice felt her face giving way. The mask she had worn for two months just collapsed. Her mouth started it, folding into a stupid shape as two huge sobs erupted from her guts, like volcanoes.

'What he said,' she whispered. It had all gone now; something was flowing out of her that she had no control over.

Tara stood up. 'Nick, would you leave us, please,' she said. The man nodded and turned. He was gone from the room so quickly Alice felt herself relax a little; he had been so frightening.

'If you want to, you can talk. You're safe here,' said Tara.

'How did you know?'

'How did we know you were raped? We didn't. You just told us,' said Tara calmly.

'I didn't.'

'You didn't say it, you showed it.'

'I didn't,' protested Alice. She could feel that the face she was speaking through wasn't her own. This face was twisted in a way she had never felt before. She was so confused; she was pleading with this strange woman for some sort of explanation for her madness and she didn't seem to be getting anywhere. 'I want to know how you knew what he said to me.'

'The man who raped you?' asked Tara.

Alice nodded, and just the fact of her nodding made her sob more. The man who raped her. She had never used the word to herself before. Is that what had happened, then? Was she a woman who had been raped? Was that what all this was about?

'He said the same things that Nick said to me just now, is that what you're saying?' asked Tara.

Alice nodded again, and more sobs emerged.

'Okay, well, I'm really sorry about that, Alice. I had no idea. Let me explain. Nick uses a character when he has the helmet on, so he just uses phrases and terms that we know, from research, that a lot of men have used when they assault women. The reason we did that particular exercise was because the most common form of assault is by a man we know.'

Alice nodded again.

'Now, no one here knew what had happened to you. We didn't plan anything to upset you, and I'm real sorry we did. I feel very responsible for what has happened to you, I really do. If you need to talk about it, just go right ahead. We're here for you. Anything you say in this room is utterly sacred, it will never be repeated. I guarantee that. Can you verify that Daisy?'

Alice glanced at the concerned face of the woman sitting next to her. She nodded. 'I absolutely promise.'

Alice took a deep breath and started talking.

Chapter Twenty-Six

'Barney, for fuck's sake, mate, what's been going on!' shouted
Nick when he dumped his bag on the kitchen floor. The place
was a shambles and stank of stale dope smoke. He could hear
thumps and noises coming from Barney's room above. He stood
looking at his unopened mail which had been tossed on the floor
beside the fridge. He picked it up – a letter from Tiffany, three
bills, a letter from his mum and a brochure about home
insurance. He'd been back in England two months and it already
seemed like two years.

'Hi, Dad,' said Barney, sloping through the door. He was the
same height as Nick but half the weight – a great, long, lolloping
lad. He was wearing hugely baggy jeans and a droopy, unwashed
long-sleeved orange and black T-shirt. His feet were half encased
in a massive pair of trainers, the laces obsessively undone.

When Nick had first seen Barney on his return from America
he could hardly believe the difference. He knew the change had
started before he had left the country. The different smell, the
increase in body weight, the endless sleeping. He had read an
article in a magazine in America about the sudden eight hundred
per cent increase in testosterone that boys of Barney's age
experienced. Eight hundred per cent in a few days, and people
wondered why boys went off the rails. The fact that any of them
stayed anywhere near the rails was far more amazing.

Barney had moved into Nick's maisonette permanently just after he'd arrived back from America. Barney was a constant, round-the-clock background worry for Nick. The place seemed relatively untouched for the first few days after his return, but it wasn't long before he realised that Barney had been making a supreme effort to tidy up, which gradually faded into total chaos.

Barney had been waiting for him at Heathrow, which made the journey back into London far less wearisome than he had anticipated. He had been delighted by the surprise, seeing this lanky kid holding a piece of cardboard with his name written on it standing in the crowd at the passenger exit.

They had embraced, Nick feeling the size and strength of his son's body. It was so amazing to think this was once the little lad who had held his hand on the beach not so many years ago.

Having Barney in the maisonette had been good on the whole, although he clearly wasn't used to looking after himself. All Nick seemed to do at home was shout at him to pick his clothes up, clean the bath, wash his cereal bowl in the morning, put stuff back in the fridge, get a new bog roll out when one was finished, tidy his room. He could feel an attack of orders coming on as he stood in front of the boy.

'What's up?' asked Barney with a half-smile, not unlike the one Nick saw in the mirror.

'The place is a shithole again. What are you on?'

'Nothing,' said Barney. 'I'll clear up.'

A young girl walked into the kitchen, her hair half over her face. She must have been Anglo-Indian or something, Nick thought. She looked different from the traditional Indian women who lived in his area. More street, more dangerous — very pretty, jet-black hair and a hundred earrings.

' 'Lo,' she almost uttered.

'This is Sooty,' said Barney. Nick looked askance.

'Short for Sutupa,' said the girl.

'Oh, right. How d'you do,' said Nick, offering his hand. The girl shook it with the smallest, limpest hand he could remember.

She had clearly just pulled her clothes back on. He couldn't believe it – she didn't look a day over thirteen. He checked his watch – it was 9.15 in the evening.

'Where d'you live?' he asked.

'What's it to you?' she said flatly.

'Well, it's late and you have to get home.'

'I'm all right, I live just off the Holloway Road,' said Sutupa, not so hostile this time.

'Right,' said Nick. He filled the kettle. It felt like it was time to sit down with a cup of tea and work all this out.

It was the last thing he needed after the day he'd had, working with Tara in the sweaty training room at the old school in Holborn with Daisy. He knew he had to support women in their struggle against male oppression, but Daisy just wasn't like Tara. She had no oomph. He had seen Tara working and she had oomph to spare. How anyone expected Daisy to be able to teach he had no idea. But then it wasn't down to him, he wasn't involved. There were half a dozen women he'd met since he'd been back in England who came and watched occasionally and who seemed to know what was going on. Nick had managed to remain blissfully unaware of all the organisation going on. He felt involved, he wanted to express his opinions, but they weren't wanted because he was a bloke. Simple as that. If he'd had a fanny they'd be all over him.

Then, just as he got started showing the stunning woman from the insurance company what they did, she had to have a wobbly and he had to sit downstairs in his suit feeling like a wanker for an hour while Tara workshopped the woman's problems. He had felt annoyed. He wanted to stay, not to say anything, but just to be there. Maybe it was because she was so tasty-looking. Such amazing eyes, he couldn't help notice, but thin as a fucking rake. She looked dirty, not physically dirty, but prepared to get dirty in bed, like Tiffany only older and more intelligent. She had nervous, thin, white, nail-bitten hands. No ring. She had shoulder-length dark hair and a slightly beaky nose.

Nick had once wanted to write a song about girls with big noses. Sally had a big conk; Tiffany had a healthy-sized hooter. This Alice woman had a sexy nose, a great mouth. She was, in Nick's book, as tasty as it was possible for a woman to be in real life rather than in a magazine.

And she shook when he stood near her, she visibly shook. When he went back into the room, Tara asked him to stand motionless on the floor while Alice walked around him with her. When she had calmed down enough she felt the material his suit was made from. Nick felt like a shire horse being patted by a nervous child.

Alice sat down and watched as Tara and Nick went through another exercise in front of her. She seemed to cope with it a little better.

They sat on the floor and helped her write down the basic danger areas and frailties of the suit. The whole rigmarole was to enable Tara to get public liability insurance and personal injury insurance for Nick. What should have been a minor irritation had become a major hassle.

Alice told them it all looked a little lethal. She was eventually encouraged to try landing her knee in Nick's padded crotch. She found this very hard to do, but on her third attempt she made contact. She nodded; she seemed to have cheered up a little.

Nick had smiled at Alice as she left. She looked at him from under the curtain of her hair. She did make contact, but it was very brief. Nick watched her walk out. He looked at Tara. She said nothing.

Now he was looking at Sutupa – similar kind of countenance, slightly hunched, bright-looking but fucked-up.

'How old are you, Sutupa?' he asked.

'Nearly sixteen.'

'Which means you're fifteen, which means if you and my son are having sex you're breaking the law.'

'Dad!' said Barney. He was visibly blushing. Nick couldn't tell anything from Sutupa; she didn't seem to blanch.

'Well, someone's got to talk about it,' he said. The kettle boiled and he filled the teapot. 'Tea?'

'Yeah,' said Sutupa without hesitation. He noticed Barney glance at her as she said this.

'You want some, Barn?'

'All right,' said Barney. Nick glanced at him. 'Please.'

The three of them sat around the table Nick had bought at the junk-yard on Liverpool Road. It was old and worn. Nick had sanded it down in their small back garden and it now looked okay.

'We're not having sex, all right,' said Sutupa after sipping her hot tea. 'My mum wouldn't like it.' She laughed after she said this; clearly her mother had little hold over her.

'I'm sure she wouldn't. It's just you can get in a lot of trouble if you're not careful. Look what happened to me.' Nick ruffled his son's hair.

'Dad,' said Barney.

They sat in silence for a while. Nick didn't really know what to say. He hadn't adjusted to the fact that he no longer needed to talk about Action Man or the Power Rangers with his son any more.

'So, what are you guys into? Like, what sort of music and shit like that.'

Sutupa laughed under the mop of her hair.

'Dad,' complained Barney.

'Well, I was just trying to be friendly. Did you guys meet at college?'

'Dad, how can we meet at college? I don't start there until September and even then it's only if my GCSE results are good enough,' said Barney.

'All right, clever arse. So my calender's up the duff. Where did you meet, then?' asked Nick with a laugh.

'Street,' said Barney. 'Sooty's in a gang.'

'Shut up,' said Sutupa. She was smiling, looking at her tea.

'Well, it's true,' said Barney. He clearly wasn't having a good time.

'What sort of gang?' asked Nick.

'Just a gang,' said Sutupa. It seemed that she didn't want to talk, but she kept sitting there as if she were waiting for the next question.

'Right. Like the Crips and Bloods and all that shit?' asked Nick.

'Sort of,' said Sutupa. 'Street Sistas.' She spelled it out for him. 'S-I-S-T-A-S.' Clearly this was important.

'What d'you do, then?' asked Nick after a few moments' silence.

'Do?'

'Yeah, what d'you do? Go round mugging people, stab other gang members, spray your name on the side of trains? Drive-by shootings? What?'

'Nothing like that,' said Sutupa

'Well, what, then?' asked Nick. He was smiling, trying not to sound aggressive.

'We just hang with each other, share stuff. Go out. You know what I mean?'

'Okay. Well . . .' Nick looked at his watch.

'Dad!' said Barney. 'It's all right. I'll walk home with Sutupa.'

'Don't have to,' she said.

' 'S all right,' said Barney.

'No one dare touch me, you know what I'm saying.'

'Street Sistas protect you, is that it?' said Nick.

'Better believe it,' said Sutupa. She stood up and pulled on the black quilted bomber jacket she had been carrying.

'Way to go, girl,' said Nick, trying to sound like Corville and failing slightly.

Sutupa and Barney sloped out of the flat and Nick started clearing up. Something about the girl had cheered him up. She was young and street hard but somehow unfettered with the politics that had become his bread and butter. Even though she communicated in monosyllabic grunts most of the time, he found her more enjoyable to be with than Daisy. Nick had decided on the way home that he really didn't like her and wasn't going to take any more shit from her.

Although he had been back in England for a couple of months, it felt like ages since he'd had a shag. He knew it didn't really matter but he missed the closeness. The parting from Tiffany had been very confusing. He'd never had a love affair that just naturally fizzled out before – no tears, no recriminations, equal levels of guilt on both sides, with plenty of reassurance that this wasn't necessary. Parting, in Nick's experience, had usually been due to a row, or he'd had a huge desire to get away and had made crap excuses. Something had happened with him and Tiffany which he decided must be very rare in anyone's life. They had both changed at the same time. When they had first met, they had both been lost – he escaping from his life in England, working in a meat-market bar in San Francisco, she escaping from her mother and doing the worst thing she could possibly do, working as a stripper in the Crazy Horse.

When they met a second time, although nothing on the surface had changed that much, they had both resolved whatever it was that was driving them crazy. Nick had found something to do at last; Tiffany accepted that she was a bright woman and that trading on her body was going to lead nowhere.

After getting over jet-lag, seriously short of money, Nick had spent three nights back on his old stamping ground outside Trash. It was fun for about ten minutes, the same old crowd outside the door: Farson, the black guy with shoulders wider than a fire escape door, and Mickey, with an arse wider than a street. Nothing had changed. They spent the night, every night, passing dumb-ass comments on the people they let into the club, every phrase containing an offensive or politically incorrect idea. At one time Nick would have found this amusing and would have joined in – maybe a little half-heartedly, but it passed the time. Now he just found it tedious and annoying, and he started to see the young women who almost fell into the club as potential victims of the violent, lustful appetites of his colleagues.

'Look at the arse on that slag,' said Mickey within minutes of greeting Nick. 'She deserves a good shagging, mate, I'll tell you.'

'Why d'you say that?' asked Nick. Mickey looked at him over the heads of some excited teenagers whom he passed through the cordon.

'What you on, Nicky, mate?' he asked, genuinely confused.

'I just wondered why you thought she deserved it?' asked Nick. He tried to smile.

' 'Cos she's a slag, you cunt. That's why. What better reason d'you want?' said Mickey, always on the edge of aggression.

'Fair enough,' said Nick.

'What happened to you in the States, Nicky boy? Them lezzos cut your balls off or what?' For some reason Mickey found this very amusing and laughed out loud as he looked through a teenage girl's bag. He pulled out a packet of condoms and waved them in the air. 'What you got these for, darlin'? You on the game?'

The girl looked shocked and disturbed.

'How much for a quickie out the back, eh?' Mickey laughed again and pushed the horrified girl through the door without listening to her complaints.

'Has he always been like that?' Nick asked Farson when Mickey went into the club for a break.

'Worse than that usually, guy,' said Farson, who was at the opposite end of the fun scale to Corville. With Farson everything was serious and heavy – he was married and had two kids, he was very into responsibility and Christianity, and thought the people who went into the club were beneath contempt.

'Mickey's got no respect for anyone, guy,' said Farson. 'What d'you expect? He's got no beliefs, he's got no morals, he's basically an animal in a suit, you know what I'm saying?'

Now Farson laughed, but it was a dry, dead laugh. Nick felt very depressed – the pleasure of the male company he had enjoyed in San Francisco had brought the misery of his old occupation into stark relief. He made weak excuses about not turning up but eventually the guilt got the better of him. For all his chain-smoking offensiveness, Frankie Jessop had been good to Nick over the years.

'I can't cut it any more, Frankie,' Nick said to his old boss one lunch-time. He had asked to have a meeting with Frankie. Frankie told him not to be a wanker, any of his boys could see him whenever they wanted. They were sitting in the Roma coffee bar just off Tottenham Court Road, directly under the offices of All Areas Security.

'I'll go mad if I have to stand outside that doorway with Mickey,' said Nick. 'I tell you, he needs help Frankie. He's sick.'

'I know it, Nicky boy,' said Frankie, dragging on his cigarette and coughing heartily. 'But he's been working that door longer than anyone. I can't just drop him, you know that.'

'Yeah.'

'What happened to you in America, then? You look different, mate.'

'Oh, did a self-defence course, mate.'

'Fucking hell, what you want to do that for? You're well hard already, aren't ya?'

'No, it's for women.'

'What you on?' asked Frankie, stubbing out a cigarette and lighting up another.

'It's a self-defence system for women.'

'What you want to do it for, then, you big poof?' laughed Frankie. Nick noticed his long yellow teeth. Frankie Jessop really was an extremely ugly human being, but still, for some reason, very likable.

'No, it's like a system for teaching women to look after themselves,' said Nick. This was the first time he'd tried to explain what he'd been doing in San Francisco. 'They get to actually spar with a bloke, yours truly, and I wear an impact suit, like a big padded suit so the women can punch and kick without me getting injured.'

'Fucking hell,' said Frankie, his bacon sandwich half chewed in his aghast mouth.

'So they get to experience what it's actually like in a real fight. They don't punch the air, they punch me. It's really effective. You know, there are over six hundred police-verified cases of women who knocked out their assailants within the first five seconds of the assault taking place. And you should see the way the women change during a course. Some of them start out like total fucking wrecks – they can barely stand, they cry and shake when I go for them. I say the most evil stuff to them, shit even you wouldn't say, Frankie, and let's face it, that's going some. And after a few hours' coaching, they really fight hard. They'd give anyone we know a run for his money in a real rumble, you know what I'm saying? It's really effective.'

'Fucking hell, mate,' said Frankie, washing down the half-chewed sandwich with a massive swig of heavily sugared tea. 'The bitches are bad enough as it is, no need to go round encouraging them.'

'Oh, come on, Frankie,' said Nick. 'It's not like you get beat up by women every day of the week.'

'It's all the same, mate. Fucking women's libbers are taking over the shop. Look at the fat-slag security lezzos.'

'The Very Wide Women?' asked Nick.

'Cunts, mate, very wide cunts. They've taken over half the gigs in town. They don't need protecting from blokes, mate, they'd fucking chew you up for breakfast, Jesus, Nicky boy. I had no idea you'd gone over to the other side.'

'I haven't,' said Nick. 'What you on, Frankie?'

'I've had it to here with ladies,' said Frankie. 'They're always moaning about being hard done by while they're busy taking over the joint. Makes me pig sick, mate, all these lezzos and sour-faced women's libbers. And you've been over there in America getting the shit beaten out of you 'cos I s'pose one of them flashed a bit of pussy at you and you was finished.'

'No way, mate,' said Nick, knowing that in Frankie's eyes a lesbian meant an ugly woman who couldn't get a bloke, not, as Nick had seen, some seriously attractive women who just weren't interested in men. 'It's just not like that, mate. I wish I could explain.'

'You'll never explain it to me, mate,' said Frankie bitterly. 'I've seen too much.'

Nick couldn't give up. 'Look, the women I've helped teach are just, like, ordinary women, some well tasty, some you wouldn't look at, but, you know, just normal. They're not all lezzos or feminists, they're just scared of being raped, and some of them have like actually been raped and they don't want it to happen again.'

'Oh yeah, they've always been raped, haven't they. That's the threat they hang over your head. One wrong move and they shout rape and that's it, you're banged up for eight years with nothing to shag but pretty boys.'

Nick cast his mind back, trying to remember what Frankie had done time for. He had assumed it was some financial crime, a bank robbery or raiding a cigarette warehouse, not rape. He didn't feel like enquiring.

'I done time with a lot of blokes who were accused of rape, and I'll tell you something for nothing, Nicky boy, three-quarters of the poor fuckers had never done nothing wrong. Just some vicious bitch of a wife or secretary, or some old slapper of a barmaid who'd decided to have a go at them if they stepped off the straight and narrow. It's that simple, it's her word against his. That's why I never have anything to do with the ladies any more, Nicky. Never touch 'em, mate.'

I bet you're flooded with offers, thought Nick as he watched Frankie raise one buttock cheek off the red plastic stool he was sitting on and let rip a noisy fart.

'I dunno what to say to you, Nicky boy. You know I respect

your work. There's plenty out there if you want it, odd days here and there, and if you done that bodyguard course like you kept promising I could get you some serious money, looking after Arab geezers, getting some snatch for them when they want it. It's a pot of fucking gold, mate, believe me. Shit to work for but rolling in money, Arabs, you know what I'm saying?'

'Well, it's good to know, Frankie, but it looks like this self-defence thing is really taking off. We're teaching it just around the corner.'

'Where's that, then?' asked Frankie, now tucking into a bowl of suet pudding and custard and barely paying Nick any attention.

'Over Holborn way, in some old school that's been converted to sort of studios and that,' said Nick. He could see that Frankie wasn't interested. Whatever it was that made Nick excited about Winning Strategy had failed to ignite the mountain of a man he was sitting next to.

He finally bade farewell to the man who had employed him for over eight years. He walked back out on to the street and took in a lungful of fresh London air. It was still good to be back. He loved America, he loved San Francisco, he probably even loved Tiffany a bit, although that had gone decidedly pear-shaped in the weeks before he left, but London was where he lived.

He shouldered his enormous bag and headed back to the training room. Their first course was over-subscribed to a huge degree. Four women journalists had booked, all writing articles for glossy magazines. There was talk of a TV news crew coming to record what was going on. It was exciting, and Nick had failed to communicate this to Frankie. But then he was talking to an old lag, a bitter, fat old man who hated women, so Nick accepted that it wasn't altogether surprising. However, he had an evangelist's depression – he couldn't believe that someone wouldn't catch on when he spoke about what he'd been doing.

'Hey, Nick, how are you doing?' asked Tara when he entered the room.

'Okay,' said Nick. 'Where's Daisy?'

'She's gone for something to eat. Can we talk?' asked Tara.

'Uh-oh. Can we talk. Sounds very Californian. Of course we can, we talk all the time.'

'Okay, well, I'm kind of concerned about Daisy.'

'Me too,' said Nick with a feeling of relief. He wasn't the only one who had noticed after all.

'No, I mean, I'm kind of worried about you and her. She feels very intimidated by you, which is not good.'

'Oh, right. Does she.' Nick felt slightly angry. He knew he only had to stand up for Daisy to feel intimidated – she was a wimp. 'Well, what can I do?'

'Good call, Nick. I guess you can help her a little more. She's good, Nick, really she is, and if you two guys are going to work together when I'm not here, it's got to gel between you, there's got to be immense trust.'

'Wait a minute. What d'you mean we're going to work together?' said Nick, genuinely alarmed.

'Eventually, I mean. I can't stay here.'

'Why not?' said Nick, already realising he was being stupid, but he'd never considered doing this job without Tara at the head of the class. The whole picture started to change.

'I'm just here to help get things running. That's what Daisy and Yolanda are here for.'

Yolanda was some woman from Brighton Nick had met twice who was sending out leaflets and taking phone calls in the tiny office at the top of the building.

'They'll take over completely when I go back to the States,' said Tara.

'Fucking Ada,' said Nick.

'I wish you wouldn't say that,' said Tara.

'Sorry. But I like working with you. I've always worked with you. I never even thought about working with anyone else. I don't know if I can. I just assumed I'd work with you and that was it.'

'You don't like to spend a lot of time thinking about stuff, do you, Nick?' said Tara with a smile.

'I dunno, but I never thought about this,' he said. 'But you're right. I think Daisy's too . . . well, she's not strong enough to take a class. She's not like you. People listen to you when you talk. It's really hard to listen to Daisy, she's got such a little voice.'

'Which is why she needs your help.'

'What can I do, for God's sake? I'm just the punchbag, aren't I? Not allowed to say anything.'

'Of course you are. You do speak in class, Nick, don't go childish on me.'

'Sorry, but you know, if I start suggesting things, it's going to look like I'm taking over. That's the trouble with Daisy – she's got no initiative. No drive. She's not driven, not like you, Tara. I mean, you are totally driven, which is what galvanises people around you.'

'Nick, I know Daisy can do it. I've seen her. She just needs a bit of patience and support, and maybe you not yawning when she talks.'

'Did I do that?'

'You did.'

'Shit. Sorry,' said Nick. It was true that Daisy had a soporific effect on him, but he knew that yawning while she was talking must have seemed pretty mean.

'Okay. I'll do my best. But I'm really thrown by all this. Why did I think you were going to live here?' asked Nick.

'I have no idea,' said Tara with a grin. Nick stared at her, feeling like her lover and knowing that at the same time he never would be. He did love her, however; he'd fallen completely in love with her and now she was leaving.

'I'm gutted,' he said.

'That's sweet,' said Tara. They embraced momentarily, a professional therapeutic embrace, Nick realised, when he noticed that Tara kept her groin well away from his, but an embrace nonetheless.

'D'you want me to talk to Daisy, then?' he asked after they broke the embrace. He felt embarrassed and wanted to sound casual.

'No, it's okay, I'll deal with it,' said Tara, and she walked to the other end of the room and stretched her calves by leaning against the wall.

It hadn't been brutally done, but it had been firm. Nick had always felt carefully excluded from the organisation and time-tabling arrangements of the course. He didn't mind, but occasionally he would have liked to have been consulted. He'd thought about this situation a little – every now and then, when he caught the 14A bus back up the Caledonian Road, he would 'mull it all over' as he sat on the top deck. It was a woman's thing, it was their gig and he didn't have a say in it. Tara was totally in control. That was okay; in the end it enabled him to have a good time, to do good work in the class and to let them have the headache of arranging the whole thing.

'So what time d'you want me here on Saturday?' he asked as he lifted the giant bag.

'Ten okay? We'll do a warm-up and a pre-class group.'

'Sure,' said Nick. 'Well, I'm off down the gym. See you, then.'

'Okay,' said Tara. She walked across the mat and embraced him again. 'I'm so proud of you, Nick. Really,' she said, her mouth close to his ear. This time he found the embrace acutely sexual. He fancied Tara regardless of whether she fancied him. He didn't want her to go back to America and the brainy Adrian, he wanted her to stay with him in England, for them to teach together and maybe, one day, after a long, long time, be together.

No, it would never happen. He embraced her strongly, feeling the slender power in her back.

'I'm really glad I met you,' he said. 'Even though you keep me out, you've given me something to live for.'

He held her for a while as what he'd just said seemed to fly around the room and come back to his ear.

'Fucking hell. Did I just say that?' he exploded. 'What have you done to me, Tara Kennedy? Jesus H. I'd better get a pair of sandals and start eating fucking lentils.'

'No danger of that, Nick,' said Tara. He picked up his bag and ran for the door.

'I'm going to get a burger, buy the *Sun* and go down the pub and get completely pissed.'

'See you Saturday,' said Tara.

Chapter Twenty-Seven

'Hi. My name is Tara Kennedy and I just want to say I am really excited about this class. It's the first Winning Strategy class to be held in this country and I don't think it's going to be the last.'

Tara explained the process of the class and then told her story: Brazil, a hot Saturday night, insects everywhere, cockroaches, flies, bugs of all shapes and sizes. No streetlamps. Even now, after hundreds of repetitions, it hadn't become merely an anecdote. Although she rarely thought about the event from one month to the next, the telling of the story could still bring up strong emotion.

She looked around the room — the same collection of ashen faces, the looks of shock and bewilderment as they heard her tale. This was a more mixed crowd in terms of race than she would have expected back home, but other than that, pretty much as anticipated. She passed the tissue box to Nick.

He said his piece, rehearsed and a bit stiff, but he was looking around the women as he spoke. His face looked open, his hands clasped gently on his lap. He passed the tissue box to Daisy.

Daisy was thirty-two. She had a four-year-old son and no history of sexual assault. She was a lifelong feminist and had been involved in many campaigns in England. She had worked at a rape crisis centre for two years, which made her very aware of the scale of the problem. She was training to be an instructor like

Tara, and was really convinced that the system they were teaching was ground-breaking.

The tissue box was passed to a dark-haired woman in a pair of yellow jogging pants and a red T-shirt.

'Hello. My name is Jenny and I'm forty. I've never been raped, but I know what it's all about.'

'I'm Jane. I'm twenty-seven. My best friend committed suicide two years after she was raped by a stranger in her flat. The bloke's never been caught and I want to be ready for him if I ever meet him.'

'I'm Carol. I'm thirty-seven. I've got two kids. My husband left me and before he left me he beat me regularly. Everyone thinks that wife-beaters are working-class but my husband is a corporate lawyer. He never raped me, as far as I can tell, although sometimes it felt like it.'

'I'm Zena. I'm twenty-four. I'm, um, I don't know what to say. I was raped. I don't know how to talk about it. I don't think I can fight but I don't know what else to do. I am so scared all the time, of everyone. It would be nice to be not scared. I dream about that. I think I do trust the man, I don't think anyone would be here or let him in if they didn't know what he was like. Oh, yes. I was given a venereal disease when I was raped which I didn't do anything about for too long. I felt it was my fault, but by the time I went to the doctor's it was too late and it's made me infertile.'

'My name's Grace and I'm forty-three. I've never been raped, but I had a man wank himself in front of me on the train once, but, well, that made me laugh because his penis was really small.'

'Hi, I'm Maria. My dad raped me when I was a little girl. Well, I was eleven. He killed himself later on. When I was eighteen. I'm sort of over that, but I have a little girl of my own now and I'm so scared for her. I want to know if it's possible to really fight back. I want to know what it feels like to really punch someone, or whatever it is we're going to learn. I want to be able to do it but I don't think I can. I feel so weak and I look at the man – sorry, it's Nick, isn't it, I can see your badge now – and I look at how strong he is. I mean, blimey, how am I going to fight that? So it'll be interesting.'

'Um, my name's Dana. I'm thirty-one. I've never, you know, I don't have a history. I was mugged and had my bag stolen, and I've been threatened with assault more times than I can remember. I don't want to hurt anyone else but I'd love to know how to stop them hurting me. I'm always scared and I don't think this is going to work. I'm too fat to fight, basically. That's what I feel.'

'I'm Joan and you're not too fat, Dana. Sorry, couldn't help saying that. You look gorgeous. I'm Joan, as I said, and I've never been assaulted and I feel really lucky. I know all the statistics and I've talked about it with my friends. I don't hate men. Most of the men I work with are great, really great people, and I think what the man is doing here is amazing, really. So I'm really happy to be here, a little apprehensive but, you know. It's good.'

'My name's Deirdre. I'm fifty-eight and I'm married and I've got three children and a grandchild on the way. I feel a bit old to be here. I've never been raped. I've got a rather bad back so I'm very worried about rolling about on the floor with a big man. Sorry. You know what I mean.'

'I'm Robyn. I'm nineteen. I'm a student and I'm really scared about being here, but when I heard about it I knew I had to come. I've been threatened with rape once, but I was lucky and got away in time. I kind of do hate men. Although I'm het, it's very hard not to hate them as a group, you know?'

'Oh God. You're all so amazing. I'm just Hilary. I'm thirty something. A bit dull, no kids, boring job, never been raped. My husband is a wimp but quite sweet. I can't believe I just said never been raped like you'd say never been kissed. I hope you know what I mean. That's it, really.'

'I'm Carly. I'm twenty-one. I've been raped loads but that comes with the job. I'm a sex worker, a prostitute. I work in massage parlours down here and on the streets in Manchester. I'm from Macclesfield, as you can probably tell. Um, me dad raped me first when I was ten, then a load of lads from the estate when I was thirteen, so I started charging for it. Basically. I think all men are complete cunts, to be honest. I certainly don't trust him. I can tell, believe me, they are all the same. Bastards. The idea of being able to beat the living shite out of one of them is dead good, so as soon as I heard about this I was well excited. I tell you, most prozzies would die to get on this course. We are that stuffed with being set on by bastard men. I tell you, the fucking tide's gonna turn. I fucking hate men and I spend all me working life underneath the bastards. There's irony for you. Sorry, I swear a lot, but it comes with the fucking job. There you go, lass.'

'Oh, I don't know how to follow that. I'm Linda, I'm thirty-three. I'm a writer and journalist. I don't really hate men, but I suppose I see a more acceptable side to them. I'm very interested to see if I can actually fight. I have three brothers so I spent a lot of my childhood fighting for survival, but I've never been in a serious fight. I don't have a history of sexual assault.'

'My name is Alice. I don't know if I can talk about things the way everyone else seems to. My life has taken a slight turn for the worse since it happened, so I suppose it was. A rape, I mean. I can't talk about it. I'm kind of numb inside and I suppose I am hoping that doing something like this will help burn out the numbness. I don't hold out much hope, though. I'm really grateful to Tara for letting me join the group.'

The tissue box was passed back to Tara.

'Thank you, everyone,' she said. 'You know, one of the things people warned me about, before I came to England, was how reserved everyone was here. When we hold an opening circle in America, pretty much everyone is open about their lives. We're used to talking about stuff. You've seen Oprah Winfrey, you know what we're like. And people said, oh, the English, they're so reserved and polite, they'll never tell you anything. Well, thankfully, what a load of old bollocks.' A big laugh swept through the room. Tara smiled. 'I just want to thank you for being so honest and for feeling safe here. This is what is so good about what we do. You are safe here. Safe to fail, to learn and to help each other. Okay. Let's do it!'

After a twenty-minute warm-up Tara could see that the group was ready. Nick entered the room in his suit. She noticed the journalists looking at him very carefully. Some of the women moved to the far side of the room to keep away from him.

'Okay, Nick is back, and, as you can see, he looks a little different. You may have seen pictures already but I know it's not the same when you see it for real. He is wearing what is known as an impact suit. Let me show you what this means. Nick, if you please.'

Nick stood directly behind Tara.

'I'm going to use my elbow to punch Nick in the stomach. If I did this against any of you, you'd have to go to hospital — broken ribs, ruptured spleen, liver damage, any number of injuries. This is why he wears such elaborate protection. Watch this.'

Tara slammed her elbow suddenly into Nick's suit. Although he stepped back to regain his balance he stood behind her, smiling.

'And if you don't believe that, watch this.'

Tara turned to face him. This time she landed her knee in his crotch, lifting him off the ground by four or five inches. Again Nick kept smiling.

'Now, the only person in this room who can tell us how much that would hurt is Nick.'

'It would hurt so much I wouldn't be standing again in under two hours, and then only to hobble to a hospital to have my ruptures seen to.'

'And how do you feel now?' asked Tara.

'A little warm but very comfortable, thank you,' said Nick.

Many of the women laughed. Some looked as if they were going to be sick. Tara pressed on.

'Now, Nick, if you'd put your helmet on.'

Some women sniggered as Nick slipped the giant, almost comic helmet into position.

'As you can see, Nick's face is almost completely invisible inside there. He can see and hear you, you can hear him, and this is the most important rule. When his helmet is on, he's an assailant here to attack you. When it's off, he's Nick Gardener and he's here to help you. Okay. What I am trying to show you is that if you follow what we say, you won't hurt Nick. I don't want him hurt because he's a very valuable asset for what we do. That's why he is so heavily protected. You can hit Nick as hard as you possibly can and he won't be injured. That's what you're here for. Okay.'

Tara and Daisy organised the class, explaining that they didn't want any of the students sitting down between fights, they wanted to keep the energy up. Nick gingerly went through the first exercise with Jenny.

'Do you have any injuries?' asked Tara, standing in front of her and holding her attention one hundred per cent.

'No,' said Jenny.

'Have you had any martial arts experience?' asked Tara. She knew already who did have this experience, but it was a ritual at the start of a fight.

'No,' said Jenny. Tara looked over her shoulder towards Nick. 'No martial arts experience, no injuries. Jenny is ready.'

She watched as Jenny's polite English face folded in terror as she felt Nick's powerful arms encircle her. She froze, looking at Tara for support.

'Remember what I explained. Hands up, breathe. No!'

'No,' said Jenny rather politely.

'Louder. Shake the walls,' said Tara with a smile.

The 'no' came; it was always there. Jenny had started breathing. 'No!' she screamed, her face now burning with concentration. She had found the fight, the fight that was in all women. Sometimes buried deeply but always there.

'Find your target,' said Tara. Jenny looked down, raised her foot and stamped. She hit Nick's padded foot with her toe, stretching her tendons dangerously as her heel went towards the floor.

'Make sure you hit with the heel, like I showed you.'

The second blow found its mark. Nick pulled back a little.

'Great. Now reverse elbow-punch,' said Tara. Jenny managed this a little better. Nick folded obediently.

'Heel palm,' said Tara, always staying right at her student's side. Jenny missed his head altogether the first time – something the size of a dustbin and she missed. It often amazed Tara how it was possible.

'Focus, find the target, don't just lash out.'

The second blow hit well enough.

'Knee to the groin,' said Tara; Nick was already in a convenient legs-spread position. The first exercises were done one move at a time; there was barely any attempt to simulate a real attack. Jenny's knee found its target with stunning power and accuracy. A cheer went up from the other women. Nick folded on to the floor. He knelt with his head drooped conveniently in the way for Jenny's knee.

'Knee to the head!' shouted Tara. Jenny's knee slammed into the padded helmet. Nick was over, on his back in the unconscious posture. Jenny jumped up and down in delight.

'Wait, you're not finished,' shouted Tara above the excitement.

'Sorry, sorry,' said Jenny. She adopted the posture as best she could, looking around the room. 'Look. Assess. No!' she said, and ran off the mat.

'And now what?' asked Tara.

'Dial nine nine nine!' shouted fourteen women at once. Nick sprang to his feet and took up his opening position. After nearly two years of planning, thousands of phone calls, letters, e-mails, faxes, explanations and presentations, the first woman in England had just knocked out the first padded assailant. Tara tried her best to savour the moment, but already the second student was walking on to the dusty surface of the blue mat.

Chapter Twenty-Eight

Alice felt nauseous as she watched the big, grey-clad creature walk up behind the other women in the class. When everyone had gone to join the line as the class started, she had hung back in order to be last. It reminded her of nothing more than gymnastics at her old school, an activity she hated with a vengeance.

She had never made any connection between what had happened to her and the concept of self-defence before her initial visit to assess the padded assailant. She had never considered it was necessary to defend herself because no one had ever threatened her. Even Peter didn't threaten her; he just did what he did in such a matter-of-fact way he didn't need to threaten.

Now she was about to stand on a mat with this huge, violent man who was going to grab her. In front of her was this strange woman, Tara. Incredible woman, that was all Alice thought as she had listened to her story of the rape in Brazil. To survive that, God knows what horror she went through.

When Tara explained that she always held a place free in classes for special cases, Alice fell for it. She was aware enough to wonder if this was a clever sales pitch, but she had found out from conversations before the class started that there was indeed a sizable waiting list.

She had spent the entire day with Tara and Daisy. She had missed her flight to Scotland and never spent the bright summer night on the oil rig. She had rung in sick, the first time she had missed a day's work in eight years. She spent the time in bed, watching trash TV and trying to eat something. She failed, and now, standing in the queue, getting gradually nearer the front, she felt weak.

Far sooner than she wished she was next up. The woman in front of her, a very big black lady, took quite some time to punch the grey creature. She ran to the side and called out 'Nine nine nine'. Alice reminded herself that she needed to do this, if she ever got that far.

'Okay, Alice,' said Tara, holding a welcoming arm out towards her. She was like a swimming teacher. It was as if she were saying, 'There's nothing to be afraid of, you'll only drown if it goes wrong'.

'Okay, Alice,' she said again when Alice stood before her, shaking. 'Have you got any injuries?'

'Only to my head,' said Alice with a nervous laugh.

'Oh, okay,' said Tara, her face very serious. Alice saw at once that the silly joke was inappropriate. 'Sorry. I have no injuries.'

'Any martial arts training?'

'No,' said Alice.

'No injuries, no martial arts training. Alice is ready,' said Tara.

Alice could feel the shadow behind her; her back tingled in expectation. It was terrifying. Before she felt the man she jumped forward with a scream. She tried to laugh to cover it up, but the laugh was already a cry.

'I'm sorry, I'm sorry,' she sobbed.

'It's okay,' said Tara, no criticism apparent. 'Take your time. We'll go again.'

Alice looked down as the two huge arms engulfed her. She felt herself arch automatically as the man's body came into contact with her. It was as if the merest brushing against him would cause injury. He felt like pain. He gripped her, his huge muscles completely in control. She felt herself shake against him; there was nothing she could do. Everything was swimming through her mind at once, including, she found to her amazement, a strong sexual urge. She hadn't had any contact with a man since Peter. She could sense the size and strength of this body behind her, and yet it was too terrible.

'Okay, Alice, breathe. Shout no.'

'I can't,' she muttered after a moment.

'You can, I've heard you. The way out is through, Alice. I know you can do it. Shout no. Come on, breathe in.'

The man didn't loosen his grip. She could hear him breathing; it really was someone actually holding her. What could he have been thinking? Could he feel her shake? It was all so embarrassing. But did he actually want to hurt her? How could something as nice as sex also be so horrible? She didn't want him there, this ugly great insect man.

'No,' she said.

'Mean it. Tell him this has to stop, Alice. No! Come on.'

She breathed in. Terror, pain, self-pity, the anger on Peter's face. It wasn't fair, she didn't ask for that, it was wrong. Wrong.

'No!' she screamed. 'No!'

'Great. Now find your target,' said Tara, her face only inches from Alice's. Alice looked down and there, conveniently in her line of sight, was the clown-like grey shoe of the monster. She stamped. She stamped on a man's foot for the first time. She could feel the impact – she had hurt him! He pulled his foot back, his grip weakened. She yanked his arm up as she'd been shown. She could feel him resist; she felt so weak, so useless. She tried again, pulled his arm up, felt the hairs on his arm against her lips. It was all too much. The room started to sway.

'Bite,' said Tara. 'Remember, don't really bite, just shout bite.'

'Bite,' she said as loud as she could. She looked at his arm and imagined actually biting it, really hard, drawing blood. She really could hurt him – his arm was only a hair's breadth away. She wanted this to be over, but then that was what she had felt when Peter was smashing her head against the door of his Ford Mondeo. She wanted it to be over, she knew it soon would be, and it was, and now she was here, with another man forcing himself on her.

'Bite!' she screamed. He pulled his arm away, and before Alice could think she had smashed her elbow into him. She wanted him away; she felt him move, this big, ugly devil. She turned, as she'd seen Tara and thirteen women do before, her hands up in front of her face, looking at him. He towered over her, huge and threatening.

'No!' she screamed, and poked at his huge insect eyes with her stiffened fingers. His head jerked back. She'd hurt him, she'd managed to inflict pain on him. He was Peter – she could see Peter's stupid, ugly, handsome face. Her little fingers in his eyes, to tell him. No! She could see his face, creased up in pain. Listen. No! The man was standing with his legs apart. She lifted her leg and tried to knee him there. She couldn't seem to reach. He was so much taller.

'Try again,' said Tara, who was somehow still right by her side. 'Aim for the very back of his body, the shoulder blades, that's where you're aiming for.'

Again she lifted her leg. She made contact, her lower thigh thumped into the man, she heard the breath leave his body. He fell to the ground. She felt something lift, a weight or a shadow, as she watched the figure crumple before her. She had smashed Peter's large testicles. Those prized organs, so carefully pro-tected, so loved by her at times, held in her hands so gently. No, not this time, this time he was wrong. This time she said no and he was going to stop.

'Now the head,' said Tara, softly, right beside her. 'Aim for the back of his head. The blow needs to go through his head. Full impact.'

Alice took one step back as she'd been shown and then

landed her knee in the man's great grey head with all the force she could manage. As she felt the impact on her knee she realised it was quite something. She might be weak, but she could still walk — her legs were strong enough to hold her up, they were strong enough to do damage.

She felt it and it was true. The man lay down with his hands up beside his head. She had knocked him out. She had been in a fight with a man and she had won. She knew they had all cheated, she knew the man had stood in the right position to allow her to hit him, she knew Tara had been by her side through the whole experience, but she had done it with her body and she could feel it. She didn't know it, she could feel it physically.

'Look. Assess. No!' shouted Alice, a smile emerging on to her face. She ran to the side of the mat, feeling light. She looked at the smiling, cheering faces of the other women, who were all clapping. They had all been watching and she had not been aware of them for a second. She had done it.

'Who you gonna call?' shouted Tara. Alice wanted to say her mum, but she stood frozen, trying to remember.

'Nine nine nine!' shouted all the rest of the class.

'Oh yes, sorry, call nine nine nine,' said Alice. Then she fell over.

Chapter Twenty-Nine

'That was amazing. Really. I never thought we'd do it,' said Daisy. 'I feel so high after that. After all the hassle we've been through to start up. Brilliant.'

Nick noticed he was nodding; he was doing that nodding thing because he wanted Daisy to know he felt the same way. He'd managed to have a quick shower before the closing circle. He and Tara had stood embracing in the middle of the mat for what seemed like ages while Daisy swept the floor.

They sat in a tight circle in the centre of the mat – Daisy, Tara, Nick and a journalist called Frances who had been sitting on the sidelines as an observer. Tara and Daisy had explained to him that they were only allowing two journalists into the class. One to participate, whom they therefore couldn't talk to outside the class, and one as an observer.

The class had gone much faster than he thought. It was hard work but nothing he couldn't handle. The closing circle of the group had been an amazing turnaround; even Carly the prostitute thought that Nick was pretty amazing.

His whole body glowed with good feeling. It was like the best work-out he'd ever had at the gym combined with an immense sense of wellbeing about himself. At last he felt as if he'd done something that was actually useful.

'I feel absolutely brilliant,' he said. 'I don't know what else to say. That's it. We've started. All I can see in the future is millions of classes like this and it's brilliant. I even get paid. I can't believe my luck.' He flopped backwards, laughing.

Tara laughed and touched his arm affectionately. He didn't even mind that – it was a bit naff and New Agey, but he felt she meant well by it.

'And Daisy,' said Nick as he sat back up again. 'You did really well, your session worked great, it was good to work with you and we're going to make a kicking team.'

He looked at Daisy in a completely new light. Everything glowed, everything was good.

Daisy spoke of how she had enjoyed the class and how much she had learned, and that she thought Nick was amazing and did really well. She poured praise on Tara and commented on her boundless energy. She was really keen to go back to San Francisco and complete her instructor's course.

Tara said she was pretty bushed but elated that the class had gone so well. She predicted problems with certain students, but nothing insurmountable. They went through the students one by one. Nick remembered them all, including Dana, the huge black woman who didn't think she could fight – her blow had knocked him halfway across the room.

'Zena is a bit of a problem,' he said. 'She's not really making contact. There were a couple of blows she gave me I really couldn't register.'

'I know, she's very weak. She's got no drive, poor kid,' said Tara. 'I've talked to her a little, told her she really needs to eat a lot the day before she comes.'

'What about Alice?' asked Daisy.

'Oh, wow, did you see the way she dropped at the end?' said Tara. 'I don't think I've ever seen that happen.'

'She was okay, though?' asked Nick.

'Yeah, she was fine. She had a drink and she seemed a bit woozy, but a hell of a lot happier than when she came in.'

'She was good,' said Nick. 'If anything, I would say she was the most frightened. She was really shaking when I first held her.'

Tara nodded. Nick smiled to himself. He didn't mind the nodding any more. He also knew that the closing circle wasn't the place in which to express his desires, to tell the class that he fancied Alice something rotten. He wasn't having a problem working with her – the helmet seemed to act as a foolproof system for excluding those sorts of thoughts. When he assaulted her it was just the same as with anyone else. When he took the helmet off it was hard not to keep looking at her. Her dishevelled appearance, her strangely attractive fingers were fascinating to him.

'And the closing circle was such an amazing turnaround,' said Daisy. 'I'd seen it in America, but I thought it'd be so cynical here. I thought everyone would be sneering and saying it didn't really work, even then.'

Tara was nodding again, her evangelism undented. 'Sure, but they can feel it. Their bodies were telling them this shit is for real. And they all liked you, Nick,' she said, turning to him. 'Boy, the look in their eyes. Deal with that, old feller.'

'I'll do my best,' said Nick. It was true – one by one they had all said thanks to him for being there and for being so patient and strong and kind to them. He had hoped Alice would be a little more expressive, but she only mentioned him in passing.

They finally said farewell amidst a flurry of arrangements and promised phone calls. He humped his heavy bag down the stairs and walked along the street alone. As he waited for the 14A bus on Tottenham Court Road, Frances the journalist suddenly joined him. He had said goodbye to her outside the building on Cheyne Street, but she must have followed him.

'Hi, Nick,' she said nervously. 'Is it possible for you to, well, join me for a coffee or something?' He smiled at her, not believing what was happening. 'There's a couple of questions I'd like to ask,' she added.

He looked into her eyes. She was young, red-haired and

slightly strange-looking. Not an immediate beauty, but there was something attractive – the eyes maybe. He checked his watch, as if he had anything else to do. He agreed and they went to Cranks vegetarian coffee bar, a far cry from his previous lunch with Frankie Jessop in the greasy spoon around the corner.

Frances bought him a coffee and sat in front of him with her notebook and tape machine.

'Thank you so much for your time,' she said. 'I think it's amazing. What you do. It looks so painful. You must be very fit.'

Nick nodded. He hadn't been sure before but now he could sense she was coming on to him. It was unbelievable – so soon, and from someone who hadn't even actually done a class, just watched one.

'How did you get into it? Did you have a friend who was raped or something?'

'No, nothing like that,' he said.

'I'm looking for an angle,' said Frances, her flame-red hair in a curly mass on top of her head. He'd never slept with a redhead before. He put that thought out of his mind, although of course, strictly speaking, she wasn't a student. 'I just don't understand what would attract you to it in the first place.'

'Well, nor do I really,' said Nick. 'But my life wasn't going anywhere before, and you know, it feels like I'm doing some good with this. That's a new feeling for me.'

'And what, you were in a men's group or something?'

'Come again?'

'Oh, I thought I heard that you were in some sort of men's group thing.'

'No. Bloody hell,' said Nick. 'No, I've never done anything like that. I worked with a few other blokes in the States, but it wasn't a men's group. No, Tara saw me sort out a rumble and asked me to go to America with her. I love going to America, thought I was getting a job there, ended up back in bloody London, so there you go.'

'Amazing,' said Frances. 'And can I ask about your personal life? Are you married?'

'No, not in the least.'

'Oh, right. Are you heterosexual?'

'Bloody hell. 'Course. What d'you think?'

'Oh, okay. So you're also a single, straight man. That's amazing.'

'Why's that?' asked Nick, a smile all over his face.

'Oh God, I'm going to regret saying this I'm sure, but you are incredibly attractive,' said Frances, a small flush appearing on her face.

'That's very kind of you,' said Nick. He didn't know what else to say. He had already run through five different scenarios connected with sex, sofas, the surf on a tropical beach, a white miniskirt, her legs wrapped around his head. Normal run-of-the-mill stuff.

'I know what the teacher said about no socialising, but this is professional, you know. My talking to you now. I mean, I need to get something for the article. Mainly.'

She smiled at him; he smiled back and shrugged at her. This was more embarrassing and was happening earlier than he had expected. Tim had told him to expect these kind of approaches from time to time. There were no ground rules, it was up to him, but his life could quickly turn to shit if he followed his dick instead of his brain.

'I mean,' said Frances, 'I have to use the fact that I'm a journalist to my advantage sometimes, don't I?' Her eyes glistened as she stared into his. Her whole being giving him the come-on in no uncertain terms.

'Well, um, Frances, I know strictly speaking you're not a student.'

'But I want to do the course now I've seen it,' she said.

'Sure, well, you know. It's a rule we strictly adhere to, you know what I'm saying?' Nick felt himself flailing, as it would be so easy to slip between some nice linen sheets with this woman.

'You know, the classes put everyone under a lot of stress. It would be unfair on both of us to do anything to jeopardise that.'

'Would it?' she asked softly.

'Yes,' said Nick, trying to put on a sad, resigned smile. He didn't want to be cruel.

'Oh God. I never thought that if you said no, it would make you even more attractive,' she said after a moment's thought. 'Why can't all men be like you?'

It was ridiculous, Nick knew it was. As he sat on top of the 14A he smiled. All his life he'd been a bloke, someone that a few women fancied because he was the way he was, not bad-looking. He looked after himself, took care with his grooming, but he wasn't a ladies' man. Just common-or-garden cleanliness, that was how he saw it. However, he had always felt that a lot of women despised him, even if they did it discreetly. After his trip to America things had become much clearer – he understood that in so many ways he represented a threat to women. His haircut, his dress code, his boots, his aftershave. He was a large, strong, clearly lustful man. Someone who was out for a shag if he could get one. Since he had started actually assaulting women in the classes he had noticed that all women, even ones who didn't know what he did for a living, reacted to him differently. He decided it was because of some subtle change in his demeanour. His outlook had changed and therefore the person he was perceived to be had changed. More women smiled at him, not because they fancied him, but because he was a friendly face, a safe person in a sea of danger.

On the other hand he wasn't getting any. Since he had left San Francisco, with all the possibilities that were simmering away there, not even counting Tiffany, he hadn't so much as had a sniff of anything. It looked like his son was getting some; he hoped Barney was being careful. Sixteen – he could remember being sixteen, kissing Sarah Chisolme and watching as she took her top off in the little house on Wingfield Street. It was so quiet and warm, so slow and wonderful.

He just succeeded in getting off the bus before the doors closed and it left his stop. His bag was so enormous it managed to get stuck in everything. He popped into the all-night super-market opposite the bus stop to buy some milk and bog roll.

'Yo, Dad,' said Barney. Nick turned to see his son with two other kids his own age — a lanky, skinny black boy and a short, tubby Asian boy.

'This is Richy B. and Jaz,' said Barney, introducing them. The black boy shook hands, his grip loose and fluid. Jaz just nodded.

'What's going on, then, guys?' asked Nick, dropping two cans of baked beans into his basket.

'We're going to the movies,' said Barney. 'Just buying some crisps and stuff.'

'What are you seeing?' asked Nick.

'The thing with Bruce Willis.'

'And Wesley Snipes,' said Richy B. 'Kicking film.'

'What time you back?' asked Nick.

'Dunno,' said Barney.

'I'll tell you. Back by ten thirty.'

'Dad!' complained Barney.

'I mean it, man,' said Nick, hauling his basket up on to the checkout counter.

'But it's a Saturday night.'

'Exactly. That's why I want you back home,' said Nick. 'Ten thirty, Barney. Okay?'

'Okay.'

'I'm serious,' said Nick.

'Okay.'

Nick left the shop with the three lads, feeling peculiar to be noticeably shorter than one of Barney's new friends. He was still just taller than Barney, but it was only a matter of time before demands for Barney to be home on time would be irrelevant and rather sad. He'd met these lads at his new college. His GCSE results had been spectacular — he'd passed all of them without trouble. Barney's mother was beside herself that he wasn't attending a better sixth-form college, meaning one in Oxford, but it was clearly what Barney wanted. Seeing as he'd only been there a week he was pleased the kid had made friends.

He said goodbye to his son and watched for a while as the three lads walked up the tree-lined street towards the Screen on the Green. It was a lovely warm September night. Barney was obviously excited, feeling cool to be hanging with black boys, wearing the same clothes and trying to speak the same way. He was a good kid when all was said and done. Barney and his mates didn't look threatening; they looked friendly and pretty innocent.

When he walked through the door of the maisonette, the last remnants of the warm glow he had experienced from being in the impact suit deserted him. The place was in a terminal state. Dirty shoes right by the door, piles of free newspapers and mail all down the corridor, which was covered in London dirt footprints. There was a wet towel at the bottom of the stairs. The phone was ringing; he couldn't even find it. It was under another pile of clothes and old newspapers and magazines.

'Hello, it's me,' said Sally. He hadn't spoken to her in more than three months. There were about fifty messages left in that time, but she'd never rung when he was home. He knew by the phone bill that Barney was ringing her every day.

'Who's me?' asked Nick cheekily. Sally didn't respond.

'I'm worried about him, Nick. He's not doing anything.'

Nick took a large breath, smiled and said, 'Hello, Nick, how are you? I'm fine, thank you, very happy, just started an amazing new job. Oh, really, and what's that? Well, I help train women in a self-defence class. How marvellous. Thank you, and how are you? I'm very well too.'

'He's not studying as far as I can make out,' said Sally, as if none of the previous tirade had ever been uttered.

'What d'you mean?' he asked. This was a part of his life that was never going to end, until one of them died.

'He's supposed to be studying for his A-levels.'

'He's only just started!' exclaimed Nick.

'If he slacks off now and starts using drugs, well, he just can't. You see, Barney is not like you, Nick, he can go to university and complete his education, that's all,' she said snappily. 'The thing I've been working towards for the last fifteen years. Teaching him to read and write, to add and subtract. Hours and hours, Nick. I don't want all that wasted just because he thinks it's cool to hang around with his useless father.'

Nick felt the old belly fire ignite. He chewed his lip to prevent himself saying anything. He held on as best he could. Sally spoke on regardless.

'I've been speaking to the senior man at the college. I know him. That's how Barney got the place.'

'Is it?'

'You don't know anything about him, do you?'

'I bloody do,' said Nick, doubting the truth as he spoke.

'He told me Barney started very well, very good attendance, but it could easily change. He seems too relaxed, it's all going to go wrong unless you're very careful. He says you're much nicer since you've come back from your holiday, which means you're too soft on him.'

This time Nick laughed. She couldn't talk to him without showing her spikes. From what he remembered it was impossible for her to communicate with anyone without the intention to hurt.

'You are amazing,' he said. 'Hats off, mate.'

'Well, what are you going to do? Where is he now?'

'Who?'

'Barney,' she spat

'Oh, I dunno,' said Nick.

'What d'you mean, you "dunno",' she said. She always fell for it. Act thick and drive her crazy.

'I dunno where he is, I'm too thick to remember. Oh no, wait a minute, that's right. I think he's taken loads of drugs and gone bungee jumping on a special day out for Paedophiles with Aids. Yeah.'

'How can you be so flippant about your son's education?' she hissed without humour. 'His future depends on his getting good grades, for Christ's sake. He'll have to come back here.'

'Sally, shut up. Listen. The boy's good, he's well, he's happy. Dangerous word to use in your presence, but there you go. He's going to college, he spends hours in his room reading and writing. He's got a girlfriend, he's gone to the movies with some friends who seem fine, and he'll be back by ten thirty. We're going swimming in the morning, then we're having lunch with his mates from college. I am happy for him to grow up different from me and be bright, but I'll be much happier if he grows up nothing like you. Uptight, narrow-minded and miserable.'

'What d'you mean he's got a girlfriend?'

Nick laughed again. Insults never penetrated Sally's thick hide.

'She's Anglo-Indian, she's in a gang and she's called Sutupa.'

'Oh my God.'

'She's tiny but well hard, I would say. He seems pretty smitten.'

'Oh my God. She's not one of your ghastly cast-offs, is she?'

Nick shook his head. 'No, she's fifteen. Too young even for a dedicated old perv like me. And how are you, Sally?'

'What?'

'I said how are you?' he repeated, happy to have thrown her again.

'Me? I'm fine. Of course I'm fine,' she said after a moment's hesitation. 'If he's out late with some awful Indian girl he's not going to do any work, is he? He'll fall behind, he'll see how you loll about and sponge off people and he'll think it's a good idea and he's finished.'

'You are an unmitigated cow, aren't you? He doesn't want to come back to you because you're a fucking nightmare to be with. Haven't you understood that yet? Jesus, I'd have thought with your intellectual prowess you'd have sussed that out by now. He needs to be with me, and believe me, having him here is not my idea of a good time. He's a lazy fucker when it comes to housework. He's clearly never had to look after himself with you and your fucking awful mother dithering around him all his life. He's had a shock here because he has to do all his own laundry and washing up, he has to cook his own food and clean his own room.' Nick looked around the bombsite of the kitchen as he spoke. 'He doesn't like it, but he has to do it, because I have to do it as I don't have a wife or a cleaner to rely on.'

'Finished?' asked Sally after a moment's pause.

'We'll never be finished, Sally. We hate each other too much. I have less respect for you than anyone else I've ever known. To others, you might be Professor Sally Mulberry. To me, you're scum.'

He put the phone down and punched the air.

'That was brilliant,' he said out loud to himself. The phone rang again. He picked it up and slammed it down. It was part of the ritual. For the next hour, as he cleared up the disgusting mess of his home, he kept the phone unplugged. As soon as he plugged it in it rang. He picked it up and put it down again, then picked it up and dialled Tiffany Smooth.

She wasn't home. He left a message.

'Hi. It's me, Nick,' he added. He didn't want to sound like Sally. 'Miss you, babe.'

He hung up. He didn't know what more to say. He sat at his kitchen table and went through his bills. He was lonely and depressed, that much he knew. He wasn't having a good time but it didn't seem to matter quite so much as it once had.

He went upstairs into his bedroom, which was relatively unscathed by the Barney invasion. He pulled out his bottom drawer and lifted the small pile of magazines from inside. He looked at them, convinced that he'd left *Sperm-Soaked Babes* on top. But *Trailer Trash on Heat* was top of the pile. His heart raced momentarily. It could only mean Barney had found them. Maybe he'd shown them to Sutupa. She'd be horrified – they'd both think he was a total perv. The covers of the magazines were so, well, so gory. He sat down on the bed with them on his lap, flicked through their familiar pages.

It was all so weird, still having raging feelings of lust and yet being so much more easy in the company of women. There was no connection between what he was looking at and the class he had just undertaken. Or if there was, Nick couldn't find it. He knew that if the women in the class had been aware that he was looking at a picture of a woman being fucked in the vagina and the rectum at the same time by two men, while a third had his penis in her mouth, they might think slightly the less of him. That was what made it so attractive – the fact that looking at it was still so wrong.

But then, fuck it, this was sex; what the women in the class objected to, quite rightly, was violence. And yet, that night in San Francisco with Tiff, when he had started crying in the middle of a totally kinky fuck-fest – wasn't that close? Did she really want to do that or did she let him because of some other agenda? True, she didn't struggle to stop him, but then she couldn't really, with her hands tied together. And the woman in the pictures he was looking at, he could con himself that she wanted to do what she was doing, or having done to her, but when he looked into her eyes they were the eyes of a nineteen- or twenty-year-old, virtually a kid. Having a man's erect penis in your mouth must be a bit shocking, the first time, and *Sperm-Soaked Babes* only featured very young women. He threw the magazines on the floor, but their glossy allure was too powerful, and finally he put them to the use for which they were created.

Chapter Thirty

Alice Moreton opened the door to her apartment and stared in horror. The first thing that went through her mind was burglary. They had wrecked it; they could still be inside. She adopted the defensive pose that Tara had taught her that afternoon. Her heart rate went up; she was super-aware. Then she was very scared, then she felt faint, all within a few seconds of opening the front door.

Nothing happened. She could hear the clock her father had given her softly ticking in the kitchen. It slowly dawned on her that she hadn't been burgled, this was just the state she had been living in for the past few months. She stood up and sniffed to cover her embarrassment. She closed the door and picked her way along the corridor. The mess hadn't mattered up to that point; she hadn't even noticed. She glanced at the mirror leaning against the wall. She had taken it down and turned it to face inward. She shook her head and picked it up, looked at herself again. She smiled and hung the mirror up.

She went into her kitchen and started to clean. She vacuumed, washed, ironed, stacked, put away and dusted for four hours. At the end of the whole process her apartment was clean and tidy again, like it always used to be before the rape.

She could say it to herself now. She had been raped; she had just told fifteen other women, and a man. That man. She hadn't been able to stop thinking about him all the way home. She felt light and excited. Never, in all her life, had she even seen a man like that, let alone met a man like that.

He was so completely good. Time after time he was beaten by angry women, and he came back for more and more and more. To see that happen again and again, it was so incredibly sexy. There was something about the undeniable strength of his spirit which made her hot. Maybe it was that she knew she could thrash herself against him, grind at him for hours, and he would just watch her with those fantastic eyes. She threw her head back and laughed at the thought. It was so preposterous.

Not only was he a sex god, he had taught her so much. She sat in her old armchair with a cup of tea. There was no sound in the house, except the ticking clock. Actually, now she thought about it, Tara had taught her, she knew that, but he had made it possible to learn. If Peter tried that rape again she would be able to stop him. Even big Peter, even with him on top, she knew she could stop him, really hurt him enough to stop him.

She suddenly wanted to ring Peter Welbeck and tell him she wanted to land her knee in his big ugly bollocks and see him fold up on the ground beneath her.

She picked up the phone and dialled his number from memory. She got his answering machine.

'Hi, Peter here, can't take your call, usual drill after the tone.'

The beep sounded and Alice said, 'Hello, Peter, this is Alice Moreton. Remember, the one you raped in your car? I haven't forgotten. I never will.'

She hung up, only then noticing that she was very agitated. 'You bastard,' she screamed at the dead phone. Then she started crying again, thumping the huge red pillow her aunt had given her for her twenty-first birthday.

'I've started!' she said to herself between sobs. 'I've started to get back. I will get back. I will.'

The sobs overcame her and she buried her head in the cushion.

Then the phone rang, she looked up, swallowed some sobs and became frightened again. She knew it must be Peter. He'd got her message and rung back – he was going to do something, she had scared him and he was going to attack her again. Why did she ring? Why? She looked around the room for help but there was none, saw the answering machine which she'd smashed a few months previously. She couldn't switch that on. She looked at the phone, still ringing. Slowly, she moved and picked it up.

'Hello,' she said quickly.

'Alice, it's May here,' said the old familiar voice. 'I'm sorry I haven't been in touch for so long, it's just been pretty hellish with Sam.'

'May, May, oh God, I'm so pleased to hear from you. Can I come and stay?' said Alice before she had any notion of what this might entail.

'Blimey, of course you can,' said May. 'That's why I've rung. David has taken the bloody baby to his mother's in Yorkshire. This is the first night I've had off in over six months, that's why I'm ringing everyone I know. I feel like I've just climbed out of a hole in the ground.'

'So do I,' said Alice. 'But for rather different reasons.'

Alice double-locked her flat, got back in her car and drove to May's house in Luton. She had only been there once before – May had moved just before she'd had the baby. It sounded like hell to Alice, and from what May had told her it was hell. She didn't look at a map but followed her nose, and didn't take a single wrong turning. This gave her an immense feeling of satisfaction as she remembered how she used to be. She could remember less and less of the period that had passed since she was raped. It had become a fuzzy blur, a numbness which she felt she had just fallen out of. She had never undertaken any form of therapy, sought any type of help or made any effort to deal with what had happened to her that day. She realised how stupid she had been, to imagine she could just forget something so horrendous, just pretend it hadn't happened. When she heard the other women's stories and realised how much violent hatred there was in the world, she just felt lucky to be alive. What if he'd really got carried away and killed her? That must be how it happened. She trusted men implicitly, always had — they had never behaved in a way to make her think otherwise. Until Peter. The bastard. How could he do that? She imagined them both as babies, her a little girl in Tewkesbury, him a little boy in somewhere like Leicester — she couldn't remember exactly where he came from. Did his mum look at that chubby six-month-old boy in his cot and think 'One day you'll rape a girl in the front seat of your car, and you'll get away with it'.

Did her dad wonder, as he washed her tubby little tummy in the bath, that one day this self-same girl would be held down in a choking grip and raped by a personal-insurance-selling rugby player? It was all so absurd.

She pulled to a halt outside May's house and ran up to the front door. The two women embraced.

'Too long,' said May. She held up a picture of a small baby. 'Okay, there he is.'

'He's grown,' said Alice, not sure if this was the right thing to say.

'Yes. Now, let's talk about anything other than fucking babies.'

'Fine by me.'

Chapter Thirty-One

As Tara got off the train that night in Brighton, she was looking forward to her welcome at Yolanda Tintern's house. The class had been successful but exhausting, and she couldn't sleep on the train. The presence of three teenage boys who rough-housed together loudly in the opposite seats did not put her at her ease.

It was still her habit to run through three or four attack scenarios. She couldn't help it – she no longer even bothered trying to help it. She allowed her mind to race through how she would disable one so brutally his injuries would dissuade the others. As it turned out the three boys did not even cast her a glance.

She looked out of the window into the night sky. The clouds looked beautiful in the sunset. However, she felt more tired than she could ever remember being. It wasn't the course – she was more than used to that – it was some deep tiredness she couldn't define. Maybe it was just getting old. She would have to stop teaching at some time but she couldn't imagine any other way of life. Teaching was everything to her, it was all she thought about. She missed Adrian, maybe she missed sex. It almost felt like that – it was as if the tiredness were in her belly and her sex. Tara breathed a deep sigh. She needed a break, she needed to get away from crying women and blue mats and dealing with so much fear and anger. She recalled Nick's face after the first session that afternoon. He had looked magnificent, so radiant after he had accomplished his first solo session. He had behaved impeccably, never interrupting her but always being where she needed him to be to help.

When they had embraced after the class she felt enormous, unthreatening warmth from him. It wasn't something he'd learned — the power was something that had been allowed to the surface through his training. How could she have a break? She didn't have the choice, she couldn't just up and leave the whole organisation. Whatever her capacity to spot a natural ability in men was, she had it and she had to use it. She had seen Nick Gardener in the most unlikely circumstances. He'd done everything he could to prove her wrong, and yet in the long run she had been right. She smiled as she remembered him. Such a big man and so gentle. The way he patiently showed some of the less competent students the right posture for a leg kick, always asking if it was all right to put his hands on their legs to guide them. He still didn't have the experience of someone like Tim, but he was a natural. And very good-looking, if you liked that sort of thing, which she never had — but she did notice.

She walked the short distance from the train station to the house, found her key and entered. Yolanda was in the kitchen, sitting alone, reading the paper.

'Hoorah! The conqueror returns!' said her landlady as she entered the kitchen.

Yolanda and Daisy were the two women who had originally brought her to England to set up the course. Yolanda had run innumerable charities and self-help organisations and was managing the British arm of Winning Strategy with aplomb.

'Sounds like you had a good day,' she said.

'Fantastic.'

'Tell me all about it,' said Yolanda, handing her a cup of tea. Tara sat at the big messy kitchen table as Yolanda busied herself making a stew. Cats brushed against her leg as Tara described the class and told her about the students and their strengths, the ones she was worried about and how wonderful it was that Daisy and Nick worked so well together at last.

'And how was your lovely boy?'

'Sorry?' said Tara, not sure who she meant.

'The lovely Nick. Was he a good boy?'

'He was wonderful.'

'I knew it. He's so gorgeous, isn't he?'

'Is he? I guess so,' said Tara. 'Didn't know you were interested, Yolanda.'

'Who? Me? Heavens above, girl, I'm old enough to be his mother. But you . . .'

'I'm sorry,' said Tara. She had never found Yolanda particularly easy company.

'Oh, I'm speaking out of turn, am I?' Yolanda asked with a deep laugh.

'I don't know,' said Tara.

'Oh, come on, Tara. It's written all over your face.'

'What is?'

'You and Nick. And he's crazy about you. It's so romantic.'

'Is he?' said Tara, genuinely concerned. 'I don't think so.'

'He is, of course he is. Come on, I mean, you chose him, out of all the men you could have chosen, you picked a dreamboat. Okay, the big muscles aren't exactly my taste, but he is so dreamy-looking. Lovely eyes.'

'Are you implying there's something going on between Nick and me?' asked Tara quite sternly. She had not been expecting this.

'Not implying, no. Just observing. You're not telling me you don't fancy him?'

'No, I don't fancy him,' said Tara very clearly. 'I found Nick because of what he does, not what he looks like. He's become a truly gifted padded assailant, a very rare thing indeed.'

'And he smells so wonderful. Oh, and those armpits. Darling, when I saw those I thought I'd died and gone to heaven. How you can stay in the same room as him when he pulls off his T-shirt . . .'

'I'm not in the same room as him normally,' said Tara, remembering the time when Nick had got changed into the suit when Yolanda and Daisy were talking to a journalist in the training studio a week earlier. He had been momentarily naked. She could remember seeing his naked buttocks, his powerful legs, his broad, muscular back, but she had barely allowed herself a glance. Surely she didn't fancy him – surely she'd know if she did. Yolanda's tirade was so transparent – she fancied the pants off Nick, that was what all this was about.

'Yolanda, you seem to have forgotten about the fact that I live with a man in San Francisco.'

'Oh yes, I know. But this is different, isn't it? Come on, admit it, Tara. You're tempted.'

'Yolanda, what do you think is going on?' said Tara, getting exasperated.

'I'm not going to say it, Tara. Really, if you're being that dishonest with yourself then I don't see why I have to be the one who has to deal with all your denial.' She was laughing as she spoke; somehow it didn't sound accusatory or aggressive, just peculiar.

'Are you saying I'm in love with Nick? Is that it?'

'No, you're not in love with him. But you want a baby, don't you?'

'A what?' said Tara, unable to believe what she was hearing.

'There you go. I knew you'd respond like that. Admit it, Tara. You want to have a baby and you've told us that Adrian can't really . . .'

'Yolanda!'

'Well, I can't help speculating,' said Yolanda as she put a large bowl of thick vegetarian stew in front of her house guest. 'I mean, why not?'

'That's so out of line. I work with Nick, it's a professional relationship. I am not about to jeopardise that with some, well, some unfocused desire to have a child.'

'Okay. If you say so,' said Yolanda. 'D'you want another cup of tea?'

'No, I do not want a cup of tea, I want a beer.'

'Oh, I haven't got any beer,' said Yolanda, slightly crestfallen.

'Let's go out for a beer. Is there a nice bar near here?'

'Well, there's a gay bar down at the end of the road. Is that okay?'

'A gay bar would be just the thing,' said Tara with a bright smile. 'Then if I look at a man you'll know I'm not trying to get pregnant. Goddammit.'

Tara took a spoonful of Yolanda's steaming stew. It didn't look great but it tasted amazing.

'Hey, this is good,' she said.

'Isn't it?' said Yolanda. 'Anyway, I'd have thought you'd be too tired to go out.'

'I'm too wound up. Now that I've been relegated to the mother-to-be pile, I need a drink.'

They walked together down the hill to the pub. It was small and packed with noisy young people, some clearly very gay men and a large contingent of lesbians. Tara felt slightly overwhelmed as she walked in, but was quickly engrossed in conversation with women who'd seen her talk at the conference. She'd certainly made a big impression in the small town. She bought a bottle of Bud for herself and a cider for Yolanda, turned from the bar to be met with the doe-eyed stare of a young woman, one she remembered meeting after her conference appearance.

'Hello, Tara,' said the woman with a big smile.

'Hi there. How you doing?'

'Good,' said the woman. 'I hear the class went well today.'

'Yes, it was very good. News travels fast.'

'I know one of the women you're teaching. She's over the moon about the whole thing.'

'That's good,' said Tara, taking a pull at the bottle of Bud.

'It's good to see you again.'

'Thanks,' said Tara. She now remembered that the woman's

name was Claire and she had a little baby girl. 'How's your daughter?'

'I'm so flattered you remember me. God,' said Claire. Tara began to regret asking. Then the woman continued, 'She's fine, she's sitting up and holding things now. They grow so fast. I've hardly got over the birth and she'll be walking soon.'

Tara smiled as she heard this, watching Claire's face light up as she spoke about her offspring.

'Tell me, Claire, is the father of your child . . . well, is he around?'

'No, not really. He helps financially. You know I'm gay, don't you?'

'Sure. I kind of guessed you might be,' said Tara with a gentle smile.

'We used artificial insemination.'

'Did you?' said Tara. 'My God. Did you have to go to a hospital or something?'

'No, we did it at home. It was pretty easy, but then I've known the father for years and years, since I was a child. He's gay and very sweet, and rich, which makes life a bit easier.'

'You're lucky,' said Tara.

'D'you want a baby, then?' asked Claire.

'I don't know. Sometimes,' said Tara. 'Not now, though. The thought of having to get up early tomorrow morning when I've had a day like today . . . boy, am I grateful I don't have to worry.'

'Yeah, they take up your time,' said Claire. 'I haven't got used to it. My mum's looking after her tonight. This is only the third time I've been able to go out for a night since she was born.'

'That's tough.'

'Worth it, though.'

'I guess so. If you say so,' said Tara.

'I thought you were straight, though,' said Claire after a moment's silence.

'Me? Oh, I am. You mean why am I in this bar?'

'No. Why d'you want to know about how I got pregnant?'

'Well, I live with a wonderful man who's infertile. It makes life real complicated.'

'I bet it does. Men are a bit sensitive about stuff like that.'

'I think some women are too,' said Tara, noticing that she was in the unusual position of defending men.

'Yeah, you're right. So, are you thinking of having AI, then?'

'I hadn't been. No. I don't think it's suitable for someone in my position.'

'Well, if your boyfriend didn't mind, if he understood and, you know, he was mature enough to love the child, there's no reason not to, is there?'

Tara was very tired all of a sudden. She had felt elated when she first entered the bar, but the two discussions she'd had that evening were laying heavily on her spirit. It was almost as if Yolanda had planted a seed which was rapidly making roots and starting to shape the way she saw her future. And the roots were big and dark and went deep.

She stood in the corner of the room and watched Claire from a safe distance. She was the mother of a little girl – she seemed so complete, a young woman talking and laughing in a smoky bar. She hadn't become another person, she had just made a new life inside her. Tara Kennedy started to actually wonder what that would be like for the first time in her life.

Chapter Thirty-Two

Nick opened the yellow-painted door of the lock-up garage and revealed a shape covered in a tattered dustsheet. He pulled the sheet away with one jerk and revealed an equally battered white Triumph Stag. He hadn't been to visit his car in over a year. Although it was in the crime-infested badlands of north-west London, behind a row of shops in Pinner, no one had so much as broken one of the garage windows to have a look inside.

'Oh, wow, it looks amazing. I'd forgotten what it was like,' said Barney. Father and son had travelled on the Underground to Pinner on a Monday morning. According to Barney, he didn't have anything important at college that day and Nick had just finished a weekend intensive as a padded assailant. One five-hour class on Saturday, the original group who had by then completed four of their six classes, and a beginners' class on Sunday at the offices of a large publishing company. This had been particularly exhausting because Tara and Nick had had to carry a crash-mat floor with them, hiring a van and loading it up, then unloading it, setting it up, doing the class, repacking the van, driving back into London, unloading and returning the van. He didn't get back home until nearly eight o'clock, finding Barney and Sutupa and two other young women in his kitchen. Barney was cooking, making an incredible mess, but clearly having a great time. He presented his guests with his 'world-famous savoury pancakes' which were seemingly well received. He apologised to his dad – he hadn't bought enough stuff to make him one. Nick shrugged and got a takeout, as usual. Sweet and sour pork balls and special fried rice. Both the other girls in his kitchen were in the Street Sistas – one was very fat and not noticeably communicative, another teenage grunter; the other was tall and, Nick guessed, Greek or Turkish or something Mediterranean, with very dark hair and a heavy build. She was Nina, and she chain-smoked and coughed a lot. He wasn't overly impressed with either of them. They seemed sullen and proud of their ignorance, laughing at each other's stupidity. He didn't say much, just watched Barney trying to blend in, seeing him tread carefully through a con-versation only to be teased cruelly by the women. Sutupa seemed far more involved with the other women than with Barney – she almost seemed embarrassed by him. Without any warning that Nick could see, the four of them sloped off. Nick demanded that Barney be back by ten that night, a command which he obeyed.

The interior of the car looked pretty good, but it was clear to anyone that there was a severe rust problem around the wheel arches and along the sills under both doors.

Nick knelt down and poked his finger through the body-work.

'Funny bunch of girls you had round last night,' he said eventually. 'Is that the Street Sistas, then?'

'No, there're loads of them, that was just her posse.'

'Right. Sutupa seems well different, though. I mean, she's a bit brighter than the rest, isn't she?'

'I think so. Yeah. And better-looking. Monica's a bit of a lard mountain, isn't she?'

'Big girl,' said Nick, smiling. 'She ate your savoury pancake in one mouthful.'

Barney laughed. Nick stood up.

'I've bought my sander. I just need about half a ton of filler and some paint, then I can get this heap through its MOT and sell it.'

'You can't sell it, Dad. This is a classic car.'

'It's a knob-wagon, Barn. I'm too old for that shit. I need a nice estate, like one of them big Peugeots so I can get all my stuff in the back.'

'Oh no!' wailed Barney. 'I've always loved this car. Remember when you came to pick me up in it? It's so loud.'

'It's got a great engine, true, there's nothing wrong with that.'

'Mum just went totally, totally ballistic, seeing you that time, driving in a white sports car.'

'Oh yeah, I'd forgotten about that.'

' "What's he doing wasting money on rubbish like that? What about your school fees?" All that stuff, and I was just so pleased you'd spent money on this and not the stupid Dragon School. It was brilliant, Dad. I've never forgotten that day, roaring down the motorway with loud music on, and everyone just looking at us. It was fantastic.'

'That was about the last time I drove the bloody thing. It failed its MOT on about three hundred points. Masses of rust, no brakes to speak of, no wipers, headlights pointing all over the shop, tyres as bare as a surf lifeguard's arse. It's a total embarrassment, Barn. The best thing I can do is get it road-worthy and try and flog it. Should be worth a couple of grand, shouldn't it?'

'And some,' said Barney.

They went to a nearby car spares shop and bought everything they needed. Nick had a small amount of money in the bank again for the first time he could remember. He wasn't exactly raking it in, but then he was so tired after a class that all he wanted to do was sleep. He didn't go out, didn't spend hundreds of pounds boozing because he couldn't stand his life and needed to bury it in a pub. He didn't spend money on clothes he didn't need; he just seemed to save money.

It felt good to be fixing up the car, and Barney was surprisingly good at body-filling, working really carefully and methodically at each part, removing all the rust and slowly reshaping the bodywork.

Nick got to work on the brakes, stripping them off, grazing his knuckles, straining his neck as he slowly removed the old pads and applied the new ones. He removed the battery and connected it to a charger. He drained the engine and gearbox and refilled them both with the correct oil; he changed the oil filter, the spark plugs and points and the coolant. While Barney sanded down filler on the rear wheel arch, Nick went to a nearby public phone and called around tyre suppliers to find a set of tyres. He found a second-hand set at a wrecker's yard not more than a mile away. Worth the risk, he decided.

'Let's take it for a spin,' he said when he returned.

'What?' asked Barney.

'I've found some new tyres down the road. Let's chuck the big jack in the back and go and get them.'

'But, Dad, the car's totally, like totally, illegal.'

'I know, but it's only a mile away.'

'But what if you get caught?'

'I won't. I'll drive really carefully, you big wuss,' teased Nick, climbing into the driver's seat and turning the engine over. To his utter delight it started first time, a little roar and then a reassuringly smooth tick-over. 'Hop in,' he called to Barney, and they pulled out into the alley.

He'd forgotten what a pleasure the car was to drive – a powerful engine, no roof, a sunny morning. Beautiful. They cruised along suburban roads, under the bushy green plane trees, Barney laughing and Nick checking the route in his *A to Z*.

They found the breaker's yard beside a huge railway siding. Sure enough there was a set of five RS 720 16s in a pile. They looked new, mounted on alloy wheels which would have cost as much as Nick's car. For the price the oily individual with the greasy hair was charging, they could only have been stolen. Nick worried slightly that he was being a negative influence on Barney

— he could hear Sally's horrified tones coming through the ether. On the other hand, they were affordable and would make the car sell. He handed over a hundred pounds in cash and set about changing the wheels.

Barney and Nick stood back when they'd tightened the last bolt. The car was transformed. The bodywork was still a patchwork of grey filler and ochre rust-proof paint, there was no soft top and the roof frame looked a bit bare folded up behind the seats, but it was on the way.

'Kicking,' said Barney.

'Just a respray and it'll be roadworthy,' said Nick. 'I might get a professional to do it.'

'Oh, Dad. I can spray.'

'That's what I mean. You can spray your name on a wall. I want someone who can put on a coat of paint that looks smooth.'

'What's the point if you're going to sell it?'

'Well, it looks pretty funky, doesn't it? I might keep it for a while, just to piss off your mum.'

Barney jumped up and punched the air. The two men hugged briefly. The greasy yard-owner agreed it was a tasty motor and definitely in the classic car league. They returned to the garage following the same back route, avoiding busy intersections and police cars.

By the time they got back it was getting late. They ate fish and chips as the two of them filled and sanded the last of the bodywork, then locked the garage and went home.

'I've had a brilliant day, Dad,' said Barney when he had come down from his bath. 'Thanks.'

'Me too,' said Nick. They watched TV together. Nick drank a cold beer, Barney had a glass of milk and went to bed. Nick lay in the silence of his bedroom after his bath and gave himself time to think before doing anything. He had had a good day too. For the first time he could remember he was feeling satisfied at the end of a day instead of drunk or depressed or horny. He loved what he was doing, the classes were amazing, and he had a kind of glow which seemed to engulf him for days after.

The phone rang. He wondered whether it would be Sally, but on the other hand it could be Tiffany. She would be awake. He rolled off his bed and searched for the phone in the mess on the floor.

Chapter Thirty-Three

'It's Alice, from the class,' she said nervously. She had sat alone for hours trying not to phone, everything in her day-to-day life told her not to be so stupid, but there was something else pulling her, filling her mind with the shape that was him. Him, that man, that Nick Gardener. Even his name smelt of musty strength, a big shoulder, a smooth, strong chest. It wasn't just that all the women in her class had a bit of a crush on him. This was something else. Alice had been through all the men she knew, all the men she had ever known, and this one was so much better than any of them, better than all their best aspects combined. She knew in her heart of hearts she would never meet another man like him, this was the one, and somehow, just somehow, she had to just meet him and talk. That was the drive – the sheer urgency of not losing him. Plus there was the contact list, given to everyone in the class. Every phone number and address of every student, as well as Tara and Daisy and there, in black and white, Nick Gardener. She had his number right there in front of her. How could she do anything other than ring him? It must have been meant to happen.

'Alice, how are you?' he asked. Such a lovely voice, not too rough, but not smarmy and knowing.

'I'm fine. I just had to ring you.'

'Oh? Why, what's up?'

'Well, I just had to ask you. I can't sleep or think straight. I just needed to ask you a few things.'

'Ask away,' he said. He sounded happy enough to talk.

'Well, you're not with anyone, right?'

'Right. Not now. I'm all on my old lonesome.'

She thought that was a little naff as a reply but she was over-brimming with forgiveness.

'But as a regular thing,' she pressed on. 'You're not with anyone as a regular thing?'

'As a regular thing, no. But Alice, you know the rule.'

'I know, I know the rule,' she said quickly. He was referring to something Tara had said in the introduction to the first class. No socialising between teachers and students for a year. It seemed so cruel.

'The thing is, well, I'll be honest with you, Nick.' She wanted to use his name, she wanted to say his name again and again. What was happening to her? She hadn't felt like this since she fell in love with Edgar Biddulph at college. 'I have very strong feelings for you, and I don't know what to do with them.'

'Okay. I see,' said Nick. 'But you understand why that rule is there, don't you, Alice?' He'd used her name — surely that meant he felt the same.

'I do. I don't think I agree with it altogether. If you imagine a scenario where two people like each other, then that isn't really any one else's business, is it?'

'It's just a safety thing. If other students knew you and I were involved in some way, it could create stresses in the class which really shouldn't be there. I think the rule has come about through experience, you know — they've been doing this a long time in America.'

'I know.'

'Plus there's a thing called transference which I didn't understand until I saw it take place. You are so pleased that you've made all this progress and your mind sort of won't let you accept that it was you that did it, not me or Tara or Daisy, but you. So you kind of transfer all that good feeling on to someone else, when actually it's down to you. So really, what that means is the feelings you think you have for me are not really, well, real. D'you see what I'm saying?'

'I accept all that. But is it against the rules to find out if your feelings are reciprocated? That's all I need to know, just to put me out of my misery.'

'I don't want you to be miserable, Alice,' he said. He was flirting. The cloud lifted again. She could hear him smiling. What did that mean, though? Why was he being so roundabout? She had noticed the way he looked at her – he always made a point of saying goodbye after each class. She'd always made a point of taking a long time to get changed, suddenly needing to relace her training shoes or find something in her bag before she left, giving her a few more seconds in his presence. And was he having an affair with Tara? They seemed so close. She had seen them embrace after a class and her heart sank, but then she thought they might just be very open and intimate with each other because of all the therapy they must have done.

'What does that mean?' she asked.

'I can't say, Alice, but I'd like to keep in touch with you.'

Alice held the phone to her chest and pressed both lips together. He did have feelings for her. Her heart and mind raced through a sunny future together, the two of them hand in hand. She was falling hopelessly in love.

'Oh my God,' she said. 'I knew it.'

'But I cannot do anything about it for a long time. Okay? And neither must you. Please, Alice. I want to be able to teach all the students in the class at the same level. Including you. You're doing really well and I don't want to jeopardise that. Okay?'

Alice agreed not to make life difficult for either of them, promising anything he asked, as long as they could meet up some time after her course was over. She hung up and wailed into the night. She had been so lonely for so long. Once so sought-after, especially as a student, she had men hanging out of windows for her, comparing her with Helena Bonham Carter. She knew she had been a dark beauty, but in recent months she had felt like a dark shadow, something people avoided. She had wanted them to avoid her. Now she wanted to go to a party and scream her happiness at everyone.

The course had certainly made her life at work more bearable, and she had done a mass of overtime to catch up on all the work that had piled up while she'd been whatever it was that she had been. Already she couldn't remember it. It was more like a colour than a feeling – not even a colour. Maybe a filter over that part of her past. It was masked, probably some clever psychological way of protecting her from the pain of what had happened. Her big fear now was not men, not even walking along a street alone at night. Her big fear was not being able to have sex with a man she liked. Always a highly sexed woman, Alice hadn't masturbated since the attack. She had barely touched herself at all, just the most cursory of contacts when she bathed. All the things she'd read about rape, and she'd read a lot, seemed to say the same thing. It was as if the rape took sex away from the woman – she didn't miss what she didn't have. She had no drive. The man in the impact suit was the first hint that there was anything there at all. Maybe it hadn't been stolen, it had just shrunk to nothing in order to survive.

But if she got into bed with this gorgeous man, and he was erect and strong and above her, supported on those wonderful arms . . . What if it hurt now, what if it wasn't nice? She didn't want to find out, but she had to. Would he be gentle with her or would he just turn into the same sort of brute that Peter was? What was it about the men she liked? She had been approached by soft, gentle, kind, considerate men all her life. She found them utterly unappealing sexually; even socially she found them slightly annoying. She always went for slightly dangerous-look-ing, big men. In sex, she recalled, it was always a fairly submissive role she took – pinned down, underneath, feeling the man's body in control, making her body do whatever he wanted. She liked that – she wanted a man who would show her how much he was turned on by her. If he was genuinely connecting with her, it didn't matter what he did – anything was permissible and that was incredibly exciting.

She felt she knew that Nick would be connected with her – he was so honest and strong and not scared. She had watched him carefully when he didn't have his helmet on, the way he looked at all the women – not lusting after them, seeing them all equally. He was so brave, so incredibly sexy, and he had eyes that made her melt.

That night Alice masturbated for the first time since her assault and then she cried herself happily to sleep.

Chapter Thirty-Four

The graduation ceremony came around far faster than Tara had expected. Somehow the sheer inertia she faced getting the first class off the ground had seemed to slow time down; the first three classes took for ever. The last three flashed by in no time, and she was already involved with four other groups. Daisy had taken on her first class with Tara as an assistant and everything had gone pretty smoothly. Nick had proved himself an expert padded assailant, and she had noticed a massive improvement in his attitude as the classes progressed and he gained more experience. He was utterly involved with each student, never forgetting a name after a class, remembering each move and each problem they had encountered. He was very open and affectionate, and to complicate matters she had met his son.

It was after a class during the week. A gangly youth was waiting nervously on the street outside the Holborn Centre building. Nick had greeted him warmly and introduced him. The son, like the father, was alarmingly strong-featured and handsome, tall and gentle-looking with a strange, half-shaved, half-long hairstyle. They had an Italian meal together in a three-storey self-service eatery just off Tottenham Court Road. She learned the story of Barney, and how he had been brought up by his mum but was now living with his dad, and he was fantastic.

It was all too neat. Even as she ate her lasagne verde, Tara was imagining a teenage American boy spending time in London with his biological father. What an adventure for him, very like her own life in so many ways, brought up on the West Coast of America but coming to the old country at that crucial and exciting time in her life. She stared at Barney, imagining, concocting without a care in the world.

Barney stood and left them to get some coffees.

'Good-looking lad, isn't he?' said Nick when he was out of earshot.

'He's wonderful. Such an amazing boy, when you think how boys can be.'

'Yeah. All right. Steady,' said Nick with a big grin. 'But you know what, much as I despise her, his mum's been brilliant. It's not me — he's a really bright kid and he gets that from her.'

Tara felt ever more confident. She nodded seriously. 'You're no slouch, Nick, don't self-deprecate too much.'

'Okay, but he's an academic. He'll probably get into Oxford or Cambridge or something. Barney's a real brainbox. Spends all day reading. I mean, I can barely write my name and I never read anything other than comics.' He smiled.

They discussed the coming week. Eight separate classes and the graduation ceremony on the following Sunday.

Barney rejoined them carrying a tray of coffees.

'Barn, mate, you're coming to this graduation do next Sunday, aren't you?'

'Um, I don't know,' said Barney.

'What, you going to see your mum?'

'No way. No, I just, well, I should be doing my homework and everything.'

'It's only a couple of hours, mate. I think you'd really learn a lot. I know I have. It's an amazing thing to see the first time.'

'I'll try,' said Barney. He seemed to have closed up. Tara stopped her face reacting — whatever was going on between these two, it was nothing to do with her.

They left the café and walked into the bright sun of the busy London street. Tara breathed deeply, sensing the toxic fumes. She had become increasingly aware of her body, of the monthly changes and pressures. She realised these feelings had always been there, she'd just never bothered to notice. After her period she would keep a very low-key mental note of when she was ovulating, just imagining how it would be if she could arrange something.

She had stayed up late one night to phone Adrian at work, just before his regimentally timed lunch break. She got straight through.

'Adrian, how would you feel if I found a way to get pregnant?'

'Wow, who you gonna screw?'

'No one. No, I mean, I've just met a gay woman who had an AI baby, and everything seems to be pointing in that kind of direction for me. I just want to know what you think.'

'Oh, wow. Just hang on a minute. I'm adjusting from phase space to infertility and babies and artificial insemination and real mulchy organic stuff. It's a big gap, Tara. I mean, you know how I feel about having a baby. I really want one. I guess I was dreaming along the lines of adoption.'

'Sure, we could always try that.'

'Or this artificial shit. Maybe that's a better route.'

'So, you'd think about it.'

'Sure.'

'The fact that it was from another man's gene pool, is that like a real big factor?'

'Pretty big. It's what our cultures have been built on for the past five thousand years. But heck, I'm a modern guy.'

'Oh, Adrian, you'd consider it?'

'Sure, hon, if you think we can swing it.'

'And you'd be okay with me getting morning sickness, getting fat, needing a back rub and a pot of Ben and Jerry's Cherry Garcia ice cream at three in the morning?'

'So what's new?' said Adrian. She could hear the smile coming nine thousand miles down the line.

'Come over for the graduation of my inaugural class.'

'To London?'

'Sure, why not, you got money, don't you?'

'Plenty of money, no time, hon.'

'Make time. Really. It would be good.'

'Okay. I know a guy at Stanford who is actually in the process of trying to create more time. I'll speak with him.'

'Will you come?'

'I'll try.'

Tara had slept so well that night, she worked better than ever the next day. She could feel that her teaching was at an absolute peak. She was so in tune with each student; she saw results that surprised even her.

Now they had completed their first course, and Daisy was becoming a really competent teacher. When she returned from her final training in San Francisco she'd be running top-quality classes. Tara could go back home, which meant she wasn't really blowing any working relationship with Nick, as such. It wasn't as if she were sexually propositioning him, not at all. She wasn't exactly sure of the physical technicalities, but she was sure it could be done with dignity. They would have to have a mutually arrived-at parenting agreement. Although the child wouldn't live with its biological father, she had no intention of trying to hide its biological roots. She'd want Nick to acknowledge the baby – not support it financially, just be there, somewhere in the background. She didn't know how far in the background – they'd have to agree to work it out as they went along. It couldn't be that complicated.

Tim Renaldo had arrived a day before the graduation, and she spent an hour with him at the airport. They had coffee in a café full of Japanese tourists and they talked about the class and Nick and eventually she mentioned her intention to have a baby. Tim was delightfully supportive, agreeing whole-heartedly that

Nick would make the ideal biological father. Tim had had a vasectomy at the age of thirty-eight when he decided then he didn't want any more children. He was yet more delighted when Tara suggested he could be godfather to the forthcoming child. He was only slightly disconcerted when she casually informed him that Nick, as yet, had no inkling of her plans. He laughed, agreed that this aspect of the plan might have been unwisely overlooked.

All this was swilling about in the forefront of Tara's mind as she sat in the opening circle of graduation day for the first class. Those same fourteen faces who had sat in this very room only five weeks before, scared and pale, full of foreboding and anxiety. She scanned them as she sat there – confident, outward-looking, happy, talking with each other busily, swapping phone numbers and promising to keep in touch. She glanced at Nick. He was kneeling with his hands in his lap, a position he used to find intolerably uncomfortable, one that Tim Renaldo had shown him as being the least threatening male position. He looked wonderful, carefully watching the students as the last of them joined the circle. Daisy was busy looking through notes, and slowly, without Tara saying anything, the room fell silent. All eyes were upon her.

'This is great. You have been such a fantastic group,' she said, looking at each of them in turn. 'Our first class to graduate – it's a really exciting day for all of us. Your friends and family members are going to join us for the last hour but we'll start by running through every exercise we've done over the weeks. Before that, I just want to take time to check in, send the tissue box around the circle, see how everyone is feeling. Okay? Daisy, you go first, okay?'

Daisy spoke briefly about how good she felt about the class and her new job as teacher and how she hoped they'd all keep in touch and come back for more advanced classes. She passed the tissue box to Jane.

'I'm just so happy. Doing the course kind of let me say bye-

bye to my friend – you might not remember, the one who killed herself. But this has been such a lot of fun as well. I want to thank you, Tara, you're just amazing, and Daisy, thanks so much for all your time. And of course, Nick. I never thought we'd all fall in love with you. It's brilliant what you do and if only – I think this is what we all feel – if only there were more men around like you.'

'It's just fantastic. Jane said what I feel too. Just the level of confidence, the fact that I don't have to think now when we have a fight with lovely Nick. It's just there, all that body memory stuff is so true. My body knows what to do even if I'm freaking out. Thank you.'

'I feel so much less angry. That's what's a complete surprise to me.'

'I'm free, that's all I feel. Free from so much shit. It's been fantastic.'

'I'm a different woman to the one who sat here six weeks ago. Thanks. I'm still scared, but it's a fear that is my friend, not my enemy, and I can never thank you enough.'

'Can't go back and beat the shit out of my dad, but other than that, you've really helped me deal with a lot of bad stuff. Thanks. And thank you, Nick, you've been so brilliant.'

'I'm not too fat to fight, I've learned that, and I've actually lost a bit of weight. It was great when you said that my kicks were the strongest, Nick.'

'This is so exciting and depressing. What am I going to do next Saturday? No class. This has been such a brilliant experience.'

'Well, everyone's said what I feel. I think it's a very good course. It's really shown me what I can do, I feel more confident. Thanks.'

'Excellent. I'm so high from all this, and meeting such a fabulous bunch of women and not being made to feel like a boring student. I still hate men, except Nick. There must be something wrong with you, Nick. Thanks, Tara, you rule. Brilliant.'

'My husband said I'd turned into someone completely different and he feels he's got to get to know me all over again. It's been great and I'll be lost for what to do next Saturday too.'

'It's been very hard to work while I've been coming to this. I keep thinking, one wrong move, you bastard, and I'll give you a roundhouse kick in the nuts you won't forget in a while. What's weird, though, is all me punters are being real nice to me. It's like I must be different or something. And I never thought I'd say this, but you're not a bad bloke, Nick, for a bloke. Thanks, Tara, you're not bad for a Yank either. And I'm not swearing anything like as fucking much as I was, don't know if you noticed.'

'I just want to say thank you, and you can read my piece in next month's *marie claire*. They're doing a really big section all about the system and Tara, and Nick. You can all read my copy to check if you feel okay with it. So thank you, and I feel fantastic.'

Alice, sitting next to Nick, was the last to get the tissue box.

'I feel very lucky because I became a victim and got over it really fast. I suppose the whole thing took about ten weeks. I think all the women here have been amazing. I'd like to thank Nick, of course – who wouldn't? – but especially Tara.'

Finally the tissue box, unused and pristine, was passed back to Nick Gardener. He smiled, his eyes glinting.

'I'm a bit choked up, to be honest. I'm just an average bloke. You should ask the mother of my son about what a wonderful bloke I am, just to get some balance.'

A laugh from the circle of women. Nick told them they were all a top-notch bunch of scrappers and congratulated them on their efforts. There was an embarrassed but nonetheless genuine series of whoops and hollers from the women. Nick went out of the room and Tara commenced the warm-up.

After a fairly mundane two-hour course which basically reminded the students of each sequence they had learned in the previous weeks, everyone joined in putting chairs out and preparing the room for the spectators.

Apart from Adrian and Tim Renaldo, there were two television crews, ten journalists and a handful of celebrity women among the tightly packed crowd of friends and family that lined one side of the room. Nick's mother had turned up – a very stately woman with a kind face. She sat near the back and didn't look overly happy to be there.

Tara introduced herself and Nick, and then each woman went through a set routine, Tara standing on the side with a whistle, no longer needed by her students' side, Daisy keeping order in the line, officially keeping the energy up. She didn't need to – the women were at full power. To say the evening was explosive would be an understatement – the crowd were constantly on their feet, cheering and screaming on their friend or partner. Some of the men in the audience were in tears; most of the women were. One of the cameramen was being hugged by his producer – the recording had to be completed by his assistant. Tara knew that what these people were seeing was so clearly genuine, so obviously as near to real as it was possible to simulate, that the emotions it stirred up in an observer were very hard to cope with.

At the party afterwards, held in the same room, but now strangely different with the crash mats in a large pile in one corner, Tara decided to make her move.

Nick was standing talking to students, drinking a bottle of beer. She had watched him with his mother. There seemed to be a lot of distance there – his mother had left very early and they didn't kiss. She waited until he was slightly lubricated because she guessed he'd be softer and more receptive then. He'd been interviewed by the press until his voice was hoarse; he'd talked to friends and partners of students and behaved himself beautifully.

Tara had managed to excuse herself, taking a back seat and quietly encouraging Daisy to come to the fore and deal with the press. She spoke to two women, one apparently very well known; both told her of sexual assaults they had experienced and how incredibly hopeful the class made them feel. They were both signing up to take it and would do all they could to spread the word.

Tara noticed that Alice was standing very close to Nick. She knew that if something wasn't already going on there, they were certainly going to break the already flimsy one-year rule soon.

'Nick,' she said when she reached across him for a potato chip. 'Can I have a word with you?'

'Sure,' he said, and excused himself from the women he was surrounded by. They walked together to a quiet corner of the room. Tara was embraced twice by students as they walked, but eventually she had him alone.

'Nick, I have something to ask you which is very sensitive, very difficult to deal with, and I would beg you to be considerate in your reply.'

'I haven't slept with Alice. Okay? I said no.'

'Nick, that wasn't what I was talking about, but thank you for being so obedient to the one-year rule. You've got to be about the only guy who ever has.'

'Oh, what?' said Nick.

'I'm not talking about you and Alice, although I have to say it's pretty damn obvious she's got the serious hots for you, boy.'

'Yeah, well, it's a bit mutual.'

'Oh, that's so passionate. So English. It's a bit mutual. You fancy her.'

'Yeah, all right. She's driving me crazy. But I'm being good,' said Nick. He took another swig from his bottle and cast a glance in Alice's direction.

'Listen,' said Tara. She took a deep breath. Jumped in. 'This is something far more complicated. Um, I want to have a baby.'

'Oh.' Nick looked at her, his blue eyes telling her quite clearly that he had no idea how to react and no idea what her wanting a baby might have to do with him.

'Okay, now you're not going to be able to speak for a few minutes, so I'll spell it out to you. I want to have a baby and Adrian, the man I love and want to be with for the rest of my life, has a sperm count so low, no one can be bothered to count it. I spoke to Adrian the other day, and he's cool about it. That's why he's here. He's seen more graduations than is necessary for a computer scientist. However, as you can imagine, for an infertile male there is a lot to deal with, so there's kind of a great need for sensitivity around this area. However, this problem can be overcome if I can find a sympathetic male donor to help me.'

'Fucking Ada,' said Nick. 'You're not . . .'

'Yes, Nick. I am.'

'Fucking hell, Tara. You want me to give you a baby,' he whispered.

'Well, not a whole baby, just some sperm.'

'Jesus fucking H. Christ almighty,' said Nick, covering his face with one hand. He looked at her through his fingers. 'Just some sperm. Fuck me, Tara. I mean . . . oh, this is all too much. I mean . . . I'll have to think about the – what are they? – the implications of what it means if you and I have a kiddie, but what a fucking offer.'

'Nick, let me put one thing straight right here and now,' said Tara with as kind a smile as she could manage considering what he was obviously thinking. 'We're talking AI here.'

'AI?' said Nick slowly.

'Artificial insemination. I'm not looking to get laid, okay?'

'Oh, right,' said Nick, the flush suddenly draining from his face. 'What, you want me to . . .'

'Well, we'll have to look into the technicalities, I don't know exactly how it works, but I know people who've done it. You kind of fit the bill because you've already got a child and you're a good age for fathering and we know and trust each other. That's why I asked you, and believe me it was not easy.'

'No, I s'pose not.'

'Think about it a while,' said Tara.

Nick laughed and gave her a hug. 'You are a bloody strange woman, Tara. This is the second time you've walked up to me with the weirdest suggestion I've ever heard in my life.'

'How d'you mean?' she asked, not quite following what he was saying.

'In Brighton, you know, when we met, and now you want me to toss off on to a warm spoon so you can slip it in and get yourself up the duff. I've got to hand it to you, you're no conformist, that's for fucking certain.'

She smiled at him. 'So you'll think about it?' she asked.

'I don't know how to think about something like that. My thinking muscles aren't overdeveloped, you know what I'm saying? Fucking hell, Tara. You're a nutter.'

This time Tara hugged Nick. The students were right – he was magnificent.

Chapter Thirty-Five

Nick stumbled in through his front door, slightly drunk, utterly happy and slightly excited. He pulled his gigantic bag behind him and more or less collapsed on to Barney's bike, which as usual was blocking the hallway.

'Sorry, sorry, come in, come in,' he said. Alice stood on the threshold.

'Are you absolutely sure?' she asked, a big smile across her gorgeous face, her hair a mess on top of her head, her eyebrows strong and prominent above two limpid dark eyes.

'Yeah. I'm just embarrassed because I live in such a dump and you're such a class act. Still, it'll be educational for you, to see how trash lives.'

'Don't worry. I don't live in a palace.'

'No, but I bet your place is really nice.'

Nick hooked his bag up on the special wall hooks he'd attached a few weeks earlier. He had done a lot of work in the flat – it looked far more lived in, and with all Barney's books lining the shelves in the front room it appeared a little more as if he had a brain as well as a body. He stumbled into the kitchen which for once wasn't too much of a mess, breathed a sigh of relief and put the kettle on. Alice walked in quietly behind him.

'It's a nice place. I can see you and your son are really happy here.'

'Yeah, we are.'

'Is he here now?'

'Should be,' said Nick, checking his watch. 'If he's not there's trouble. I 'spect he's asleep. We shouldn't make too much noise, I s'pose.' He hiccoughed as he spoke and excused himself. They looked at each other for a while. The thing Nick had noticed about this woman was that she looked better the more he looked at her. She had looked, he now realised, as rough as anything when he'd first seen her, although even then she was seriously tasty. The phone rang. Nick turned and looked at it. He checked his watch and decided it must be Sally.

'I've got an answer service. I'll check the messages later,' he said, staring at the ringing handset. He threw two teabags into a teapot from an unnecessary distance and took two mugs off hooks under the shelf above the sink. Alice sat down at the kitchen table and sighed.

'I feel very nervous,' she said.

'Yeah, me too. I think.' Nick stopped himself.

'What?'

'I think we should, well, have a cup of tea and sort of . . .'

'What, leave it at that?'

'For now. Yeah. I think I'm kind of running downhill, you know. All this has happened so fast, meeting you, and I'd like to take it slowly.'

Alice swallowed and sat silently.

'Okay,' she said. She stood up.

'No, no, don't go. Please,' said Nick, his hands outstretched to her.

'I have to go,' she said, looking at the painted floorboards. 'I have to go and think.'

'Oh, but Alice, please don't get offended. Bloody hell. It's not that I don't want to. I just made a really serious commitment, you know, not to socialise for a year. And I know it's bollocks but I promised and it makes everything I'm trying to do look a bit shit if I just jump into bed with you at the first opportunity.'

'I'm sure you're right,' said Alice. She stood motionless for a while. 'No, you are right,' she added after a large sigh. 'I shouldn't try to use you as my salvation, should I?'

'Bloody hell,' said Nick. 'I don't know about that. Stop for a tea, though.'

Alice smiled and sat down. 'Look,' she said, 'I just feel I was meant to meet you. That's all. That day I walked into the class when you were with Tara, I thought you were horrible. You looked disgusting, but then I was half insane at the time.'

'Yeah,' said Nick, realising he was going to have to hear this, like it or not. He poured the tea and got the milk out of the fridge. There was plenty left, so Barney hadn't drained it all over his Kellogg's Sustain as he normally did.

'But then when I worked out what you did, you know, because of what happened to me, it was all so, well, so obvious. That's why I'm here, really. I know we shouldn't and I really respect Tara, honestly. I thought she was a bit of a pain too when I first met her, but I think she is an amazing woman.'

'Yeah,' said Nick.

'So, I just want you to know, you know?'

'What?' asked Nick.

'Well, that I like you above and beyond the fact that you're a fantastically good-looking man who I see as a saviour and who basically helped me save my life, and I'll never be able to thank you enough. I'd do anything for you, Nick, you know that.'

Nick thought, even through the haze of alcohol, as temptations went this was a pretty big one. He sat and listened to Alice talk for another hour until his eyes started to close. The phone rang twice during that time and they ignored it easily. He felt happy, but the happiness was tinged with lower abdominal tension. He decided this was because she was there and all the time she was there the chances of them shagging like two dogs on the kitchen floor were pretty high.

She left after midnight. He'd called a cab for her. They kissed on the doorstep. He knew she would be able to feel his erection because she pressed against it with her leg. He watched her get in the cab and drive off into the night.

Many hours later, Nick couldn't tell how many, the phone entered his world, slowly and insistently. It rang and rang and rang. He went through fifteen different dreams, talking to Sally, to Tara, to Tiffany, even to Alice, talking to Frankie Jessop, to his mum, to his brother in Australia. Then he slowly came to, realising that it was actually a real telephone. His telephone.

He stumbled around, holding his throbbing head and feeling the aching muscles in his stomach and back. He picked his watch up from the floor by the bed – 2.33 a.m. Pitch black outside. It wouldn't be Sally. Annoying though she was, she never rang that late. Tiff wouldn't ring – she knew about the time difference. He went down the short flight of stairs as best he could, entered the kitchen and stubbed his toe on the fridge. By now he was in a panic. If the bloody thing stopped ringing just before he found it he'd go ape. Bloody cordless phones. He'd seen it earlier – bloody Barney could never put anything away. He found it resting on an empty mug on a stool that had been pushed under the kitchen table. How the fuck did it get there?

'Hello?' he said, through a thick haze of sleep.

'Is that like Barney's dad?'

'Yeah. Who is it?'

'It's Richy B., man.'

'What time is it?'

'It's late, man. You gotta come. Barney's had his arse mash up, man.'

'You what?' said Nick, alarmed. 'He's here, isn't he? Where is he?'

'In hospital, man.'

'What you on, son? Has there been an accident? Which hospital?'

'Whittington. I been ringing you all night.'

'Why's he there? What's happened?'

'He got mash up. You gotta come, man. He wants to see

you.' The phone started beeping; the money was running out in the call-box.

'Fuck. What's your number? Is he hurt?'

'Come, man. Whittington hospital. Quick.'

The phone went dead. 'Fuck, fuck, fuck,' said Nick. He rubbed his face and stood confused for a moment. This was all too weird. He looked at his watch again as if that would help. It didn't. He looked at his old answering machine, sitting unplugged on top of a pile of newspapers, waiting to be junked.

He dialled 1571.

'BT Callminder. You have eighteen messages. Hear them?'

'Fuck,' said Nick.

'I'm sorry, I didn't understand that. Would you like to hear those messages?'

'Fuck,' said Nick, switching off the phone. He always checked his messages when he came in. Always. But not tonight. He went back upstairs.

Barney's room was a mess, but there was no Barney. He went back into his bedroom and started pulling on clothes as fast as he could.

He clattered back downstairs, pulled on his old leather jacket, slammed his feet into a pair of Blunstone elastic-sided boots, and wrenched his front door open to find a police officer walking up the steps towards him.

'Evening, sir. Mr Gardener?'

'Yeah, Nick Gardener, yeah. What?'

'I've come to inform you about your son . . .'

'I know, I've just had a call.'

'We'll take you up there, sir.'

'Oh, blimey, thanks, mate,' said Nick. He climbed into the back of the panda car.

'Your son's all right, sir. Not in any serious danger. It was a very nasty assault nonetheless.'

'Oh, Jesus. Poor little kid,' said Nick. He was so confused, angry and crying at the same time. Barney had turned into an innocent little four-year-old in his mind, standing in the park watching the big boys play rough games. He still needed his dad there to protect him, and what had happened?

Nick felt he needed help, desperately – someone, even Sally. He didn't want Alice to be put off; she'd think he was trouble. Bollocks, he thought. He couldn't hack this shit on his own.

'What happened?' he asked after listening to a police radio message about an incident on City Road.

'He was attacked by a street gang, as far as we can fathom from eye-witness accounts. Girls.'

'What d'you mean, girls?' asked Nick, rubbing his eyes to try to make sense of everything.

'It's becoming a bit of a problem. Girl gangs, I suppose you could call them. Mind you, this is the first time I've come across anything like this,' said the officer.

'Oh, I have,' said the driver. 'Remember that old geezer we found down by the canal?'

'Oh yeah, that was girls, wasn't it.'

'Mind you, he was a paedophile,' said the driver.

'You mean a gang of girls beat up Barney?' asked Nick, desperate now for any information.

'That's right, sir. About eight of them, from what we can gather. We're hoping your son'll be able to give us some clues as to who they are.'

'Fuck,' said Nick, staring out of the window at the orange-lit buildings of Liverpool Road floating past.

Ten minutes later he ran into the Whittington hospital's accident and emergency department. He enquired about his son at reception and on being asked to take a seat explained he couldn't sit down knowing his son had been assaulted and was lying in hospital.

He did everything he could to keep his temper – he used eye contact and slowly delivered words, trying everything in his power not to sound aggressive, which was what he was feeling. Just before he completely lost it he was led to a cubicle by a tired-looking nurse. The department was very busy – a few people with split heads lying drunk and blood-soaked in corners; a wild, skinny white girl falling out of a vomit-stained miniskirt, swearing at anyone who passed; a couple of terrified-looking young men with makeshift bandages around their heads and hands.

Nick was shown into a curtained-off area and was confronted with the sight of his sixteen-year-old son, barely recognisable as his face was dark blue and swollen, especially around the left eye.

'Oh, Jesus fucking Christ,' said Nick, looking for something to touch, a hand to hold, anything. Barney had a drip in his right arm; his left arm was broken and had been hastily set in a plaster bandage. So much must have happened while he was sleeping only a mile down the road.

The tired-looking nurse returned. 'You're the father, I take it?' she said, her lilting Irish accent strangely soothing in the craziness of the department. Nick nodded. The nurse felt for Barney's pulse in his neck, then checked the drip.

'He's not quite as bad as he looks. The broken arm is the worst thing but it's only a minor fracture. The rest is bruising, except he's lost one tooth, poor fellow. He's had a CAT scan and the brain seems to be fine. That's what we really worry about in cases like these. Everything else gets better in time. There'll be a doctor here in a while but as you can see we're pretty pushed. I'm sorry I can't tell you anything more at the moment. Okay?'

'He's going to live, then?' said Nick, his eyes already filled with tears.

'Oh, Jesus, yes, he'll live. Don't worry. He's only a wee young lad, he'll recover very quickly. He's not unconscious, he's had a little something to help him sleep. His face will be pretty painful in the morning. As soon as we've found a bed he'll be transferred to a ward. You know what it's like.'

'Thanks,' said Nick. The nurse smiled at him and left. Nick sat with Barney, holding the tips of his right hand.

He had no idea how much time passed, but when he left the curtained-off cubicle the department seemed quiet. He found his way to the men's room and took a leak, washed his face and hands and looked in a mirror. He looked rough, but not as rough as Barney. He felt something swell up inside. Like vomit only hotter. Anger. That was what it was, of course. He was fucking furious. His anger showed in his face; it was creased in ways he'd never seen before. He looked well hard as he stared at himself in the mirror. Like a killer, a nutter, someone on the run. Something had happened – he'd been propelled back into something more basic as he'd sat with his little boy in the noisy A & E department. Mind you, he thought, he didn't look as rough as the fucking bitches that hurt his boy. He'd tear their fucking little spastic heads off. Fucking Street Sistas, they were as good as dead. They'd never be able to look out for each other enough. One by one they'd find themselves in fucking hospital with their legs broken. He wouldn't rape them or have any sexual contact, he wouldn't steal their money. This was going to be male violence pure and simple – he'd set the standards for male violence. He would only cause injury; they'd have no excuse. None of them would be able to accuse him of any sexual offence, just actual bodily harm. It would all take place in daylight with witnesses. He'd carry a picture of Barney as he was in hospital. He'd show people what these slag bitches had done. He'd hold the little cows by the hair, occasionally smashing their heads against something solid like a lamp-post, then when he was ready, calmly break their fucking legs. Mash them up serious. They shouldn't be in the least bit surprised when they came out of a newsagent's one evening to find their fucking teeth punched down their throats. He could feel the impact as he thought about it.

He punched his right fist into the palm of his left hand and looked at himself. Even he found what he was looking at frightening, but what did they expect? These fuck-head teenage slags had decided to go against the grain and use violence to solve a problem, whatever the fuck their problem was. This was what he'd been told women never did. Men were violent and women had to learn to retaliate. Bollocks.

He held on to the sink to steady himself. He felt a knot of pure pain in his shoulders, a knot of over-controlled muscles. Muscles that wanted to exert themselves suddenly, unexpectedly, and in the direction of a bunch of fuck-faced little cows. He was so incredibly and overwhelmingly angry. He had never before felt this level of pure fury. Someone had hurt his child. He decided this allowed him, without thought or remorse, to become an animal. The normal rules of social conduct no longer applied. He was a dog that had slipped its leash – mad, bad and extremely dangerous to know. That little bitch had sat in his kitchen, she had let him pay for her fucking pizza. Well, she'd soon be street pizza. He'd rip her fucking nose-rings out and shove 'em up her arse. She'd soon be a dirty bit of rag lying bleeding on the path, no idea what hit her. The sheer force of his anger would spread her over the fucking road like strawberry jam. The Street Sistas were about to get decimated. Cry havoc, you little fuckers, thought Nick Gardener, run home to mummy, you little twats – because then he'd have the excuse to mash up family as well.

Chapter Thirty-Six

The opening circle of the Monday evening class was a very different experience for Tara, and, she assumed, for Nick. Apart from the fact that it was a new group of students, this was their second class, and there was always a danger of a morale drop. Most students hit a wall of insecurity as the exercises got harder.

Nick had arrived late and looked very tired. She had guessed that once again the year-long no-socialising rule had been broken and he had probably gotten himself laid by the sensuously beautiful Alice.

She asked if he was okay just before she opened the class. He said he'd had some trouble with Barney but everything was fine. She was just about to try to find out what had happened when Daisy interrupted. She wanted Tara to go through the running order one more time to make sure she hadn't forgotten anything. The new batch of students was being taught by Daisy – Tara would be assisting, on hand to deal with any crisis. Daisy had excelled herself in the first week, and Tara felt sure she'd be fine.

Out of the fourteen women, only two divulged any history of assault.

In the opening circle of the group a young woman called Michelle told the tale of how a young man she knew tried to get her to spar with him. He started to be really rough, telling her that he could beat her no matter what she learned. She explained that this man wasn't normally violent or even very competitive, but something about the fact that she was learning to fight must have really upset him.

Although Tara had heard this kind of story before, she knew Daisy might be thrown by it. She was wrong.

Daisy said, 'You might find it best if you kept what you're doing in the class fairly close to your chest. Yeah? It's always hard to judge people's response. The training touches on a lot of raw areas, you know, painful stuff in human experience. Some men may not know how to handle the emotions involved.'

Tara noticed Nick take an involuntary breath as he heard Daisy say this. She noted it but thought nothing more about it.

'Okay,' said Daisy after the tissue box had finished its circuit. 'This week we're going to be trying some different moves and Nick is going to start vocalising more. He'll start using abusive language, he'll start making noises when you get good impact. Try not to be put off by this, try not to get panicked. Always look for a target, don't worry about what he's saying to you. Some of the things he says will be very disturbing, very frightening. He's in fact using language that we know, from research, has been used by men during assaults. That's why he says these things, pretty horrible things. We want you to be able to function even though what he says is repulsive. A man will often use these terms either to get himself off or to gain vital moments during a struggle. Many women freeze when they hear this stuff. We don't want you to.'

The class, once it got under way, was slow and hard. Daisy worked well, was conscientious, utterly focused and right on the game. Nick fought harder, grabbed more aggressively, held on for longer than he had in the opening classes. Tara noted that his vocalisations were possibly two classes ahead of where they should have been.

'Hey, darling, how's that slimy little cunt, eh? Not tight enough for me, bitch. I'm gonna fuck you in the back door, darlin',' he said as he pulled a woman to the ground.

Tara would normally advise against using the word 'cunt' this early in a course, but there was no way she was going to intervene – she would see if Daisy said anything in the break. This wasn't the normally supremely sensitive Nick she had grown used to. Plus his vocalisations when women made good strikes against him were a little over the top.

To hear a person suffer pain was a very strong block women had to go through. When they landed a blow on a man and he groaned in agony as he fell to the floor, they had a natural tendency to stop, or sometimes even to enquire if he was okay. They had to learn to ignore these feelings and inflict further pain, until the man was incapable of harming them.

A woman called Queenie opened the second exercise. She was a hippie chick in her thirties. Nick came up from behind and pulled her roughly on to the floor. Statistically this was the most common way for a man to attack a woman. Daisy taught the women not to resist, not to try to keep standing, to use the man's weight and strength to their own advantage.

It was a system that worked incredibly well – three or four moves, twisting the body into a position where a target could be seen and a blow achieved. Once the students had got over their initial discomfort on the floor, they realised that they were safer, that their legs were lethal and the man really didn't stand much of a chance.

Queenie fought well, speedily grasping the concept and managing to carry out what was asked of her. One by one the women went through the exercise, Nick responding expertly – never too aggressive, never backing off until they had made a full impact blow.

'Let's take five,' said Daisy after the last student had completed the primary exercise. Nick took off his helmet, spat out his gumshield and took a long swig of Evian water from a large bottle. He and Daisy retired to a corner of the room. Tara checked that a couple of the more timid students were okay and then joined them.

'Great class, Daisy. Really good work,' she said.

'Thanks,' said Daisy, wiping herself with a towel. She looked at Nick. 'How you doing?' she asked quietly, squatting next to him.

'Fine. This is the best thing I could do, Daisy. I've had a bit of a rough night, but I can still do this. It's great,' said Nick. He didn't look at her. Tara tried to sit beside him as casually as she could.

'Can I take some of your water?' she asked.

'Sure,' came the dead reply. Nothing, not a glance in her direction. Maybe something had gone wrong between him and Alice. She almost hoped this was the case, because what really worried her was what she had said to him at the party the night before. Maybe he'd thought about it and felt offended, maybe he didn't want to talk to her about it and was blocking her out.

'You okay?' she asked.

'Sure,' he said. 'Just a bit tired. I'm fine. This is the best thing for it. Hair of the dog.'

'What's that mean?' she asked. Although familiar with the phrase, she wasn't sure if he meant he actually had a hangover.

'Getting the helmet on and sweating it out. It's a fucking life-saver today, believe me.'

'Something's happened?' she asked quietly.

'Nothing I can't handle.'

'I'd like to talk after the class, Nick.'

'I'm busy,' said Nick. He wasn't opening up to her, didn't look at her, just poured the bottle of water over his head and wiped his neck with a towel. Tara felt a strong need not to give up.

'Look, if you need to talk, you know, I don't need to go to Brighton tonight. I could stay with Daisy maybe.'

'I'll be okay.'

'I'm always on the end of a phone, Nick. You know that.'

'Thanks,' he said. He'd cut her off. Damn him, he was blocking her out. What could have gone so wrong so quickly? It must be her demands, she'd pushed him too far. There was nothing she could do about it. Not now, in front of a class. She stood up and smiled.

'Okay, let's get back to it,' she said. The women clambered to their feet. Nick pushed his gumshield in, pulled his helmet back on and the class continued.

Chapter Thirty-Seven

It was a hot class – Nick was sweating buckets inside the suit. He felt more uncomfortable than usual. The shoulder straps were digging into him, every part of his clothing was soaked in sweat.

In the last exercise of the day he was approaching women from behind as they walked along. He was concentrating well, trying to make each assault slightly different. In the moments between fights or when he was having a quick drink and a cool-down, he was amazed by how he managed to concentrate so well. The suit was an amazing thing – he didn't think about Barney lying in hospital for a second. He didn't consider the women who had attacked his son.

As soon as the helmet came off, though, the images, the thoughts and the anger surged back in. He felt as if he was about to burst. He couldn't seem to breathe out enough – it was easy breathing in, but air seemed to stay in his lungs.

'Come here, you little minx,' he said to a young woman called Helen. He had grabbed her hair quite aggressively. She spun around and elbowed him in the side of the head. He wasn't quite ready for it and the blow sent his brain jangling about in his tired skull.

'Oh, you want it rough, do you, bitch? Okay, then,' he said, taking a swipe at the woman. She fell to the ground and delivered a well-aimed and very powerful groin kick. Nick lost his balance and fell awkwardly, his tiredness getting the better of him. Then Helen shuffled forward. He could see her through his gauze; he started to get up but she hit him with a scissor kick which slammed his head back down on the mat. That was enough. He put his hands to the side of his helmet in the unconscious position, then immediately felt another blow land on his helmet.

He heard Daisy blow her whistle as the third very powerful scissor kick came raining down. He could hear the woman screaming at him. She'd lost it, she wasn't listening to Daisy. He turned his head to see what was going on just in time for the fourth frenzied kick to land on his helmet, only this time, unfortunately, his hand was between the helmet and the woman's shoe. The pain was intense and immediate.

'For fuck's sake!' he screamed as he pulled away. He could see Daisy's shoes right next to him. Why wasn't she stopping this? It was crazy – the woman had lost it.

Suddenly her heel smashed into his eye gauze. He was completely unprepared and his head hurt like fuck. This, decided Nick Gardener, he really didn't need. Whatever had protected him before was gone now; whatever clever little boundaries he had managed to construct in his head which kept everything tidy had just broken down. This stupid little bitch was belting seven types of shit out of him and she had to stop.

He sprang to his feet only to feel the woman punching his back. She got a fist in at the side of his protective padding near his kidneys and sent a spasm of pain right through his body. He spun away from her and frantically fumbled with his helmet. As he removed it the sound of screaming came to his ears with a vengeance. The woman was shaking off Daisy's attempts to calm her. He could see Tara coming up fast from behind her, but Nick couldn't stop himself.

'Will you listen to the fucking whistle, you dumb-fuck bitch!' he bellowed right in her face. 'When the fucking whistle blows,' he screamed, pushing her with open palms on her shoulders, her face frozen, her mouth open in horror, 'you stop hitting me, you aggressive little cow. Do you fucking understand?'

'Okay, Nick, okay. She's stopped,' said Tara, stepping quickly between them. 'It's okay now, let's take five. Okay, everyone, it's a hot day, let's take five.'

Nick threw the helmet furiously on to the mat. He saw his gumshield lying on the floor, blood on it. The little cow had made him bleed. Then he felt the pain in his hand – she'd ripped the skin off his fingers.

'Fuck you!' he shouted, his vision blurred with tears. 'All you fucking awful women!'

Chapter Thirty-Eight

Peter Welbeck had a very resonant voice, a slight Midlands accent in a received-pronunciation framework. Quite deep, with a breathiness about it, as though he had just climbed five flights of stairs before he spoke. His voice seemed to have a smile, even on the phone – he spoke with a grin permanently attached to his face which he presumably felt gave him a jaunty air.

His voice was also chilling and deadly to Alice Moreton's ear. Just before she left for work one morning, late, which was not usual for her, the phone rang. She picked it up without thinking.

'Hello, Alice, didn't think I'd catch you.'

The bottom fell out of her world.

'Alice, hello. It's me, Peter.' A jaunty lilt to his voice.

'What d'you want?' Her voice sounded dead even to her.

'Oh, you sound down in the dumps, baby. What's up?'

'What d'you mean, what's up?'

'Alice. It's Peter.'

'I know who it is,' she said. 'What do you want?' As soon as the words had left her lips she regretted them.

'Well, I was wondering if you were free for lunch. I'm in town.'

'I'm busy. I don't want to see you.'

'Oh, come on, Alice, don't be like that. I got your message and I was really depressed by it. I thought you'd got over all that nonsense. It was a misunderstanding – you know I didn't mean any harm. I'd never hurt you. Blimey, I'm half crazy about you. Please don't be daft about it.'

'I don't ever want to see you again. Okay?'

She slammed the phone down and looked at her hand, so far away somehow, and shaking so much. She held on to her kitchen table and breathed as deeply as she could. She walked to the sink and drank a glass of water, anything to stop the wave of maddening terror that had ripped through her. There was nowhere to hide.

She picked up her car keys and went to her front door. She looked through the spyhole – there was no one on the landing. She gingerly opened the door, half expecting Peter to make a rhino charge at her at any moment. There was no one around, just the familiar hollow echo of distant traffic and the smell of floor polish.

She drove to work, constantly checking to see if anyone was following her. She took a completely different route – not that Peter knew which way she drove to work, but he was intelligent enough to guess.

She parked in the underground carpark beneath her building and checked her mirrors before she got out. He could be waiting for her there. She took the lift up to the office and breathed a sigh of relief. Everything was buzzing away as normal, except there was a huge bunch of flowers on her desk. She smiled when she saw them, felt a flush develop on her cheeks when she realised half the office had seen them too. She pulled open the little square envelope attached to the wrapping, assuming that the flowers were from Nick. She had to blink and read the name twice before the truth dawned. They were from Peter Welbeck, with much love. At the bottom was the word 'Lunch?'

'Bev,' said Alice to the secretary she shared with another assessor, 'can you bin these for me.'

'Sorry?' said Bev.

'The flowers. I really don't want them. Can you chuck them out, please, I've got to get on.'

'Oh, what a shame, they're lovely.'

'They are not lovely, they are frightful. Now take them away. Please.'

'Okay, okay,' said Bev, carefully picking up the enormous package.

Alice listened to her voicemail. Among the mass of business enquiries and a message from her mother were three communications from Peter Welbeck. Why had he suddenly turned up? She hadn't heard from him in . . . she didn't know how long, but a long time.

During the morning he rang three times. Bev asked if she could put him through. Alice refused to take his calls. She asked Bev to get her lunch for her, and when the day was done she rang her mother and asked if she could stay the night with them in Tewkesbury. Her mother was naturally delighted.

Chapter Thirty-Nine

'Hear you wanna beat up on a bunch of little girls,' said a familiar voice when Nick answered the phone. It was Tim Renaldo.

'Fuck me, news travels fast, mate. Who told you that?' asked Nick, still lying in bed even though it was 10.30 in the morning.

'Oh boy, the tangled web we weave,' said Tim. 'I'm at King's Cross train station. How far is that from your place?'

'Oh, man. Fancy some breakfast?' said Nick, feeling the first ray of sunlight leaking into the grey desert of his shut-eyed world.

'I could eat a whore,' said Tim with a laugh.

Within half an hour the two men had met at the Café Rouge in Islington. Tim had asked for a posh breakfast and that was the poshest place Nick could think of. They embraced warmly on meeting.

'I need a coffee and a big breakfast. I need to take a dump real bad. Planes really screw up my bowels for days, man.'

'Thanks for all that information,' said Nick. They sat at a window table and ordered.

'What happened to your boy was shit, man,' said Tim once they had settled. Right in there, noticed Nick. No messing.

'How d'you know about it?' he asked.

'Tara rang me and told me and I thought, fuck it, this is a man who needs some support. You know?'

'Tara told you? But she doesn't know. I haven't told anyone.'

'You live in a cosy fucking world, brother. While you were at the hospital with your boy last night, the phone lines were buzzing. When was he beat up? Sunday night?'

Nick nodded.

'It's been non-stop since then, man. What d'you think, people just carry on as normal? Tara Kennedy is not the kind of woman who thrives on lack of information, you know. She rings around.'

'Who?'

'Your mother, of course. Tara's real spooked. She don't dare ring you man, and believe me, that has never happened before.'

'My mum! Oh, blimey, I don't believe it,' said Nick. 'I thought, if Tara knows, she won't let me work, and then. . . . Oh shit.'

'Oh shit indeed,' said Tim.

'It's kind of blown over already. My boy's out of hospital today. I've got to go and get him later on. I still don't really know what happened.'

'And you're mad as hell.'

'I don't know. I just want to sleep. I don't feel anything.'

'It's pretty clear to see, man. You're mad as hell. And in the class yesterday . . .'

'You heard about that?'

'Of course I heard. You've got an important job now, man. People are gonna talk about you. Get used to it.'

'I feel sorry about it now. I really do,' said Nick. 'I don't know what to do – I haven't slept all night. Probably feel the same as you, you know. Jet-lagged and spaced right out.'

'Better than drugs, man,' said Tim with a hippie smile. The coffee arrived and the two men sat in silence for a while. Nick was reminded of the time when they had sat in the café together on Haight Street. It seemed like a lifetime ago, before he got into all this mess.

'Fuck. Why did I ever listen to you?' he said finally.

'Oh, it's my fault,' said Tim with a grin. 'That's real good. You English guys are so smart.'

Nick laughed. He knew it wasn't Tim's fault, he knew that whatever negative thing had happened at the Monday class, whatever had happened to Barney, the rest of his life had taken on a delicious new complexity which brightened his every waking moment.

'No, it's my fault,' he said after a moment's thought.

'It ain't your fault either, bud,' said Tim. 'It's those fucking bitches that took chunks out of your boy. That's who I blame, man.'

'Yeah, but Tim, don't say that kind of thing. That's what I've been trying to stop myself thinking.'

'And I bet it hasn't worked.'

'Well, it's so complicated, isn't it? I mean, what's happening when a bunch of girls, a gang, you know, they pick on a kid and beat the shit out of him? Break his arm, for fuck's sake. It's weird.'

'Girl gangs are big in the States, man. Shooting each other, car jacking, dealing crack, all the same shit the boys do.'

'I never even heard of it until a few weeks ago.'

'Kind of a rude introduction to the phenomenon, eh?' said Tim with a sad smile.

'But what does it mean? For us, I mean?' asked Nick.

'For us?'

'Blokes like us, who do what we do. I feel like a traitor.'

'Oh, man,' said Tim, shaking his head.

'I do!' said Nick. 'There am I, teaching women how to beat up men better. But look at what happened. Those women don't need teaching how to fight, they need teaching how to fucking well control themselves. It makes me want to think the un-thinkable.'

'And what's that?' asked Tim, suddenly showing more interest.

'That women are spoilt rotten – stuck-up, over-confident nightmares. Bossy know-all fuckers with an argument for everything so they can dupe us into thinking they're right and we're just a bunch of mugs who resort to violence when we don't get our own way. They're just as fucked up as we are.'

Tim nodded all the way through this.

'Will you stop nodding!' said Nick rather more forcefully than the other customers in the Café Rouge felt comfortable with. Tim nodded with a smile and then stopped himself and looked shamefaced.

'Sorry, man.'

'Well, what are they on? Fucking women have utterly screwed up my life. Sally, that's my boy's mother – total fucking nightmare. You couldn't design more torment without resorting to thumbscrews, and she virtually got herself pregnant. I was too green to know any better. Then Tiffany – you remember the girl with the tits in San Francisco? Shit, I mean, the best sex I have ever had. I never knew sex could even get that kinky and intense, but she was barking mad. The tattoos – there was no clear skin left, hardly.'

He felt a little pang of guilt. Tiffany was one of the sanest women he'd ever known.

'Then Tara. Fucking hell, Tara is completely barking. She wants me to jerk off into a cup and let her make a baby with my spunk! I mean, for fuck's sake! Tara is the ultimate fucking nightmare woman. She drives me fucking crazy!'

'That's because you're in love with her.'

'What?'

'You're in love with her, man. That's cool. We all are.'

'What are you talking about? She's a fucking nutter.'

'No way.'

'Way, Tim. Come on. You guys are all so smart,' said Nick, impersonating Tim rather well. 'What d'you mean we're all in love with her? She's so distant and screwed up and weird. She's so efficient and, you know, utterly obsessed with her work.'

'And she's amazingly beautiful and charismatic and loving and we all dream that maybe we'd be the guy that would turn her head. But Adrian's an amazing guy, so I know there's no hope of that, and I don't let it affect me, but, man, you'd have to be blind or gay not to fancy Tara. She's stupendous, upstanding and gorgeous. Come on, Nicholas, admit it. You're a bit in love with her.'

'I'm not. Oh God. What a mess,' said Nick. He buried his head in his hands again, trying to force out the teeming swirl of emotions that sloshed through his mind, trying to order them so they didn't seem so overpowering. 'I can't stand all the fucking mess. I've got to stop to try and sort it out. I've let things slip for so long, just gone along with what everyone said, and now it's all gone so wrong. I just want to tidy up my brains somehow.'

'Life's a mess,' said Tim quietly. 'That's what we live in. A mess. Our lives define mess. It's what our generation is here to do. Make a mess. I have two children with two women – it's a mess. I shouldn't sleep with students and I do and I'm slightly in love with a totally unavailable woman. It's a mess. I have a flea-bitten old dog, my car is a wreck, I live in a dump and it's a mess. But I love my kids, I'm pretty healthy and I try not to hurt people. I help people protect themselves and I respect others who do the same. Like you. Your life's a mess, your kid got beat up by girls, you've got more women throwing themselves at you than you know what to do with, you're slightly in love with a woman who wants you to father her child. If you haven't just started an affair with, and let me emphasise this point, the most beautiful woman I have ever seen in a class anyplace, then you soon will.'

'I will not,' said Nick darkly.

'You've just started to do something you really enjoy doing and you're very good at, and okay, so you blow it during one class a little. No big deal, man. Work it out and keep going.'

'I shouldn't have done the fucking class. I should have told someone. I should have told Tara. But I didn't want her to see that side of me. I thought I could butch it out. The helmet has always kind of, well, protected me before. It's always been a really clear line – helmet off, just normal, helmet on, Hannibal, but still in control, you know, and suddenly, yesterday, this stupid fucking woman just wouldn't stop.'

'I knew it,' said Tim, holding his tired-looking face in both hands. 'Tara said a student ignored the whistle.'

'She ignored the whistle,' agreed Nick.

'So you are real angry inside.'

'I'm not sleeping. I think it through and know there's no use being angry. I think I'm sort of over it and then, well, last night the hospital gave me Barney's clothes, the ones he was wearing when they attacked him, and they're all ripped up and covered in blood. I mean, fucking hell. It's wrong, isn't it?'

'Yeah, it's really wrong, man. Don't matter who does it to who for why, it's wrong. But so is busting a student's confidence. Still, I know what it's like, man. Sometimes you just want to stop being beaten by women, that's all. Sometimes you get so goddamn sick of the whole thing.'

Nick smiled. He knew that if there was one person who'd understand what he'd been through this was the one. Tim's breakfast arrived – eggs Benedict with a side order of fries.

'You see, I can remember thinking as this silly cow was pounding away at my head. I thought, why should I take any more of this? What the fuck is all this about? Surely it was the women who weren't "dealing with their anger". Why were they taking it out on me and my boy? Two men who hadn't really done anything bad. I felt a lump in my throat, you know. I was actually really sad. That was what was so weird. Then I looked through the eye protectors and I saw her face. She's a really cute girl but her face was like twisted into ugliness. I thought, fuck you, lady. Took my helmet off and gave her what for.'

'You didn't hit her?'

'Pushed her. No, I didn't hit her. What, is she saying I hit her?' asked Nick, worried as to what the implications might be.

'No, she thinks it's all her fault, she's full of remorse,' said Tim through a mouthful of breakfast.

'I didn't really hit her, just kind of impact-pushed her.'

'Impact-pushed. Oh, you guys are so smart. Impact-pushed. What did Tara do?'

'She just told them to take five and took me out of the room.'

'That girl is so cool,' said Tim with a smile. 'Man oh man, just nothing seems to faze her.'

'She was pretty mad when we got outside. We kind of had a fight.'

'Oh, man,' said Tim. 'She's real upset about it, but the stories tie together real neat. I guess you're both telling the truth.'

'Who are you? Judge fucking Dredd?'

'Yeah, man, the facilitator, armed and dangerous,' said Tim with an eggy smile. 'Man oh man, this is good.' He took another mouthful and then said, 'Tara didn't tell me what happened between you, though. When you say you had a fight, you mean like you came to blows?'

'No, a bit of pushing, then I said I'd had it and I tore off my kit and left. I just got the hell out of there, went to see Barney.'

'Your boy?'

'Yeah. Should have been with him anyway. I shouldn't have done the class.'

'So you keep saying. Then what happened?' asked Tim, furiously pushing food into his mouth. 'Sorry,' he said through a mouthful of eggs Benedict when he registered what Nick was looking at.

'It's fine,' said Nick. 'I went up to see my boy. I was in a total state 'cos I'd rung his mother Monday morning and she went totally ballistic. Blamed me, said I'd set it up to try and make him more aggressive – amazing theories she came up with, all bollocks, of course, but it still gets to you when it's your own kid.'

He remembered the look on Barney's face when he had walked into the ward after leaving the class. His son, normally a cheery-faced kid, had so many weird colours on his face. He looked a little better than when Nick had first seen him on the Sunday night, his bruising now receding, the previously swollen closed eye now slightly open. His broken tooth still looked bad, and his arm was in a plaster bandage which had a very well-drawn caricature of Barney emblazoned on it in orange felt pen.

'Richy B. did it,' said Barney with a new lisp caused by the missing tooth. 'What you doing here?'

'Come to see you, me old mucker,' said Nick. 'Brought you some comics.' He fished out two Judge Dredd comics he'd chosen in a Charing Cross Road store. It cheered him up to see how positive his boy's reaction to them was.

'Excellent,' said Barney, trying a smile. 'Mum'll hate those.'

'Is she here?' asked Nick.

'You missed her by a couple of minutes, as always,' said Barney. 'She wants me to go back to Oxford.'

'You're going to go, aren't you?' said Nick glumly.

'For a bit. Until I'm better.'

'I can't believe this has happened,' said Nick. 'Can't even give you a hug, can I?'

'Rather you didn't, Dad. It's all a bit sore.'

'Why, Barney? Eh? Why?'

'What?' asked his son, almost annoyed.

'Why d'they do it? What happened?'

'Do I have to talk about it?'

'Have you told your mum?'

'As if I could keep it from her.'

'Well, for fuck's sake, you can tell me, Barn. You know you can tell me anything. It's driving me crazy not knowing. I wanna go out on the streets and kill the little fuckers,' Nick said conspiratorially. 'You know what I'm saying, Barney? No one hurts you, mate. You might be a lanky sod but you're still my kid.'

'I know, Dad,' said Barney.

'Every time I go out the front door I'm looking for them. Every time I see their spray-painted name on the walls I'm that close to killing the next tough-arsed-looking street kid I see.'

'Please don't make it any worse, Dad. Mum said it'll get in the papers when it gets to court. I don't want to walk around as the boy who got beaten up by girls. Not because it's some sissy thing, I don't mind that, it's just I don't want to become some sort of icon. You know what it'll be like, a tabloid story that proves women are getting more violent and all that sort of rubbish. I just don't want anyone to know.'

'Well, what's going to happen to the bitches that did this?' Nick asked, looking around to check that no one could hear him say the word bitches.

'The police say they know who they are, they're still deciding whether to charge them with actual bodily harm. Looks like they will. But that's not going to solve anything, is it?'

'You can't just let them get away with it, Barney.'

'It's my fault. Well, it isn't, but . . .' Barney turned and looked out of the window. Nick was bursting to ask him what had happened but managed to stop himself. He had got to know his son pretty well over the years, was still marvelling at how complex this once little fellow who used to toddle along beside him had become. After a few moments Barney turned to face his father, a tear running down the cheek below his good eye.

'I don't like fighting, Dad. The posse got really mad when I said they were morons. Except I didn't say that. I said that fighting was for morons and it never solved any problems. Just made them worse. And then they said that meant I thought they were morons and no one abused them, and as Street Sistas they'd had enough from sexist blokes and all that stuff. I got angry when they pushed me and said it proved they were as stupid as men if they used violence. I should have shut up and walked away, but they made me so depressed. They behaved like football oiks, really moronic. Like Nazi thugs. It wasn't Sooty, though, Dad – she tried to stop them.'

'What? It wasn't the little girl I met?'

'She's not a little girl, Dad. She's nearly sixteen.'

'Well, she looks about twelve, but we won't go into that.'

'Look, I just want to forget it. It was my fault, I shouldn't have said they were morons.'

'But it's gone really wrong, mate. I've been called a lot worse and I didn't go around putting people in hospital.'

'It's different for them. They're bottom of the heap, Dad. Black women in the inner city, absolute bottom of the heap.'

'You sound like your mother now.'

'But it's true, Dad,' said Barney. 'Doesn't matter who I sound like if it's true.'

'All right. I know it's true, but it's no fucking picnic if you're a white bloke. What I can't believe is that no one tried to stop them. Why didn't someone wade in?'

'Sooty did.'

'Well, fat lot of good she did. Look at you.'

'It was like a joke that's been going on for ages. Sooty told them I was a pacifist. They were teasing me, calling me a mummy's boy and all that shit. I don't mind that. I get that at school. I've been beaten up more times than I can remember.'

'What? When? You never told me.'

'You were never there. It's because I decided to be non-violent.'

'Oh, fucking hell.'

'When I was twelve I read all about Gandhi.'

'When I was twelve I couldn't read,' said Nick, almost to himself.

'Okay, but I knew he was right,' said Barney, his eyes alive beneath the fading bruises. 'All the violence just leads to more violence. It doesn't solve the problem, Dad. I respect what you do, I think you do it for the right reasons, but I think it's wrong. Teaching people how to be more aggressive is only going to make the whole world more violent. Sooty agrees with me – she's just scared of crossing the other Sistas. We just got talking on the street and I said I was a pacifist and that I'd signed the peace pledge.'

'What's that?' asked Nick.

'It's like a pledge you can sign if you're a pacifist. It means you pledge never to bear arms no matter what. If there's a war, I'll just go to prison or be shot straight away. No messing.'

'Very convenient,' said Nick.

'Well, they laughed at first, but Jeannie took offence because I said that violence was the way lower life forms solved their problems.'

'So Jeannie's the one, is she?'

'No, Dad, she's not the one. It's my fault because I shouted at them when they shouted at me. I wasn't a very good pacifist. I was a bit aggressive. They kept calling me a wimp, or a poof, they called me a sissy and a tosser, and I just said there's always someone tougher than you so violence was pointless. Then they started hitting me.'

'And you didn't hit them back?'

'No. I tried to do what Gandhi's followers did. Let them exhaust themselves with their violence and hatred until they could see they would never defeat me.'

'Oh, Barn, mate. I dunno much about Anglo-Indian history but I know there were like millions of followers of Gandhi, not just one martyr trying to do it on his own.'

'Amounts to the same thing.'

'Blimey, you're either a nutter or one tough-assed little kid.'

'Probably a nutter,' said Barney with a gap-toothed smile.

'No you're not, mate. You're just one very unlucky fucker. That's all. Jesus. It's so fucking unfair.'

'I know.'

'I'm so sorry, Barn. I should have been there. I should have come with you.'

'You can't always be with me, Dad.'

'But fuck, they're not defending themselves against some violent bastard that oppresses them, they've picked on someone who's weaker than them, or more intelligent and not into fighting. That's not bravery, that's disgusting.'

'I know, Dad, but you have to see it in context.'

'The context I see it in is that you got injured by some ugly fucking people, actually. In the end it don't matter that they're women – they should still go down.'

The two sat in silence. Nick didn't want to hear his own voice – he sounded like a retired boxer, bullying his pansy son for not fighting back. But everything in him wanted to shake Barney, ask him, 'Why didn't you take one of them out, you limp-wristed little tosser?'

He left the hospital more angry than when he'd arrived. He stormed back down the Holloway Road, imagining smashing the Street Sistas' faces in. His body twitched as he imagined them being foolish enough to threaten him or challenge him in some way. He pictured himself grinding their faces along brick walls then temple-punching them when their heads were held up against something solid like a lamp-post. Watching them flop to the ground, kicking their limp bodies on the pavement, stamping on their thin arms and breaking the bones. He imagined pulling their hair and ripping their clothes, leaving them half naked and then seeing their breasts, and punching them in the face and then seeing their little panties and pulling at them.

He stopped and checked his thoughts. What he had just been doing was having a rape fantasy. For the first time in his life he had had an actual violent rape fantasy. Not even a sex fantasy involving a woman he fancied whose clothes he was ripping off. This was a fantasy about women he hated, whom he found vile and beneath him, scum bitches, loud-mouthed slags who deserved a fucking good hiding. He was thirty-six years old and it was the first such fantasy he could clearly remember. It wasn't anything to do with sex; it was everything to do with violence and power. He rubbed his tired eyes and went home. He lay on his bed alone and cried and cried as he had never cried before. His mother and father were in his mind's eye, his little brother. He could see himself wearing shorts in the old school play-ground, being punched by that fat kid in his class. Little Barney copping a thump at the indoor playground off Highbury Fields that miserable rainy Saturday when he'd come to stay, Tiffany with her ever larger and uglier tattoos – everything in his head made him cry. But mostly it was his loneliness.

'I messed up, Tim,' he said over the table at the Café Rouge. 'Stuff keeps going through my head that I can't handle. It's never happened before.'

'You had rape fantasies, right?'

'How d'you know?'

' 'Cos you look a little guilt-ridden and you think you're kind of special because of what you do and you really shouldn't have rape fantasies. Am I right?'

'Sort of.'

'But so what? So you have rape fantasies. You rape anyone, Nick?'

'No, mate. Bloody hell.'

'Okay, you ever had murder fantasies?'

'Yeah, but that's different.'

'How so?'

'Because, well, because I never get close to murdering anyone, you know what I mean? I've never got close to shooting someone, or stabbing them, or beating them to death, but I guess I have got close to raping them. It's just when sex gets really heavy. I mean, you know, the whole thing with the line between sex and rape. I've sailed close, I know that. And yesterday I was walking along the street and I was imagining really violent rape, not just sort of kinky sex, but smashing a girl's face in, ripping her clothes off and raping her.'

'Okay, I hear you. That's cool.'

'It isn't cool! For fuck's sake, it is anything but cool. I swear to you, I've never done it before. I've imagined playing games, I've played games, but always it was sex, with someone I liked, who wanted to do it too. This is about hate. This anger inside me, this anger about women. All fucking women. That's new. I don't remember that from before doing the course.'

'Or is it before your son got beat up by girls?'

'I don't know. How do I find out?'

'I don't know either. Take a break. You can't do any more classes for a while, that's for sure.'

'But I've got to pay the rent,' said Nick.

'I'll pay your fucking rent, Nick,' said Tim, seemingly genuinely angry for the first time. 'You need a break, man. This is very heavy shit and very heavy shit cannot be put away and forgotten while you're a practising padded assailant.'

Chapter Forty

'How about we just forget about babies for a while and act like tourists? I've never been here before,' suggested Adrian as they walked along the beach at Brighton. It was early in the morning. Tara was tense because she sensed that Adrian was bored. Whenever she saw him away from work for more than a few days she feared he was on the brink of boredom, and when Adrian was bored he disappeared. She looked at him and smiled. Of course, it was a great idea. She wasn't sure she could do it, but she needed something to take her mind off her plight.

'Okay, just for a few days. I'll have to make sure Daisy is okay with the classes we got lined up, but I'll try.'

She'd spent the better part of the previous two days talking to Tim Renaldo, who had agreed to take over the classes that Nick wasn't doing. He would also talk to the three men who had come forward in response to the request Tara had made on the TV feature that had covered the training system. There was no question that running a programme as big as the British one required a great many more trainers, and in particular a great many more padded assailants than they had.

Finally, after more attempts than she wanted to remember, Nick agreed to talk to her on the phone. He didn't want to meet her, as Tim tried to explain, because he didn't want to say the wrong thing and he knew he was going to.

He rang her early in the evening just as there was a nice mood developing between her and Adrian, but that had to wait.

'Hi, it's me.'

'Hi, you. How you doing?' asked Tara, pleased that he was informal enough to say 'me'.

'Pretty bad.'

'I'm real sorry about Barney. It's so unfair.'

'Yeah.'

'How's he doing?'

'He's okay. Tough boy. Must be made of rubber.'

'Do the police know why it happened?'

'Nah. It's just an incident, isn't it. They've arrested the ringleader. They're charging her, but the rest have gone to ground. I've spoken to someone who saw it, though. Bloke who works at the cinema. They were jumping up and down on him, Tara, kicking his head like a football. They were a pack of wild animals.'

'It's terrible, Nick. It's just horrendous.'

'And it was girls, Tara. I know that's not politically correct and I know it's not possible, but that's what happened. It was girls.'

'I know. I mean, it is unusual but that doesn't excuse it,' said Tara. 'But did Barney tell you what started it?'

'He's a pacifist.'

'A what?'

'Exactly. Means he won't fight, no matter what.'

'No, I know what it means, it's just I haven't heard the term in a while,' said Tara, wondering for a second if this was the truth, remembering her talks with prison officials who worked with rapists and how they would live in utterly convincing denial for years on end.

'Seems he shouted at them that violence was for morons and they took that as a come-on,' said Nick. 'I'm sure he wound them up. He winds me up but he's only a kid, he don't know what he's talking about half the time. His mother has filled his head with a lot of half-baked hippie feminism shite, and look what happens to him.'

Tara could feel the anger coming down the line, aimed at her. She had to deflect it, not let it settle on her shoulders, otherwise she and Nick were finished. He would have to leave the training programme. She would have to find someone else and train them from scratch. She would have to find someone else to father her child. It was a difficult moment.

'Nick, I know this might be difficult to hear, but the balance of violence is still so heavily weighted against women.'

'Yeah, it is difficult to hear,' he said bitterly.

Tara spoke carefully, softly. 'Okay, what's happened to your son is the exception, right? A non-violent man abused and beaten by violent women. But this is a one-off, Nick. It's happened before but it's so rare. I called a police colleague in San Francisco and he only knows of three incidents like this in California in the last year. It's very rare. That doesn't mean it isn't terrible.'

There was a silence. Not a good sign. 'Nick?' she said after a while. 'Are you there?'

'I'm just not sure any more. Not sure what I'm doing is the right thing.'

'You mean being a padded assailant?'

'Yeah. You know, what my boy said really made me think,' he said. 'The reason he didn't come to the graduation Sunday night was because he doesn't agree with what we do. He thinks we make the world more violent. And 'cos he didn't come, he was out on the street, and because he was out on the street he got beat up.'

'Well, I've heard the argument that we make the world more violent before but I don't agree with it,' said Tara, knowing she was on dangerous ground.

'But what's it all about? We teach a bunch of nice middle-class women how to fight back, but what if one of them throws a wobbly and kills some bloke? And we've taught her how to do it. It just raises the stakes, don't it. I mean, I've always had Gandhi down as a bald hippie, but he had a point, didn't he.'

'He was a truly great man who treated the women in his private life pretty appallingly.'

'I might have known you'd say that.'

'I'm sorry, Nick, it's a well-documented fact. That doesn't negate what he did internationally, but we've got to move on — we can't go back to demure housewives and brave soldiers, you know. Men and women have got to adapt. I care about you absolutely, Nick. I really do. We've become close doing this work because of its very nature. It's so emotional and stirring that it either tears people apart or brings them together for ever. It's not about making people violent, Nick. I think you know that.'

'You know what I think. Women are more than capable of violence,' said Nick. 'Even if they don't do it physically, they fuck your head up with mental violence, with emotional violence. It's men what are the weaker sex. We don't stand an earthly. Look at me and Barney's mum — she's brought him up totally as she wanted, I didn't have a leg to stand on, and okay, Barney's turned out pretty good on the whole. But I reckon it's women who need to sort out their attitude. And now I've got a job where I teach women to fight in really like ultra-violent ways. Barney may only be sixteen, but he's got a head screwed on his shoulders. He doesn't like what I do 'cos he thinks it encourages violence, and I'm beginning to think he's right.'

There was no arguing with a man this set in his anger. Tara didn't know what it was like to feel that protective towards a child, but she could imagine. She knew that Nick was in real pain. The only hope was that the passing of time would allow him to continue his work. She cursed the stupid girls who had carried out the attack. Of all the people they could have picked on. Nick ended by saying he didn't want to see her, or Alice, or anyone for a while. He needed to be with Barney and work out what he was going to do.

✻   ✻   ✻

Tara and Adrian had been staying at Yolanda's house on the steep hill for five days. Adrian was growing increasingly uncomfortable among the clutter. Tara explained to Yolanda that they were taking advantage of the proximity of Tara's mother and going to see her in Cambridge.

As soon as Yolanda dropped them at the station they breathed a huge sigh of relief. It wasn't so much that they didn't like their rotund host, it was just that staying in someone else's small house was tough, whatever they were like – plus Tara and Adrian's taste did not run to cats, curtains, teacups and toast at every turn. They bought two paper cups of cappuccino and climbed aboard the train.

Late that evening they walked out of Cambridge train station in the rain and saw a pair of bright Volvo headlights flash at them. Tara's mother climbed out and greeted her warmly. She shook hands with Adrian and they climbed into the car.

'At last,' said her mother. 'You've been in the country for months and this is the first time I get to see you!'

'I'm so sorry, Mom,' said Tara. 'I've been real busy but it's bad of me not to have come sooner.'

'It's so good to see you, baby,' said her mother. Tara noticed that she sounded more English and looked younger than she remembered. 'So Adrian, hi there. We meet at last.'

'It's an honour, Mrs, um . . .'

'Call me Maria. Everyone does. Now, Gordon is so thrilled you're coming. He's cooking right now. I hope you're hungry. You know what he's like – he's used to cooking for his three enormous boys.'

'I'm starving, Maria,' said Adrian politely.

It was a fairly long walk from the carpark through the college cloisters to the apartment Tara's mother lived in. As they made their way quickly through the heavy rain, Adrian stared around at the Gothic splendour surrounding them. Tara had forgotten quite how beautiful her parental home was.

Tara introduced Gordon. He was so splendidly Australian,

with a huge chin, tall as a house, and very fit-looking. Closely cropped grey hair covered an enormous head.

'Mate, good to see you,' he said to Tara, embracing her warmly. 'This must be Adrian. Come in. Get that vile British weather off your clothes. How these people live here is beyond me.'

They had an amazing meal of chicken, couscous and vegetables, drank dry white wine and ate bread that Gordon had made himself. The conversation was fast and amusing. Adrian seemed on top form, very ready to talk and be interesting about his work, which was not always the case.

When they had finished, Adrian and Gordon cleared the dishes and disappeared into the kitchen, deep in discussion about chemical computer mapping and academic politics. They had many colleagues in common. Tara sat down on the floor next to the fire. Her mother lit an extravagantly long cigarette and settled in a high-backed armchair.

'Can't believe you still do that,' said Tara, fanning her hand in front of her face.

'Keeps me slim, darling,' Maria said with a smile. 'Anyway, we've got to die of something. Your generation are so timid, scared to live.'

'Oh yes, sure, look at all the heroin users,' said Tara. She prodded the fire with a poker. This seemed to stop the conversation short, which was not what she had intended. There was some basic communication block between Tara and her mother. She knew it was there but wasn't sure where it came from although she had been very upset at her mother's response to her father's death. She seemed to recover so quickly, was remarried within two years. It didn't seem right to Tara, and she knew from her time in therapy that there was still a great deal of unresolved anger against her mother residing inside her other-wise peaceful interior. She sighed, wondering how two people could get to this point. She glanced around at her mother and realised at once that she was the subject of her close scrutiny. She smiled, took a deep breath and spoke. 'Mom, I want to ask you something.'

'I know where you can buy some heroin, if that's what you want,' quipped Maria. 'All the students are using it again. It's become terribly fashionable.'

'Mother, please,' said Tara. 'This isn't easy. Just listen for ten seconds, will you? I want to have a baby.'

'Darling. That's wonderful,' said her mother, kissing Tara with smoky breath. 'When?'

'No, this is the thing. I want to have one, and so does Adrian, but he can't. Well, he can but he's got a very low sperm count. Like uncountable.'

'Oh, you poor, poor thing. And you and Adrian are back . . .?'

'We never really stopped. I love him very much, Mom, I don't want to find someone else who can . . . you know.'

'Fine, darling.'

'So I am considering artificial insemination.'

Her mother was silent for a moment. This time it was she who was looking into the fire and Tara who was studying her.

'Is Adrian aware of this?' she said after a long while.

'Yes. He wants to be involved in the whole thing.'

'Well, that's marvellous, darling. Isn't it? Are you going to get Dr Trent to do it?'

'Mom, he's about ninety-seven!' exclaimed Tara. Her mother was referring to the old family doctor from Palo Alto who had looked after her as a child.

'No, I don't mean that, I mean actually carry out the operation,' said her mother.

'It's not an operation. It's really straightforward.'

'Oh, I see. Well, who will . . . I mean, goodness, I have no idea how you do it,' said her mother, fanning her neck in mock embarrassment. 'Who will actually administer the . . .'

'Sperm, Mom. Adrian and I are going to do it.'

'Goodness me, how very modern. And where do you get the . . . the, you know, the sperm from?'

'Someone I know. That's what I wanted to talk to you about. I don't know if it's a good idea.'

'Oh, it gets steadily more intriguing,' said her mother, blowing a blue cloud towards the ancient ceiling. 'And how exactly does this donor, um, deliver his, um, his donation?'

'Mother! I don't know. He just gives us a little dish thing.'

'Oh, I see. We're not talking about some kinky orgy here.'

'No, we are not.'

'No Adrian with a video camera recording the magic moment?'

'No!'

'What a shame.'

'Mother!'

'Well, your generation is so timid. Everything has to be so safe.'

'So you don't think it's a bad idea?'

'It's completely mad, darling, completely daft, so yes. Why not? It would be so lovely to have a nice grandchild. Is the man, well, the biological father, is he a nice fellow?'

'He's perfectly fine. Not really like Adrian, in any way. But he already has a very handsome son and I think he's happy to help.'

'How on earth did you ask him? In my day you barely asked a boy for a kiss, let alone demand sperm from him.'

'I just explained the situation. It's quite businesslike. I kind of wanted to know who it was, not just buy a frozen test tube from some dubious character in California.'

'Well I never did,' said her mother, tossing the remains of her cigarette into the fire. 'Adrian must be a very good man. Very mature. Your father would never have stood for anything so intrusive in our marriage.'

'Well, you were very lucky – you had me.'

'Yes, we did. Two of the finest minds on the West Coast and we develop a child who can run fast, swim deep, teach women to fight but can barely write her name.'

'Oh, that's so not true.'

Tara's mother leant forward and brushed her cheek. 'If you think it'll work, and you think Adrian can deal with it, please, Tara, go ahead. You're the best thing that ever happened to me. Still, to this day. And I'm married to Gordon, which is not bad, let me tell you.'

'I needed to ask you because it's so weird I kind of wanted it to be a family decision. D'you understand that?'

'Absolutely, darling.'

'That's so great, Mom. Is everything good for you?'

'It's wonderful, darling. Really. We just need a grandchild. All Gordon's boys are either gay or too keen on their work to procreate. It's down to you, darling.'

'Looks like it,' said Tara, feeling warm inside. Maria stood up and embraced her tall daughter.

'So, I might be a grandma after all,' she said.

'You just might,' said Tara.

'What are you going to have, a boy or a girl?'

'I don't think we can choose,' said Tara, unsure of her mother again.

'Oh, I thought you might have worked out how to do that as well.'

Chapter Forty-One

Alice drove home from the airport feeling happy, singing along with her radio and tapping the wheel as she crawled along the M4. Her car was a reassurance to her when she saw it in the long-term park at Heathrow – her shiny Golf, still new enough to be smart.

She had just flown back from Scotland having finally made the trip to the oil rig that she had meant to undertake weeks previously. After blowing out her first visit, her boss had managed to reschedule. The original assessment, done by a local firm in Aberdeen, had not been good enough for the Lloyd's group who were covering the enormous structure. When they were asked whose opinion they wanted the group had no hesitation in mentioning Alice's name.

She was proud, there was no point denying it. Her assessments had been proved to be very sound over the years. She had always warned of the risk of helicopters going down in high winds, and they had done; she had said oil rigs would not break their moorings and float off, and they hadn't.

The visit to the rig was just what she needed – isolation and a view from her small sleeping quarters in the humming metal structure that brought instant solace. The smell and buzz of the place always made her feel safe. Her father had worked in the oil business in Canada and Alaska when she was a girl and she had grown up with the smell.

Her tiny cabin on the rig had looked west. She was just able to make out the low dark hump of the shoreline fifteen miles away. The sunsets during her two nights on the rig were breathtakingly spectacular. She sat looking through the thickly glazed windows, the rollicking surf just audible below her, the long strips of high cloud a deeper red with every moment as the dully glowing sun slowly sank out of sight. She wished she could live on an oil rig full time, do all her work there. It was the nearest thing to a space station there was – such a peculiar combination of high technology and ancient loneliness. She didn't like ships because she suffered badly from sea sickness, but a rig didn't move, and it allowed her to appreciate the beauty and majesty of her surroundings.

In the report that was on her laptop hard disk, also backed up on an encrypted zip disk that she had surface-mailed and a downloaded version on the office mainframe, she had described the rig as very safe. It was clear where the fires came from. She listed the kinds of accidents that would have to occur in order to get the disasters that had overtaken such places in the past. Virtually all of them would be caused by deliberate acts of vandalism or sabotage, and she warned the employers in her report to take great care in their dismissal procedures, making sure there were no aggrieved parties on board. She knew her report could end in criminal proceedings against an employee who'd been fired – she didn't want to think about what that might mean. She'd done her job, that was all.

After nearly an hour and a half of driving through the dense urban traffic she pulled her car into her space outside her apartment building. It was just getting dark, but it was a pleasant early summer evening. As soon as she'd stopped the engine she could hear birdsong. It was relaxing to be back. She climbed out and stretched, looked up at her apartment windows and felt good about being home. She had just ducked back into the car to get her laptop when she felt something very close behind her.

'Hello, Alice. Long time no see,' said a chillingly familiar voice.

Before the adrenalin hit, before the fear rushed in and took her breath away, using the full force of her small lungs and the maximum range of her vocal cords, Alice Moreton shouted, 'No!'

The noise echoed around the neighbourhood. The volume surprised Alice as much as it did Peter Welbeck.

'Alice, calm down,' he said. He seemed very big as he stood so close to her, somehow bigger than Nick was even with his impact suit on. 'It's only me. I've missed you.'

'Move away from me. You're too close,' said Alice, still very loudly indeed. Peter made a face as if he were in pain, as if he were putting up with a child in a tantrum.

'Alice, calm down. What's the matter?'

'Move away from me now!' she said, emphasising the word 'now' with a stamp of her foot. Peter Welbeck smiled, shook his head slightly, not sure what to make of the whole thing.

'I just wanted to talk to you. What's happened? Maybe I can help,' he said, touching her lightly on the shoulder. She let her laptop slip to the ground and took up the defensive stance, her hands up in front of her face, her elbows tight into her body, legs bent, feet apart, well balanced. Her eyes locked on to his face, so close. He laughed.

'What are you going to do? Kung fu me or something? Alice, I just wanted to see you. I've missed you. Don't be silly.' He was smiling. He looked so harmless. Was he really trying to hurt her or was she crazy? No, she wasn't crazy, he should back off. She had made it very clear that that was what she wanted.

'Move back. You are too close,' she shouted, her breaths coming hard and fast.

He smiled again, then, in a swift movement accompanied by a lecherous grin, he embraced her. 'Come here, you silly little rabbit,' he said gently into her ear. 'Let's go up to your place.'

Alice stood, frozen, her arms up in front of her, her hands reaching only to Peter's upper chest as he smothered her face in wet, slobbering kisses. He was huge — that was what she'd liked about him in the first place. Just the sheer physical size of the man. Now he blotted out the world. He was too big, he had to go. But how? She knew she couldn't reach his eyes with an eye jab; she had to do something else.

She didn't know why she did what she did, but she could hear Tara's voice speaking to her. 'Keep breathing, go soft, turn around.'

She did as she was told, allowed the tension and resistance to his grip to slip a little, then she turned around in his arms, still keeping her arms raised.

'Oh, baby. That's better,' said Peter softly, his nose nuzzling into her neck. 'You always did like it dirty.'

Her flesh actually crawled. It felt as if the very skin he was touching was trying to move across the surface of her body to avoid him. His arms were still encompassing her. She slowly lifted them up as she'd been shown. 'Lift up his arms like you're taking off a T-shirt,' said Tara's voice. It was as if her body knew what to do. Peter's arms came up easily — there didn't seem to be any resistance. She felt the hairs on his forearm brush her lips. With one swift movement, using her canine teeth by turning her head slightly to the side, she bit into the taught flesh. To her surprise she suddenly felt her teeth join as her mouth filled with blood. Before Peter Welbeck really started to scream in pain, before he had time to pull his arm away, Alice's right arm was stretched in front of her. It snapped back mechanically and her elbow made devastating contact with his abdomen. The sound was phenomenal — the low, guttural grunt as she smashed the wind out of his lungs. He buckled forward with such violence his head made contact with hers and sent her sprawling to the floor. She was dizzy and felt sick. She had no idea how, but as she made full contact with the ground, her body arranged itself into a defensive position, left leg bent and anchored into the ground, right leg curved back, ready. She pulled up her dress to give her legs room to move.

Peter Welbeck stood up. He was holding his right forearm with his left hand, blood everywhere.

'You fucking little cow,' he said as he managed to pull in a breath. He looked ugly. He stepped towards her, one, two steps, raising his huge foot. He was going to kick her but his leg seemed to move so slowly.

Her heel found its target as her leg lashed out. 'Aim for the back of his body, full impact,' she heard Tara's voice say. Five hundred and fifty pounds per square inch of pressure on his penis and testicles, and Peter Welbeck folded in two. No words escaped his mouth, only a low, pitiful groan as he sank. His head flopped to one side as he landed on his knees. Alice shifted her position quickly to bring his slowly recovering head into line with her leg.

Again her heel sprang forward like a missile and made brutally powerful contact with his temple. Unfortunately for Peter, Alice's car was right next to him and his head then made secondary contact with that, leaving an unsightly dent in her front driver's side wing. He stayed where he was, didn't seem to react. She pulled her leg back and kicked again, this time hitting him on the jaw. Again his head smashed into the wing of her car, this time leaving an impact splatter of blood on the silver paintwork. Peter remained motionless, his face expressionless. Still he didn't go down. He was on his knees, his hands covering his genitals, blood everywhere from the wound in his arm, but he wasn't unconscious. She moved slightly for one last blow, and with her fingernails gripping the cold tarmac, she bellowed 'No!' as her heel found its target. This time the impact was so intense it hurt her foot; through the hard leather heel of her shoe she felt a sharp jab. Peter Welbeck collapsed on to himself; his blood-stained face rolled towards her, his eyes unfocused, his mouth open.

Alice pulled herself away, scrabbling backwards on her hands and feet like a demented crab. She was breathing and crying at the same time. She stood up, immediately adopting the defensive pose, looking around. The street was empty, no one around. She looked down at Peter lying in a heap by her car. He wasn't moving.

'Look, assess, no,' she said to herself. She then gingerly approached her car, maintaining her position, picked up her laptop carry-case – her mobile was in the front pocket.

'Police, fire or ambulance?' said the operator within two rings.

'Police and ambulance,' said Alice.

Chapter Forty-Two

The reassuring purr of the large engine pulled him along the narrow redbrick street from his childhood, the recently resprayed bonnet of the Triumph Stag rising impressively as he touched the throttle.

He pulled up outside number eighty-four. That was what he'd always called it – number eighty-four. Anyone who knew him when he was a kid knew which street he meant. A tiny little area, all he knew, and it was enough. He couldn't remember any hankerings for travel. The world expanded he decided, until you were about thirty, and then it shrank again.

Nick opened the boot and pulled out a huge bag full of washing, walked up the short path from the street and knocked on the old blue-painted front door. He could hear his mother's slow, thunderous approach along the narrow hallway. This house hadn't changed noticeably since as far back as he could re-member. He and his brother Mark had both been born in the nearby hospital where his mother had worked all her adult life.

'Hello, dear,' she said as she opened the door, kissing him on the cheek. He returned the kiss fleetingly.

'All right, Mum,' he said, and carried his bag up the narrow stairs to his old childhood room.

He slept for something like ten hours the first night he was at his parents'. He was completely exhausted. On the Saturday morning he woke up as he heard his father's ancient Briggs Stratton motor mower start its short trips up and down the patch of neat lawn in the back garden.

He joined his mother in the small kitchen. She'd already made him a cup of real coffee.

'Thanks, Mum,' he said, sitting on one of the creaking high stools. At least twenty layers of paint adorned its 1960s legs.

'So, are you seeing Barney today?' she asked casually.

'Don't know. Could you ring up? I don't want to talk to Sally.'

'Oh dear. You two are never going to resolve this, are you? You're such an odd lad.' His mother had always called him a lad. 'Your brother is so right and proper, going out with Helen for nearly three years before they got married, and then they waited another two years so that their house was ready before they had a baby.'

'Yeah, but he had to go to Australia to do it,' said Nick.

'What does that mean?' asked his mother tersely.

'He's such a mummy's boy – he'd never do anything out of order in case he upset you. He was shagging himself stupid in Australia, then he'd write you letters making it all sound like he was some sort of saint. Bloody hell, Mum.'

'I'm sure you're not right,' she said. 'He's such a lovely lad, and such a good father. Have you written to the twins recently? It was their birthday the week before last.'

Nick grimaced. He'd completely forgotten – not that there was anything in his life to help him remember. He'd never actually seen his twin nephews other than in dull family snaps of two babies lying on a wooden floor.

'I don't know, Nicholas,' said his mother with an enormous sigh, the sort of sigh only an enormous woman can manage. 'I know you're not a bad lad, but this fighting business . . . well, I don't know what to say. It looks awful, and what's happened to poor little Barney is dreadful. It seems this kind of bother follows you around. I was always worried about you meeting your match.

I know you're a big strong lad, but there's always someone bigger.'

'What are you on about, Mum?' asked Nick. Nothing he had ever done had pleased her; nothing he'd ever done had even been noticed by his father, who passed the window every now and then, walking behind his trusty green mower, lost in thought. 'I'm bloody amazed,' said Nick. 'I thought you were chuffed.'

'I'm not sure what I think. It's very impressive, I'll grant you that, and they obviously all worship you, but it's left a funny taste in my mouth. I'm not sure.'

'But Mum! What I'm doing now is the first truly useful job I've ever had. It's changed the lives of millions of women in America. I'd have thought you'd be well chuffed. You saw what it was like at the graduation thing. You saw how strong those women were.'

'I know how strong the women were who beat up my grandson,' she said flatly.

'I know, but it's different, isn't it?' Nick was slipping; he could feel this new lease of life he'd been given slowly leaving him. For some reason he expected his mother to help him believe. She turned and looked at him, her features smooth under the pressure of her bulk.

'If you want an honest opinion, dear, it all looked a bit violent to me. You've always been attracted to things like that. Your kick boxing and your funny kung fu business, and then your awful job with that crook, wearing that dreadful suit and standing outside on the street waiting to get in a fight. I used to lie in bed worrying about you. All it would take would be some idiot with a knife. It happens all the time. I've seen the result.'

'But look,' said Nick, his head in his hands, 'just forget about Barney for a moment.'

'You have for most of his life,' said his mother, cruelly. Nick breathed in, trying to recover from this onslaught. She was right, of course, but then she didn't know how well the two of them had been getting on before the beating.

'All right. I know I've screwed up on that score.'

'You haven't screwed up anything, you just weren't there for him. That's all he needed. A dad, like your brother is for the twins.'

'All right, Mum. But I've changed. Barney has been living with me and we've talked and, you know, we've really spent time together. He wants to be with me. His mother just turns on the guilt and does his head in, which we know in this family doesn't work, does it?'

'Tell me about it,' said his mother in a chilling reprise of his own phrase.

'And I've really got my life together. I've started earning money, I've done up the flat a bit. Got the wheels back on the road, all kosher.'

'Such a silly car.'

'It's like a new lease of life, Mum,' said Nick, oblivious of her criticism. 'And I feel good about myself, I feel I'm actually helping people for the first time. I'm not supposed to tell you this but four of those women you saw at the graduation had been raped. We have a group therapy session thing at the beginning of each class and they talk about it. I had no idea, Mum, honest. I know you think I'm a thug what goes round beating people's heads in and raping chicks, but I never did. I had no idea all this stuff was going down. Honest. Some of them could barely talk, they were scared to leave their houses. And now look at them – really confident, really useful members of society again. They haven't become violent, Mum, they've just learned how to try and stop people abusing them any more. It's a feminist thing, for Christ's sake. It's what you've been on at me about since the year dot. Blimey.'

Nick's mother wiped a blue J-cloth around the edges of her already spotless sink. Deep in thought, she looked out of the window at her husband. 'Maybe you're right. When you first told me about it, it all sounded so implausible. I don't know. I just wish you could get a job with the ambulance service or something.'

'You always wanted me to do that.'

'I can just see you in the uniform. They're tough lads, most of them. Wonderful job they do.'

'Mum, I had to find me own way. I haven't done that bad. I've never been in prison, I've never hurt anyone who didn't deserve it. I've looked after my kid a bit, now and then, put up with his awful bloody mother. Cut me a bit of slack, why don't you.'

His mother smiled at him, put the J-cloth down and gave him a gentle cuddle. 'I know you're doing your best, Nick. I know.' She held him at arm's length. 'And you have lost weight, you lucky little bugger. How d'you do that?'

'Stopped eating crap, took more exercise and wore an impact suit. I sweat buckets inside that bloody thing. Ninety fights in five hours – great weight-loss regime, Mum, you should try it.'

'So, you're not going to give it up, then?'

'No, Mum, I'm not.'

Nick remembered the telephone conversation with his mother the night after Barney was beaten. His darkest hour – he'd sworn he'd never do another class. Somehow, in convincing his mother that what he'd been doing was right, he'd won the argument he couldn't have with himself. He went back to bed, feeling better. He tried to sleep but his mind wouldn't let him. He was having thoughts and feelings. He masturbated and imagined doing it into some sort of glass receptacle to help Tara have a baby. He imagined she was there helping him, egging him on as she did the students in a class. He imagined Alice helping him, then he imagined the whole class of women, fourteen of them, all gathered around chanting at him to come. It was glorious – they were cheering for him, like at the end of *The Full Monty*, only this was the hard-core version. Hundreds of women, clapping in time with his strokes, chanting and scream-ing for sperm. They all wanted to see him come; they wanted that stuff.

He turned and lay on his back after he'd finished, his face

wreathed in a huge smile. It was the most confusing sexual fantasy he'd ever had.

After a quiet lunch with his mum and dad, during which he heard about the local football team, he got on his dad's old pedal bike and rode down Headington Hill towards north Oxford. The sun was out, low but bright. It was a delightful late September day – there was a stiff breeze but it seemed to follow him rather than blowing in his face.

He pedalled down the High, through the throngs of students who all looked to him like they should still be at school. He wound his way through Cornmarket, where he was meant to get off and walk. He didn't – it still felt like fun to risk it. He rode past Martyrs Memorial and eventually Browns Café, following the route he'd taken every day when he was eighteen. The café still looked much the same from the outside. He peered in, saw a waiter who looked Barney's age and realised how stupid it was to expect to see anyone he knew still working inside.

Ten minutes later he pushed his father's bike up the path at Barney's maternal grandparents' house, the first time he'd been there since Barney was two weeks old. This house too seemed remarkably similar – maybe a little smarter than he remembered but essentially unchanged. He knocked on the door, saw movement inside. Completely unexpectedly his heart jumped a little when Sally opened the door. She looked amazing.

' 'Lo,' he said. Her face was frozen; she put her hand over her mouth and stared at him.

'Hello there.' She spoke slowly through her fingers. 'What on earth are you doing here?'

'Came to see the boy,' he said. ' 'S he here?'

'Yes.' She held the door, clearly not about to let him inside. 'Goodness me, Nicholas. How long is it since we've actually seen each other?'

'I dunno,' he said, finding it hard not to immediately adopt the 'thick' persona he always used on the phone. He decided to shrug it off. 'I would estimate about fifteen years, Sally.'

'Fifteen years. Long time.'

'It's all relative. You look good on it, though.'

'Goodness, a compliment,' she said. An awkward smile flashed across her lips. She had great teeth — something had happened to her teeth. 'That's a bit of a shock,' she added.

'Accepting a compliment gracefully is a sign of maturity and high self-esteem,' said Nick with his winning smile.

'Oh, I stand corrected,' said Sally. 'Well, you don't look so bad yourself. Your hair's receding a bit, but that suits you.'

'Thank you,' said Nick. 'So Barney's here?'

'Yes, but . . .'

'But what?' he snapped.

'Well, he's resting. I don't know that . . .'

'Sally, I'm his father, right? We have established that by now, I think. He's been living with me for the past four months.'

'I know, and look what happened.'

Nick smiled. 'We'll never change, will we?' He wanted to be generous. It was so strange to reattach a face to the voice he had fought ever since Barney was born. Before that even, ever since sperm met egg.

But here he was again, standing looking at her. Sally had returned to looking how she had been before she was pregnant, tall and slim, her hair cut short, her teeth fixed up or polished or something. She was wearing a mini-dress, a black thing with no sleeves. She looked pretty good. Her neck was long and, well, he had to admit it to himself, kind of inviting.

'Well, we have changed a bit,' he said. 'For the better.'

'So Barney has been telling me. He showed me an article from the *Guardian* about you. I didn't know you'd become a self-defence teacher.'

'I'm not, I'm a padded assailant.'

'Goodness.'

'It's a very different role, Sally. I work in a subordinate position to a woman. Imagine that.'

Sally smiled. 'How is it you've never told me about this?'

'Because you've never asked and you've never allowed me to tell you anything about what I do,' said Nick, feeling his temper rising.

'You may have a point there,' she said with a slight shrug of complicity. Nick felt himself soften again. He realised they were actually talking to each other for possibly the first time ever. But then he was standing on her doorstep and she wasn't letting him see his son.

'So I can't come in. Is that what you're saying.'

Sally glanced over her shoulder down the dark hallway, then stepped outside, holding the door ajar.

'It's not Barney, it's really Mum and Dad. I think they'd get a bit of a shock seeing you after all this time. They're both a bit ancient.'

'I'll be polite,' said Nick. 'It's all water under the bridge now, isn't it?'

'I don't think so,' said Sally icily. 'You may be blessed with good luck elsewhere, but your name isn't too crash hot in this household.'

Nick noticed a movement behind Sally. He nodded in the general direction and Sally snapped her head around. Her tiny, frail old father pulled the door open a little. He really had changed. Nick remembered him as a small man with a thick mop of dark hair. Now standing at about half Nick's height, he looked like the five-thousand-year-old man.

'Who is it, dear?' he asked with a delicate smile in Nick's direction.

'It's Barney's father,' said Sally brusquely.

'Hello, Nick, old chap, how the devil are you?' said the old professor without needing to pause for a second to remember his name.

'I'm all right, Professor, thank you very much.'

'Marvellous. Lovely to see you again,' said the old man, and he went back into the house. Nick smiled at Sally. Sally scowled at him humorously and opened the door.

'He's completely off his trolley, poor old thing,' she said as she walked swiftly down the chilly hall and up the stairs. Nick followed, trying to remember the layout of the house. He felt old, being in this place he hadn't seen since he was in his teens. The years that spanned the gap had been long and hard. They had left a mark on him – he wasn't the same person.

Sally opened a huge dark wooden door and revealed a room totally unlike the rest of the house, bright and cheerful, the sunlit windows giving a tree-filtered view of the similar Victorian Gothic houses opposite. The room was huge, with a high ceiling, spanning the width of the building, and half of it was a kitchen. He had no memory of this room at all.

'Bloody hell,' he said as he looked around. He realised he was standing in a really nice flat. Barney hobbled into view from around the corner.

'Bloody hell,' said Barney. 'Fancy seeing you here.'

Father and son embraced gently. Nick felt himself relaxing by the second. Barney's familiar face, now almost fully recovered, was a welcome site in what had for so many years been his Mordor, his forbidden castle of the night.

'I should get beaten up more often,' said Barney. 'Cup of tea, Dad?'

'Bloody hell,' said Nick. 'All right.' He kept turning in circles, taking in the enormity of the room.

'Of course, you haven't seen it since Barney was a tiny baby,' said Sally. 'We did this about . . . what must it be? Thirteen years ago. Mum and Dad live downstairs now. I've got the rest of the house. Come on, I'll show you around.'

Nick followed Sally to the door, glancing back at Barney. They exchanged faces of comic horror and imminent death.

Sally's guided tour was fast but friendly. She opened the door to her bedroom, completely redecorated but still recognisable. This was where they had made Barney. Nick stopped for a moment and smiled – it was almost as if he were saying farewell to the cocky, fit young man of his youth. In this room – this was where it had happened. It came back vividly. He turned and looked at Sally, who he suddenly realised was looking at him quite intently.

'I suppose it's a little odd for you, isn't it?'

'A little,' said Nick.

The bathroom was delightful, with a large pile of matching towels adorning the shelves, ointments and pungent soaps in baskets, top-quality fittings and pricey tiles on the walls. It was spotlessly clean and looked wonderful.

Barney's room was equally impressive – a bed up on a platform, posters of girl bands on the wall, books like he'd never seen on the shelves. He had thought there were enough books in his maisonette on Offord Road, but that was nothing compared to this.

'I never encouraged him to read. I didn't have to. He just consumes books,' she said.

'Tell me about it. My place is full of them.'

'Did you ever read any of them?'

'Don't make me laugh,' said Nick.

They joined Barney in the kitchen. Nick sat on a tall stool that faced the breakfast bar.

'You look okay, Barn. Much better, mate. How you feeling?'

'My arm hurts, that's all. Got a dentist appointment this afternoon. I'll be okay soon.'

'They've charged another girl,' said Sally.

'Have they? D'you know who it is?' Nick asked. His son nodded and said nothing.

'Barney doesn't feel good about it.'

'No,' said Nick quietly. 'I know, but I think it's the right thing.'

Barney stood up and smiled at them both. 'I'd just like to point out,' he said with a smile, 'that as a form of psychotherapy, seeing the two of you sitting there together is strangely good. More strange than good, but definitely good. I'm just going up to my room to finish my book if you need me.'

He walked out, smiling and winking at his father.

'Bloody hell,' said Nick when he'd gone.

'Bloody hell indeed,' said Sally. 'So, Nicholas Gardener, bane of my life, how come you turn up like this and confuse everyone with your good looks?'

'I just came to see Barney,' said Nick.

'You could easily have arranged something. Your lovely old mum could have come and picked him up. I see her every now and then — she's been a good granny, all things considered.'

'I know, I know.'

They looked at each other for a while.

'This is weird,' said Sally. Nick nodded. 'You've changed, haven't you?'

'I think so,' said Nick. 'So have you, though. I couldn't believe me eyes when you opened the door. Amazing. Are you going out or something?'

'What d'you mean?'

'Well, dressed like that.'

'Oh, no,' said Sally, slightly embarrassed. She flushed and looked away. Maybe she was acting, he couldn't tell; maybe she was taking the piss. However, he found her embarrassment charming, strangely alluring.

'Sorry,' he said. He wanted to hold her. Sally, the arch bitch. He must be going off his rocker.

'So, what are we going to do?' asked Sally. Nick's heart fluttered gently.

'What about?' he asked.

'Our son,' said Sally.

'I don't know.'

'He still wants to live with you.'

'Does he?' said Nick, surprised.

'That's what he says. He told me he was really happy at your place and you get along really well and teach him loads of things I don't know about.'

'Bollocks. I couldn't teach him anything.'

'I think you have, just by being who you are,' said Sally, her voice a little tight. 'You know how much it hurts me to let him go but I think I've got to. He's grown up so much since he's been with you. He needs to be with you, Nick.'

'You could come and visit us, though. If you wanted. I mean, my place is a fucking sty in comparison to this gaff, but you'd be welcome.'

'Would I?' asked Sally with a grin.

' 'Course,' said Nick, now feeling embarrassed himself.

'Well, I just might. I've driven past it a few times.'

'You never have.'

'I couldn't help it. I just wanted to see where Barney was living.'

'You can't tell from outside. It's not as bad as it looks. Honest. I've done it up since I've been earning a few quid. It's still embarrassing. You know, a bloke my age that doesn't own anything. Well, I own me car, but . . .'

'I've heard about the car. Barney's very impressed.'

'It's a runner again. I'll give you a spin in it if you like.'

'I might take a raincheck on that,' said Sally.

'I can't believe I'm sitting here.'

'I can't believe you're sitting there.'

'We've both been stupid, ain't we?' said Nick.

'Yes, although I think I have a little more justification for my anger.'

'Fair enough,' said Nick, deciding for once not to take issue with anything she said.

'But I admit I haven't behaved well all the time,' said Sally. 'I can see that, you know.'

'I was too young to have kids. I was so stupid, so selfish. I look at little kiddies now and I get a lump in the throat 'cos I think Barney was like that once and I never saw him. I mean, I only really met him when he was six.'

'I know.'

'My mum gives me so much earache about what a crap dad

I've been and how my fucking wanker of a brother is the greatest dad on the earth. And anyway, things are really different now. My new work is so amazing. You should do the course, Sally, really you should, you'd really get off on it. It's brilliant. I've seen the transformation in women's lives.'

'You just said "women" then. Like it was natural.'

'Did I?'

'I've never heard you say anything but ladies, babes, chicks, totty, skirt. Something dreadful like that.'

'Oh, well, I say women now,' said Nick without malice. 'I've learned a lot doing this course. I've had time to think about what I do and who I am. All that shit. I was embarrassed at first, but I got over it. I can cry now. I could never do that before.'

'You've never cried.'

'Yes I have, in public too. Tough enough to cry. That's what they say in California. Mind you, they are a bunch of wankers, but the best sort, you know what I mean?'

'Nick Gardener crying. I find that hard to believe.'

' 'S true.'

They looked at each other in silence for a moment. 'Hello again,' said Sally Mulberry.

'Hello,' he said softly.

Chapter Forty-Three

'You're very lucky, Ms Moreton, he's not pressing charges,' said the police officer. 'And I've just got off the phone from the DPP's office and neither are we. We don't have enough to put a case together. We're not charging Mr Welbeck either as we have no evidence of the initial assault you allege, and as you never reported the assault, that's that effectively. Case closed, as we say in the trade.'

Alice was sitting with Tara in the interview room at Highgate police station where they had been anxiously waiting for two hours. She had run through the possible outcomes of Peter laying assault charges on her. She knew the rape would be widely reported – everyone would know, her life would be in tatters. She had talked it over with Tara and they had gone through the possibility of the story being picked up by the tabloid press. When the police officer closed the file on the table in front of them and slapped the palm of his hand down on top of it, they both breathed a sigh of relief.

The relief was short-lived for Alice, and she felt herself starting to cry again. Tara held her gently, but it was no solace. She needed to be alone in her flat. She needed time to have passed between this moment and the rest of her normal life, but then her normal life was part of this now. She didn't believe she would ever recover.

When the police had arrived at Alice's apartment block the previous evening they discovered Alice in tears, sitting on the steps. A few yards away an unconscious Peter was lying in a small pool of blood beside her car.

An ambulance came and took Peter to hospital. Alice was then arrested and taken to the police station for questioning. She was checked by a woman doctor who showed no sign of not believing her story. Her solicitor arrived and told her there was nothing to worry about and she was glad she wasn't representing Mr Welbeck. Then she spent the best part of twenty-four hours trying to sort out the situation. Alice slept badly in a cell – it was so much quieter than her bedroom which always had the constant rumble of North Circular traffic in the background.

Initially she was interviewed by a very sympathetic woman police officer who was clearly impressed with what she had done to Peter, although officially she made no comment.

When her solicitor returned in the morning, she was questioned by two male officers who were less sympathetic and at one point accused her of luring Peter to her house with the direct intention of doing him harm. They implied that Peter had told them she was upset because he dumped her and that she had carried out a premeditated, completely unprovoked assault on him. This kind of questioning was not something the Winning Strategy training had given her any preparation for. Her only remotely similar experience had been at the enquiry into the South Acton rail crash where she was called as an expert witness.

Tara, who had been informed of the circumstances by Alice's solicitor, arrived later in the day. From what Alice could gather from Tara's behaviour, this kind of police involvement in a case was not something she was used to either.

'He's very lucky that Ms Moreton is not pressing charges,' said Tara sternly. 'Let me inform you, in San Francisco, the police department would have treated this woman as a victim of an assault, not a perpetrator.'

The police officer looked at Tara, then at Alice, shook his head and sat down at the table between them.

'Am I free to go?' asked Alice after a moment watching the police officer tidy his papers.

'Yes, you are. I'd only like to suggest that you take care and report any future threats you receive to us. We don't really like people taking the law into their own hands, Ms Moreton. Mr Welbeck is a big man and you were very lucky you didn't get more seriously hurt.'

When Alice left the police station she took a deep breath. It had been her first contact with officers of the law other than asking directions.

Tim, the American padded assailant, was waiting for them on the street. He smiled at her and gave her a huge hug.

'You are one tough lady,' he said. 'We are all so proud of you.'

'I didn't do anything really,' said Alice. She walked with them briskly through the bright afternoon sunshine, two tall lean people, so sure of themselves, so confident. Although she'd won a fight with a fifteen-stone rugby player, she felt as confident as a three-year-old who had lost her mum in the supermarket.

'I could just hear Tara's voice in my ear,' she said. 'And I really didn't want him near me.'

The two tall Americans nodded and smiled. Alice looked about her, at the busy streets, the endless noise of traffic. Her head still hurt from lack of sleep and the big bruise she had on the back of her skull where Peter's forehead had hit her.

'It's been so weird. I need a holiday.'

The three of them went to a pub on Highgate Hill. Tara and Tim had coffee but Alice had a beer. They talked about her work, fascinated to hear what she knew about the safety of everyday things. She had never really explained her work to people outside the field before, always feeling they would find it very boring.

After an hour Tara said she'd have to go. They embraced.

Alice felt blessed. She had been through an experience that could easily have been even more devastating than it had been, but she had been supported all the way by these strange, strong people.

She sat down again, feeling very reassured that Tim was with her. She was not looking forward to being alone.

'Nick told me a lot about you,' said Tim. Alice smiled. 'He said you were a kind of special person.'

'I haven't heard from him since . . . well, you know about what happened to his son.'

'Yeah, bad business.'

'I've never met his son so it all felt a bit awkward, you know? It'd be even worse now, after what I've done. Tara told me what happened – sounds like it's made a bit of a mess of everything.'

'Sure has. I was meant to be here for five days. I been here two weeks already.'

'Did Nick tell you I, well, I sort of made a pass at him?'

'He mentioned it,' said Tim with a wry smile.

'I feel awful about it now. I was so high after the end of the class, I just felt I could do anything. I know he was tempted, I could see it in his eyes.'

'Yeah, he was real tempted.'

'But he didn't respond and I'm glad now. He told me all about transference and he was right. Now, after what happened yesterday, well, I can see, it was me that cured myself, with Tara and Nick's help. I still feel sick about it, though.'

'About what?'

'What I did to Peter Welbeck.'

'The guy that assaulted you!' said Tim. 'You really don't need to be, Alice. Man oh man, he had it coming, and what better place for it to come from?'

'But I was so mad, I wanted to kill him, I really did. I was so lucky I didn't. Imagine what would have happened if . . .'

'Well, you didn't. He's already out of hospital, Tara says.'

'Yes, apparently. But don't you ever worry about that? What you've taught me is lethal, or it could be. Isn't there a very big risk of a law suit, especially in America. You know, some day, some woman's going to kill some rapist, and then what happens?'

'I really don't think it's likely. Like about ninety per cent of women we've taught who are assaulted don't even get to a physical contact stage. You were one of the very unlucky ones.'

'I don't know,' said Alice. She had been awake half the night in her cell wondering if what she had done was right, if maybe she should just have let Peter do what he wanted and forgotten about it. At least he wouldn't be concussed and lying in a hospital bed. At least he'd have been arrested, not her.

'I need a break,' she said after a long silence.

'Ever been to northern California?' asked Tim. His smile was delightful. Alice felt very happy to be in the pub with this kind-faced, grey-haired old hippie.

Chapter Forty-Four

Tara had decided that Brighton depressed her a little. Although she'd spent a lot of time there in her life, she had never really just sat and listened to the place, to the sea. She sat on the beach until the discomfort of sitting on a pile of round rocks roused her from her thoughts. She stood up and nearly toppled over as she tried to get her balance on one of the mounds of pebbles that made up the beach. It was the soulful nature of the sea throwing itself limply on those big pebbles. It was the fact that someone had decided that it would make a nice resort. A rocky beach that was virtually impossible to walk on in bare feet and agony to lie on without a major-league air-bed.

But she was excited. It was going to happen. She almost felt sick with the tension. What if he changed his mind? What if he couldn't manage? What if Adrian changed his mind and grossed out on the whole thing? What would they do? She wanted Adrian to do what only Adrian could do, but they had to concentrate. Adrian had said it was better if she was kind of turned on, but he didn't know if he could handle it. She knew it would only take the slightest upset to make her decide it was all a really bad idea. So far Adrian had behaved impeccably. Not only had he arranged to take three more weeks in the UK and work remotely, logging into his mainframe in Palo Alto at night-time, he had organised the whole AI thing. He had taken it on as a scientific project, done the research, procured the equipment and booked the two rooms at the Grand Hotel on Brighton's seafront.

She was desperate to be alone and yet she wanted everyone she knew around her. This might be the last time she would ever truly be alone, she thought. If it worked, she'd always have someone there; even if they weren't with her physically they would always be around.

She saw three young boys playing together by the waves, their thin white English legs nimbly picking their way across the slippery stones. They were throwing rocks into the surf and making explosion noises with their mouths. Tara picked up a large round pebble and threw it as far as she could into the sea. It went quite far, surprising even her. The boys stopped and looked at her; one of them swore under his breath.

'You throw the javelin or something?' one of them asked.

'No, I don't,' said Tara. She smiled at them, expecting them to ask something else. They lost interest in her so she kept on walking and the boys very quickly resumed their game. Maybe she'd have a little boy with thin white legs. What would she do with him all the time?

She got back to the hotel just as it was getting dark, climbing the impressive steps and entering through the huge swing-doors. She glanced into the bar and saw Adrian talking to Nick at the bar. He was there; he'd kept his promise.

She walked up to the two men feeling incredibly aware and open. She wanted to do something so badly and she wasn't sure what it was.

'Hey, babes,' said Adrian, embracing her. 'We were just starting to get worried. Thought you might have decided to leave all of us and swim out to sea.'

'I don't think so,' she said, wishing she could think of a witty retort. Nick stood up and embraced her too.

'I'm so sorry for all my rubbish,' he said. 'Just had a brilliant class today, went really well.'

'That's good. I must ring Daisy.'

'She said to tell you everything's brilliant. Really good group. We did some really good work today.' Nick held her at arm's length, a huge smile across his face. He knew, she knew, they both knew everything, and it was a wonderful, special, exciting, beginning sensation. Tara felt exposed and vulnerable, but she knew it didn't matter. She was pretty sure she didn't want to have sex with this man, but she loved him all the same. She embraced him again.

'I'm so sorry, though,' he said again.

'Hey, you were right,' she said quietly into his ear as they held each other. 'Women can be violent, women can be real pieces of shit. They can kill and torture and maim – they just can't rape, that's all.'

'I know, I know,' said Nick quietly. 'I've thought about it a lot. I'm sorted now. Really. Spent time with my boy, and his mum. That's all been a bit of a surprise, I can tell you.'

'I thought you hated his mum.'

'I did. Well, I still do, but I sort of hate the woman who rang me up all the time. Now we've met again, well, it's different. We've both changed a lot, me especially, I suppose. She wants to do the course but I said I wouldn't be involved. She'll have to wait until we've got another padded assailant.'

'That's great news, Nick,' said Tara, feeling it was about the worst news she'd ever heard.

'What's up, hon?' asked Adrian.

'Well, she's not going to be happy about this, is she?' said Tara, feeling as if her eyes were red-rimmed from crying even though they weren't.

'What, you mean what we're here for?' asked Nick. 'She doesn't know anything about it. Doesn't need to.'

'But that . . .'

'No. It's nothing to do with her.'

'Well, if she finds out, she's going to be upset. At the moment you're father to her child and no one else's.'

Tara noticed Adrian scratch his temple in the way he did when he was upset. She touched his arm. 'Sorry, babes, but you know what I mean.'

'No, Tara,' said Nick firmly. 'I won't be the child's father, Adrian will. That's the whole point. Your kid will grow up with its mum and dad, that's what's so good. Sure, when it's older it can come and meet me or whatever, but Adrian will always be Dad. Always. I'm a crap dad anyway. You should ask my mum — she'd tell you.'

Adrian was looking at the floor, nodding slowly. Tara swallowed, her eyes stinging with tears.

'This is fantastic, Nick, that you're doing this for us. Really. I think it's incredibly brave of you.'

'Or stupid,' said Nick. 'I think if I wasn't so thick I'd never do it, but I can't think of a good reason why not.'

There was another silence which Tara felt acutely.

'Oh my God. I don't know what to do now. D'you guys know what to do?' she asked.

'We've been over it,' said Adrian. 'It's pretty straightforward. We've got the adjoining rooms, it's fine. And it may not work.'

'I know. I know. But I've kind of got a feeling it will,' said Tara. She looked at the two men in front of her and smiled. 'I'm real tired,' she said. The smile was very fake, she could feel it not really working. 'I guess I'll go up and take a bath, then.'

'Okay,' said Nick. They all stood up. There was another silence and then they all burst out laughing and embraced. Tara, Nick and Adrian in a tight huddle in the front bar of the Grand Hotel in Brighton. It was a moment that would remain with all of them.

As soon as the lift doors closed Tara grabbed Adrian by the shirt and looked into his face from two inches.

'What the hell am I doing here?' she moaned.

'Getting pregnant?' said Adrian with a smile.

'I must be crazy. What's going to happen? What's he going to do?'

'Honey, you know what he's going to do. It's all pretty basic.'

'I know. I guess I've tried to make it a policy not to think about that aspect of the whole thing.'

They got out of the lift and walked along the corridor to their room. Adrian opened the door, switched the light on and showed Tara into the bathroom. There on the sink unit was a pile of towels, a small circular glass dish and a long-spouted clear plastic syringe.

'Oh my God,' said Tara. She stood and looked at the equipment with a mixture of womb-twitching horror and utter fascination.

'Got it mail order from a place in Chicago,' said Adrian, picking up the syringe. 'Found it on the Net pretty quick. I think it's based on an old-style turkey baster, but it's kind of more hygienic.'

'Oh my God.' Tara picked up the little glass dish. 'What's this for?'

'Nick's sperm goes in there.'

'Oh my God!' she said, putting the dish down rapidly. 'What have I done?' She sat on the toilet, holding her head in her hands.

'You haven't done anything, babes,' said Adrian, putting an arm around her shoulder in an unusual display of affection. 'Not yet, you haven't.'

'Oh God. Ade, tell me I'm not totally crazy.'

Adrian guided Tara to the bed, made her lie on her back, and then set about giving her the best massage she'd ever had. It was his one concession to the world of the physical – he gave exceptionally good back rubs, concentrating on each little area for ages, removing tension, slowly working his way up and down her back.

Tara fell asleep, not for long because she was woken by Adrian, who was moving around on the bed. He had clearly been lying next to her reading a huge wad of computer print-out. It was all over the floor.

'Are you working now?'

'I've kind of got to, babes. But I think it's time to get ready. I didn't want to wake you but I think it's all nearly . . . you know.'

'What is?' asked Tara. Adrian nodded in the direction of the adjoining door. Tara listened. Nothing.

'What's he doing?' she asked. She glanced at Adrian, who was smiling at her.

'I'm sure he's got it all worked out. He came and got the little dish about twenty minutes ago when you were asleep.'

'Oh my God. He took the little dish!'

'Well, what did you expect him to do?'

'I don't know. It's all so . . . Well, it's so personal.'

'You wanted sperm from someone you knew. That's a kind of personal request. I suppose he could have put it in a little plastic bag and surface-mailed it to you.'

'Adrian!' said Tara. 'For God's sake. This is serious.'

'I know. All I'm saying is be calm, babes. It'll work better if you're feeling relaxed. Now go take a shower and get back on the bed. I'll make sure you're ready.'

Tara stood in the shower, letting the water hit her full in the face and run down her back. She heard a knock on the door and almost fell over as she scrabbled to get out of the shower stall. She threw on a hotel bathrobe and opened the bathroom door. Nick was standing in their bedroom wearing a similar bathrobe. He was holding the dish with a funny grin on his face. 'This is for you, Tara,' he said. He was looking at the floor. 'It has got to be the most embarrassing present I've ever given anyone, but you know it's given with hope and the best feelings in the world.'

Tears were pouring down Tara's cheeks. She hadn't felt them approach; they just seemed to come. She sheepishly took the dish from him, shocked by its warmth.

'I had it in hot water before, um . . .'

'They last longer if they're warm,' said Adrian.

Nick smiled at Tara and blew her a kiss. The door closed behind him. Adrian took the small sperm-filled dish from Tara's hands and placed it on the bedside table. He pushed the nozzle of the syringe into the glutinous substance and pulled back the plunger. Adrian looked up and smiled at her.

'Relax, babes. Everything's going to be fine.'

Chapter Forty-Five

Nick clicked his door shut and turned back into his room. He was clean, tingling clean from a hot bath. He was tired, hollow tired from a full class, the journey to Brighton, two beers and a wank.

He looked over at the table. There in all their glory were his four hard-core pornographic magazines, bought for him so long ago in San Francisco when he was someone else — *Jizz-Glazed Cheerleaders, Sperm-Soaked Babes, Girls Who Like It up the Ass* and *Trailer Trash on Heat*.

He picked them up, flicking through each one and taking a last look at the series of images. They had helped him do something quite difficult — they had helped him fill the little glass dish when the very idea of it was about as stimulating as old cheese.

He sighed and wondered what was happening in the next room. It might as well have been ten thousand miles away, he felt so completely excluded. He jiggled the magazines up and down a few times. What was he going to do with the bloody things? He'd kept them for so long, and they had always been a slight worry in the back of his mind. What if Barney had found them? — it was possible he had. What if Sally found them? — which she definitely would if she came around to his place. He didn't want to imagine it. It made him the person he no longer felt he was.

He looked around the room. There was a built-in set of drawers next to the table. He pulled the bottom drawer out; there was nothing inside. He lifted the drawer to disengage the runners that supported it; the drawer came free and he pulled it away.

Revealed underneath was a small pile of pornographic magazines, left there by a previous occupant. Nick smiled. Dull minds think alike, he thought. He picked the magazines up. *Fiesta* – women leaning up against road signs with their knickers on display; a *Men Only* – women in soft focus, legs-spread poses in beds of impossible beauty; *Shaven Haven*, a magazine dedicated to women with no pubic hair.

He put them back in and added his collection to the pile. His were so much better anyway. The other magazines were so naff. Who'd buy them?

He carefully refitted the drawer and closed it. The magazines were still there, still close to him, but they would soon be out of his life. He sighed again. He felt very miserable. He wanted to ring people – Sally, his mum even. He didn't want to talk to Barney because he might just have made Barney a little brother or sister and it would be hard not to tell him. Maybe one day, in say five years' time, he and Barney could fly to America and visit Tara and the baby, who'd be a little boy or girl by then. And Barney would be . . . well, he'd be twenty-one, so he probably wouldn't want to go with his stupid old dad. It was all a bit of a fantasy.

He went into the bathroom because that was the only place he could go. Stretching and checking himself in the mirror, he noticed his eyes looked really tired, but he didn't want to lie down on the bed. He felt sleep would evade him. He turned on the bath. He'd worked up a bit of a sweat having a wank – might be good to have another bath, and there were so many towels there it seemed a shame not to use them.

He ran the bath until it was close to overflowing, dropped his bathrobe neatly in the corner and looked at himself in the full-length mirror. It was a little clouded so he wiped it clean with a towel. He looked all right, a bit skinny in the legs maybe, but his stomach was pretty flat, upper body good, hair a bit thin but not going grey. Dick quite big now he came to look at it, not bad really for someone who'd just made a baby. She was a lucky girl, that Tara — the baby should be a beauty.

He stepped into the bath and slowly let the water engulf him. Back to work tomorrow, big class in the afternoon, then he'd arranged to go to the movies with Sally and Barney. Sally was staying over. He wondered if he could get horny. Judging by the last couple of times he'd seen her, he didn't think it was going to be a problem.

Chapter Forty-Six

Daisy sat down on the mat and Nick joined her. The class was full – fourteen women, three of them with their fees paid by a TV production company who had made a documentary programme about the course.

Daisy introduced herself and explained the arrangements. Nick thought she sounded good, better than he'd expected. It was so hard to compete with Tara and her wonderful delivery, the way every word she said somehow counted, had impact.

Daisy finished up by introducing Nick. She passed him the tissue box. He sat in silence for a moment, looking around the room.

'Well, you've heard that I'm called Nick. I'm here as a padded assailant. Over the next five weeks we are going to get to know each other really well. This is an incredibly intense course. It's going to change your life; it certainly changed mine. All I really want to say now is that I'm so proud to be here, so proud to be a part of what for you is going to be a difficult but incredibly rewarding time. People have asked me what I can possibly get out of being beaten up by women – they think I must be crazy. But let me tell you, when I see someone go from the fear and frozen inaction of their first class to the frighteningly rapid response of their last, it makes you wonder. If we can unlock this kind of stuff in people who are like convinced they are incapable, imagine how that could be used for good in other areas. This course isn't just about defending yourself, it's about changing the way you see yourself in the world. Convincing yourself that you are allowed to be there, on the streets, in the shops, where you want to be. I know this sounds all Californian and, you know, really meaningful, but it's true. I just want to thank you, right now, for allowing me to be your padded assailant. Thanks.'

He passed the tissue box to the young black woman on his right. The stories unfolded – the abuse, the rapes, the beatings. The men who intimidated and threatened, the fathers who used fear and secrecy to cover their crimes, the brothers and uncles who never spoke. The boyfriends and their threats. The long-endured fear and the deeply entrenched hatred and distrust of men by so many women – it was all there in the opening circle. Nick listened, totally in the moment, finding his eyes stinging with tears as a woman broke down and expressed her utter terror at having to get up in the morning and face the world, and men, all over again.

When the circle was completed he left the room and prepared himself, relishing the fit of his impact suit as he slowly armoured himself. The jockstrap and steel box, the leggings, the crotch-piece with shoulder straps, the chest and back protectors, stomach guard, structured shoulder pads, elbow pads and gloves. Then the oversized T-shirt and baggy trousers, the padded shoes, and finally his well-worn, sweat-smoothed helmet.

Nick Gardener was a padded assailant who knew how to do his job. He entered the room with the blue mat and started to do it.